Medicine at Crooked Hat is a sequel to A Pocket Full of Glory by Patricia Rose

The second novel in the American Sojourner Series.

"I dedicate this book to all my relations with much love"

"Mitakuye Oyasin"

Each soul must meet the morning sun, the new sweet earth and the Great Silence alone.

OHIYESA
Santee Dakota

Medicine At Crooked Hat

Patricia Rose

Chapbook Press

Schuler Books
2660 28th Street SE
Grand Rapids, MI 49512
(616) 942-7330
www.schulerbooks.com

Medicine at Crooked Hat

ISBN 13: 9781943359158

Library of Congress Control Number: 2015957522

Printed in the United States by Chapbook Press.

1

"The Bear"

The bear moved slowly down the incline, his powerful body progressing as streaks of sunlight dappled his coat. The wind whispered through the pines as a covey of quails flew above the grizzly. Shila watched as the great bear ambled out of sight. It was late autumn in the Sierra Nevadas. Shila was hidden in the thick pines and out of the scent from the bear. He considered this good medicine and the second time he had seen the bear that year. He would never forget that this was the bear that had marked him with a scar his blood brother.

Shila was a Shoshone of the Gabrieleno Clan. He was tall and muscular with long black hair that reached beyond his waist. His eyes were his most prominent feature, they were hazel in color. Not the dark brown as was usual for his tribesmen. His people were moving their encampment to the Amaragosa River Valley as winter would soon be approaching. Shila was a young man of twenty years, and was called a brother to the bear. He was to be a wisdom keeper like his father; already he carried the medicine of a healer in his spirit. It was said on the day he was born, a red tailed hawk landed by his mother's lodge. Then encircled it three times before flying off toward the mountains. His father saw this and knew his son would be different. He thought about why he had chosen to come to the mountains that day. He had spent the early morning hours praying to the Grandfathers. Giving honor and offerings of tobacco to their spirits. He had requested for a vision of how to help his people. Things were changing from the old ways of his father's youth.

Many of the young men of his camp wanted to go up against the white men that were encroaching on their ancestral lands. They were angry and wanted them gone from their mountain home. Shila thought about how the land was already changing. From the white man searching for gold. They were coming up from California. His cousin Many Horses, told how the rivers were being poisoned and fish were dying and many of the wild birds and ducks; found dead along the shores. Mud slides and cutting down of the great trees were only part of the devastation these men had wrought in

1

their wake. These were some of the things he prayed about on this day. Shila loved and respected the great earth mother. He could not understand how men could be so disrespectful of her and take from her without giving back. This he thought was a sign of some kind of madness that could not be cured.

2
"The Family Tree"

Ansleigh stood looking out the door of her cabin. As she stood there a group of deer ran across the clearing into the wood. If only I could follow them she thought. I envy their freedom. Ansleigh was a young woman of nineteen thin with pale blue eyes and blonde hair. Which hung down her back wild and unkempt. She was fair skinned and pretty with a soft voice. She was dressed in a man's shirt and trousers. Three years she had lived here as a trapper's wife. She still missed her sisters and the loss of her son a year ago. Pennsylvania had been her home.

She grew up Ansleigh Chastine Riley, the daughter of a school master. Jacob Riley from Ireland. He was a young man with an education and a spirit for adventure. He came to America to discover his dreams. He was of medium build and fair complected with dark brown hair and green eyes. Her mother had been a wild and stubborn woman by the name of Rebecca Sykes. She was a small boned woman with auburn hair and blue eyes. There was something mercurial about her. Rebecca was fond of telling stories of her youth and her Great- Grandfather Peter Sykes. Who she adored. He had a large horse farm and how he had survived the Great American Revolution. Her Great- Grandmother Chastine Beaumont had been badly burned in a barn fire and spoke in French and taught her songs and dances. She told her wondrous stories about Baptiste a fiery stallion and famous race horse.

Rebecca often talked about her grandmother's dearest friend a Cayuga Indian woman by the name of Echo Hooks. Ansleigh vaguely remembered the stories of her coming to the old school house one Summer. She was teaching the children about horses. She was elderly and had long gray braids that hung down her back. Her two sons, Benjamin and John were there with their families that day. It was said that her oldest daughter Onatah had married a young architect and moved to Europe. Her husband Johnathan Lancer had written several books in his life and ended up joining Congress two years before he died. Her maternal Grandmother Anne Sykes never married she was the second born to Peter and Chastine Sykes. Getting pregnant at sixteen and dying in childbirth with Rebecca. Their first born, her Great -Aunt Marin married a map maker and traveled the country. They settled in Boston. She never got to meet her. Rebecca missed her youth and died of consumption when Ansleigh was still a child. Her father never remarried. Ansleigh Chastine was the youngest of three girls.

Two of her sisters were to be married and were living in Philadelphia. She first met, Thomas Andrews her husband in an open field behind her father's school.

She had been there that day reading to the young girls in his classroom. She often helped her father at the school. It was a warm afternoon and the children were being dismissed. When Ansleigh thought she saw the figure of a man walking across the field.

She was curious so she decided to see who he was. He was tall and dressed plainly in an ill fitting suit and a crumpled hat sat lopsided atop his head. He was barefoot with his boots tucked up under his arm. His hair was dark brown and shoulder length. His eyes blue and he had a look of something untamed about him. "Excuse me sir, are you looking for someone?"

"Yes, actually I am taking a walk to clear my mind." "Are you troubled then?" "You could say that, I just lost a chance for head'n west working for the Brighton Prairie Schooner Company. Wore my best suit." he said as he ripped off his jacket throwing it on the ground. "I hate cleaning up and being a dandy just to impress an old fart behind a desk." Ansleigh covered her mouth to muffle a laugh. "Beg pardon miss, I meant no disrespect I have a bad temper." "So I see. What kind of job was it?" "They wanted men to ride rough shod as scouts and sharp shooters on the trails heading

3

up in the Sierra Nevada Mountains. I want to go west I always have." "So go."

He looked surprised at her response. "It isn't all that easy my mother's ailing. It takes money to move across the country." "Why weren't you hired? You seem rugged enough." "That's not it. I was late getting to the hiring office and all the open jobs were filled. I made a fool of myself begged the man to hire me. I told him I would do any kind of work. He was having none of it. So I took off run my horse so hard he took a spill. He's around here somewhere I hope he don't come up lame."

"Ansleigh! Ansleigh is that you? What are you doing out here?" Her father came up behind her eyeing the young man warily. "This young man seems to have lost his horse, run away on him." "Thomas Andrews sir." He offered the school teacher his hand. Mr. Riley declined to offer his. "Ansleigh you need to get back to the school. I'll be along shortly." "But father." "I said I will join you later! So lad why are you here?" "What she said is true I am looking for a sorrel horse. I rode him hard and he tripped in a chuck hole. I hope he didn't come up lame." "You need to move on I don't like strangers around the school. We do understand each other?" "Yes sir we do." With that Thomas picked up his jacket and walked off. Later that day at home Mr. Riley explained to Ansleigh that proper young girls did not talk to strangers. Especially one who was standing in the middle of a field. "Why anything could have happened" He chided.

Her oldest sister Katherine just shook her head and said she was too much like her grandmother and just as stubborn. Ansleigh kept to herself when it came to her feelings. She would ask Katherine about their mother often. Katherine told her stories about happier times. When they would go to the horse farm and Great Grandpa Sykes would take them for rides in his dog cart. Great Grandma Sykes would sing in French and would make the best desserts she had ever tasted. She told her that their family servant Myniah Way had taught her how to bake. Martha was the shy one and had her mother's red hair. Ansleigh wasn't born until after her father forbid anyone to go to the farm. Ansleigh wondered what her mother had done.

4

Because Rebecca would cry when they talked of the farm and her family there.

The only bond Ansleigh had with her past was a well worn memory book that had belonged to her great grandmother Chastine Beaumont Sykes. It was full of dry pressed flowers and a journal of events that took place in her life. Stories about Peter Sykes and their children Marin and Anne. She told of Myniah Way the family servant and her best friend Echo Hooks. Ansleigh treasured this book.

3

"The School Picnic"

Ansleigh met Thomas again later that week at the market place in Kingsessing. He was looking at a set of traps. "Do you come here often?" She asked walking up behind him. He startled at her voice. "You surprised me." He said. "What would you need those for?" She asked him coyly. "These? The truth of the matter is my Uncle is a fur trader, a darn good one. I use to go to Canada with him in the winter. He and my father took me with them. I just got to thinking." He paused in mid -sentence. "Thinking?" "There is a lot of game to be had in the Sierra Nevadas. I'm a pretty decent trapper. I heard they're paying good money for buffalo hides as well. Thought I might still head west" "What about your mother?" "She knows. My Aunt Clara said she would take her if I would send her money every month for her care. I already gave her money from my last job." "So when do you plan on leaving?" 'I hope within the month. I need to take care of my mother's affairs. When my father died. He left us in debt." "Ansleigh there you are Father is looking for you." A tall brunette with deep blue eyes and delicate features had joined them. Along with a shorter, plumper red haired young woman with a pretty face. "Mr. Andrews this is my sister Katherine and my sister Martha."

"Good morning Ladies." Thomas said as he tipped his hat. Katherine took Ansleigh by the arm whispering in her ear. It was obvious Ansleigh

5

was upset by what she was hearing. As she pulled away from her sister and walked boldly into the market- place. "Sorry Mr. Andrews." Katherine apologized. "Ansleigh can be so rude at times."

Katherine walked away with her sister Martha. "Nice meeting you." "You too." Thomas returned. He watched the young women as they disappeared into the crowd.

Ansleigh found herself attracted to the young man and wanted to know more about him. Unlike her two older sisters who did everything their father expected of them. Right down to his hand picking their husbands. Martha was to marry a Wainwrights son who was dull and witless. Katherine, she knew favored a young man who worked as a blacksmith. Quin James rugged and dark haired with a disarming sense of humor. "I'll have no one with dirty hands courting me daughters." He would say. We are respectable folk and I'll not have it changed at the tip of any man's hat." He had a rotund balding accountant by the name of Mr. Portly chosen for Katherine. She wanted to protest but feared her father's temper and of course the dowry he had promised the two young men.

The school where Mr. Riley taught had an annual picnic each year when the classes were over.
Many of the boys were needed out in the fields to help their families. Ansleigh loved this time of year. She would go swimming and gather wild flowers from the woods to take home and set on her mother's grave.

Ansleigh was almost seventeen but felt older somehow. Her father frowned on her unbridled nature. Yet he knew she was the most like her mother, which he found irresistible about her. This fact made him prone to be over protective of her. Deep down he never wanted her to marry.

The picnic was held outside of the school building with tables set up with all kinds of food.Mr. Riley had a black servant in charge of the tables.

He would fan flies from the food and chase children away who liked stealing sweets off the table. Thomas was there as his niece was one of the students. He had promised to join her. It also gave him an excuse to see Ansleigh again.

6

She made him feel something inside. An awakening of emotions he was uneasy about. His breath would quicken when he saw her and all the things he was going to say to her vanished. He would end up thoughtless and vague. She was walking in his direction and he quickly ducked behind a tree to watch her privately. She was talking to a student and smiling. Her hair hung loose about her shoulders and she wore a pale blue dress. As the sun glanced off her face, her eyes deepened in color. He was content to stand there indefinitely. When he heard a voice. "Mr. Andrews how nice of you to join us." It was Katherine. "Yes my niece Mildred has graduated this summer." "Mildred, such a nice young girl she is too." "She is the first person in her family to read." He said proudly. "Something you can be grateful for. Have you talked to Ansleigh?" She inquired. "No, I haven't seen her." He said awkwardly. "Might I suggest you take her for a walk other wise father will be watching your every move." She looked directly at him while saying this.

This surprised Thomas as he wasn't expecting this from her. "Thank you then I shall." He said.

"Do enjoy the food we'll talk later then." Katherine walked on. The day was coming to a close people were picking up their belongings and gathering their children. Thomas walked Mildred to a carriage that would be taking her home. She hugged him and thanked him for being there. Her parents had been to busy working the fields to be there for her. Thomas waved her off and headed back to his horse.

When she appeared as if from nowhere it was Ansleigh. "So would you care to walk with me to the river?" She teased. "What about your father?" "That is why I am asking you. He is seeing Mrs. Bailey home she is almost a hundred you know." "Really? I should live as long", he joked. "Come on then!" Ansleigh said as she grabbed Thomas by the arm and started running toward the river. It was a humid afternoon and the flies were biting.

The heady scent of wild phlox and milkweed filled the air. Ansleigh suddenly stopped and stared straight at Thomas. "So I thought you would have left by now." "I leave in two days time. I am riding horseback and camping along the way. I figure it will take me at best over a month to get

7

there." "Do you care to swim?" "Swim?" Thomas looked at her oddly. "I am not dressed for that."

"Who wears clothes?" Ansleigh said laughing as she took off her dress standing there in her chemise. His mouth became dry and his heart started to beat rapidly. She was even more beautiful than he had imagined. He quickly flung off his clothes and joined her in the coolness of the water. She squealed with delight as she splashed water into his face. They were like two children discovering water for the first time. When they finished playing, Ansleigh went and sat on the river bank with the sun behind her. Thomas stood in the water staring at her. "You act as if you had never seen a woman before." "I have never seen one as beautiful as you." Thomas sat next to her pulling on his trousers. "I hope you don't think I do this all the time. In fact it is the first time I have ever done anything like this." "I think you would wait until you were married at least." Thomas said teasingly. "I feel very drawn to you." She said.

"As long as my father has a breath in his body; no man will ever call me his wife. You are leaving and I will never see you again." The tears started welling in her eyes. Thomas suddenly felt her vulnerability as he took his jacket and covered her shoulders. He leaned into her and taking her chin in his hand he tenderly kissed her on the lips. "I need to get you back before your father comes looking for you."

They both dressed in silence and walked hand in hand toward the school. Mr. Riley was sitting in his buggy. "What is this Ansleigh? Where have you been and your hair all wet." "She slipped and fell in the water it was an accident really it was Mr. Riley." Thomas blurted out. "I was there to pull her out." "Thank Providence for that father." Thomas knew that Mr. Riley was not believing his story but he let it go. "I will be thanking you lad for your help. I hear that you are leaving town. I'd say the sooner the better wouldn't you?" With that Ansleigh climbed into the buggy next to her father and they trotted off down the road. Leaving Thomas with all kinds of emotions he had never felt before.

4
"Vision Quest"

The dog was slinking along the side of his mother's lodge. When Shila approached the dog it stood looking at him then cowered as he ran off into the woods. Kachiri his oldest sister laughed. "Little brother you have a way with animals. That old dog has been hanging around our camp all summer. He has bitten two of our children. But Father won't let us kill him. He said that his spirit would stay if we do that." "Kachiri that dog was beaten by a white man and left to die." "How do you know such things?" Asked Kachiri. "I saw it in the dog's eyes." "Come you two I have a meal prepared, it is time to eat, and it grows late." Their mother Hapisteen scolded as she peered from out of the teepee's entrance. It was late summer. Shila was just sixteen and learning the ways of the Grandfathers with Fox Healer the medicine men of their tribe. "I will be leaving tomorrow and heading high into the mountains. Fox Healer has asked me to do a vision quest." "When do you start fasting then?"Asked his mother. "By the dawn I will not eat for the rest of the week." "Be sure to drink plenty of water." Kachiri said. "Remember how sick Many Horses got when he came back from his quest in the spring. He had a fever and almost died." "That is because he did not respect the spirits and he was eating. I know because he told me." "It is a serious thing not to be taken lightly." his mother chided. Shila ate quickly then thanked his mother and left to find his father. There was a full moon and the biting insects were everywhere. Shila reached down and found wormwood in the thickets and rubbed the leaves on his arms and face to repel them. He saw the camp fire glowing in front of his grandfather Grey Elk's lodge.

There sat his father River Tree and his grandfather both smoking their pipes and talking. River Tree was the son of Grey Elk. He was tall and thin. His hair long and braided. He had an aquiline nose and piercing black eyes. He was intimidating to some. As Shila approached his father asked "Are you ready, my son?" "I think I am Fox Healer is a hard one to please." "You will do well Shila. You are a spirit warrior in your heart I have always known that since you came to us." his grandfather said as he passed his pipe to Shila. He took a puff and then offered the pipe to the four directions. "Fox Healer tells me he thinks you will have a vision." His father told him. "It is something I have prayed about this is my first vision quest and I want to be prepared." The three men sat and talked about Shila's quest as the evening wore on. Shila went back to his mother's lodge. Laying on his blanket he looked up at the lodge poles and wondered how things would go.

He slept little and before he knew the birds were singing up the dawn. Shila gathered his bag and pipe and silently crept out of the lodge, when he felt his mother's hand reach for his. "May you have many spirit blessings my son" Shila kneeled down and stroked his mother's face softly then left. Shila was trying to remember all the things that Fox Healer had taught him as he walked into the mountains. He spent the first day walking and climbing. Drinking little sips of water from his gourd as he was taught. He found a small cave the first night. It had been a bear's habitat he could tell by the broken branches and animal bones strewn on the floor of the cave. The next morning he was up at dawn and as he was getting ready to leave, he looked up and saw a red tail hawk peering down at him from a pine tree. It flew down and headed north. Shila saw this as a good omen. He decided to follow where the hawk led. It was a hot day and Shila thirsted but knew to drink only what he needed. His stomach started to hurt from hunger. He was hoping to find the spot where he was to do his vision before the night fall. He spotted the hawk once more as the sun was setting.

It had brought him to a clearing in the woods. A rocky bluff over looking a ravine filled with a dense underbrush. This is it Shila thought to himself as he waved to the hawk. "Thank you little brother." He set up camp preparing a fire from twigs he had gathered. Using a mineral stone from his pouch he struck it until a flame ignited. He laid out his blanket and looked out into the orange sky as the sun was setting. He began chanting and praying asking for guidance for his spirit journey. He had one night of sleep before he would begin. The next morning he was up and prepared himself and thanked the mountain and the trees for their shelter. He smoked his pipe and offered it up to the Grandfathers. He then sat cross legged and closed his eyes. It was much more difficult then he had imagined. He was hungry and the sun was beating down on his back as the sweat trickled down his face. He wanted to scratch and his legs kept cramping. He could hear old Fox Healer telling him to pay attention and learn patience and endurance. Your body can be your greatest enemy at times he had warned him. It keeps your spirit from being free to fly.

He kept dozing off which he knew he was not supposed to do. He fought to stay centered. He drank small sips of water to stay awake. He was grateful for the evening as the air was cooler and he was more alert. Odd he thought how he could hear so many sounds in the night. The rustling of the trees in the night air.

The barking of the coyotes and the singing of crickets. He looked out at the sky and the stars were in a profusion of lights over head. He pulled his blanket around his shoulders as he sat there. Thoughts of his family and his childhood streamed through his mind. He was still fighting off the need to eat. As the dawn came he was growing sleepy and he struggled to stay awake. As he sat there. He felt something come up behind him. He knew it was large by the way it moved and the sounds of its breathing. He didn't budge just closed his eyes and started to chant. The large bear took its great paw and knocked Shila over sniffing of him and licking Shila's neck.

He still wouldn't move and the bear lost interest and ambled off. Shila felt something warm trickle down his neck. It was his blood where the bear had used its claws to push Shila over. He saw this as his first sign. He left it alone and went back to his sitting position. He started to go into a trance state after that. He saw a great grizzly and the bear talked to him. He told him that men were coming to take over their mountain home and that things would not be good. Shila would be a wisdom keeper and a healer like Fox Healer. The bear had left a scar on Shila's neck as a reminder of his vision. Then Shila felt a strange pulling as he felt his spirit leave his body. He flew like a bird to a great water fall that cascaded down the mountain side. He saw a beautiful white woman with long flowing hair, the color of the sun. She was floating in the air over the water fall. As he approached her, she smiled. Her eyes were blue like the sky and her skin white like that of a dove. He felt as if he had known her from someplace in his life. She took his hand and they went to a large settlement, it was dark and a grave sense of gloom lingered over it.

She told him he would be tested here and his gifts as a wisdom keeper and healer would be needed. This place was a threat to Shila's way of life and he was to be ready for all the things that would befall his people because of it.

She then disappeared. Shila was then drawn to a place of brilliant light, where he saw many people of his village that had died. His great-grandfather and his little brother were there. They were happy to see him. Shila knew he was in the after life. He thought perhaps he too had died. His great- grandfather told him that he was still needed on the earth. But he wanted to show him things that were to come. It was with great pain that Shila saw men cutting down the sacred trees, killing off all the buffalo and poisoning the great waters. Towns and cities were taking up all the land and the white men were everywhere. He saw into the future where there were strange looking objects that men rode around in. There were great silver birds in the skies and the land was scarred. There were large rivers of black roads with no grass as far as the eye could see. He felt the great earth mother was dying as she cried out for help. He felt such pain in his heart at seeing this. It was then that he came back into his body as he opened his eyes a gray wolf was standing near him. It was a female and she was whining, he saw where a splinter of wood was protruding from her foot. He talked softly to her as he walked over to her. "Baya -ish be still." He gave her some of his water. She lapped it up and then laid down. Shila took his knife and worked the splinter out of her foot. She never moved just kept watching him with her eyes.

He took some herbs from his pouch and wrapped her foot. Using a strip of leather he tied it all in place. She then stood up and looked at him and howled limping off into the trees. In some strange way Shila felt this was a spirit message that he was here in this life to help others. It was then that he realized his vision and his purpose.

5

"Ansleigh & Thomas"

Ansleigh stood on the porch of their house, she had a satchel tucked under her arm. She kept looking behind her. Her heart was heavy as she wanted desperately to say good bye to her sisters. But she couldn't take the chance. She was going to stick to her plan to go out into the night and find Thomas before he left. As she stepped down off the porch, she felt his hand grab her. "Where do you think you are sneaking off to this time of night?" It was her father and he had been drinking. "Let me go father!" Ansleigh warned him. "So you want to run off? You are so like her, after men and their attentions." "How can you say that about her? She was a good woman everyone says so." "Those who didn't know her like I did." "What are you talking about?" "William Clark a common horse trader worked on your Great Grandfather's horse farm. She was in love with him. She wanted to leave me and go with him." "I don't believe it." "It doesn't matter Ansleigh. I kept her reputation in tact and Mr. Clark was escorted by gun point out of Kingsessing. You were born a few months after that. Who's to say he isn't your father."   "I am not going to listen to any of your lies"Ansleigh said as she stepped down off the porch. I won't let anyone defile you." He pulled her to him. She pushed him so hard that he fell. "I am sorry Ansleigh please don't go. I didn't mean to say those things." She saw her chance and she ran off into the night. She was crying so hard it was difficult to get her bearings in the darkness of the trees. She knew where Thomas's Aunt Clara lived and was hoping to find him there. When she reached the farm house she saw Thomas at the barn, he was busy packing his supplies onto his saddle.

13

She didn't know what to say she just stood there watching him. Thomas had this feeling someone was there. He turned around and there stood Ansleigh with tears streaking her face. "Ansleigh what are you doing here?"

"I'm going with you." "What are you saying? What about your father? Your family?" "It's done I have left and I ain't looking back. I want to be with you. I am a good worker and I can help you." "I don't know Ansleigh, I really like you, but I planned on this trip alone." Her tears started welling and Thomas was weakening he couldn't bear to see her in pain. He took her in his arms. Ansleigh felt this hot flush of desire fill her. His eyes, his lips, his hands on her. She breathed in the night air and went limp in his arms. Their lips sought each other out. He lifted her up into his arms, laying her gently down on the hay. Their desire and lust became all they knew. They lay there for a while looking into each other's eyes. Thomas stroked her face.

"I guess I can rent a horse for you to ride once we get to the valley. It's a day from here. We have to ride double and it will be slow going." "I have some money." Ansleigh said as she reached into her satchel. "I made it sewing for some folks I know." "You better hang onto it for now. We'll need more food." "I brought some bread and jam and some of my father's jerky." "Well I guess you thought of just about everything didn't you!" teased Thomas. Ansleigh looked at him. "I know it won't be easy, but I want to get as far away from my father as I can." "Did you ever think he might set the law out look'n for you?" "I don't know maybe. But I am leaving here one way or the other." "I suggest we get a head start because he most likely will be look'n for you."

"Have you set things right with your mother?" "We already said our farewells." Ansleigh and Thomas gathered their belongings. Thomas pulled Ansleigh up onto the back of the horse and they started out.

Mr. Riley went to the local Sheriff's office first thing the next morning. He made out a report about his daughter missing possibly abducted by one Thomas Andrews. There would be a bounty of course on his head. He wanted his daughter back safely. The sheriff contacted an ex-lawman he knew and set things in motion. He never told his daughter's Katherine or Martha about what he had done. Katherine knew that her sister had ran off. She wished that she herself, had that kind of courage. She did not love the man she was about to marry in the fall. She still loved the young blacksmith whom she saw in church every Sunday. Their eyes would meet often and she dreamt about being with him. It was noon the next day before Thomas and Ansleigh stopped and took a break. They were both exhausted from their long ride. The horse was in need of rest as well. "We'll stop here and take a nap. I will go and fetch water" Ansleigh literally collapsed on the spot. She had never been so sore in her life. She had blisters on her bottom and all up and down inside of her thighs. Where the sweat of the horse had chafed her skin.

Thomas set up a small campfire to cook trout he had managed to catch in the stream. The smell of the fish woke Ansleigh. She was ravenous. "I thought that would bring you around." Said Thomas smiling. She reached in her satchel and brought out what was left of her bread. They both took turns eating with their fingers out of the skillet. "I have to admit I never thought fish could taste so good. She said. "Don't get to use to it." Thomas replied. "There will be days when we will both be hunting for food." "I know but I don't regret coming with you." "Let's take a rest the horse needs to stretch and eat. They both laid down on a blanket Thomas had brought. Holding each other they soon fell a sleep. They woke to rain drops falling on them. Thomas groaned, "Just what I didn't want. It could be worse I guess at least the weather is holding warm."

They quickly packed up their camp and saddled the horse. "We are a few hours ride to the valley, we should get there before dark." Thomas gave Ansleigh his jacket to wear. It was slow going and the rain was unyielding. The kind that stings your face. By the time they had reached the horse ranch in the valley they were both soaked to the skin.

A tall lanky man with a long grey beard greeted them at the gate. "You look a might tired there Missy." "We are just out of Philadelphia." Thomas told him. "Riding double? Ain't to smart there Laddy Buck."
"That is why I am here want to see if you have a horse I can rent for the girl." "I wish I could help yah, but we quit do'n that awhile back. Folks was

15

keep'n the horses not return'n them to the post. One fella ended up gett'n shot over the deal so me and my brother called it quits. I kin sell you a nice little mare though. She's bit slow and yah have to kick her in the ribs to keep her go'n." "I didn't bring money for horse trad'n" Thomas scowled.

"I can use some of my money to help" said Ansleigh. "No, that won't be necessary." "Look here young feller you look like yah have a strong back. Tell you what. If yah ain't in no big hurry. I have some broken fence posts needs replac'n. Willy my brother broke his arm last week fool'n with a calf. I am short handed. You help me and I will give yah a good price on that mare. What do yah say?" "I don't know." Thomas mulled it over in his mind looking at Ansleigh. "Yeah I'll do it."

"Haggerty that's ma name" as he shook Thomas's hand. "Come on up to the house, get out of them wet clothes my missus will feed yah." The house was once an old Hotel where travelers laid over from their coaches. Ansleigh saw a faded sign that read The Brown Horse Inn still hanging from the porch. Shot full of holes where someone had obviously used it as target practice. Haggerty noticed her looking. "That was from a shoot out nigh onto twenty years ago. Story goes a fella brought his squaw here to spend the night. Inn Keeper weren't hav'n any redskin on his premises. She was married to a white man. Well sir, her husband was all liquored up and started shoot'n at the Innkeeper killed him dead. He then started shoot'n at everything in sight. They said everyone cleared out and him and his wife ended up spend'n the night and cleaning the place out. Look'n at that sign I guess he wasn't too good a shot."

Haggerty's wife was pretty rough looking, she was one of those people you have to think about as to what gender they are. She had her hair cut like a man and a small mustache grew under her nose. She wore pants and suspenders and a man's shirt with knee high leather boots with spurs. "This here be Ella my missus." Haggerty said as he spat on the floor. She reached over and knocked his hat off his head and in a gruff raspy voice said. "That ain't no way to be when we have company and you know it. Now get outside and bring in some more fire wood. It's gonna get cooler out I can feel it."

16

In the corner slumped over an older man sat puffing on a pipe. His arm was wrapped in a sling. "Willy," he said. "Welcome to what's left of the H&W Ranch." He looked up and over at Ansleigh "Handsome woman you have there son. Best keep her close to your side in these parts." "I plan on it sir."

Ella spoke up "I hope you kids like chicken cause that's what we're hav'n." Ansleigh and Thomas weren't going to argue. It smelled great. A couple of work hands came in and sat at the table, hair parted faces and hands washed. Hands in their lap as if waiting for a signal to eat. Ella looked at both Thomas and Ansleigh.

"Go out and wash your hands then get back in here" she barked. The meal was amazing, it was some of the best chicken Ansleigh had ever tasted. With sour dough biscuits and gravy. There was even a berry pie for dessert. Ella started talking about her days as a cook on a wagon train.

She said you had to be good or they'd shoot you or worse, leave you for the wolves. That is where she had met and married Haggerty. Willy never married. He liked drink'n too much he told us.

Ansleigh helped clear the table and did the dishes for Ella. She had already made a good impression with that. Ella put Thomas and Ansleigh up in the loft area. "You two are hitched ain't yah?" "Yes mam", Ansleigh blurted out. As Thomas and Ansleigh settled in for the night they felt they had run into some luck with getting the horse. Ansleigh said she would help wherever she could so maybe they could get the mare at a really good price. Thomas could not help noticing how she kept wincing as if in pain. He asked her what the problem was. She hiked up her skirt and he saw the blisters on her thighs they were bleeding. "Green Horn that is what you are. By the time we reach Nevada you will be as tough as nails." He took out a tin of ointment from his pack and rubbed it on her legs. "I know it hurts" he said. But it will get better. You need to wear pants when you ride." He pulled her to him kissing her softly on the lips. They both fell into a much needed sleep in each other's arms.

"Night Wing"

Shila watched silently as the young elk grazed through the under brush. He slowly pulled the arrow from its sheath. Pulling back on the bow he said a quick prayer and let the arrow find its mark. The young elk dropped at once. Shila had made a clean kill. He walked over and kneeling he touched the elk thanking it for giving its life that he and his family might live. He gave a prayer offering and thanked the Great Spirit for this gift. He quickly dressed out the elk leaving its heart as an offering to Mother Earth. He then laid the elk across his horse and headed back to camp.

It had been a month since his vision quest and Healing Fox had spent a week talking with him about his vision. He told Shila that it was a powerful one, as few men were allowed to see the future as he had. Shila had reoccurring dreams about the white woman and the bear. The wound on his neck was deep that the bear had left. You are now a brother to the bear he was told and carry bear medicine. They are great healers, you will be asked to use these gifts many times in your life said Healing Fox. "I hope to serve well." Shila said quietly.

"This is good." River Tree said as he helped Shila take the elk from his horse. As they pulled the elk down they heard a woman scream. Shila knew his sister's voice. He quickly grabbed his knife and set out to find her, his father was right behind him. There in the center of their camp was Kachiri. Night Wing had her by the arm twisting it.

"Let go of Kachiri!" Shila demanded. "Why should I? She was chosen for me. Is that not so River Tree?" he spat out his words angrily. "You have been drinking that poison.

It takes your mind." Spoke River Tree "I use to respect you Night Wing, you and your brother. But you have brought shame to our camp." Kachiri pulled away from his grasp. "You go to the darkness of your drink and dishonor the Grandfather's by laying with other women." "My sister is right you have lost respect with many."

Night Wing threw Kachiri on the ground. Shila immediately drew his knife to Night Wing's throat. "No, Shila that is not the way of the Wisdom

Keeper. Let Night Wing feel his shame that is punishment enough." River Tree helped his daughter up from the ground. Night Wing stood up to Shila."You will not touch me like that again. Watch your back young one." He threatened as he staggered off into the darkness.

Kachiri told her brother to heed Night Wing's words. "He has a dark heart. That is why I refused his offer to be my husband. He is a brave warrior and is loyal to our people but something in him is dishonest I have felt it for along time." "If he ever touches you like that again he will have my anger to face." said Shila. "You must learn to control your anger Shila it will be a constant obstacle for you to overcome on this path."

"Anyone can be angry, it is the wise who know how to use it for its true purpose." "Kachiri it is you who are wise." He said as he took her hand. They both entered their lodge and Kachiri told her mother of Night Wing's threat. Shila's mother Hapisteen was of the Lakota people she listened then spoke. "His people are not from the mountains he came from a place of many lakes. His grandfather Lame Wolf was the leader of the Raven Clan. He was a bitter man and not liked by many. He had a thirst for blood and was known to have killed many white men and people of his own clan as well. He liked power and I am afraid that is where Night Wing learned his ways.

Sometimes we carry things from our ancestor's and it may not be good. It is best Kachiri that you do a sweat and cut the cord between you and Night Wing the sooner the better."

Shila built the sweat lodge with help from his father. They used young saplings along the ravine near their encampment. Fox Healer helped too. He asked that Shila and Kachiri both be cleansed. Shila for his anger and Kachiri in the cutting ceremony. Fox Healer was known for making the sweat lodge fires hot. Shila and his sister sat praying, their bodies cleansing from the pores, sweating in the intense heat. Fox Healer poured water on the heated rocks and the steam rose permeating everything. After praying Fox Healer had Kachiri take a knife and cut a leather cord denouncing Night Wing and any ties they had. She cried as she chanted and left silently crawling out into the cool night air. Her father was there to give her water to drink and wrap her in a blanket. Shila was to stay longer and to ask

19

forgiveness for letting his anger lead to violence. As the fire grew hotter Shila chanted even louder, soon he saw the great bear. The bear was sitting in the place of Healing Fox. The bear showed Shila many men of all colors. They were drinking until they were drunk. A dark force surrounded them making them prisoners and stealing their minds. This force was very real and corrupted the body. He then understood why Night Wing had behaved the way he did.

Shila thanked the bear for the vision and was once again looking at Fox Healer. He nodded at Shila letting him know that his sweat was over. Shila then crawled out and felt the cool night air and his mother was there to give water to him and Fox Healer. The lesson was over.

Shila asked his grandfather Grey Elk where Night Wing was getting the drink that made him crazy and what was it?

"It is called whiskey." he told him. "The white man prizes it highly. They make it from corn I am told." "Corn? But how can that be? Corn is a good plant." "You must learn Shila that there is good and bad in our hearts. It is not the fault of the plant. It is how we use our thoughts that create what is good or bad for us do you understand?" "Is there a cure for this thing called whiskey?" "I have seen some men go mad drinking it, some die of a sickness it causes, if you do not stop.

My fear is that too many of our young men have been exposed to it. Trading their furs and knives for it. I have held councils with the other clans asking for help in solving this problem. The white man is clever he knows the drink will destroy our people.

They want our land and will stop at nothing to take it from us." "I will not let this happen Grandfather." "I know you mean well Shila but it is not that simple. Once the greed and craving for more enter our hearts it is already too late."

7

"Crooked Hat"

August Mayfield was a skinny, colorless and mean spirited man who was blinded in one eye. He had a jagged scar that ran from his brow to his cheek. His hair was gray and he had a scraggly beard and gray eyes. He came to the mountains in search of gold. Leaving California behind because he had killed a man and his family over a strike dispute. He knew he was wrong deep down in his soul. Ever since the incident he kept looking over his shoulder as if something or someone were after him. He had picked up a partner by the name of Harp Miller in his travels. Harp was a big man large boned and ugly. He was missing two of his fingers. They had been shot off in a gun fight when he was a younger man. Harp, never knew of August's past. He was more interested in having a companion on their treks through the Sierras. August was tight lipped only talking when necessary. Harp liked that about him. As he himself had a short temper and didn't like being bothered by too much talk.

They had been traveling for about a week when they came upon a small encampment.

A little woman with wild dark hair and a face full of freckles and a broken nose ran to fetch her husband. When she saw the two men ride into their camp. A fat and balding man with a long gray beard climbed out of a make shift tent. He was pulling up his suspenders while his wife aimed a shot gun at the two men.

"Now look here mam." Said Harp "Put that thing away before someone gets hurt."

"Looks like I'm the one that's got the upper hand espece' d'idiot!" August pulled out his gun and shot the rifle right out of her hand. Wounding her. She started to bleed profusely from her hand part of her finger was dangling. "See here mister, we got no quarrel with you, what'd yah go and do that for? Can I at least tend to ma wife?" "If she keeps her trap shut."Said August as he and Harp dismounted their horses. Keep that damn bitch under control or I will. The bearded man quickly ripped a part of his shirt off making a tourniquet for her bleeding hand. The woman stood silent never moving or saying a word. When he was done helping his wife. He looked at the two men. "Nate Townsend and this here's my wife Maizey." "So do you have anything worth eat'n?" asked August as he started rummaging through their personal things. Harp went into the tent

21

and came out with a bag of jerky. "Can she cook?" asked August. "She's a fine cook." Nate added "But how do yah expect her to do anyth'n with her hand all messed up like that." "You are lucky that I was in a good mood or you would be standing over her grave. I asked can she cook." "I kin cook I have some beans and biscuits on the campfire. Jist made it this morn'n." Harp, grabbed a hold of the hot lid and dipped his hand into the hot mixture. Scooping it up into his mouth. "Wooo...ee that shore is hot but damn good." August found a tin cup and helped himself to the stew. Nate and Maziey just stood there staring.

"If it ain't too much to ask why are you two here?" asked August. "We're head'n ta Nevada territory for winter sets in. Why yah ask'n?" "Seems ta me if your gett'n ready to move on, you have some permanent looking fixtures here. Like your sett'n up a cabin?" "Oh that ain't nuth'n it were here when we found this place." Harp walked over and looked at the half- finished building. "Pitch still fresh on them logs.

"I'd say less then a month August." August took his gun and forced open Nate's mouth with it and cocked the hammer. "Now how's about telling the truth for I make your wife a widow." Nate started to shake "Look mister I ain't got nuth'n you'd want here." Maizey looked at him as if to keep him from saying anything more. "So Miss Maizey what you think'n?" asked August as he ripped off her bandage. She started bleeding again. "I can watch that all night how about you Harp?" "Sure thing she'll bleed out like an old cow after butchering." "We are planning on build'n a little place here. It's near water and we can farm it." "Ha!" August laughed. "Farming rocks that's what you will be do'n! Now tell me the truth or I will put a bullet through your wife's eyes right now." "Tais-toi!" (*Quiet*) Don't yah say a thing" Maizey warned. "I cain't let them kill yah Maizey. Truth is we found us a little gold here." "Now you're mak'n more sense." said August. "How about we all take a little walk and you show me this here Coyote Hole." He threw the bloody bandage at Maizey and she wrapped her hand. They all walked up the side of a high ridge and came upon a small cave. Nate had a torch he lit and the men followed him. August kept his gun on him the whole time. After walking a few yards they saw a huge boulder with a streak of gold running through it. August saw where Nate had been

22

chipping away at it. "Holy Cow" said Harp I never! That is one hell of a
lode. How much are you getting out of here a day?" "It's slow work.
Maizey and I kin only work so much."

August was more then happy about their find. "So Mr. Townsend you
have a claim to this here site or are you one of them claim jumpers?"
"Maizey and I found this on our own. We already went to Pig's Poke and
put in the paper work on it. So who else knows about this Glory Hole?"
asked August. "Me and ma wife and that assayer at Pig's Poke."

As they walked back to the camp he told Nate that he would let him and
his wife live under one condition. That Nate keep working the site and that
Maizey did the cooking for the camp. That there was more then enough for
everybody and he was being generous sparing their lives. "Of course we will
have to keep you tied at night so I can get some sleep." "That's right" said
Harp "Wouldn't want my throat slit while I was a sleep."
"Harp and I will help yah finish the cabin. We can all get real cozy yes sir,
Harp I think we found what we were look'n for."

Maizey spent that night sewing her finger with horse hair. It eventually
healed but she would never be able to use it again. She hated the two men
and when they weren't looking she would spit in their food before serving
it. True to his word August and Harp helped Nate finish the cabin before
the snows came.

Maizey and Nate worked tirelessly at the cave excavating the gold each
day. Harp, would take turns with August watching over them to be sure
they didn't try to escape. By the first snow they had four pouches full of
large and small nuggets dug out of the boulder. August being a greedy man
decided that there was probably more gold in that cave, he wanted to buy
some explosives and see what they would find deeper in the ground. He
said that it was taking way too long at the rate they were going. So August
and Nate set out to Pig's Poke Mining Camp to buy supplies and some
black powder. They turned in only half of the gold they had been gathering,
as not to draw attention to their bounty. The assayer asked Nate where he
was getting such rich deposits as it was some of the finest gold he had seen
in them parts. He told him luck he guessed as there really was only a

23

shallow hole he had been digging away at the past year. The assayer told him he found that hard to believe.

"Gold this pure comes from a big lode usually." August quickly asked Nate to ask about his claim papers. The assayer said "Yes sir, I got them right here, look it over. Everything is legal now. You got yourself a proper claim. But if I were you I wouldn't boast about it. You got yourself some really rich ore and any claim jumper would be gunning you for it." Nate thanked him and quickly left with August. "Next time we come here we're gonna mix in some other minerals so it's not so rich. Don't want them vulture's gett'n into our claim." They went to the store and bought supplies and some black powder explosives. August was in a hurry to get back. They managed to get through that first winter. August tied Nate and Maizey up every night. He would never trust them. There was a lot of drinking on the really heavy snows while they were all held up in the cabin. August would go berserk some nights and start shooting up the cabin and howl like a demented wolf. Maizey was terrified of him. She knew that someday she would figure out how to get away from him, but not before killing him. They did set off the explosives during a winter thaw and just as August had predicted there was a large vein of ore that went down into the ground. He knew they were going to be very rich with this discovery. He also knew that they were going to have to get more help to work this mine.

One night when they were all eating. August said he had an idea. "Me and Harp have talked about this a bit. We need to take on more hands to set up a proper operation here. We're think'n about sett'n up our own camp. Maybe a small town from that. With access to the river and flat land north of here. It is ripe for the pick'n." "How you gonna get people to work it?" Scoffed Nate.

"Oh I know some fellas from my army days. I can send a post. If they saw this set up they'd be here quicker then flies on a horse's ass." "Aint right,"grumbled Maizey this here camp belongs to Nate and me.

August reached over knocking her off her chair to the floor. "Shut your trap and fetch me some more coffee." "A town you say." Harp laughed. "Kin I be the mayor?" "Why not." said August. "What shall we call this here mining town?" Maizey poured August a cup of coffee Nate never said

24

a word the whole time. He felt shame for not defending his wife. His cowardice was like a sickness that ate a way at him. "So what do you think we should call this here town Maizey?" "Porc charcutier (*big pig*) she spat. August twisted her arm. You best quit talk'n in that French lingo for I have to hurt yah!" Just for a moment Maizey wanted to throw the hot coffee in his face, she often fantasied about such things. "My daddy always said that when a man don't speak the truth and he's a cheat and a liar and steals things, ain't his that he wears a crooked hat." August started to laugh. "I like it Maizey, I am gonna let you have this one. "Crooked Hat." Harp first thing tomorrow I want you to make us a sign carve it nice and big. "Crooked Hat" Population Four. Yes sir we are in business." August said as he scooped up another fork of grits and gravy.

8
"Heading West"

Ansleigh and Thomas spent a month at the H&W Ranch. Thomas ended up doing more then mending fences, made repairs on the house and built a new manger for the horses and chopped wood for their winter stock pile. Ella had become very fond of Ansleigh. "You know I cain't have children,"she told her one day. "But Haggerty loves me just the same. He's enough to keep me busy most days that and his no account brother. You and Thomas plann'n on hav'n children?" "I don't know haven't given it much thought." "You want to have them while you are young and strong. I could see myself hav'n a daughter like you." "That is so kind of you to say." Ansleigh was taken by this remark and tears appeared. "I didn't mean it to hurt you child." "No, it's just I miss the memory of my mother she died young." "Come here."Ella said as she gave Ansleigh a hug. "If I were you, I'd get hitched before you plan on hav'n any little ones." Ansleigh's mouth dropped. "I didn't live this long not to know a thing or two. It don't matter none to me, but it might out there where your head'n. Child needs a proper name. I never knew who my pap was and my mother died penniless.

25

Work'n in a dirty old tavern cooking and clean'n for strangers. But she was good to me and she taught me how to be a survivor.

She was someone I could set store by. She was the best cook I ever knew. I don't know what you and that young feller are runn'n from? But yah need to be careful." Ella was so much more then Ansleigh had given her credit for. She had wisdom and strength she admired.

Thomas told Haggerty that it was time that Ansleigh and he got started again on their journey west. Haggerty told him he was more then impressed with all the young man had done for them. He told Thomas that he and Ansleigh would be sorely missed after they left. The day they decided to leave the weather was turning cooler. Leaves were changing on the trees. Ella had fixed them an extra special breakfast that morning. It was hard for Ansleigh to eat as she was choking back tears. "Eat your food honey, its gett'n cold. You'll need your strength for that long ride a head of yah." Thomas told them how much he appreciated their hospitality and kindness while they had been there. That he wouldn't forget them anytime soon. Haggerty said his feelings held the same.

When they got their gear together Ella had stocked quite a few provisions in a leather satchel. "That'll keep yah fed for a week or so." She said. When Thomas and Ansleigh walked out on the porch Willy stood there with their two horses all saddled up ready to go. As Thomas finished packing the rest of his gear on the saddle he pulled out some money to give to Haggerty.

"So what do I owe you for the mare and saddle?" he asked. "Put that away you have more then earned that horse." "We want one thing from yah." Ella said. "You name it." Ansleigh said as tears filled her eyes. "That you send us a post and let us know where you are and how you are do'n. Kin yah do that? You kids will always have a place here with us." Ella said. Then quickly walked away into the house. Ansleigh had ill prepared herself for the weather that lay ahead. Ella knew this and gave her a heavy wool jacket, gloves and hat. Telling her she would need it soon as fall could be bitter cold at times.

26

The mare was slow and true to Haggerty's words, Ansleigh had to keep urging her to keep up with Thomas. The one good thing about the horse was she had a lot of stamina and could keep going after Thomas's mount was tiring. They rode for a full day after leaving the ranch. The sun was out and Thomas said it made more sense to travel while the weather held. They set up camp under a canopy of pines. Thomas had brought a tarp and made a quick lean to for the night.

Ansleigh had fallen a sleep while still in the saddle. He carried her off the mare and covered her with a blanket while he set up camp. Ansleigh woke up and was starving. She looked over at Thomas and he was sitting by the fire he had built smoking his pipe. "I am sorry Thomas, I was so tired." "I know," he said grinning. "I will make a range hand out of you yet." "Let me fix you something to eat." "That sounds like a good idea." He said as Ansleigh set about pulling food items from Ella's pouch. They ate dried fish and hardtack which they washed down with coffee. "I want to reach Ohio in two days time so we will be riding hard for the next two days are you up to it?" "Yes, I will do my best wearing your trousers has definitely helped with my blistering." "Good let's get some shut eye then. I want to get an early start."

By the next morning it was raining hard and it was cold. Thomas and Ansleigh had to pack the camp away wet. He draped a blanket over Ansleigh telling her it would help somewhat with the rain. Ansleigh was miserable but she never let on. She stayed behind Thomas all that first day. The rain stayed with them until dark. Thomas knew they had to set up camp to dry out all their clothing and blankets. Ansleigh was shivering so bad she couldn't stop shaking. He made her sit right next to the campfire. They both stripped off their clothing and lay naked under the tarp. It was their body heat that kept them warm so they could sleep.

It was better going for them the next day it was sunny and cold. Most of their gear was dried and they quickly packed and were on their way West again. They reached Ohio by nightfall. Ansleigh was getting better at setting up camp and was able to help Thomas. That first day in Ohio brought a new set of problems. They had come to a river that Thomas did not see printed on his map. He had no idea how wide or long it was. He knew they

27

would lose a day's ride if they tried to go around it. The only way was across. He worried about Ansleigh because fording rivers was dangerous. "I want you to strip down to your under garments." He told her. She asked him "Why?" "If you lose the horse heavy clothing will only drag you down into the water an easy way to drown." He warned her. She didn't question him and did as he asked. They both crossed at the best spot they could find. Thomas was in the lead. "Now if I go down, you keep go'n do you understand? Get to the other side. I will take care of myself."

They eased the horses slowly into the water. The mare started to panic. She reared up and Ansleigh was left floating in the current. The water was deep as they had come upon a drop off. Ansleigh was trying to fight the current and she started to panic and her head went under. She felt the shock of the cold water and her limbs went numb. She was taking in water and unable to breathe. Thomas jumped off his mount and swam toward Ansleigh. His strong arms pulled her up to safety and he swam to the shore. The horses had managed to swim across to the other side.

Ansleigh was coughing and spitting up water. Thomas made her undress and he built a quick fire on the shore. He rubbed her body down and made her drink some whiskey from his pack. He soon had her in a blanket.

She started to cry. "I am holding you back Thomas I am sorry I don't mean to be so much trouble." "Hush now." he scolded her. "Your alive ain't yah that is all that matters. We do have a problem though." "What is it?" asked Ansleigh. "We lost the pouch with the food Ella gave us." "What are we gonna do?" "I am going to find a tree branch and make a fishing pole. You can start digg'n for worms once you get rested." "I am fine Thomas really I want to help." They spent the rest of that day trying to catch fish. They did manage to catch half a dozen Suckers. Which they pan fried over the campfire and ate as if their lives depended on it. Thomas took care of the horses and dried out their gear again. Exhausted they fell asleep by the campfire without setting up their lean- to.

9

"Katherine's Escape"

Katherine was breathless as she ran across the back of the school house. Quin was waiting for her with two horses. She kept tripping over her baggage. She had brought what she thought she would need for their journey. When Quin saw her, he dismounted his horse and walked over to her. She threw her arms about his neck and they kissed. "We have to leave while we still have light. I know a small inn we can stay at tonight. I have already paid for the room under Mr. And Mrs. James." Katherine smiled. "Father, would love that." "You know we will make this right as soon as we are on our way." "I love you Quin." "I know I love you too." He said and they kissed once more.

Katherine couldn't believe she was doing this. Her wedding to Mr. Portly was one day away and she was eloping with Quin James the local smith whom she had loved for so long. She knew her father would be furious but she didn't care. She refused to stay and be in a loveless marriage just to satisfy her father. But she did feel pain on leaving her sister. Martha had married the wainwright's son the month before and was living with his mother. She didn't tell Martha of her plan to elope. She feared her father would have found out and tried to stop her. Quin was leaving behind his family business but he knew his oldest brother would make it work. Katherine was all he cared about. With out her in his life he felt as if he were nothing. They had made a plan to marry in Ohio. He had a cousin he wrote to there about his intent. Then they were meeting up with a wagon train in Indiana that was heading west.

Katherine was so hoping in her heart that she might be able to find Ansleigh once they journeyed west. She was also three months pregnant and did not want to tell Quin.

Jacob Riley was none too happy upon finding his daughter Katherine gone from his home. No one had to tell him what had happened. He knew that she had run off with the local blacksmith. He was enraged that two of his daughters were now gone and he had to live alone in his big rambling house. He had to deal with a very angry Mr. Portly who accused him of lying about the dowry and that his daughter was no more then a common whore. At which point Jacob punched him in the face. He told Martha what had happened and that he was going after Katherine to bring her home. He asked that she might keep an eye on the house while he was gone. And to work with the children at the school until his return. In fact he told her to move in with her husband as they would have a lot more space and privacy. Martha told him she would and to please keep her informed of his whereabouts. It was agreed. Jacob Riley had approached a retired Army Colonel who went by the name of Johnson to travel with him. He said he would be fully compensated for his troubles. It was agreed and they left within the week. He had decided to go on horseback so he could stop along the way to talk with people. He was ill prepared for the rigors of travel as he had become soft over his years as a school master.

His first week out he was in constant pain from saddle sores. Camping and sleeping on the hard ground proved almost too much for him. But his will to find his daughters kept him motivated. Katherine and Quin did make it to Ohio and spent a week with his cousin. They were married by a local Judge. Not what Katherine had dreamed of but at least she was marrying for love. After they were married Quin was anxious to get started west. They had two days ride to reach the Wagon Train before it left its starting point. Ansleigh and Thomas had toughened into their long journey west. They had become adept at catching rabbits and quail to eat. Ansleigh was also becoming a good rider and learning how to care for the horses. One night when they had reached Missouri, they come upon a camp. An old miner was busy skinning a rabbit. He looked up as they approached. His eye sight was poor as he squinted into the dark. "Be you friendly?" He asked. "I am an old man with harm to no one."

"You have nothing to fear old- timer." Said Thomas. "We are look'n for a place to bed down is all?" Thomas introduced himself and Ansleigh. "I could use the company." The old man said. "My name is Nicholas Barnes. I have jerky and I have rabbit on the spit there and another ready for roast'n. There's coffee if you want to call it that." He laughed. "Help yerself." Ansleigh and Thomas had hearty appetites and soon were eating rabbit and

30

finished off the bag of jerky. Ansleigh passed on the coffee it was black as ink.

Nicholas told his story of how he used to be married and had two sons somewhere back East. He had lived most of his life in New Hampshire. He lost his wife to the fever and raised his boys till they left home. It was then he heard of the great gold rush out West. So he decided to sell his farm and he headed out. He never had any luck he said finding the big lode. But he made enough off from nuggets he found panning. It became an obsession with him. Thomas asked him where he was going from here. "I am slowly working my way back to the Old States. Miss my boys. I want to die on home soil. So where are you two headed?" "We're headed west."Said Ansleigh. "Thomas wants to hunt buffalo." "It's no life for a woman specially if you plan on young'uns."

"Haven't really thought that far ahead." Said Thomas as he choked down another cup of coffee. "Say young fella do you go by the name of Andrews?" "Yes, but how would you know that?" "Don't want to upset yah none. But a week back I had a visitor in my camp. None to friendly that feller I kin tell yah." "So?" Thomas wanted to know what this was leading to. "This here fella is a ex-law man goes by the name of Clegg. He told about a young couple fitt'n your looks that a Jacob Riley hired him to find." "So how much is the bounty?" Asked Thomas. "Two hundred dollars." "I can't believe Father would do this." "Don't surprise me none. So you say that was a week ago?" "There abouts he has a buckskin horse and this feller is tall with a big black moustache and he wears a hat with a Eagle feather tucked in his band. Cusses someth'n fierce. He's a mean one. So if I were you two I'd keep my eyes open at all times. He's a head of yah and that's good." Thomas looked over at Ansleigh. "I guess we better get some sleep, morning comes early." He thanked Nicholas for the warning. They both slept lightly that night. Ansleigh lay next to Thomas while tears silently rolled down her face in the dark.

31

10
"The Mining Camp"

Her name was Huittsu (*little bird*). She was small with high cheek bones and large doe shaped eyes. Her Great Grandfather Bear Heart had started Shila's clan. She was of the marrying age and had loved Shila since as far back as she could remember. She smiled every time she saw him. Most of the women in the camp knew how she felt. But Shila was distant with her. He seemed more interested in learning the medicine ways then being involved with women. But that did not stop her from trying too win his favor. Shila was now in his nineteenth year and had done two more Vision Quests since his first.

He was restless and told his father that he felt it was time for a change. River Tree knew that his son was young and eager and ready to explore his world. He asked him if he had thought about marriage. "You know Huittsu loves you it is in her heart to be your wife." "I know Father, I am very fond of her. I cannot tell you why but she is not the one."
"How do you know this?" Asked his father. "Spirit has someone I have not yet met chosen for me."
Shila's father respected his son's reply and did not mention it again.
It was summer and Shila decided to look for healing plants and took supplies to spend a week a way from camp. Many Horses wanted to go with him. Shila told him it was best he go alone. He had known Many Horses since they were children. Many Horses respected Shila and was his closest friend.

He was a sturdy young man and held the distinction of being the best bow maker in their village. The young women all vied for his attentions. But he only had eyes for one.

The first two days Shila went along the river banks looking for Buffalo Berries and Arrow Leaf. He really wanted to find Hop Sage and Colts Foot which he used in his pipe for prayers. One morning as he was heading up the side of the mountain ridge. He heard mens voices. He dismounted from his horse and lay down flat crawling to the top of the ridge to see who they were. There below him was a small encampment with a group of white men walking about and working from a tall structure made of wood. Water was washing down it. They were busy using their hands to sift through what looked like dirt at first. But then he realized it was what his father had told him, was gold. It was then he spotted Night Wing. He was talking with a thin white man who had a scar running through his right eye. The white man gave Night Wing a bottle and he was given two beautiful wolf pelts in exchange. Shila knew it was the whiskey that his grandfather told him about. He also knew where he was getting it from. He noticed several tents and a large central cabin were at the center of this encampment.

He saw women and children and dogs. A corral with horses and cows. A sign which he could not read or understand was erected at the entrance to this camp. Shila spent the rest of that day looking for more healing plants, but his mind kept going back to the camp and all the people he saw there. He felt this was a bad omen. His grandfather told him how white men lusted after gold and killed each other for it. After he gathered the healing plants Shila returned to his camp. He told his father about what he had seen and that Night Wing was trading with the white men for whiskey. River Tree said that he was not surprised. He also told Shila that Night Wing was causing problems with the young men of their camp. He was sharing his whiskey with them then taking their knives, beadwork and other items to trade with. The elders did not like the behavior of the young men as respect was lacking in their actions toward them. He told Shila that a council was being called in two days time and a Chieftain from another clan was coming to talk.

The night of the council had arrived. All the men and women were gathered around a large fire pit. Their leader, Grey Elk sat at the center flanked by River Tree and Shila. The women sat in the inner circle as well. Night Wing was there sitting with his father Red Bird. Fox Healer said a prayer to the ancestors and passed the pipe around the circle. Night Wing refused to smoke it. His father looked at him sternly. He knew this was a major sign of disrespect to the people. Grey Elk spoke "We wish to welcome Deer Strike of the Raven Clan. He is here to help us come to a decision about the whiskey that is causing many problems in our encampment among our young men." Deer Strike thanked Grey Elk for inviting him to sit in the council. "I am here to represent my people. I know in the past there were hard feelings between us.

I cannot take on the wrong doings of my Uncle Lame Wolf. He was a man of great power but it was that very power that destroyed him. I believe in following the red path and healing the wrongs that have been done." "You mean you are a coward and take the easy way. My grandfather Lame Wolf was a brave man and many warriors respected him." "That is true Night Wing, and yet he thirsted for revenge. He did not follow the path of living right and respecting all beings." Said Grey Elk. "He brought the whiskey and poisoned the minds of the warriors in our clan." Said Red Bird. "You are my son and I am proud of you but my father was wrong. He is with the ancestors now. I can only hope his spirit has found peace." "Father, how can you bring shame in front of all the elders?"
"How can there be shame?" Asked Grey Elk. "When a man speaks the truth there is no shame."

"I have sat in silence long enough about this problem." Deer Strike spoke with anger. "I have watched two fine warriors become weak and sick from this whiskey. One near death as he cannot walk or talk with a clear mind anymore. Even our children are curious about this drink. I have been told they are getting this whiskey from white men not to far from here. In a village called Crooked Hat." "It is so." said Shila. "I saw it myself."

Grey Elk shook his head sadly. "How do we keep our young men from going there?" "I think if they go there and bring back this whiskey, they should be punished." Said River Tree. "How can you tell a man what to do? It is his right to live his life as he is free to do." Said Deer Strike. Shila spoke up. "If they want to harm themselves with this whiskey, then they are also harming others by their actions."

"Our children look up to their elders for guidance is this not so?" "What are you saying?" Asked River Tree. "If they wish to be under the spell of this drink then they must go from here. Take their lodges and live alone as it is the path they are choosing. The people should not have to suffer

34

because of their selfishness." "What if they wish to return?" Asked Red Bird. "Then they must be willing to give up the whiskey and regain their personal power." "Shila has spoken with much wisdom." Said Grey Elk. The men and women in the circle all trilled in high pitched voices to show their favor in what Shila had said. Fox Healer said he would spend time praying to the Grandfathers for a sign that this is the right thing to do.

"You think you are special you talk and are a man of little action," spat out Night Wing. "You will not tell me I have to leave this camp. I will drink the whiskey as I am a great warrior and was in battle when you were still at your mother's breast." He lunged at Shila and pulled a knife on him. "Come let me see how brave you really are. Or are you going to hide behind Fox Healer as a child." Shila could feel his anger rising. Soon the two men were wrestling over the knife. Night Wing lashed out and ripped open Shila's side. The blood started to flow. Kachiri begged her father to stop them. "This I cannot do, Shila must prove he is strong or no one will respect him." The men fought long and hard. Rolling into the fire pit and knocking over stacks of drying meat. Shila could feel his bear energy rising in him. He picked up Night Wing over his head and threw him into a brush pile, he grabbed the knife and held it high over his head trilling a war cry. He brought the knife down hard into the ground just inches from Night Wing's face. "I am through with this."

"You must seek your answers from the Great Spirit. You will not bring your whiskey into our camp. Or you will have to face me." With that Shila walked off holding his wounded side. Kachiri went chasing after him.

11

"Vineyard"

Ansleigh and Thomas were only two weeks away from Nevada. Soon to be out of Utah. They had become toughened by their journey. Ansleigh had overcome her problems with saddle sores and was muscular and fit from her riding. She and Thomas had become very close during this time. They had been vigilant watching for the gunslinger that the old miner had warned

35

them about. They had come across a few campers on their journey and exchanged food and conversation. They asked about Clegg but no one knew of him. Thomas had decided to stay in Utah as a camper had told him of the Bison hunts that were taking place in the Beaver Valley area. He was told the government would pay three dollars a hide and more for hooves, bones, and skulls. He had a Springfield rifle in his possession it had belonged to his late father and was a good musket loader for killing large animals. He was told that his father had killed elk and bear with it.

Ansleigh wanted to keep going as she was weary of riding. Thomas told her it wouldn't hurt to stay and make some money before arriving in Nevada. He told her they would need a place to live once they got to the mountains. She wondered where they would get the tools they needed for killing the Buffalo. Thomas said they could rent a wagon in Vineyard and she could take a long needed rest. A fellow traveler had told him they had a small hotel there. It was a hot day for the fall season when they reached Vineyard. Thomas and Ansleigh were in need of water and food. There was a mob of men gathered in the main street. They saw two men who were facing each other hands on their gun belts. Before Thomas had dismounted his horse both men lay dead in the street.

They had killed each other with one shot each between them. There was whistling and cheering going on as many of the bystanders had obviously placed bets on the fight. A tall lanky man with a tin badge gathered what looked like his share of the bets. He told everyone to break it up. A small dark man with swarthy skin and a hunched back came out of the crowd to drag the bodies out of the street. The man with the badge gave the little man a couple of bills and walked off.

The stench of the town overwhelmed Ansleigh. She was use to being on the open ranges and mountain areas where the air was pristine. Flies were everywhere and manure lay open in the street and out houses profusely lined the edge of town. There were tents and lean to peppered throughout the area. There was a tannery with wagons full of Buffalo skulls and dismembered body parts lined up to be emptied. She became ill and before she could get off her horse she vomited quite violently onto the street below. Thomas quickly pulled her out of the saddle. He heard a voice.

36

"This ain't no place for a lady. Specially one as purty as you." Thomas stood there with Ansleigh in his arms.

"Sheriff Patch I'm known as in these parts." "Thomas Andrews and this here is Ansleigh. What happened with those two men?" "Two drunks? We get shoot'ns like that bout everyday cept Sunday."

"They sober up on the Lord's Day a lot of good it does um. Most of um here to make money off the buffalo hunts or miners that are broke look'n for money to keep panning. So what brings you to Vineyard?"

Thomas set Ansleigh down and she leaned into him for support. "We are heading to Nevada territory and the mountains to trap. Thought I would try buffalo hunting myself." "It ain't as easy as you think son. Lotta fellas get killed if they don't know what they are doing.

"Those bulls can run you through if you let um. They can knock a horse right out from under yah." "I told you Thomas we need to forget this." said Ansleigh. "We are here to stay." Said Thomas. "Where is the hotel I heard about?" The Sheriff laughed. "It ain't much two or three to a bed and you have to pay for clean sheets. And it ain't cheap." "I guess we'll chance It." said Thomas. "Where can we get something to eat?" "There's a small kitchen at the whore-house pardon my language miss." Said the sheriff as he tipped his hat at Ansleigh. "The food is good there. I wouldn't feed my dog at the hotel."

The hotel was a two - story building with a balcony. A sign that read Rider's Hotel hung from the roof. There was a small bar set up in the entry way a few men were leaning against it. As soon as Thomas and Ansleigh entered all eyes were on her. Thomas looked around for a desk clerk. The small swarthy man with the hunch back approached him. "Mr. Beety at your service, are you looking for a room?" "Yes in fact we are." Said Thomas. He couldn't help staring at the man. "You are in luck because I do have one left. One of the previous renters is shall I say departed." "Were those the two men I saw in the street earlier?" asked Ansleigh. "Yes miss. I am the hotel clerk and the undertaker both, here in Vineyard." Thomas paid the little man and they followed him up the stairs to a small room at the end of the hallway. The heat was suffocating and the bed had a filthy coverlet that smelled of cattle manure stretched across it. "Sheets washed this morn'n."

Said Mr. Beety. Ansleigh pulled them back they were gray and full of holes. "It's the best I can do." Ansleigh fell across the bed saying "I don't much care." and she quickly fell asleep. They did eat supper later that day and true to the sheriff's warning. One look at the hotel food had Ansleigh and Thomas out the door.

They found a little house on the outskirts of the town where a Mrs. Fairdale was the proprietor. She took them to the back of the house into a dining area. The food was the best Ansleigh had eaten since her stay with Ella. Mrs. Fairdale was talkative and asked them several questions about there being in Vineyard. She told Ansleigh that she could make a lot of money with her pretty face and eyes. But of course seeing she was already taken. It wasn't going to happen, such a shame too she said because she told Ansleigh that she was a real looker. Thomas thanked Mrs. Fairdale for a great meal and quickly escorted Ansleigh from the premises.

Jacob Riley looked down at the blisters on his palms and his back ached from an old battle injury. When he was a lad in a fight during the Ulster rebellion. He thought about Rebecca and how beautiful she was when he first saw her at the harbor in Philadelphia. He had just arrived from Ireland. Eager to find his way in this new America. She was with a friend and they were picking fruits from an open market. Jacob walked up with a duffle slung over his back. Rebecca's green eyes caught his and he was smitten. He smiled at her. "Hey Riley you best plan on call'n it a day we can set up camp here. You won't last much longer sleep'n in the saddle." Said Johnson. The two men settled in the camp; they made a small lean to and Johnson went to hunt rabbit. Jacob set up the camp fire. He was getting better at such things as Johnson was a competent man and Jacob was learning a lot from him. They had been gone almost three weeks.

Johnson taught Jacob how to hunt, and forage for edible plants. They would play cards and drink coffee at the campfires every night. Jacob told Johnson how much he loved his daughters and wanted them near him and he couldn't abide with their running off. Johnson would just look at him and say nothing.

They had one lead on Ansleigh when they met a couple of miners at a campsite. They told them they definitely met the couple that fit their description. They told them they were heading into Nevada Territory and had at least a week's head start. Jacob was holding onto hope that he would find her.

The morning air was cool and there was a haze covering the valley. There were several hundred bison grazing peacefully as the sun started to rise in the East. Thomas could feel his heart beating against his shirt. He had his rifle ready to fire. A small band of men were mounted next to him as they looked out over the valley. Ansleigh was waiting in the wagon parked under a group of Scrub pines. One of the men whispered it was best to walk in quietly behind their horses as the buffalo spooked easily. And they did not want to start a stampede. The men slowly dismounted and started to walk down into the lower valley area. Thomas hoped he would get a buffalo he was sweating and his stomach was queasy as he followed behind the other men. As the sun rose it was blinding and he was trying to see in the distance. But all he could see was the sun's bright halo. Then it happened one of the horses lost its footing and slid down the slope. The other horses started to whinny. The bison startled and began to move.

"This is it!" Shouted one of the men. Thomas heard a gun shot but he couldn't see a thing. He mounted his horse and headed into the chaos. Buffalo were thundering across the valley floor and men were riding along side of them taking aim and shooting. A large bull spotted Thomas and started his charge. He remembered the Sheriff's warning and tried to pull his horse back from the on coming bull. He then aimed his rifle at the beast and shot him right between the eyes. The great bison dropped and slid right into Thomas's horse and he fell off onto the ground.

His horse was rearing and Thomas struggled to calm him and hold him in place. He quickly placed a strip of cloth with a number he was given into the bison's ear. So he could claim it later. That is if someone didn't steal it from you first. He got back on his horse and ran along side the herd trying to get another buffalo. He saw a young cow who was limping along and couldn't keep up with the others. He aimed his rifle and shot her she dropped right there. He dismounted and tagged her. Ansleigh had walked over to the edge of the canyon looking down she saw the bedlam and violence before her eyes. Something deep down inside of her was affected by all of this bloodshed. Innocent creatures being killed and carnage everywhere. She had to look away.

Thomas finally came and fetched Ansleigh he was excited and his eyes were wild. "We must bring the wagon quick before the scavengers lay claim to my kills. Four Ansleigh I killed four bison today." Thomas grabbed the reins and they rode down into the kill area. Ansleigh looked about as men were carving the animals with large knives and blood was spilled everywhere on the once green grass. Thomas found his bison and quickly started carving into them brutally hacking away at their skins and bones. He was covered in blood as he smiled up at her. "We can celebrate tonight a few more days like this will more then pay for this trip. Ansleigh sat in the wagon as if in a dream she suddenly longed to be back home with her sisters. Working in their garden and walking with the students.

"Ansleigh don't just sit here help me get these carcasses on the wagon." Shouted Thomas. She did as he asked and soon she too had blood on her hands. It felt wrong to her in ways she didn't quite understand.

They made their way back to the tannery and waited in the long lines till their wagon was emptied.

They paid them cash and Thomas rented the wagon for the week. When they went back to the hotel. Thomas wanted to drink to celebrate Ansleigh told him she was tired and needed to rest. He ignored her and she left him. She washed herself in the hand basin and soon the water was blood red. She couldn't seem to get it off her skin. As she lay on the bed in their room. Her mind kept going back to the look of terror in the bison's eyes as they were being slaughtered. She fell into a nightmarish sleep. It was dark by the time Thomas got back to the room.

He was drunk and still talking about how exciting it was to face death and win. He rolled over on top of her and took her roughly and with great passion. She could still smell the blood of the bison on him. It was at that moment she lost all respect for him.

40

12
"The Hanging Tree"

Crooked Hat was taking on more immigrants as the months passed.
August had changed the cabin into an office. He had hired an assayer from
back east, a Mr. Jensen. Whom he paid handsomely. Houses were springing
up along the main road of the town. Harp was now the Mayor but August
was the real power behind the throne. Nate and Maizey had opened a small
cafe to feed the workers. It was no more then a shack that seated twenty at
a time. It housed two Rumford cast iron cooking stoves. They called it
Maizey & Nate's Café. They had a Chinese man working in their kitchen by
the name of Ki. They were finding it hard to keep up with the demand for
food. Even though they were being paid by August they had to give him
profits from their kitchen. They no longer had to be kept in captivity as
August warned them his hired guns would kill them at a moment's notice.
He had hired two gun men from San Francisco to keep order. It was simple
if you caused problems you were either hung or shot.   August seemed
to take pleasure in watching men hang. There was a saloon- hotel and a
brothel called Mrs. Jacks. They were building a general store. Even though
there were still plenty of tents set up from the transient workers. They had a
small office for the Coach lines next to the Livery stable. In the back was a
large stockyard with cattle and horses.

Maizey and Nate were building a small house on the edge of town. To
get away from the drunks and gunfights. Maizey still thought of the time
she would kill August. It would then bring her the revenge she sought. She
knew Nate did not have the stomach for it and she despised him for that.
August would sit up late nights in the saloon.

By lantern light he would write and sketch out the plans for his town. He
never thought about the possibility of the land belonging to someone else.
Until one afternoon. Harp came running into August's office. "August you
best get yourself out here." "What are yah carry'n on about? Spit that
tobacca outta your face and talk plain." Harp grabbed him by the arm and
headed out the door. There on horseback were three men. They were
Spaniards. "What is that yah want from me?" The two younger men spoke

in broken English "Si, Senor, we are here to speak for our father." Said the youngest. Then the other young man spoke. "My father wants to know how it is you are building on our land."'" August laughed. "What in the Sam Hill are you carry'n on about? I am standing on my land. It is you who are trespassing. Unless you have some kind of paper work. I suggest you leave for I lose my temper."

The older gentleman listened to his son's as they translated what was being said. He told them what to reply. "My father is Valdez Aquilar. My family has owned this land for over 100 years. We do not need paperwork." "You come here and start ripping apart the land. I know what you do." The youngest told August. "It is none of your damn business what I do. Now get to hell out of here before I have to kill you." Harp, was standing behind August aiming a rifle at the three men. August pulled his rifle out and aimed it too. One of the young men repeated his father's words. "This is not the way of a gentleman." "I never said I was a gentleman." August spat on the ground. The two young men had their hands on their guns as well. It was a stand off as no one moved or said a word. Just then the two hired guns appeared and flanked August.

The old man told them perhaps they could come to an agreement. With that August shot him in the chest. He fell from his horse.

The two young men were then grabbed from their horses by the gunslingers. August had them dragged to the outskirts of the town to his hanging tree as it was named. Both of the Spaniards were hung. August told the people who had followed them out to the tree. That if anyone had any problems with him running things than this would be their fate. People were afraid of August Mayfield and he liked that way.

13
"Winter Wedding"

Ansleigh was growing tired and restless with her life at Vineyard. She was tired of the drunks and daily brawls. She ate lunch every day at the bordello with Mrs. Finley. She was trying to convince Ansleigh to take a job with her. There were times when Ansleigh was tempted just to provoke Thomas. Thomas had made more then enough money for their move. She started to nag him about leaving, because she was ready to move onto Nevada. She didn't like this killing nature that he had. He grew even more removed from what he was doing killing buffalo he thought was fun. She did not see how he could be so callous about this whole affair. She told him she was going home that she had, had enough.

Thomas was very fond of her and did not want her to leave he said they would marry and leave for the mountains. He was ready. Just before they left Vineyard, they had Mr. Peevy perform a marriage ceremony at the local saloon. Sheriff Patch and his wife attended. Ansleigh felt in her heart she had done the wrong thing. But there was no turning back. She wasn't going to return to her father. Life is hard she told herself and she had to accept that.

So on a cold winter's day they started out Thomas had bought a pack mule to carry buffalo hides and supplies for their journey. They were less than two weeks out from Nevada. Ansleigh felt a sense of freedom and release after leaving the town behind. She told Thomas that as far as she was concerned she hoped he was done with killing the buffalo. He told her that it was over and he was glad to be heading into the mountains again. They were slowly moving through passes laden with deep snows.

Scrub pine and cedars and rocky cliffs loomed over head. Ansleigh felt as if nature were purifying her after her long stay at Vineyard. She was so grateful to be free from the heaviness of heart she felt while there. She was full of hope that this would be a new beginning for her and Thomas.

Clegg was a self obsessed man. He also was very fastidious. He was tall and angular with a large black mustache, and his eyes were deep set. He shaved and bathed every day whether it was in a nearby stream or a hotel room. His clothes were always impeccable. He bought new shirts and pants when he worked in the cities. The only thing he never changed was his hat with the single eagle feather in the band. Given to him by a Kiowa. He didn't like working in the mountain ranges he preferred the company of men. But he needed money to head into California. So he took the job from Mr. Riley. Thinking it would be easy enough to find the young girl. But found out soon enough it wasn't going to be all that simple. He had under estimated Thomas and found that he was going to have to earn his pay on this one.

He had been a scout during the War of 1812 and a good one at that, he could track any man or horse for miles. He was thinking about doubling back as he felt that he had a lead on the young couple. It was then that he came upon Crooked Hat. He decided to stay a day or two then head back.

14
"The Sharpers"

Justice Rowena Hamilton and her brother Charles grew up in the slums of London. Their father was a dock worker. Who was killed on the job. Their mother was mentally ill and they ended up in a Poor House. She died of Pneumonia two years after they had arrived. Leaving Justice and Charles to fend for themselves. They learned quickly about survival and the art of the con in the years that followed. By the time they were old enough they were sent to work as servants for a wealthy landowner. Justice was a lovely girl and their new master took advantage of this situation. Charles wasn't about to let this go on, so the two of them ran away. Living in the streets of London as pick pockets and thieves. Sleeping where- ever they could find shelter. Eating restaurant garbage and always one step away from the law. As fate would have it. They picked the pocket of a young man. Who had in his possession two tickets for passage on a Clipper Ship bound for America.

They saw this as a stroke of luck and boarded the ship heading to New York. Upon arrival they worked the streets until they found employment. In a local factory working long exhausting hours. They rented a room from a factory worker they met. This man also happened to be a good card player and taught Charles the game. Charles was a quick study and very good at poker. They would earn a few dollars playing late in the evenings after work. Charles taught Justice, how to play as well. During this time Charles decided to join the Military and headed south to fight in the Indian Wars. Justice stayed in New York.

She met a wealthy widow at a social event who was looking for a companion. She found Justice's beauty captivating. Justice soon learned etiquette and how to charm people with her smile and quick wit. She was taught the art of dancing and playing the piano. The widow reveled in her intelligence and eagerness to learn. They loved playing cards together even though the widow lost most games. Charles had returned from the wars to find his sister. He couldn't believe her transformation. She astonished him. She had grown fond of her mistress and did not want to leave her new found security.

Charles had a plan of working the River Boats in New Orleans. There was a lot of money to be had on the gambling vessels. Justice was torn about leaving. But the widow died shortly after Charles's arrival. Leaving Justice a small inheritance. They ended up going to New Orleans where they lived for several years then onto Jefferson City, Missouri. It was there that Charles saw in the newspaper an article about Crooked Hat and it's rapid growth with opportunities for wealth.

On one hot July day a coach pulled up in front of the Crooked Hat Saloon and Hotel. A couple stepped out; they were well dressed. The gentlemen held his hand up to help the young woman down from the steps. August was sitting on the hotel porch smoking his pipe when he almost tipped his chair over as his feet hit the floor.

The most beautiful woman he had ever laid eyes on was stepping from the coach. She had black hair done up into ringlets framing an oval face, with thick black lashes and hazel eyes. The kind of beauty that is rare wherever you may find it. She was tall and elegantly dressed in an ivory colored dress with a matching parasol and a large hat with roses and feathers protruding. He quickly stepped down off the porch.

"Madam, may I take your hand?" He took her gloved hand and helped her onto the porch steps. I am August Mayfield the town's founder." He said as he tipped his hat to her. "You are just the man we need to see." She said as she introduced him to her brother. Charles was a stocky man with thinning brown hair and a goatee. I am Justice Hamilton. We have arrived all the way from Jefferson City, Missouri. What brings you two to Crooked Hat? If you don't mind my ask'n?"

"Charles and I read in the paper where your little town is busting wide open. It seems your mine is very profitable." "It would seem." He said hesitantly. "I must say I am parched from my long ride. Would we be able to come in out of the heat?" "Forgive my manners but of course." "Where do you want this luggage put mam?" Asked the coach driver. "Why put them right inside the hotel lobby." Charles tipped the driver. As they stepped in out of the heat of the day, August asked the bar keep to fix drinks for everyone. "What's your fancy Miss Hamilton?" "Call me Justice." She said impassively. "Charles and I prefer whiskey if you have it with a little water."

Harp entered as they were sitting down. "What do we have here company?" He asked as he looked the young woman over boldly. "Mayor Miller, mam." As he took her hand. "Course August is the fella that really sees to things around here." "So I noticed." said Justice as she glanced over at her brother. "Mind if I join yah?" "Please do." Said Justice. August gave Harp a cold hard stare. Which made him uneasy. "I see you are kinda quiet." August observed of Charles. "Oh Charles can talk when he needs to." She smiled. Justice reached in her hand bag and pulled out papers to roll a cigarette. Charles lit it for her. August had never seen a woman smoke before. It surprised him.

"So what can I do for you?" August inquired. "Charles and I are professional gamblers."

"A couple of "sharpers are yah." August leaned into Justice "And with your looks I imagine you pull folks into your cheat'n game?" "Hold on now Charles and I run a clean game." "I've been known to play a game of poker and win but at the end of my gun. All you need is a good shooter and it keeps things in line." Said August. "Are you suggest'n we start gambl'n here at the hotel?" Harp asked. "That's my guess." Said August spitting out a wad of tobacco.

"You have drunks just burning to spend their money. Charles and I have worked many a hotel. Spent five years in New Orleans working the river boats." "Why'd yah leave?" asked Harp." "Let's say the same people get to

46

know you and it gets harder to make a win." "Justice and I can bring in more money than you can imagine." "So what's my cut?" Asked August. "Sixty to forty split." "I don't like them odds." August said staring straight into Charles's eyes. "Fifty -fifty or no deal. Besides I am furnishing you a place to stay and I'll feed yah as well. I'll even provide yah a shooter for protection." "Charles can handle a gun he was a sharp shooter in the war." Justice added. "With some of the hot heads we got runn'n around he'll need to." Said Harp. "Do you have any law men working here?" Asked Justice. "A drunk tin badge by the name of Daniels. But I am the only real law in this town. Bar Keep set up some more drinks. I think we can come to an agreement of some kind." By the end of the afternoon they had all come to a verbal contract of how it would work.

"Mr. Mayfield you need to come quick there's a shoot'n out at the site. Old Tin Pan is drunked up and shoot'n at everything that moves."

A grizzly faced barrel chested man had ran in from the street took his hat off and bowed his head to Justice. "Where's the hired guns?" Growled August. They're up at the whore house its Saturday remember." "Damn I pay'um enough they need to do their jobs." "Want I should fetchum?" asked the intruder. "Harp and I'll take care of it we need you for back up though." August said as he reached behind the bar and pulled out two Flintlock rifles throwing one at Harp. The three men started out the door when Charles called out. "I'm going too." "You'll need a gun." Said Harp. "I have the only one I need right here." He said, pulling back his coat to show his Colt revolver. Justice walked out to the porch and watched as the men walked down the center of Main Street heading out to the mining area.

When they got there an old bowlegged man with a long grey beard was shooting a gun at everything that moved. Cursing and spitting tobacco in every direction. He did all this while he sipped whiskey from a bottle. August and the men spread out around him. "Tin Pan put that damn gun away before you get hurt." "I ain't gonna stop shoot'n till I get paid!" "What you talk'n about? Men got paid yesterday at noon you know that." said August. "That snooty assayer of yourn refused to pay me?" "He can't do that he works for me." "You better tell the bastard cuz he didn't pay

47

me." "Put down your gun and I will talk to him, you need to go and sleep it off." Tin Pan swirled around aiming his gun at the men. He pulled up his gun and at the same time Charles had shot the gun from the old man's hand. "Did you see that?" exclaimed Harp. "I ain't never saw nobody that fast."

August walked over to Tin Pan reached down picked up his gun and threw it to Harp. He grabbed Tin Pan by the throat. "Now listen good old man if I have to come out here and do this again. Your feet won't be touch'n the ground. You will be swing'n from one of those trees yonder. You will get paid when I see some work from you." With that August slugged the old man in the face breaking his nose. "Let's get back to town I need a drink." He said. The men followed him as Tin Pan stood holding his nose as it bled all down the front of his shirt.

15
"The Opera House"

August decided to go into the logging business. The area he had built in was full of old growth trees. With the gold boom everyone was in need of lumber. Soon more workers were flooding into Crooked Hat. He put Harp in charge of over seeing the logging camp. The nearby river made it easy to send the logs down to Pigeon Grove. Then overland and all points West. August had been thinking of adding an Opera House. A traveling troupe of actors stopped on their way to San Francisco. They performed in the saloon to standing room only. A saloon wasn't deemed fit for a decent woman. Except for the town prostitutes who found compliant business in that crowd.

August liked the color and enchantment of the actors and their costumes. They excited his senses. One of the actresses a Miss Faye, was quite attractive he thought. She had a beautiful singing voice. This gave him an idea of the possibility of producing his own show. He could run it once a month. Build a Opera House like the ones in Boston. He approached Miss Faye after their second show. He bought her a drink. She was a petite brunette with striking blue eyes. He noticed her small hands and she had a pleasing way about her. She made him feel self conscious. Which was unusual for August as very few people vexed him.

Beatrice Mary Prohaska (Miss Faye was her stage name) was an only child who grew up in New York. Her father was a watch maker from Austria. Coming to this country in search of wealth and starting his own business. Which he did. He married a young Irish Immigrant Mary Murphy who died in childbirth.

He raised Beatrice on his own and she grew up helping her father in his clock shop. She met Mickey when they were still young. He would make deliveries to her father's shop. Beatrice loved him deeply. They secretly planned on marrying. But her father was a stern man. He wanted her to marry above her situation. He saw Mickey as a threat so when the situation presented itelf he killed him. Accusing him of molesting and raping his daughter. A fabrication and Beatrice hated him for it. After the scandal she ran off. She traveled to Saratoga Springs where she found a job working as a housemaid for the Blythe family. Aristocrats from England.

August had offered Beatrice a substantial amount of money; to perform and stay in Crooked Hat. At first she wasn't interested as she wanted to go on to San Francisco. When he told her, she would be the director and in charge of hiring performers. She accepted. Thorton Blythe her companion stayed on to help her.

August set about building the Opera House. It would also be doubling as a City Hall and Community building. The theater itself would be small with a raised platform and curtain. He had ordered a piano all the way from New York City and theater chairs. They were being shipped overland. He was excited at the prospect of this venture. He knew that they would also draw people from Pigeon Grove a near by settlement.
Beatrice had a ten year old boy, she claimed to be her brother. By the name of Zacharia that traveled with her. He started working at the hotel.

Washing bar glasses and stocking shelves, emptying chamber pots and sweeping floors. He also assisted the hotel cook, Mr. Cranston. He ended up staying with the Cranston family during the week while Beatrice stayed on at the hotel.

49

Beatrice met Justice when she moved into the hotel. Right next door to her and her brother Charles.

They met one morning at breakfast in the diningroom. Beatrice was looking for a place to sit. "Please come and join me." She heard a woman's voice. Sitting in the dimly lit room was a well-dressed woman in black. Not much older than herself. "Justice Hamilton glad to finally meet you. You are a songbird and a good one I am told." "I get by." Said Beatrice. "My name is Beatrice Faye." "Please do sit down I could use some female company, it gets tiresome talking to men all day. They think I am a prostitute here you know." She laughed. "Truth is I haven't slept with a man in quite a while." "That really isn't any of my business."

"What can I get you?" The hotel clerk asked Beatrice. "Get what you want it is on me." Said Justice. Tipping the clerk. "Just coffee, please." "You aren't trying to play a shrinking violet here? I mean, come on honey you are an actress."

"I don't like small talk." "You are straight forward I will give you that. So you are not married then?" "No, I am not. I was betrothed, many years ago to a young Irishman. "What happened?" "My father shot him." "Why?" "You would have to understand my father, he was all about money and social graces. He thought that Michael had molested me. Nothing was further from the truth. Anyway Mickey is dead and my father got away with it." "I am sorry." "Don't be, I live with it." Justice could sense the bitterness in her voice. "So how did you end up here?" Beatrice told her the story of how she had come to Crooked Hat.

After her father killed Mickey she left New York and found a job working for the Blythe family in Saratoga Springs. They were a wealthy family from England. She did housekeeping for them for room and board.

That is when she met Thorton their youngest son. They soon become close friends. He had an uneasy relationship with his father.

Thorton wanted to be an actor. They wanted him to go to medical school. He fought them about it. He went to college for two years and quit. Beatrice, liked the theater. She would spend time helping him memorize his lines. He soon had her involved with acting. She had a beautiful singing

50

voice. They were doing Operettas at a local theater. That is when Thorton met a young actor heading to Boston.

He ran off taking Beatrice with him. They lived in Boston for ten years. When they weren't doing shows they both worked. Beatrice as a seamstress and hat maker. Thorton worked in a local Book Shoppe. They read in the paper about the Gold Rush in California and San Francisco was the new mecca of the West. The place to make your fortune.

"So here we are." "What about the boy?" "Zacharia is my brother." Beatrice hesitated. "And?" Justice inquired. "He joined me after our father died." "So do you love this Thorton?" "No, not like that, he is a good friend however. He doesn't prefer women." "Oh." said Justice as her brows raised. "He is however a gentleman and a gracious man." Beatrice added. "His manners are impeccable." At that point Thorton entered the room. He was tall and had long dark hair pulled back into a tie. His face was soft with full lips and large dark eyes. One might say he was elegant for the surroundings he found himself in. He spotted Beatrice. "There you are I have been looking for you. Whom may I ask is this lovely creature?" Taking Justice's hand in his. "You my dear should be on the stage. A rose by any other name would smell as sweet." "You obviously are Mr. Blythe." "At your service." He kissed her outstretched hand. "He is gracious." Smiled Justice. "Do you mind if I join you?" "By all means please do. Do you smoke?" "Yes." Justice rolled a cigarette for Thorton and they smoked together.

"Mr. Mayfield is planning on opening our show within the month." "I hope so." said Beatrice. "I need the money." "Oh you needn't worry. He will pay you. That you can set store by. Just don't cross him." Justice warned her. "After all, I don't know too many women who have theaters built for them." She quickly swallowed a shot of whiskey. "Kind of early for that isn't it?" Teased Thorton. "It keeps me pacified." Justice told him as she ordered another drink.

16
"Grey Elk's Farewell"

The snow was deep and Shila kept losing his footing. He was carrying
his Grandfather Grey Elk's body to the scaffold that he and his father had
built for him. It was a dreary day. It fit the way Shila felt inside. He had
loved this man since he was a child. Grey Elk had given him his first bow,
and taught him how to hunt. He was the reason that Shila knew the old and
sacred language that few understood or used anymore. He was at his side
when his Grandfather drew his last breath. He told Shila to always be true
to the spirit within. To be with their people to guide them through the
trying times that lay ahead. Shila made him a promise that he would do as
he asked in honor of his life. River Tree wanted to help Shila with his father
but he knew that his son had to do this in his own way. He would bring the
people to say their farewells when Shila was finished.

Shila thought how peaceful his Grandfather looked lying there with his
face in a deep sleep facing ever out toward the sky. Shila trilled as the tears
fell and he knew that this was only the beginning of many such things to
come. He prayed and asked the Great Spirit to give him the strength that
he needed to be a true spirit warrior.

When he returned to the village Huittsu was there to greet him. She too
had been crying. Shila could hear the women keening and it only made him
more distraught. He went to find his horse and Huittsu followed him. He
rode his horse hard until finally the animal buckled and fell to its knees.
Shila knew his actions were wrong. He left the horse and started walking
into the mountains. He was angry and did not know why. As he walked into
the trees he felt as if someone were following him.

He hid behind a tree and waited. As the person who had been tracking
him walked by he grabbed her by the throat and looked into Huittsu's eyes.

"What are you doing here?" He demanded. "I was worried about you. I
wanted to comfort you." "I do not need you to be my mother. I came out
here to be left alone. Can you not honor that." he snapped at her. Tears
welled in her eyes. "I am sorry Shila I did what was in my heart. I know
how much you loved your Grandfather. I loved him too. It is not only your

loss, but that of the people as well." Shila knew she was right. He reached for her hand taking it in his.

Huittsu had wanted to be in his arms. She truly loved Shila. She closed her eyes and pulled him towards her. Shila gently stepped back and kissed her forehead. "It is the love of a sister that I feel for you. I know this is not what you want to hear but it is my truth."

"There is nothing I would not do for you." "I know this, I cannot return that kind of love. I will not take that from you if I cannot return it in full." Huittsu wept with her face buried in his coat. Shila lifted her face to his and kissed her. "You must let me go. Can you do that?" He turned his back on her and walked off leaving her alone. His anger would not leave him as he went ever deeper into the forest.

"We must be getting close to the town don't you think?" Asked Mr. Riley as he leaned over his saddle. "The old man said it was a day's ride." "I have watched the vultures they are getting thicker so I know we are near some kind of settlement. You can always tell the stench of settlements by the number of death birds that soar overhead."

Mr. Johnson laughed as he took a swig of whiskey from his flask. He then passed it over to Mr. Riley who took a long hard swallow. "Hold on there we'll soon be Crooked Hat and you can wet your whistle there."

Mr. Riley had grown fond of drinking it helped blur the reality of his loneliness. "I hope so I need a rest from this horse. I never have been fond of riding. I need to stretch my legs a bit too." Said Mr. Johnson. "I am in need of a woman's company, that old man said they have some fine skirts there." "You can have your women as for me I want to sleep on a real bed again." Mr. Riley said as he urged his horse forward. The two men were growing tired of each other and were both ready to reach their destination.

17

"A Bitter Season"

Quin and Katherine had been on the wagon train for several weeks. Katherine was visibly showing. Quin was happy about her having his child.

Yet she worried about having it while traveling. Quin reassured her that she would be fine that there was a mid-wife on the wagon train who would be there to help her. Katherine had grown homesick for her sisters and the comfort of living in a house. Her hands were calloused from the work and handling the horses.She grew thin. She had taken to bouts of crying and not knowing why. Quin was angry with her at those times. Saying she was being too soft and wanting attention that she should be ashamed of herself for acting like a child. It was at these times she hated him. Maybe she should have married Mr. Portly after all. At least she would be living in a house and enjoying the benefits of his wealth.

She didn't want this child she carried. It made her loath herself for such feelings. So when she lost her baby a little boy; she carried the burden of her sin. It was on a rain drenched night. That had hit the little band of wagons. There were high winds and a chill of snow that was coming. The mid-wife an elderly woman had all she could do to console Katherine as the birth pains were unbearable. The baby was born breach and had come way to soon. He had lived long enough for Quin to hold him but died shortly after. Katherine had drifted into a coma and had lost a lot of blood. The mid-wife told Quin to expect the worst. Katherine lay in the wagon for two days. An Indian woman was summoned and she stayed with Katherine. She chanted and used herbs to stop the bleeding. On the third day Katherine was responsive to her surroundings.

She was disoriented and kept asking for her baby she didn't remember his dying. Quin, was relieved to see her awake. He knelt down next to her in the wagon telling her that he could not bear it if he had lost her too. Katherine looked at him feeling nothing. Only her tears were there as a reminder of her lost baby.

A red fox ran through the thicket and spooked Ansleigh's mare sending Ansleigh falling to the frozen ground. She was in severe pain, her ankle and leg were swelling up quickly. Thomas dismounted and came to her side. He pulled up her skirts to look at her swollen leg. "I don't think you broke anything but it will swell and turn black. I will have to make a travois for you to ride in, you won't be able to straddle the horse anymore." Ansleigh was already in a sullen mood. She had grown so restless as of late.

Homesick more and more for her family. She had fallen out of love with Thomas and she knew she was carrying his child. She didn't want to tell him but she knew she must.

"Thomas I am growing weary of these travels. I need to find roots somewhere." "I know," he said as he spread out a blanket on the snow for Ansleigh to sit on. He gently lifted her in his arms and placed her on the blanket then set about building a small fire. "I guess this will have to do for tonight. I will see how you are doing in the morning before we travel on." Ansleigh winced in pain. He made a pack of snow and placed it on her swollen leg. "This will help a little." he said and offered her a sip of whiskey. Which she refused. "I will be all right. It looks like more snow is coming." "Yes", he said looking up at the gathering clouds. "I'll find limbs to make the travois maybe with some luck I'll snare a rabbit for our spit."

"It won't take long to put up our lean- to." With that he grabbed his rifle and disappeared into the forest.

Ansleigh sat there growing sleepy when she felt as if there was a presence near by. She looked up and strained her eyes into the growing gloom of the day. She thought she saw a branch move. She slowly pulled her knife out from its sheath holding it tightly in her hand. Just then a tall good looking young man appeared before her. His hair was long and he had fine features. He was dressed in a white blanket coat with crimsons stripes and leather leggings. He moved silently and she sensed his power. They both looked at each other for the longest time, not saying a word. She held up her knife as if to scare him off. He knelt down next to her and gently took the knife from her hand. He looked at her leg then reached into his pouch and pulled out a clay vessel filled with a grease like substance. He started to rub it on her leg then handed her the medicine. He motioned for her to keep it. He then stood up looking at her once more before he left. Then as quickly as he had appeared he was gone. Ansleigh wasn't sure that she may have had a vision, if it were not for the small vessel of grease he had given her. She hid it away deciding not to tell Thomas about this.

Thorton staggered falling from the out-house door into the mud he lay there in a drunken stupor. Just then he felt a man's boot lift his face out of the mud. "So here is the young Romeo from the acting troupe. Ahh fair Juliet it is the East from yonder window breaks." Clegg laughed as he lit a cigar. Thorton stood up wiping the mud from his face. "I must say you speak well and you know Shakespeare it seems?" "My brother was an actor my father hated him for it." Sneered Clegg.

"What do you want from me?"Asked Thorton barely able to stand. "I think you and I have some things in common." said Clegg as he looked Thorton in the eye. "I like the way you look does that surprise you?"

"It has been awhile since I met anyone that appeals to me in that way." "I am sure you are misinformed about me sir."Said Thorton. Just then Clegg grabbed him by the throat and lifted his face to his. "I know what I like." He said coldly. "You and I can make the best of this situation don't you agree? I have been watching you. I can make it worth your while. I have more than enough money and I like spending it on my friends."

Thorton felt a disquiet about this man yet was strangely attracted to him. "Come let me take you back to my room you can clean up there. What are you drinking? I will have the bar keep run us up a bottle." The two men walked back toward the hotel. August had been standing in a hedge row where he went to relieve himself. It was then he saw the two men together. "Well I'll be damned." He said as he watched them walk away and up the hill.

"I'm tell'n yah Nate, we need to ask August for more money. We should have been in charge by now.
I didn't bargain for none of this and you know it." "Things ain't that bad Maizey why yah complain'n all the time. That's all you do. August has been pay'n us. We got a good little business go'n here." "Good little business? You call it!" She hissed. "We own the mine, if you were any kinda man you woulda put a bullet between that man's eyes and we would be runn'n things round here not him and that ape Harp. Yore a coward plain and simple "le lache!" With that Nate shoved Maizey knocking her to the floor. "Shut up Maizey do you hear me?"

Maizey crawled over to the stove and grabbed a poker, she swung it at Nate hitting him across his face. She broke one of his teeth. He ran out of their house leaving her shaking with rage.

18
"Dr. Haveston"

Beatrice rolled over and sat on the edge of the bed. August reached up and touched her arm. "So are you ready for more?" He jeered. "A man needs to take care of his women." She could not bear his touch. But she kept telling herself that the money was worth it. Wasn't it? After all the Opera House marquis boasted her name. She was doing three shows a week and singing on the weekends at the hotel. August had bought her three new dresses from New York and a friendship ring he called it with a large ruby at its center. She knew his generosity had a price with it. He warned her if he caught her with another man he would kill them both. She knew that he patronized the local bordello. In fact she was rather worried as she was having issues with her health. She feared she had contracted some kind of disease of a feminine nature. She didn't want August or anyone to know about it. But she knew she had to seek a doctor's attention soon. She bent over and kissed August full on the lips cringing inwardly. "That's more like it." He said. Slapping her hard on her buttocks. "I will see you tonight at the hotel. I was told Judge Garner will be attending. I want you to dine with him. He would be a good ally to have. I am told he is a friend to President Fillmore. We need the connections. Wear that blue dress I bought you. It shows of your curves darl'n." "Yes of course." Beatrice said lost in thought. She quickly dressed and left August still in bed. He had rolled over and was soon asleep. A young woman had told her about a doctor. A Dr. Haveston who lived in a grey clapboard house on the edge of town. He shared it with a young woman. Who was an Opium addict by the name of Molly.

He treated anyone that needed his help and many people with secrets went there. Beatrice was one of them. She went to talk with Zacharia who

57

was already at work in the hotel kitchen. She told him she needed to see the doctor that day. She asked him how he was. He was depressed and told her he missed being able to stay with her. "It'll change soon I promise. I almost have enough money saved to get a place of our own. Staying with Mr. Cranston isn't all that bad is it?" Zacharia looked at her sullenly. I know it isn't easy please be patient. I will try and spend Sunday with you." With that she left.

She wore a black silk scarf draped over her hat as if she were someone in mourning. She could not chance anyone recognizing her. She walked the full distance to his home. When she finally arrived, her expectations were met. It was a grey dwelling with plain curtains at the windows drawn against the light of day. She gingerly knocked on the door. A young woman with a swollen jaw answered. She had long stringy hair that lay limp about her face her eyes were dark brown and she was excruciatingly thin. Her dress was filthy and her eyes cast downwards.

"I suppose you'll be need'n to see the doctor?" "Yes, I don't have an appointment." "Don't matter none most folks just walk on in. If he's here he'll have a look at yah. If he's been drink'n it's best you go back to where yah come from."

"Is he here? I have the money." "I can tell by your fine clothes. She said bitterly. Sit yourself down and I'll see if he's in his office." Beatrice swallowed hard and sat in a kitchen chair. Trying not to breathe too deeply. There were food stains on the floor and and a musty odor filled the air. The interior of the house was dim and lonely. Left over food and an empty whiskey bottle was on the table.

The house was very cold. She noticed a small fire place that had burned down to embers in the parlor. A perception of gloom hung heavy in this place. She was just about to leave and forget about it when a young man entered the room.

He wasn't what Beatrice had expected. He was much younger than she had anticipated. He was of medium stature with a pleasing face. Light brown hair and blue eyes. His clothes were clean and he had a look of sophistication about him. "Molly tells me you need to see me?" "Yes, if it isn't an inconvenience?" "I am sure you are here for a reason. So follow me

58

and I will see what I can do to help you." Beatrice quickly followed the doctor into his office.

She was in total shock when she entered the little room he had as an office. It was immaculate. Everything in its place. Clean towels and linens and his instruments all in neat little rows on a nearby table. "Everyone has that reaction." he said. "When they come in here. I had a very strict Professor of Medicine at the University I attended in New York. I would spend hours cleaning my instruments, scrubbing floors and polishing the basins we used." "I ...I wasn't expecting any of this really."She stammered. "No, it's all right. Molly lives in the house. I stay here and sleep on a cot in the back room. I prefer it that way.

So please tell me what brings you here?" "Suddenly Beatrice became very conscious of her situation. "Maybe I can come back some other time?" "You must feel you need my help or why else would you have come? Please Miss, sit down." "My name is Beatrice.' "You look so familiar should I know you?" "Does it matter?"She asked him. "No, not really. How then can I help?' "It is so embarrassing."

Beatrice was really confounded she found this man to be attractive. She didn't want him to know about August.

"Are you with child?" He asked her. "No, but I am having problems of a feminine nature." "What do you want to show me then? I have a sheet that I use for your privacy." Taking a deep breath she said "Yes, I will do this." The young doctor placed a large sheet between them.

He had her lie down on an examining table. Beatrice took off her bloomers. The doctor gently touched her body and noticed sores on her thighs and bruising too. You have a really nasty discharge and I notice someone has been very rough with you. You have contusions.
You can sit up now." "What is it?" Asked Beatrice. "You are not going to like this but you have contracted Gonorrhea. It is in the early stages. But if you don't treat it right away it will only become worse. You will become very sick and some people die from it." "What can I do?" she asked. "I can try treating it with Silver -nitrate. I do have a supply as many prostitutes carry the disease. If I were you I would tell your gentleman about this

59

because he is obviously the carrier." "He will kill me." "Either way you will die if you let it go."

Beatrice started to cry and she could not stop. The doctor let her cry. He then said she must follow his advice about the medicine. He gave her, her first treatment that day and told her to return in a week's time. Beatrice paid him well. He told her not to have intercourse under any circumstances. As she needed time to heal. As she left his office that day, she was in a quandary about what to do. She was very afraid of August. She was perplexed over Dr. Haveston. As he was not what she had expected? She couldn't help thinking how it was that he had ended up here.

The hotel was packed that night a group of miners were celebrating. They had found another gold lode tunneling down in the mine shaft. August was beside himself with jubilation. This meant more money and he had a dream of someday having a railroad coming to Crooked Hat. He had plans for a depot and adding another hotel for guests. He was buying everyone drinks at the bar. Beatrice was in her blue dress and had just finished dining with Mr. Garner. He had his hands all over her throughout the meal. She was most anxious to be free of him. Beatrice was asked to sing. She wasn't in the mood but August gave her that look and she knew it meant a fist in her face if she refused. Justice was drunk and kept hitting the wrong keys on the piano. Beatrice tried to sing but it was of no use. She left the hotel and walked out into the cold night air. When she felt someone grab her by the throat. It was August. "What the hell do you think you are do'n?" Get back in there and do what you are paid to do." Beatrice was afraid but she knew she couldn't do as he asked. She struggled for the right words. "Look you whore I am tell'n you one more time to get back in there." "I am sorry August but I can't. I wanted to tell you earlier. I am ill" "What do you mean ill?" "I went to the doctor's today. He told me I have Consumption." She lied. "Consumption! That is catching?" "Yes, it can be.

He told me to rest and he would keep me on a medication to help." "Damn you say! What the hell good are you to me now? You better be bedd'n down with Justice cause I don't want any kind of your crud gett'n to me." He pushed her to the ground and used his foot to hold her face in the mud. She was fighting to breathe. He reached down pulling off the ruby ring he had given her. He then spat on her and walked off. She lay there as the coldness of the night air crept over her. She wanted to die.

19
"The Hawk Lesson"

Ansleigh couldn't stop thinking about the young man she had seen. She was mesmerized by him. Something was so very familiar about his eyes. Then it came to her. As she lay next to Thomas at their camp one night. She had dreamt about him. Actually more then once. She started to recall the dreams and how odd they were. This was the first time she had been exposed to a native so close she could feel his breath. She had been very calm in his presence and felt no fear. The grease he had given her quickly took down the swelling. Thomas was surprised at how quickly she had recovered. She wondered what all of this meant and if she would be seeing him ever again.

As Thomas broke camp Ansleigh decided to tell him about her carrying his child. Thomas started to grin. "Ansleigh really? I am going to be a father. I'll be damned. All the more reason to get you settled in somewhere and out of this weather. We are in the Sierra's now and we can start looking for a clearing to put up a small one room cabin. I can have it up in a couple of week's time. Enough to keep us out of the elements till spring. When do you think the baby will come?" "The best I can figure by late spring." "If you would prefer may be I can find a small settlement to winter in." "No, Thomas after Vineyard I have had enough of people. I would rather be alone." "What about a doctor or a mid-wife?" He asked. "There'll be time for that when I am near." "I want you to rest up tomorrow and I will ride ahead to see if I can find a settlement where we can at least buy supplies to bring with us. Might as well settle in somewhere near water if we can." Ansleigh agreed.

Thomas left at dawn telling Ansleigh he would be back before nightfall. In some ways she liked her time alone. She felt a bond with the baby in her womb. Even though she had lost her feelings for Thomas, she hoped maybe the child would rekindle their relationship.

Shila had lost track of how long he had been in the forest. He slept at night under the pines building small fires to stay warm. He remembered his Grandfather Grey Elk telling him that a warrior can live in all the conditions of nature. From the hottest to the coldest days to watch his animal brothers and how they survive throughout the seasons. His anger had slowly subsided. It was because of his misgivings about whether or not he could do what was expected of him by the people. He did not want to disappoint his father or Healing Fox. But as hard as he would try, he could not control his emotions. They pulled at him and taunted the high ideals he had for himself. He prayed to the Grandfather's for answers. He had dug down into a small pit he had made himself. It was strewn with pine branches and dried leaves.

He was out of the wind and the bitter cold that had crept in. As he sat there deep in thought he looked out and saw a young hawk. It was fighting against the gusts of wind from a snow storm that was sweeping through the mountains.

It was trying to reach the tree tops and safety. Every time it attempted to go into the wind it blew him back. He made several attempts and was growing weaker with each struggle. Then it happened. The young hawk started soaring letting the wind take him with it. He no longer fought it. Shila watched as the hawk was swirled up effortlessly to the highest point of the tree. Where the hawk caught a branch and was at long last secure in its pinions.

He thought how like himself this young hawk was. He struggled with his fears and felt trapped and wanted to control his destiny. The more he struggled with it the more he was blown about like the young bird. He knew that he would have to let go and let spirit take him where he was needed. Just as those thoughts came to him he looked out again and saw his Grandfather Grey Elk in the distance. The snow swirling about him. He was smiling and nodding. He then turned into a giant eagle that unfurled its wings and flew heavenward. Leaving Shila below a small figure buried in the snow humbled by this lesson.

It was late when Mr. Johnson and Mr. Riley rode into Crooked Hat. They saw a young woman laying in the middle of the street. Mr. Riley brought his horse up short and dismounted. Walking over to her he knelt down. "Miss are you all right?" Beatrice rolled over looking into his face. "Yes, I must have fallen. Thank you for your concern." He gently helped her up. "Looks like the little woman may have had a little too much to drink?" Chortled Mr. Johnson. "No, I caught my foot in a rut and fell." "You are a pretty little thing why are yah alone this time of night?" "I must be heading home." "Can a man find a drink and a woman there?" "If that is what you have a mind to do, then that is the place. Now if you will excuse me I have to call it a night." "Are you sure you will be all right then?" asked Mr. Riley. "Where's your coat? Let me help get that mud off from you." "Leave it be. I will be fine. I need to go." She said as she hurried off down the street into a dark alley. Once in the safety of the darkness she leaned against a building and wept. She didn't know where to go that night. She knew Justice would be with August. She had to find Thorton. She walked quickly in the cold her arms wrapped about her shoulders looking for his room. He stayed at Mrs. Clancy's boarding house during the week.   When she arrived, an old woman with an embittered face answered the door. "What do you want? And what are you do'n out in the streets this time of night? Before Beatrice could speak the woman accused her of having a bad reputation. "You're one of them painted ladies up at the hotel. I know your kind." "I am looking for Thorton Blythe is he here? I am his sister." "His sister? I don't think so. You need to go peddle yourself someplace else for I have my husband show you the street." She closed the door sharply in Beatrice's face. She knew she had to get out of the cold she had nothing to protect her from the elements. It was then she thought of the doctor. Surely he would help her. She walked briskly in that direction as the snow gently fell upon her shoulders.

20

"The Card Game"

Clegg, sat in a chair next to his bed. Thorton was sprawled out on the sheets in a drunken stupor. He looked at him admiring his physical beauty. He couldn't remember how long he had preferred the company of men. His father had been a hard hearted man who died of a liver disease. Too much drink. Clegg, rarely saw his father sober. His oldest brother had left home and joined a wagon train never to be heard of again. His father would hiss every time he spoke his name. Said he would never be allowed in his home again. His youngest brother was an actor living in Boston. Clegg's mother was a nondescript little woman who never spoke. She treated Clegg and his brothers as if it was a duty rather than a joy.

He felt guilty most of his childhood never knowing why. He had a young friend Billy. They were inseparable. He had loved him for many years. Billy was killed in a hunting accident. Clegg, never got over it.

His mother was slovenly and their house smelled of dirt and whiskey. He cleaned up after his parents and became more obsessed about cleanliness as the years passed. He met a young girl when he was sixteen. Her name was Georgina. They had sex in her father's barn often that summer. He had been hired to work the fields. She was crazy in love with him. He did not love her. He felt nothing when they were together. He grieved Billy though. Clegg left home after his father died. He was eighteen and joined the Army. He fought in the South against the British in the war of 1812. While he was in the Army he learned how to track and he was an excellent marksman. After the war years he set out on his own. Traveling from New Orleans to the Eastern Coast.

In Philadelphia he met a Lawman by the name of Jack Bowls. Jack was a good looking man, strong and determined. Clegg admired him greatly. Jack deputized him and they worked together for four years. Until Jack had decided he had, had enough. He ended up marrying a woman much younger than he was. Clegg felt abandoned and he hated the sight of Jack's young bride. He some how felt betrayed. He knew then that he wanted to work alone and that his preference was for men and not women. He still thought of Billy even after all these years. In a way Thorton reminded Clegg of him.

Charles drew his gun slowly and had it pointed underneath the table at the man who sat across from him. "You damn card sharp. They told me to watch you and that hussy you're with." "You can call me any name you want but you better be apologizing to my sister." "Sister hell she's ain't nothing but your accomplice the two of you work together." Harp walked over to the table
"Does there seem to be a problem here?" "Nothing I can't handle."Said Charles. "Yeah there is a problem. You have card sharps work'n here." "Look mister, why don't you let me buy you a drink. It doesn't pay to be a sore loser." Said Justice.
The agitated man went for his gun. At that point Charles pulled the trigger and the man pulled back his hand, his gun was laying on the floor. "Now while I am still sober; if I were you I would take your backsides out of here." The man quickly picked up his gun and ran out of the hotel. "Damn it Charles I told you to keep your arguments outside of the hotel!" said August." "He was defending me is all. Nothing to get all ruffled over." Said Justice as she poured Charles a drink.
"He didn't like losing. We are two hundred dollars richer by my count. Besides what's it to you?" "Depends on who has the upper hand around here doesn't it Mayfield." Said Charles. "In what way?" Demanded August. "This man insulted my family." August was growing more agitated. He stood before Charles weaving back and forth. "If I were you, I'd call it a night." Charles said as he laughed. August pulled his gun on Charles shooting past his ear. Charles recoiled and aimed his gun quickly. But Justice lunged in front of him. "You two have had way too much to drink. You need to settle down." "Whoa there, Justice is right lets all simmer down." Harp intervened.
Mr. Riley and Mr. Johnson stood by watching as they drank at the bar. "So you say that's the fella that runs things around here?" Asked Mr. Johnson. "Yep that's him," said the barkeep. And you don't wanna cross him." "I can see that." Said Mr. Johnson. Nate was there watching as he

greedily drank down several shots of whiskey to ease the pain of his broken tooth. He didn't want to return to his house knowing Maizey was still angry with him. He wanted to run from this place. Start over but how could he? When his cowardice was always eating away at him. Instead he ordered another drink so he could slowly sink into oblivion.

Charles was livid as he grabbed his money off the table. "I'm keeping this lot. If you want your cut then you'll have to face me to get it." "That can be arranged." Growled August. Justice took him by the arm. "Come on let's you and I take a little walk." He pulled away from her but she insisted. She walked with him to his office in the back of the hotel.

She made him sit in his chair while she massaged his shoulders. "You have to understand my brother. He is very protective of me. You can't fault him for that." "Maybe so but I call the shots around here."

"So you do." She said as she rubbed deeper into his shoulders. He reached up and took her hand guiding it downwards. She tried pulling it away but he grabbed her by her arm. Pulling her into his lap.

He began kissing her. "I want to take you right here." "I thought you were Bea's man." "Not anymore. I have had my eyes on you ever since you stepped down from that coach. Now let's see what you got." He said as he twisted her head back forcing her back to arch she felt a sharp pain as he twisted her forcibly. He grinned as she winced in agony.

21

"I Don't Sit In Judgement"

Her hands were numb from the cold as she knocked on the door. Hoping someone would hear her.

Molly answered she had been drinking; a young man stood behind her. "The doctor don't take patients this time of night miss. You'll be need'n to come back in the morning. The young man wrapped his large hands around her waist. He was high from the Opium. Beatrice could see it in his eyes. "She looks purty like you." He breathed heavily. Molly kept pushing his hands off from her. "I am so cold can I just come in out of the weather?"

66

Begged Beatrice. "Come on in. I'll go to the back and see if I can get Aubrey out of bed." The young man stood by the door weaving back and forth his eyes in a blank stare. Beatrice sat down at the kitchen table she felt so cold and alone. "Molly don't be leav'n me all by myself. "MOLLY!" He hollered. The doctor appeared pulling his jacket on over a night shirt. Trying to adjust his eyes to the candle lit room. "Miss Faye? What's wrong?" I am surprised to see you here." "I am so sorry I didn't know where to go." "You look half frozen." He took his jacket off wrapping it around her shoulders. "Let me take you to my office." "Hey doc yah got yerself a real lady this time! Ain't yah!" blurted out the young man. The doctor leaned into Molly whispering "How many times have I told you not to bring him here." "Ain't none of your concern now is it." Molly said sarcastically." "Take your whore back there with yah and leave me alone!" she screamed. "I am sorry." said the doctor. "I have been called worse." Beatrice said as she followed him into his office.

The doctor gently wiped the mud from Beatrice's face. He noticed her hands were red and swollen. Let's get your hands warmed up. You may have suffered a little frost bite here." He said as he rubbed them briskly in his. He then placed her hands in a basin and poured cold water over them. He rubbed them briskly then wrapped them in a towel. "Can you feel anything?" He asked. "They are tingling." "That is a good sign. Hopefully I got to you in time. Frost bite is very painful. It begs the question what are you doing out in this weather without a coat?" "My partner threw me out. I am no longer allowed in his presence." Beatrice said bitterly. "I have only myself to blame. I know what he is." "You are talking about Mr. Mayfield aren't you?" "How did you know?" Asked Beatrice. "I saw you with him a few times when I was at the hotel. That is where I remember you from. I have heard you sing. You have a lovely voice."

"You have been there? So I don't have to tell you. I have been a kept woman. I am ashamed to admit it but it is true." "There are worse things in life then that. So you don't have to be ashamed. I don't stand in judgement of anyone." "Thank you for your understanding. I didn't have anywhere to go so I thought of you.

Maybe I took to much upon myself in doing so. But for some reason I trust you." "I am glad you saw fit to do so. There are few people that share that view. What is it you would have me do?" "I need to stay out of the weather tonight. A chair to sit in and a blanket is all I need.

I will be gone first thing, in the morning." "I will not hear of it. You can have my bed. I will sit in the chair. No, I insist." The doctor took her to his small bedroom and helped her take off her shoes. He then gently covered her with his quilts. If you need anything. I shall be in my office."He walked quietly away. She could hear him moving around.

Then she heard the sound of a bottle and his drinking from it. Even from that distance she could smell the whiskey. Who was she to judge he had come to her rescue and she was good with it. She soon fell asleep.

22
"You Can Call Me Clegg"

Mr. Riley set about asking people in the town if they had seen or knew of Ansleigh and Thomas. No one had mentioned seeing them. Mr. Johnson had taken to carousing and staying at Mrs. Jacks. Much to Mr. Riley's chagrin. So he asked about the Sheriff. People scoffed at that and he was soon to find out why. Tucked in the back of the Post Office and local Stage Coach and livery stable was a one room office with a crude jail cell. There Mr. Riley found Bill Daniels an old man with long white hair who was crippled with arthritis. He was the only law in Crooked Hat and was paid to sit in this office and stay out of August's way. He rarely arrested anyone let alone use his gun. Mr. Riley asked him about Ansleigh and Thomas. The sheriff told him he knew of them as a Mr. Clegg was in town. He had left word with him about the young couple. Mr. Riley knew that he was the other man he had hired but had never met. He left the Sheriff's Office in hopes of finding Clegg.

He bent into the cold winter wind as he crossed the main street heading toward the hotel. He suddenly had a memory of the winter Katherine was born. Rebecca was having problems with delivering her. Echo Hooks,

68

Great Grandma Sykes best friend was there that day helping with the birth. Jacob was so worried for his wife. The weather was severe and Echo had ridden horseback in the snow to help. He remembered walking through the deep snow assisting Echo with her horse. He could still see Katherine's little fingers wrapped around his thumb. As he held her for the first time. Stumbling on the hotel steps broke his reverie.

He found Clegg's room. He knocked and a tall dark man with a large moustache answered the door. Looking into his face. He asked him what it was he wanted. Clegg had a instinctive way of telling a person's nature upon meeting them. He felt Jacob's unease with him right away. Jacob was uncomfortable with this man. He noticed a good looking young man sitting in a chair near the bed. He was drinking from a bottle. "What do you want with me?" Clegg snarled. Mr. Riley cleared his throat. "I was told that you are Mr. Clegg?" "Damn right what do you want of me?" "I hired you two months ago to find my daughter Ansleigh Riley. She may be going by Andrews now." Clegg started to laugh. "I'll be a son of a bitch. You followed me here?" "No, my daughter Katherine left home too. I decided to see what I could do. Have you had any luck with your search?" "I think they are near by." "Really how do you know?" "I have been talking with some people here. Who claim they saw a young couple awhile back on horseback heading to Nevada. They fit the description you gave me." "So why aren't you out there looking for them? I paid you good money."

That was the wrong thing to say to Clegg. As he pulled Jacob up by his shirt collar, listen you gutless Irish cur don't talk to me that way! I know my job. I will find them without your help."

"I trust you will." Said Jacob gasping for his breath. Realizing this man was fearless he backed down. "As soon as the ground thaws I will be heading out it is better tracking that way. And stay away from me. I will find you, is that understood?" "Yes." "Now get to hell out of here." As Jacob left the door slammed against his back.

Thomas rode into Crooked Hat not sure where to find the supplies he needed. He went to the Mining Camp Supply store asking for help. It was there he found shovels and a saw and an axe.

69

He bought a spool of rope and a wheel barrow. He went to the General Store and purchased food supplies. Then proceeded to the livery stable where he rented a wagon to haul all his supplies in. "you here look'n for gold?' Asked the stable owner. "No sir I am a fur trapper. This is a busy town. I am surprised how it's nestled up here in the mountains. Kind of off the beaten track." "Won't be for long Mr. Mayfields plann'n on run'n a pony express and a daily coach out of here." "Really will they be hiring?" "I guess yah best come back and ask around. But stir clear of Mr. Mayfield. He's one mean son of a bitch. Less yah got money in yore hand." "I am behold'n to you for your advice.

Thomas started to work on hitching his horse to the harness. A gust of wind blew an empty bucket across the street startling the horse. It reared up and Thomas fell back holding tightly to the reins. The horse started to drag him down the street. He could feel the ice scraping his hands and ripping open his trousers. Just then a man stepped out in front of the horse. He stopped him in his tracks. "Easy there now fella." He spoke softly to him. Thomas let go of the reins standing up. His hands were bleeding and he was having trouble with his knee. "Looks like you got the wind knocked out of you." "I'll be all right." Said Thomas. "You look a little shaken. What do you say to me buying you a drink? Let your horse settle down a bit." Thomas liked his whiskey so he agreed. He thought one drink before heading back to camp wouldn't hurt. "What do you go by?" Thomas used his Uncle's name. "Jim Sutton." As he knew that he and Ansleigh were still being sought after. The stranger looked him in the eyes and said "Jim you can call me Clegg."

23

"Redemption"

Huittsu, found the moccasins by her lodge opening. They were beautiful. The bead work and detail were lovely. A sign of the horse was drawn on a small piece of leather tucked inside the shoes. She knew these were a gift from Many Horses. He had been courting her for sometime. He knew that her heart was with Shila but this did not stop him from trying to win her affections. He had made her a fine bow of cedar wood and a flute from ash wood. He would play this flute in early morning hours outside of her lodge. She kept the gifts as not to hurt his pride. She also knew that in his mind it meant she accepted his intentions. Huittsu had given up on Shila as a perspective husband. But she would never give up on loving him. She saw him frequently at gatherings and watched him often from afar.

It was an overcast snowy day and she saw Shila down by the river. He was trying to catch a fish. She watched from the shore line. He caught a trout and it flipped from his fingers. She laughed. "So you think it funny Huittsu perhaps you should join me." He flicked a hand full of cold water her way. "Shila you may be a hunter but I think you need help with fishing." He smiled at her. "You are right." He joined Huittsu on the river bank. Looking at him, she felt this great pain in her heart. The words came slowly. "The time has come for me to choose a husband." "I know." He said. A part of her wanted to embrace him as he stood before her. She remembered the first time she saw him as a child. Even then she was captivated by him. She looked at him for a long time without saying a word. "I have chosen Many Horses. We will marry when the trees bud." Shila was silent and hung his head. He took her hand in his. "He will be a good husband and a good father. You have made a wise decision."

"This may be so but he will never have my heart." With that she turned and walked away hiding her tears.

Shila did not know why he felt so strongly about not taking Huittsu as his wife. He thought about it often. Each time a strong resistance accompanied his feelings.

Healing Fox had known Shila since his birth. He was like a second father to him. He was a short man, muscular and youthful appearing for his years. His hair hung in long white braids to his waist. He wanted Shila to spend more time learning about the sacred plants to be used for healing. This was a legacy handed down by the ancients that were given to only a few.

It had been a bitterly cold winter and the natives of the village spent a good deal of time in their lodges. Shila was helping his father in erecting a lodge for an elderly woman who was very ill and was being shunned by her family. His father was now the leader of the small village. He had to make

71

many decisions involving the safety and welfare of his people. He often looked to Shila for advice as his son was a good mediator. It bothered River Tree to isolate the old woman to being alone. "Father, she has an illness that can be spread to others. Especially dangerous to the children. I will care for her here. You are doing the right thing."

Shila was heading to Healing Fox's lodge when a young boy came running up to him. "Shila, you must come with me!" What is it?" "It is Night Wing he may be dead." "Go!"Said River Tree I will finish here." Shila followed the young boy to outside of the camp. Curled up in the snow was the body of Night Wing. He was barely breathing. Two empty whiskey bottles were laying in the snow near by.

Shila lifted Night Wing up over his shoulder and walked back to the village with the young boy following. He brought Night Wing to his lodge and laid him on the ground covering him with fur pelts. He built a good fire. He asked the young boy not to say anything to anyone about this. The boy vowed his silence. Night Wing was near death. He had frostbite on his toes and his right hand. His breathing was very labored and his lungs rattled with mucus. He had urinated his leggings and was emaciated from not eating. Shila knew this was from the whiskey. He knew that he would have to remove the frozen skin or it would rot and become gangrene. There was no time to ask Night Wing if this is what he wanted. It was a matter of saving his life. Shila did what he had to do. Praying and chanting to the Grandfathers as he worked.

He stayed in his lodge with Night Wing for two days. When finally early in the morning of the third day. Night Wing awoke. He stared up into Shila's face. He was angry and tried to sit up only to lapse back from weakness. He wanted a drink. Shila gave him water from a gourd he pushed it away. "Whiskey. I need to drink Whiskey." He started to cough and brought up phlegm down the front of his chest. He cried out in pain from his infection. Shila tried to calm him. "You must rest your body is very sick." Night Wing tried to stand and fell into the fire pit. Lashing out at imaginary ghosts. He stood again only to fall. Huddling against the side of the lodge he looked like a frightened child; more than the strong warrior that he once was.

Shila sat quietly while Night Wing fought with what was happening. He looked and saw all the toes accept his big toe were missing on his left foot and three were gone on his right. His right hand was missing four fingers. He cried out and went silent. From then on Night Wing became despondent. Not eating or drinking. He would not talk or look at Shila. He lay on the pelts while a fever ravaged his body and he vomited often. Shila used the healing herbs he knew were the helpers. Chanting as he worked.

He went without sleep or eating himself. As the days went by Kachiri came and asked permission to speak with him. He let her in the lodge. She covered her face from the stench. She saw Night Wing laying on the floor of the lodge pale and near death. "Shila I see what you are doing. It would seem that Night Wing has chosen to leave this world. You must let him go. Or you will become ill yourself." "This is what I do Kachiri it is the way of the healer. You know that." "What do you owe this man? He has been your enemy for a long time." "A Healer does not see that. He only does what is asked of him by spirit. If you do not come to comfort me than I must ask you to leave."

"I will go but I will not let you put yourself in danger for this man." With that she left. Shila then fell into a deep sleep. He saw smoke rising from Night Wing's body. A dark and vile stench came with it. It saturated the lodge. The energy it brought was dark. Shila knew it to be from the whiskey. As if it were an entity in and of itself.

The Grizzly bear appeared inside his lodge. Standing on its hind legs it roared. He saw Night Wing rise and the great bear took his paw and sliced right through him. Shila woke with a start as he heard Night Wing call out. When he opened his eyes.

Night Wing was sitting up in terror touching his stomach. "The bear he killed me, he killed me." Shila knew then that the worst was over.

"Poor Nate"

Maizey was busy preparing the morning meal for the miners. When Ki walked into the kitchen out of breath. "Where yah been?" she snapped. "Got men com'n with hungry mouths to feed I need yah to start the eggs." Ki had a wild look in his eyes. He pulled on her sleeve. "Miss you come with me!" What are yah carry'n on about? I need yah to get to work!" "You come now, Mr.Townsend he dead." "What foolishness is this?" Maizey knew something wasn't right. She had never seen Ki this upset before. "Oh Alright I'm com'n." She grabbed her hat and jacket and took a lantern. As she followed Ki out into the cold morning. The sun was just starting to rise. He took her to a back alley.

There face down in the snow lay Nate Townsend. Maizey called out to him but he didn't respond. She took the lantern close to his face and then she saw the blood staining the snow. She pulled him over. His throat had been slit. She started to shake. "What we do?" Cried Ki. "Yah go back and feed the morning crew. I'll be along. Ki awkwardly tried to comfort her. "Go! I'll be fine." she said trying to hold in her grief. Maizey knelt next to Nate's body touching his face. "Yah never was much for stand'n up tah people. She slumped down into the snow laying her hand on his forehead.

"But yah took me in when my family left. Took me as yer wife, and me ugly as a dog. Never laid a hand to me. Yah were the closest thing I ever had ta love. I hope there is a place for yah tah find rest Mon ami I know I'll miss yah. She sat next to him for a long time. Maizey whose real name was Madelaine, was raised by her elderly father in the mountains of Kentucky.

He had been a mountain man living with a French woman who never spoke a bit of English. Maizey was an only child. She had to take care of her mother most of her youth. As her mother was crippled from a horse falling on her breaking her hip. She spent long days of work cooking and tending to her mother. Her father was never home. The day her mother died Maizey had to bury her and keep things going at the cabin. Her father never returned. She broke her nose and jaw from a hunting accident when the gun recoiled and hit her in her face. It wasn't long after her accident that Nate Townsend happened by. He was looking for her father. Maizey told him about her mother and her father not returning. Nate felt sorry for her situation. He welcomed her to come with him. As he was headed West and the great gold rush. Nate was twenty years her senior. She didn't mind as she was tired of living alone. So Nate took her with him and they were married in the first town they came upon that had a courthouse.

A dog rutting in the garbage brought her back to her senses. Maizey was a small woman but strong. She pulled Nate's body all the way to the hotel steps. She then went in asking the clerk to fetch Mr. Mayfield. He scoffed at her saying he wasn't about to disturb him.

Maizey took a knife from her pocket and held it to his throat. "Tu me Fais chier." (*You annoy me*) He went and got him. August was in a foul mood as he walked down the stairs into the lobby. "You got me out of bed for this." he barked at the hotel clerk.

Maizey glared at him. "Somebody killed my Nate." "What are you talk'n about?" "They slit his throat and left him to die." "Where is he?" Maizey took August out to the porch steps. "He is dead and that's a fact. I can get Bill Daniels over here." "I don't want no drunken sheriff deal'n with this. Yah know what goes on in this here town I want yah to help with find'n who dun it.

"Yah owe Nate that much. Faire des choses proprement."(*do what is fair*) Just for a moment August felt she was right but he quickly dismissed her. He had the hotel clerk help Maizey get the body over to the undertakers. Maizey never did make it back to the cafe that day.

Katherine and Quin were in Utah and the wagon train was circled in against a snow storm. Katherine was expecting a child again. She told Quin that she was through with the traveling and she needed to rest. He didn't want her to lose another baby. So he agreed they would find a settlement to spend the rest of the winter in. He sold his wagon to a young couple on the train.

He knew he would need this money to start anew. They kept one of the horses and pulled a travois with some of their belongings in it. They were told that the town of Vineyard wasn't too far off. They started out when the storm had lessened. It took them two days ride to reach the settlement. Katherine was exhausted and gratified to finally be in a town again, where she could find a real bed. When they entered Vineyard it appeared a ghost town. Several stores were boarded up. Bison skulls and bones littered the main street.

Broken wagon wheels and garbage were strewn along the sides of buildings. A pack of wild dogs scurried across their path. Prospects of living here appeared dismal at best.

They found the hotel and Quin met Mr. Peevy. As fate would have it. Katherine was in the same room Ansleigh had been in several weeks before. Quin sat on the bed next to her. "I have to find work in order for us to stay here. You do understand?" "Yes." She said as she took his hand and drifted off to sleep. Quin covered her with a blanket and quietly left the room. He decided to get a drink at the bar. As he stood there a tall thin man approached him. "So you are the young couple I been hear'n about." "News must travel fast as we just got here." "Sheriff Patch and yes it does. Not much go'n on these days." "What happened?" Asked Quin. "The buffalo are about gone and with them the speculators and hunters. Folks just packed up and left."

"So why are you still here?" "Where am I gonna go? My wife is sickly and I am too old to start over. I get my monthly pay from the government."

"I was kind of hoping to find work here my wife is with child." Mr. Peevy spoke up. "You won't find too much around here. But Karl Garrison is looking for hands on his ranch I'm told. You know your way around horses?" "Yes I do I am a black-smith." "He would most likely take you on then." Said Sheriff Patch.

"Only one problem."Said Mr. Peevy. "What's that?" Asked Quin as he gulped down a shot of hard whiskey. "Are you a religious man?" "I've been to church a few times why?" "Mr. Garrison is a hellfire and brimstone kinda man."

Mr. Peevy said as he poured Quin another shot. "He'll save your soul or die try'n." laughed the sheriff. "Even Old Nick won't have anything to do with that one." Both men laughed heartily. "I need work so I guess I can deal with him if I have to.

76

Where can I find this ranch." "Tell yah what." Said the Sheriff. "I'll meet yah in the morning and take yah out there."

Quin agreed. He paid for the rest of the bottle and took it to his room and drank himself to sleep.

25
"A Close Call"

Thomas knew that he was in the camp of the enemy with Clegg. He had to think of a way to leave as soon as he could without drawing attention to his business. Clegg walked him over to the hotel for a drink. They talked mostly about Crooked Hat and how it was growing. Thomas asked about Mr. Mayfield and the rumors of a railroad coming through the town. Clegg told him it was more than likely not going to happen. As the labor and money it would take to undertake such a feat would be considerable. "You interested in the railroad then?" he asked. "Yes, I remember when I saw my first steam locomotive. It was really something. I was all of ten maybe. My father took me to see it." He then grew silent. "If you don't mind my ask'n where you from?" "Virginia" He lied. "So how did you end up here in Nevada?" "My cousin moved out here and I came out to help him build. He is crippled." "I see." Clegg said looking Thomas straight in the eyes. "So on your journey here you didn't by chance come across a young couple goes by the name of Andrews did yah?" "No, sir never heard of them.

I traveled alone and kept away from folks for the most part, safer that way." "It's true. Man will kill yah for a bottle of whiskey these days." "Why are you ask'n?" "Bounty on their heads." Why what'd they do?" "Don't much matter to me. I just collect the money." He laughed. "Let me buy you another drink." "I want to thank you but I promised my cousin I'd be back as soon as I could. Already lost a day's work."

Clegg made Thomas uneasy as he kept looking at him unflinchingly. He wasn't sure that he believed his story. But he knew it was time to leave. Clegg walked him out to the stables. "You seem like a decent sort." Clegg said. "I'm leav'n town to do some track'n in a couple of days. Let me know where you're at and I'll stop by and have a look see." "To be honest I still get lost up in these mountains. But if you're back in town I will come and find you." "If I didn't know better I'd think you were trying to hide something." "Why would I do that?" Asked Thomas. "Yeah why would yah?" Scoffed Clegg.

Thomas quickly hitched up the horse to the wagon and bid Clegg farewell as he headed out of town. When he was halfway down the street; a man ran in front of his wagon. Thomas had to pull back on the reins. He was about to say something when the man looked up at him. It was Mr. Riley. Thomas promptly pulled his hat down to cover his face. Slapping the reins against the horse's rump. It set off into a brisk canter down the street.

Justice was late getting up from her bed. She did not feel well. She walked over to the hotel window looking out at the street below. Her jaw ached and she felt lightheaded from drinking. It seemed she drank more than was usual for her. She prided herself on keeping the upper hand when dealing with men.

But August Mayfield was a threat to her very existence. She leaned her head against the cold glass of the window. "Where have you been?" She heard Charles say as he entered her room. "You never came back last night. Did you hear me?" Justice didn't want to answer. "My head hurts Charles come back later."

He knew something was wrong as he touched her shoulder and turned her towards him. "What's this?" Her face had began to swell and her eye was blackened. "Who did this Justice?" "I drank too much and fell onto the floor last night." "No, someone did this to you and I want to know who? It was Mayfield that bastard wasn't it?"

"I will kill him for this." Justice took his hand. "Please Charles, listen. You must not say anything. Do you hear me? It was some drunk I ran into. Really, I don't remember too much about it and he is long gone." "It is Mayfield and why are you protecting him?" "I'm not. Either you believe me or you don't. But I am telling you what happened. I will be all right. I need you to go to the doctor's and get some laudanum can you do that? Please?" Charles agreed to her request but she knew he did not believe her. After he had left. She sat on her bed remembering August being in this very room.

He had spent the night. He beat her and took her roughly. She laid there next to him not sleeping until he left at dawn. She knew she was in a trap and did not want Charles to be involved for fear of August's wrath.

26

"Beatrice's Lie"

Beatrice quickly dressed and made the doctor's bed. She saw that he was no where around. She found a pen and ink on his desk. Leaving him a note of gratitude for his kindness. She used a blanket to wrap herself into and left quietly. Molly and her friend were asleep in each other's arms on the sofa. They never heard her leave. Her head was spinning as she had no idea of where to go. She decided to find Justice. She found her sitting in the dining area of the hotel drinking coffee. She had a wet cloth placed across her jaw. It was very swollen. "What happened?" Asked Beatrice as she sat next to her. "You don't want to ask, its better that way." "Charles?" "Never. He has never laid a hand to me. Why are you wrapped in that blanket?" "I need to get to my room but August has forbid me to be here."

"So where have you been?" "I'm sick and I told him so." "What is ailing you?" "I told him the consumption." Justice was taken back by her remark. "That is not good you can die from it. You will have to find someplace away from here. People will not want to be near you." "I know but I need to be free of him. This is my one chance to leave here." For some reason she could not bring herself to tell Justice the truth. "He is over at the assayer's office. I will take you to get your things." The two women went to Beatrice's room. Never knowing the common thread they shared with August Mayfield.

The sun was setting and left a red blaze of color across the sky as Thomas made it back to their encampment.

Ansleigh had the campfire going and two rabbits roasting on the spit. She was relieved to see Thomas.

He told her about the day he had and about Crooked Hat. He wanted to sleep early so he could start work on their cabin by daybreak.

79

They ate in silence Thomas was deep in thought. "What is it that troubles you?" Ansleigh asked as she started to make their sleeping area.

Thomas wouldn't answer. Once they were laying together huddled against the cold. Thomas spoke. "I saw your father today." "What!" Ansleigh said as she sat up looking down into his face. "Are you sure?" "Oh yes it was him all right. I can only hope he didn't recognize me." He told her about Clegg and his fears of him finding them. Ansleigh thought maybe it best they move on the next day. Thomas didn't see any reason to do so. He told her that he was sure that they didn't suspect anything about him. Time would tell. Meanwhile he suggested they stay clear of the town. He was tired of looking over his shoulder and would face any problems if they were to arise. With that he fell into a deep sleep.

Jacob Riley told Mr. Johnson that he didn't require his services any longer. He had paid him well and felt that he was misusing his time since they had arrived in Crooked Hat. He couldn't shake the feeling that there had been something familiar about the young man with the wagon. The day before.

Mr. Clegg was planning on leaving town and back tracking looking for Thomas and Ansleigh. He told Mr. Riley to hold his money until he returned.

He did pride himself in doing his job. To Jacob it seemed as if he were caught in time since he started this journey. He had envisioned having his grandchildren around him as he grew older.

He was bitter over his daughter's running off. Hadn't he been a good father? A provider? Rebecca had accused him of being too dominating. He had loved her so much but words never came and his feelings were frozen in his heart.

He thought life was hard and one had to survive in any way that they could. Even if it meant making decisions that weren't appreciated by others. After all it was for their own good wasn't it?

27

"The Secret"

The spot Thomas had chosen for their cabin was well hidden down in a gully. There was a bluff that looked out over the mountain range at the top of the ridge. He was really gratified on finding a small spring fed water fall on the side of the ridge with easy access. Thomas worked from sunup till sundown every day. Clearing a spot for their cabin. Ansleigh helped with what she could. Making meals and helping with the placement of the logs and fetching water from the falls. Thomas kept chiding her about doing too much in her condition. Within a week he had a stone foundation built. His hands were rough and calloused and his lips cracked and bleeding as he worked in the cold. Ansleigh was finding a new respect for him. Even though she knew he had a darker nature when it came to killing. That month of late winter Thomas worked through the weather and snow storms. Ansleigh begged him to take rest and shelter. He wouldn't stop. It seemed as if he was obsessed with his work. He had it near finished by the time the first thaw came.

It was a small cabin with one big room, a sod floor and no windows. He had made a stone fireplace for heat and cooking. He also added a root cellar to store foods. Thomas knew he would have to go back to Crooked Hat to buy cooking supplies and he wanted to make a rope bed for Ansleigh to sleep on rather than the boards he used on the sod floor.

Beatrice was struggling with her trunks and Justice was helping her. They were coming down the stairs at the hotel when Mr. Riley saw them. He walked up the stairs and grabbed one of the trunks.

"Leave the other lass, I will get it." He said. "That is most kind of you." "You're the young Coleen I saw out in the street the other night are you not?" "Yes." "It looks like you are getting ready to leave? Pity I just got here. I would at least like to buy you a drink." "You might as well." Said Justice. "August won't be back for a while." Beatrice thanked him but said she really needed to go. She wanted to be out of town before the day was over. Mr. Riley hauled her luggage out to the hotel porch.

It was a windy day and Beatrice was holding onto her hat. The cold crept into her neck and caught her breath. "Where are you going with all of this?" Asked Mr. Riley. For a moment she panicked as she really had no plans. "I need to get them over to the Coach Office." "So you lead the way." Mr. Riley said as he dragged one of her trunks across the street. As he went back to gather the other. Beatrice talked with the station manager about storing her trunks there. By the time Mr. Riley returned she was settled. She offered to pay him for his help. "No, I don't take money from women. You remind me of me girls." He told her. "You are very pretty."

"Thank you I never did catch your name." "Call me Jacob that will do." "Thank you Jacob." "You will be all right then?" "Of course." He looked at her thinking that here was a young woman in trouble. But he decided not to push the issue. He bid her farewell and headed back toward the hotel.

Beatrice knew she had to find Thorton. She went to the boarding house on the edge of town hoping to find him there.

She caught him just as he was leaving the house. "Thorton we need to talk." "Bea where have you been? Mr. Mayfield has been spreading the rumor that he fired you and that you are sick? I don't understand?" "Can we please get out of this cold." begged Beatrice. "Lets go to the café I could use some coffee. Thorton took her by the arm as they walked down the street.

The mud had hardened into deep ruts and made the walking difficult; as the wind blew and they leaned into its intensity. "Did you hear that Mr. Townsend was murdered? Mr. Mayfield is offering a hefty bounty for any information leading to the crime." Beatrice was silent. Ki was running the café and there was no sign of Maizey when they reached there. He was hurrying around while the miners barked out orders to him. "Where's Maizey?" "She not good Mr. Thorton. She lay down in house not come to work. She no come when I call her." "Grief takes a while with some. I will look in on her." "You be good man." Ki said as he scurried about trying to attend to his customers.

"So Bea what is going on? You look terrible." Thorton told her as he sat down." "I lied." "You what?" "I lied to August about my health. I told him

I have Consumption." "But why?' "I want to leave. He is a horrid man. I will not suffer his abuse any longer. I would be better off dead."

"I didn't realize he was that bad to you. He has bought you so many things." "Things Thorton things!" She said angrily. "He uses people and I am done before he is the death of me. I am taking Zacharia and leaving." "You're what?" "You heard me I am leaving." "This is how you tell me. What about the theater? Our show?"

"That is so like you to be more concerned about yourself. You have a new lover. I am sure he will take good care of you. They always do. I am taking Zacharia to California with me." "You can't take him." "Yes I can and I will. I am his mother after all." "But he's my son too" said Thorton. Beatrice sat silent then taking Thorton's hand she looked into his eyes. "He must never know you do understand that. We promised each other. Is that understood?" Thorton didn't answer her.

28

"Burning The Past"

Night Wing started getting his strength back. Shila was grateful for his improvement. Night Wing's anger was diminished somehow. He had a new found respect for Shila. Laying there all those weeks when he was near death. He observed how Shila kept calm and his patience was unswerving. He spent days feeding him and changing his soiled garments. He even bathed him. At first Night Wing fought. But his illness brought him to his knees and forced him to see with different eyes. There was no reason for Shila to do this for him. Yet he did and Night Wing was able to keep his dignity intact the whole time. He knew Shila was a true healer.

The weather was finally turning and buds were forming on the trees. Night Wing was able to take short walks around the encampment. The tribe was surprised to see a once strong warrior reduced to a shadow of his former self. He soon would tire and have to seek refuge in Shila's lodge. He wanted to go back to his tepee but knew he had stored whiskey there. He

thought he would be tempted once again to drink. He didn't want this. As he was clear minded for the first time in months.
So he decided to destroy his lodge by burning it. But not before he took something that had much meaning to him from there.

The lodge went up in flames quickly and soon a crowd had gathered. River Tree was the first one to arrive. Night Wing stood there watching his lodge as it burned, and with it went his past. He told River Tree that with spring arriving he would build a new lodge.

He had saved enough hides to reconstruct a new dwelling. One evening as Shila sat placing dried herbs into a pouch. Night Wing spoke. "I have carried the seeds of hatred in my heart for you for sometime. They went up with the burning of my lodge. I have been wrong and the whiskey took from me my soul. The Grandfathers through your help have given me another chance at this life." You do not have to say this." Interrupted Shila. "You must let me finish. I have had many days to see myself as I have become. It saddens me and brings shame to my family. For this I must give back. "I never thought I would hear you speak these words as I prayed daily for your recovery. This is a good omen." "I plan on leaving tomorrow and staying with my sister. There are no words that I can use to show my heart that you have given back to me." Shila sat silently taking in all that Night Wing had spoken. He knew that he had healed not only in body but in spirit as well.   They were silent the rest of that night.

When dawn had arrived Shila awakened to find Night Wing gone. As he rose to walk outside there by the entrance flap was a huge spread of eagle wings. Those of a Golden Eagle. It was shaped into a fan.

The center piece was beaded in an intricate design with long leather strips draped with tiny cowry shells hanging from it. Shila had never seen anything this beautiful before. He smiled as he knew this was Night Wing's way of gifting him for what he had done.

29

"Leaving Town"

August couldn't help thinking about Beatrice as he headed towards Maizey's house. It was late in the morning and he was still hung over from drinking heavily the night before. He knew he had been too harsh with Beatrice. The truth was he missed her. She was one of the few women, he would ever care for. But he wasn't about to die from Consumption. Walking down the main street of his town he felt a sense of power. A man who had risen from poverty and an orphanage as a child. He felt the world owed him something.

Reaching his destination, he pounded on the door. He was surprised at what he saw. Maizey was very thin and her cheeks looked sunken. He could see she hadn't been sleeping or eating. "You are needed down at the cafe. Ki can't run the place on his own. You need to quit feeling sorry for yourself and get back to work." Maizey felt a hot hatred filling up in her chest. "I ain't feel'n well enough tah cook. Barely make it through the day. Cain't yah get somebody tah help?" "The miners are complaining about the food. You are the best cook around and I need yah there. Look I know you miss Nate but he's gone and yah best pull yourself together." August knew she wasn't listening.

"I tell yah what. I am willing to give you full ownership of the café and yah only have to give me forty percent of the money made. I will get another cook in there to help mornings. I need yah there." "I'll think on it." She paused. "I'll be there come tamarrahh." With that she shut the door in his face.

Katherine was trying to get use to living on the ranch after weeks of living in the back of a covered wagon. Quin was glad to be working as a smith again. He was hoping that Katherine would brighten up her mood now that they were settled. True to Sheriff Patch's warning, Karl Garrison was overbearing at times and quoted from the Bible daily. He was a barrel chested man with white unruly hair that stuck out from beneath his hat. He walked with a limp and spoke with a thick German accent. Quin wanted to settle down in the area he was tired of being a restless wanderer. The ranch was nestled in a valley a butte jutted skyward to the back of their property. It was beautiful. They raised beef cattle and a few bison. He talked about wanting to stay in Utah with Katherine. She wanted to move into Nevada territory. She still held the belief she would find Ansleigh. Quin resented this but kept quiet about it. Nel was Karl's wife, she was a placid woman. She didn't trust people and resented Katherine in her home and kitchen. Katherine tried to be of help and was miserable living at the ranch. Her baby was due in early summer. She had some fears about the pain and possible loss of life again. Quin would hold her and try to reassure her that this time he would get a doctor for her. Even though he had been told the doctor in Vineyard had left with the buffalo hunters.

He decided to find the nearest doctor in the area. Even if it meant traveling several miles to get there. "So you think hav'n this baby will be of any benefit liv'n out here in this God forbidden place." Nel spoke bitterly.

She was a small woman with greying hair pulled back into a tight bun. Revealing a hardened face that belied her younger years. "I had hopes of hav'n children once. But I am barren. Kinda like this land." "What brought you here? " Asked Katherine.

"Karl and his brothers came look'n for gold. Hand me that skillet would yah." She said as she was preparing dinner for the ranch hands. "My folks come from Virginia after my mother died we moved west. My father was a minister in Vineyard before the men folk got all fired up about the buffalo hunt'n. Karl and his brother's were stay'n at the old hotel before it burned down." An odd smile came across her face as she continued. "Some old drunk set fire to it try'n to kill his unfaithful wife. Most excitement that old town had seen. Sinful lot. I use to do the laundry at the hotel. Met Karl at church one Sunday.

He's from Germany you know. I couldn't understand a word he said at first. The long and short of it he took a lik'n to me right off. We was married by my father after a few months of court'n. His brothers left head'n west." "So where's your father now?" "My father was killed by a crazy man who lost his family to the fever couple years back. Sheriff Patch shot him

86

dead. My father is buried behind the church. The church is boarded up nobody wants to claim it. Vineyard, is a dark place."

The rain was coming down heavily as Zacharia and Beatrice waited at the Stage Coach office.
Beatrice looked out the window at the muddy street. She was still having pain from her infection.

A slight fever and sore throat were nagging her that day. "Fella at the hotel says San Francisco is the city to find work. Maybe you can get another job singing? I am sure I can find work cook'n." "I want you to go to school. That's my plan. Any fool can cook. I want you to be able to read and write and make something of yourself do you hear me." "I know how to read." "Zacharia don't argue with me about this." They had been at the station since early morning." The coach was arriving late due to the weather." Is Uncle Thorton going to join us?" "Not this time I am afraid he has secured work here." Zacharia grew quiet and he sat staring at the floor. The station manager apologized for the delay. An older gentleman and a young woman were waiting there as well. By late afternoon the coach finally arrived. The driver said he had problems with the mud got stuck a couple of times on route. He was in a hurry to get people aboard while he still had daylight left to travel. Just as Beatrice lifted her satchel. She felt a strong arm lift her into the coach. She turned and looked it was Thorton. Zacharia was smiling. "What are you doing here?" She asked.
"I am going to San Francisco and you?" "What about your Mr. Clegg?" "What about him?" Thorton asked as he sat next to her. The driver called out to the horses as they pulled out. The rains had stopped.

30
"Full Moon Birth"

Huittsu had her hair braided with soft deer skin ties and little silver cones she had traded with a French trapper for. Her dress was the pale skin of an elk. She had worked the fringe along the hem and added colored beads to it. Her moccasins were the ones that Many Horses had made for her. She looked lovely. This was the month of the popping trees. Everything was green and the trees were blossomed. The camp was busy that day as the women prepared the feast for the wedding and the men made fires for cooking and played games with the children. Huittsu stood in her mother's lodge waiting for the time to meet Many Horses. Tears were forming in her eyes. Her mother took her in her arms. "I know where your heart is my daughter but this is the right thing to do. Many Horses will honor you and our family. He will be a good husband." "I know." Huittsu said quietly. "I will be a good wife to him." She then grew silent.

She heard the flute outside her lodge, it was Many Horses. He was calling her out to be with him. She came from the lodge and appeared next to him. He looked handsome in his regalia. He was fully dressed in a deerskin shirt and pants with his moccasins embellished with beads by his sister. He wore his hair long with two eagle feathers entwined. Fox Healer was there to perform the ceremony. The people gathered around as Fox Healer started to pray. They then joined hands as Fox Healer tied their hands together. Many Horse's sister placed a blanket over the two of them. Everyone in the crowd trilled loudly. When the ceremony was over.

They turned to face the people. It was then that Huittsu saw Shila standing in the back. He was smiling at her and he nodded. Again she felt a twinge in her chest. For a moment she envisioned that it was Shila next to her side and she breathed deeply into her heart.

River Tree greeted them and he untied their hands giving each one a tie to keep as a reminder of their bond. The feast went long into the night. Drums and singing were heard across the river. Shila had decided to stay outside that night sleeping under the pines. He thought of Huittsu and Many Horses and hoped they would be happy together.

Many Horses and Huittsu came back to her mother's lodge where they would now sleep as husband and wife. They had the lodge to themselves. Huittsu's mother had left food and fresh flowers for the couple and a beautiful basket she had made. The basket signified their new life together and symbolized all the events that would soon fill it. Many Horses, was shy and awkward when it came to making love.

He quickly took her and rolled over to sleep not saying anything to her. Huittsu laid there staring up at the lodge poles while she wept. Life she thought was cruel. She longed for Shila and the pain was almost unbearable.

Thomas was laughing as he chased the racoon from his work bench it had eaten his bread. "You are a brazen little fellow." he said throwing stones at the creature as it quickly climbed a near by tree. Ansleigh walked out into the noonday sun covering her eyes from the brightness. Her stomach was swollen and she could barely walk. "You look like you need to sit before you topple." laughed Thomas.

"That old racoon got into my meal again." "He likes you. Whatever for I don't know." smiled Ansleigh. "It is a fine day. So are you going into town again?" "Wasn't plann'n on it why?" "I need some more flour and cloth. I want to make the baby a blanket. Don't really have anything for it. Something new." "You know I don't like leaving you alone with the baby so close." "I will be fine."She said as she leaned against a tree to support her back. "I suppose if I leave now I'd be back by sunset." "It would be a good thing." Ansleigh said as she rubbed her stomach. "I will do it for you and my little boy." Touching her stomach, he kissed her gently. "I will bring you back some of that hard candy you like so much." "That would be nice." Thomas then finished what he was doing and saddled up his roan and left for Crooked Hat.

It was growing late and Thomas had not returned Ansleigh was starting to worry. She was afraid that someone would find them out. Thomas was careful on his visits not to draw undue attention to himself. She lit the candle on the small wooden table and sat on the edge of the bed.
She wasn't feeling well. She had sharp pains in her back and it was hard for her to breathe. She knew she had to vomit. She got up and took the candle from the table with her outside.
It was a full moon night. She bent over to vomit and was doubled up in intense pain. Water was running down her legs. She thought she was wetting herself. She knew nothing of birth no one had ever taught her. She crawled over to a low hanging branch grabbing a hold of it she beared down instinctively. She cried out but no one was there to hear her except the nocturnal creatures of the mountain.

89

She felt the power of her body as it convulsed and pushed to bring the baby to life. "Thomas!" She cried out. "Where are you?" It seemed an eternity that she was there wrestling with the branch and grinding her teeth in pain. Then it happened she strained really hard and the baby burst out onto the earth beneath her. As soon as it hit the coldness of the ground it screamed.

Ansleigh grabbed him up it was a boy. By the light of the moon she ripped the hem from her skirt and cleaned his little body of the after birth. She lifted him to her and chewed off his umbilical cord tying it into a quick little knot. She gathered what strength she had left and walked slowly with the baby in her arms. Back into the cabin and passed out on the bed.

31
"Zacharia's Healing"

Mr. Riley sat across from Clegg at the hotel. "No one has seen or heard of anyone coming through here this past month. I think they may have went on to California. I just spent the last two weeks tracking without any luck. You might as well accept that your daughter's found a new life for herself." "That's it!" Mr. Riley said as he quickly washed down a shot of whiskey. "I paid you to find her!" "You better change your tone with me. I have killed men for less." "What am I supposed to do now? I've spent the last of me savings coming here." "You should have thought about that before you started this wild goose chase. We all have to let go of something in this life. Maybe she's happy. Did you ever think of that?" "She'll end up in some God forsaken rat hole with that randy gutter snipe. She's so like her mother." "I can see now why she left." "What do you mean by that remark?" "To get away from you." "You son of a bitch what the hell do you know about a family?" "I know if you hold onto something to tight you kill it. Here buy yourself another drink." Clegg said as he flipped a coin onto the table. "We're through." With that he walked off leaving Mr. Riley alone with his drink.

Zacharia was getting sick on the coach. Thorton called out to the driver to stop. As soon as he did Zacharia jumped out vomiting on to the ground and doubling up in pain. Beatrice was very worried she had never seen him like this before. "There's blood here we best get him to a doctor." Thorton warned.

"What is the nearest town from here that might have a doctor?" Thorton asked. "I can't hold up the coach on account of the lad." Said the driver. "I gotta leave yah here." He leaned forward and spit a wad of tobacco on the ground. "What the hell are you talking about?" Thorton said twisting his face in anger. "I'm sorry but this is my job." His partner held a shot gun on them as the driver threw their trunks onto the ground below. The elderly couple looked on from the coach. Thorton was angry and swore at them as they pulled out leaving them behind.

There was a cluster of trees along side the road and Thorton carried Zacharia over to them and set him down. Beatrice felt his forehead and he was burning up. Thorton took off his coat and covered the boy with it. The rains had stopped and the weather was mild. "I am going to start walking back toward Crooked Hat. You and Zacharia must stay here. I will get back to you as soon as I can." Beatrice started to cry. Thorton gave her his gun. "You keep this with you and if you have to use it be sure you aim true." He hugged her and knelt down to Zacharia. "Look Zach I will be back as soon as I can get help."

"You need to hold on, do you hear me?" "Yes I'll try." He said as he vomited once again. "What are we going to do?" Cried Beatrice. "Be still and stay next to him, keep him covered. Thorton then looked at them both and turning started walking briskly down the road. Beatrice watched until he was out of sight.

There was still plenty of daylight left. She was afraid to be alone at night. She remembered making fires from her childhood her father had taught her.

As the day wore on Zacharia became more despondent and his skin grew cold. Beatrice was worried what if something had happened to Thorton or he didn't return. She put her arms about him and leaned against the tree. She drifted off into a light sleep when she was awakened by a sense of something or someone standing over her.

91

She opened her eyes to see a tall good looking native staring down at her. She started to cry out. He knelt down putting his finger tips to her lips. Something in his eyes quieted her. She felt no fear. He placed his hands on Zacharia's face. Beatrice wanted to know what he was doing. He starting digging a shallow grave, in which he laid pine branches, sprinkling herbs from a pouch in the furrow. He gently took Zacharia in his arms and laid him in the grave. Covering him with dirt until only his head was sticking out. He took a gourd he was carrying and made Zacharia drink from it. He then proceeded to build a fire. Beatrice sat on the ground watching as if in a dream. She instinctively knew that this man meant no harm. That he was trying to help her son. He made a smudge from a dried Cedar branch near by and continuously fanned the smoke over Zacharia's body with a feathered fan. Chanting and praying as he did so. The sun was starting to set and still no sign of Thorton. Zacharia started to awaken and to talk. The young native pulled him up out from the shallow grave. His fever was gone and he looked bright and happy.

"Mum you won't believe where I went." He said excitedly. "I saw a great grizzly bear and he took me for a ride on his back. I saw the sky full of birds and an eagle landed next to me. He spoke and told me I was going to be just fine."

"I am sure it was a dream but what really matters, is you are well."
"I feel so much better." The young native took a feather from his belt and gave it to Zacharia. It was a hawk feather. He took his hands and showed him a sign. Zacharia imitated him and smiled. Beatrice wanted to do something to show her gratitude. She reached in her bag and found some money to give him. He shook his head no. He left her some herbs in a leather pouch and mimed that Zacharia was to take this with water. She understood. Then as quickly and quietly as he had appeared he went off into the woods as they stood and watched him go.

32

"Justice Reaps Sorrow"

Thomas made it back to the cabin by dawn of the next day. He had
rented a small wagon. When he had entered the dwelling, he heard the baby
cry. He looked down at the bed. Ansleigh was sound asleep.
He gently pulled the baby up to him. "A little boy what do you know? Hello
there little fella. I am your papa. I know I am not much to look at but you
sure are a welcome sight. Did you give your mama a hard time of it? She
looks pretty tuckered." The infant slowly opened his eyes. Thomas stared
into his little face. He was a fair skinned baby with blonde hair. "Guess you
are going to need a name ain't yah?" he smiled. "Peter." he heard Ansleigh
say in a weak voice. "After my great-grandfather and Thomas after you." "It
has a nice sound to it I think." He said as he sat on the edge of the bed
holding his son. Both of them looked at the baby and it was quiet.

Then Peter started to cry in earnest. "He is hungry, hand him to me. I
don't know how to do this but I am going to try." Her breast were swollen
and sore and she pulled the infant to her. He began suckling. Thomas
grinned. "He sure knows how to handle the drink'n that he does." After the
baby was finished he fell asleep and Ansleigh asked Thomas to help her up.
She was weak and still covered in blood. "Looks like the two of yah need a
bath, and I am just the fella to do it." He made Ansleigh sit at the table as
he fixed her a cup of coffee. He then proceeded to heat a kettle of water in
the fire pit for bathing. Ansleigh was glad that Thomas was here and
helping.

Thomas let Ansleigh wash the baby. He went outside while she was
doing this. When he returned. He was carrying a rocking chair he set it
down near their bed. He then brought in a box filled with cloth and a ready
made blanket on the top. It was a soft blue with little flowers embroidered
on the edges. "Where ever did you get all this?"She mused. "They have a
General Store in town it just opened. Some fella from Sweden runs it.
Guess his wife is a blanket maker. She has a big old loom right there in the
store darnnest thing. Soon as I saw that blue blanket I knew you had to
have it." "It is lovely." she said. Placing the sleeping infant in his pine crib

93

that Thomas had made. She covered him with the blue blanket. She could still smell the fresh pine scent of the wood. Peter was sleeping serenely.

"Now my fair lady, it is your turn."Thomas told her as he helped her out of her soiled clothing. She stood naked before him. "You are still beautiful Ansleigh just like the day at the river when I first met yah." "Oh I don't feel very beautiful."She cried. "Now no tears." he scolded. He had filled a basin with warm water and proceeded to wash her gently with a cloth as she stood by the kitchen table. He even washed her hair and combed it dry.

As she sat wrapped in a blanket near the fire. Ansleigh didn't quite know what to make of all this. She hadn't seen this side of Thomas before. She suddenly felt close to him again.

Justice was losing weight and her skin was covered in sores. Some nights she would lay shivering under the blankets feeling feverish. She took to wearing scarves about her neck. August mentioned to her she didn't look well and that she should see a doctor. Charles was the one that finally took her to see a Dr. Finch in a nearby settlement of Pigeon Grove.

While she was there he told her that she had contracted Gonorreah and wanted to know who it was that she was laying with. She was embarrassed to tell him. He warned her if she didn't attend to it. She would become severely ill. Possibly die. Like Beatrice before her she was afraid to say or do anything. It was then she realized what Beatrice had done to rid herself of August. She knew that she had to say something to August even if it meant bringing herself harm. She was depressed and lonely most of the time. As August literally kept an eye on her every move. The doctor gave her a treatment that day and gave her a supply of ointment and a herbal remedy to take. He told her if there was no improvement to return and he would try and help her. She was weary from the journey. She told Charles that she had some kind of an infection. But she lied as well.

It was the weekend and the hotel was overflowing with drunks and gamblers. Charles and Justice were at the gaming table. Harp was trying to push a drunk out of the hotel because he kept pulling his gun and threatening to kill the bar-keep. "Now look fella you need ta head home and sober up." "Yah cain't make me that no account bartender watered down mah drinks I want mah money back or I'll shoot um dead." "Hand me yore

94

gun for folks git hurt here!" Demanded Harp. The drunk aimed the gun at Harp, before he could pull the trigger. Charles had shot the gun right out of his hand. "Get that son of a bitch out of my hotel." Warned August. Harp threw the drunkard out into the street. August looked over at Justice and motioned her to him. She pretended not to notice. He walked over and leaned into her taking his hand and pinching hard into her skin. "You and I need to talk." He reeked of whiskey. "In my office now."

He whispered. She told Charles she would be right back. Following August to the back of the hotel she started to feel nauseous. Her heart was pounding she knew that she must tell him about her condition. As soon as they entered his office. He threw her up against the wall groping her and kissing her neck. Please don't Justice pleaded. "What's the matter with you?" He asked pushing her a way. "Since when did you get so high and mighty?" he asked reaching for her again kissing her hard on the mouth. "I can't!" "You can't what?" She stood there afraid to say anything. Then she blurted it out. "Do this I have Gonorreah."

"What the blazes are yah say'n?" "I have the clap and I got it from you." August went berserk he started hitting her in the face and shoved her down to the floor. Calling her names and accusing her of sleeping with other men and blaming him. He beat her so bad that she could feel something break inside of her. He then spit on her and stormed out of the room.

It took all of her strength to get up off the floor but she did and she had followed him out into the saloon. August was at the bar drinking while Harp was leaned into him talking about what had transpired earlier. Sheriff Daniels, was standing at the door looking on. Justice stood in the middle of the room holding on her side. Her face was swollen beyond recognition. Her hair was matted with blood. She was weaving back and forth fighting to stand upright. She stared right at August in her hand she held a gun.

She was aiming it straight at him. He laughed when he saw her. "Well now the little Sharper has some spirit after all." Charles seeing her immediately aimed his gun at August. "I wouldn't if I were you." Warned August. Charles took aim and shot but he was shot in the back of the head at the same moment. It was Sheriff Daniels that pulled the trigger. August had been wounded in the neck.

When Justice saw her brother laying dead on the barroom floor she passed out.

33
"Healing Takes Time"

Maizey walked to the Café it was just before dawn. She still missed Nate. He would always fix her a cup of coffee while they were working and preparing the meals for the day. He use to tease Ki and poke fun at his accent. She knew it was time to get back into the thick of things. She stood for a moment in front of the café sign Maizey and Nates and decided to keep it that way. It bothered her that August had not mentioned anything to her about finding Nate's killer. So she was going to take it upon herself to find him. No matter how long it would take her. Maizey felt something sniffing at her feet she looked down to see a small spotted dog licking her boot. "Where in tarnation did yah come from? Yore as skinny as a rail." She reached down petting him.

Ki was busy filling a large kettle with water when she arrived. "Miss Maizey good see you. I have eggs and flap-jack on stove." "Salut Ki I am sorry it ain't been easy with Mr. Townsend gone."

"I know." Ki said touching her shoulder before he walked off into the dining area. Maizey threw a slice of sow belly out to the little dog. The workers were already coming in for their morning coffee.

When they saw that Maizey was back in the kitchen they all hooted and applauded her. This touched Maizey. Maybe she thought she was good for something after all.

Katherine was having back aches almost everyday. She tried to help Nel in the kitchen but it was getting harder for her to stand for any length of time. Nel had softened some what since Katherine and Quin had come to stay with them. She looked forward to their morning conversations after the

96

men had left the house over a cup of tea. "Have any names picked out for your little one?" She asked Katherine as she started to prepare the lunch time meal for the ranch hands. Katherine started to help her at the table. "You sit down I can get this. You need to take care of yourself that's a fact." "Thank you Nel I am feeling poorly today. Haven't really given it any thought. Naming the baby." "What do you want?" "As long as it's whole I don't care. I lost my son." Then she broke down and wept. Nel awkwardly put her hands on Katherine's shoulders "That's alright you let those tears come. Does a body good to cry. You don't have to talk about it." "No I want to. God forgive me but I did not want the baby. I wasn't ready. Quin and I on the run.

God took him from me for my sins. Do you believe that?" "Yes!" "I am a Christian woman but I don't think the Lord is mean like that. If Karl heard me talk'n like this, he would chastise me. But to me a loving God just wouldn't do that. You see I couldn't bare children and I blamed God for it. But the truth is I was sickly and couldn't keep them. I don't blame anybody. Besides God has given you another chance." Katherine stood up and hugged Nel.

Karl entered "What in tarnation are you two up to? I need a coffee woman." Karl was a blustery man he talked loudly and took over a room. "Sit down and take off those dang boots you are tracking mud on my clean kitchen floor."

Karl and Nel liked to bicker. Katherine sipped her tea and looked out the window at the gathering thunder clouds.

It was all over the mining camp about Charles being shot by Sheriff Daniels. Some said he had been dry gulched plain and simple. That August Mayfield didn't like Charles and it was a set up. It was all speculation. Justice was bed ridden for days. Dr. Haveston was called in she was staying at the town's brothel everyone simply called it Mrs. Jacks.

She was rooming with a prostitute by the name of Nadine. The doctor told her she had three broken ribs and a swollen kidney and a fractured jaw. He was especially worried about her right eye. He wanted to know who had done this to her, before she could get his name out. He said "It was August

Mayfield wasn't it." She turned her head into her pillow and cried. "Somebody needs to shoot that bastard and put him out of his misery." The doctor said under his breath. The doctor told her that for what it was worth he had been treating August for the clap for quite some time. He gave Justice Opium to kill her pain. He told her it would take time to heal. Justice welcomed the opium it took her out of her senses and she would float to a beautiful place far above the earth. Her pain at losing Charles was more than she wanted to think about.

The weather in the mountains was changing becoming warmer and the trees were full of blossoms. Mr. Riley had heard about Justice and decided to pay her a visit. He had secured a job at the General Store doing inventory, the ledgers and tutoring for Mr. Cederholm. A Swedish storekeeper who had just moved to Crooked Hat from back East with his family. Mrs. Cederholm and her daughters had not arrived yet. Jacob was trying to make enough money to head back to Pennsylvania. He had resigned himself to the fact he wasn't going to find his daughters. Nadine met him at the door. "Morning miss, I am here to see about Miss Hamilton and her condition?" Nadine was a willowy girl with long dark hair and a child like demeanor. "She ain't do'n to well who I may ask is call'n." "Mr. Riley she knows of me."
"I think she's stirr'n follow me."

Mr. Riley followed her down the hall. Some of the women were looking out of their doorways as he walked by. "A little early aint it, even for you Nadine." Chirped one of the girls the others laughed. Mr. Riley was feeling uncomfortable and wanted to quickly be out of there. "Yah got company." Said Nadine as she walked away leaving him alone in the room with Justice. He was shocked at what he saw. Justice peered up at him from her bed.

Her hair was matted with sweat and both of her eyes swollen so bad she could barely make him out. Her lips were bloated and her cheeks were black and blue. She was obviously in a lot of pain. "I am so sorry." he blurted out. "I had no idea."

He stood there awkwardly staring down at her lying on the bed. "Who did this to you?"

He wanted to know. She wouldn't say. "Charles do you know of my brother Charles?" She asked barely able to breathe in between the stabbing pains of her broken ribs. "I heard that he's being buried tomorrow." "Who's doing it?" "Seems Mr. Mayfield is paying for his coffin and they're holding the funeral at the town hall. They are burying him out on the flats near Carson's Bluff." "I've been out there it is peaceful."

Justice eyes were welling with tears. "And no preacher to say words over him?" "No mam." She reached for Jacob's hand. "You seem like a good man. Would you do something for me?" "Anything." He said. "Would you say some words over my brother I will tell you what I want you to say. Please!" She pleaded with him. "I can do that." He sat quietly and with great effort Justice told him what she wanted said for Charles's eulogy.

Jacob felt a great sorrow after his visit he was glad that he went to see her. He knew that he was supposed to be there. As he walked back toward the hotel that day he remembered the day of Rebecca's funeral. He had no words to speak then, he was numb inside. So Katherine did it for him.

He drank heavily that day and missed work. He barely made the funeral the next morning. They had him at the undertaker's sitting room. A few of the townspeople and miners who knew Charles were there. It was a small group. August was uneasy during the service. Harp said a few things and a couple of quotes from the Bible and they invited people to join them at the grave site. Jacob was nervous and almost decided against going. But he knew he couldn't face Justice if he didn't do as she had asked.

It was a warm day and a gentle breeze was coming across the flats. Charles was being buried under a lone pine.

As the men lowered the casket. Jacob spoke up. "I was asked by Miss Hamilton to say a few words for her brother." "Well make it quick," snapped August. He was irritable as the wound on his neck was swollen. "Justice wants to let you know that she loved you since you were a small boy. You were her hero. You were her family. There was never a time she didn't see you with admiration even during the rough times.

You always had her welfare in mind. She regrets not being here to say goodbye. But know that you will never be forgotten as long as she lives and she will see you in Glory." Jacob started to choke up on the last few words.

99

He quickly left and mounted his horse. And for a moment he didn't know where he wanted to go.

34
"Into The Shadows"

Huittsu bent down over the stream and saw her reflection she looked at her image for a while. She seemed different to herself in some way. Things were not as she had envisioned them. Many Horses was a good provider and kind to her. But she did not love him, and he knew it. She filled her clay vessel full of water to take back to her lodge. It was summer and the mountain had come to life with flowers and wild berries. The days were longer and the work was more intensive. Huittsu and Many Horses were involved with trading with Mr. Cederholm at his Dry Good Store in Crooked Hat. Many Horses was making flutes and wood carvings to trade. While Huittsu was doing bead work on purses and hair ornaments; in return they were getting food stuffs such as flour, sweet candies, cloth and some tools made in Europe.
Many Horses had been told that some of the young men in their tribe were getting whiskey there as well. Trading their furs and knives for the liquor. He knew that Shila was aware of this and was trying to intervene. Night Wing had become a hermit living near the village preferring to be alone. Shila visited him often. Taking pemmican which Night Wing loved. He told Shila he was growing restless and thought that he could help the young men who were drawn by the drink. Shila thought that this is what spirit would want of him. So Night Wing planned on helping those he could. Huittsu would watch for Shila when she was out side working. She knew it was forbidden for her to speak alone with him anymore. She missed that.
Night Wing had decided to follow three young men of his clan one night as they rode their horses in the direction of Crooked Hat. He stayed way behind so they wouldn't know they were being followed. They rode up to the back of the hotel. There in the dark Night Wing could see Mr. Miller coming out of the back of the hotel. He hid behind an out building so he

100

could watch but not be seen. The young men brought out coyote pelts and some bead work. "This ain't what I want. I asked yah to bring me some girl's purty ones. I got some fellas that'll pay big bucks for a night with a squaw." Only one of the men knew any English and that was limited. "You know." Harp said thrusting his hips to and fro. The young men looked at each other and laughed.

"No girls, no whiskey." They became agitated with him. He drew out a colt revolver and aimed it. "Don't yah be mess'n with me or you will be push'n daisies." With that he drew out a bottle of whiskey and guzzled it down in front of them. They were desperate for a drink. Night Wing knew what that was like and somewhere inside of him the thirst for it was still there. Harp, threw the bottle he was drinking from at them. They all clamored for it. Fighting over who would drink first. Harp shook his hips at them.

"Girls more Whiskey" he chanted. The oldest of the three spoke "I get girls." "You meet me in two days time. We will have a deal." Harp told them and walked off.

They mounted their horses and quickly rode out of the town. Night Wing was heavy hearted as he followed them back to the encampment. He knew that the snake that needed killing was Mr. Miller.

Kachiri had met a young man a Paiute. He lived a few miles from them in a small village. He was a knife maker and sat on the tribe's council. She met him when she was out gathering Bear Weed used for its healing properties. He was walking through the thickets looking for a plant to stop the bleeding his arm had a deep gash in it. They startled one another at first. Kachiri upon seeing his wound offered to help him. He had fallen while reaching for a honey comb high onto a branch, cutting his arm. His name she was to learn was Tocho (mountain lion). He lived in the desert regions of the Sierra Nevadas. He had been hunting the day he met her.

They used a lot of hand gesturing as they did not understand each other's language. He knew some Shoshone. She dressed his wound, she knew intuitively that she liked him. She wanted him to come to her encampment as she feared she may never meet him again. He too wanted to meet with her again.

101

The day had come for Tocho to meet Kachiri's family. Hapisteen had made a meal of venison and corn bread with Turtle soup and honey water to drink. Kachiri was nervous and excited to see him again. "My daughter has not been this excited in a long time." Teased River Tree. "He must be some kind of warrior." "Do not make fun of her heart." chastised Hapisteen. "Shila is coming? I asked him to be here." "He will be here you know that." Said her father. She had no sooner spoke when Kocho peered into their lodge. He was very tall with long braids wrapped in ermine. He was dressed in a elk skin shirt and leggings tucked into moccasin boots. His eyes were almost black and he was good looking.

Kocho introduced himself the best he could as his Shoshone was very limited. He had brought a soft deer skin as a gift to her family.

Shila was running across the meadow. He had almost forgotten that Kachiri had asked him to be there to meet her new friend. As he jumped across a ditch. He stumbled into a young woman. He had not seen her as she was bent down pulling grass. She took a hold of him to steady his steps. He looked into her face it was Huittsu. They stood there for a while looking at each other. She did not want to let him go. He walked on past her not saying anything. She watched after him alone in her thoughts. Shila liked Kocho after meeting him. He felt a strong sense of kinship with him. Kocho was a warm person with a quiet strength. Kachiri was aware of this in him. Shila told her later that she had made a good choice with this man. "I know." She told him smiling.

35
"Ansleigh and Shila"

It was hard for Zacharia to sleep at night he kept waking up from bad dreams. This disturbed Beatrice. She wasn't sure what was causing his problem. He seemed stressed about something but would not say. They had returned to Crooked Hat. They had been back for a month. On the day of the coach incident; Thorton did not return until dawn of the next day, with a buggy he had rented. Clegg was with him. He was shocked to see the

102

difference in Zacharia. He was up looking well and very talkative. He told Thorton all about the strange Indian and how he had healed him. About the bear and the talking eagle. Beatrice said he had been dreaming. Thorton agreed with her.

Zacharia was angry that they did not believe him and he did not like Clegg. He said it was real to him and that was all that mattered. In his heart he wanted to meet the young Indian man again. Beatrice took Zacharia to see Dr. Haveston to be sure he was really well. The doctor was surprised at how healthy Zacharia looked after what Beatrice had told him. He was amazed he told her because everything had indicated a bout with a serious form of dysentery. But there were no such signs. He said the Indian healer knew exactly what he was doing. Zacharia smiled and said "Yes he did."

Beatrice wanted to leave for California again. But Thorton told her she would have to go it a lone. As Clegg offered him a job riding with him on his man hunts and the pay was very good.

He told her to be patient because once he got enough money saved they would be able to go to California and possibly buy a house. She argued with him as she did not want to be in town any where near August Mayfield. She had seen poor Justice right after she returned. She saw her at the Cederholm's General Store. She was shocked a once beautiful woman was now permanently disfigured. She was blind in her right eye. Her eye lid was half opened and would not close. From the beating she walked with a limp. Her lip was still swollen from a jaw fracture. She no longer played the piano and stayed at Mrs. Jacks as one of the girls. The men would taunt her about her lips and Justice didn't care. She still grieved Charles. Beatrice did not talk to her that day as she did not know what to say to her. She knew without asking who had done this to her.

Beatrice had to find work so she offered to help the Cederholms. Batilda Cederholm and her daughters were now settled in at the store. She knew how to sew and was a hat maker from her theater days. She made a beautiful bonnet out of white cotton and added lace trim with little hand made pink roses on the brim. She took it to show Mrs. Cederholm. Batilda was a big boned woman with a square face. Her English was poor. When she got upset she would speak in Swedish. Sven, her husband was a short man. Balding with a large mustache.

His command of English was good but he had a thick accent. He liked to talk. They had two daughters Gilda and Ingrid, who were in their twenties. Gilda was pretty, a tall slender woman with golden hair and large brown eyes. Ingrid looked more like her mother.

She was large boned and buxom, her dark hair was coarse and she had thick eyebrows and a severe over-bite. Of course Sven favored Gilda and he was at odds with Ingrid. At first Batilda told Beatrice that they did not need any help. They didn't have a need for hats. When a female customer eyed Beatrice's bonnet. She wanted to know where it had come from. She wanted to try it on. She really liked it and asked if there were more? The bonnet had procured a job for Beatrice working at the General Store. She was to make many more hats in the summer of that year.

Zacharia went back to Mr. Cranston and was soon working in the hotel kitchen again. This is not at all, what Beatrice had envisioned but for the time being it would have to do.

Ansleigh was fulfilled for the first time in her life with the baby. She spent her days working from sun up to sun down preparing foods and tanning hides that Thomas brought back from his traps. He had taught her how to do this when they lived in Vineyard. She would talk to Peter as if he were an adult as they were alone a good deal of the time. Sometimes Thomas would be gone for days setting traps. She would talk about her sisters and how she missed them how she used to live in a really nice house with curtains to the windows and fresh linens on her bed. Those memories always brought tears. Thomas was good to her and she was settling in as his wife.

She felt she would never trust him again after Vineyard. The weather had turned hot and she would leave the cabin door open to let in the fresh air. They had a flock of chickens which she had to coop, the coyotes and foxes were forever getting at them. She had become a good shot with a rifle and wasn't above shooting at the intruders. They had four goats they kept for milking. She was outside with Peter one afternoon picking berries from nearby vines. When she thought, she saw someone move through the brush.

She started back to the cabin to get her rifle. When he appeared. It was the same Indian that had given her the ointment for her leg. He was shirtless and was wearing a loin cloth. His body was brown and well shaped. He was very handsome and it made her blush. Shila knew this was the woman he had seen in his vision. The flies were biting that day and the baby's arms were red from their sting. He motioned to Ansleigh to follow him. At first she stood there not knowing what she should do. His eyes were soft, so she did not fear him. He took her into the woods and squatted down near a small plant. He picked a leaf and had her smell it.

It had an aromatic fragrance. He then spit on it rolled it into a tight little ball and placed it on the baby's bites. Peter liked Shila's face and smiled at him. He picked a few more of the leaves chanting softly as he did so. Giving them to Ansleigh for the baby. He walked with Ansleigh back to her cabin. Shila felt an overwhelming need to protect her. He showed her through pantomime a way to protect herself and the baby. He suddenly disappeared and she could not understand where he had gone so quickly. Then she heard a bird like sound coming from a nearby bush.

Shila popped out at her she squealed in surprise. "How did you do that?" She asked smiling.

He took her by the hand and covered her and Peter in branches full of leaves, showing her how to bend the branches to cover her like a blanket. She felt invisible. She realized he was showing her how to hide in plain sight. She thanked him and when they came back to the cabin she signed for him to stay there. She brought out a cup with sweet tea in it, offering him a drink. Shila drank it down nodding his approval. "I am Ansleigh." she said slowly pointing to herself. Shila said her name perfectly the first time. "This is my son Peter." "Peter." he said smiling at the baby. "Shila." "What a nice sounding name, Shila." Repeated Ansleigh. She was going to refill his cup and when she turned to speak to him. He was gone. It was suddenly so quiet and she felt this strange aloneness come over her.

36

"Little Katy"

Her pain was deep and she couldn't catch her breath. She made it to the
kitchen calling out to Nel. "Oh darl'n you are ready. Where is Quin?" "I
don't know!" Katherine screamed out in pain.
"Let's get you to my room. I will have Karl fetch the mid-wife. Little Sally
White-Tail. She is good." Katherine holding onto her stomach made it to
Nel's room falling onto the bed. Nel started heating water on the wood
stove and went outside to find Karl. She found him at the barn. She told
him it was time and where was Quin? She told Karl to go and get Sally right
away. She then headed out to the pasture to let Quin know his wife was in
labor. Katherine was in labor on into the next day. Sally was there and
keeping her comfortable with herbal tea and cooling her with a wash cloth
dipped in water. Sally was an old Shoshone woman. No one knew her age
some said she was at least a hundred. Her hair was snow white and her eyes
still looked youthful she smiled a lot. It was a hot summer's day and
everyone was feeling the stress of the heat. Quin wouldn't leave Katherine's
side. He was worried about her. Then just as the sun started to set the baby
finally made its arrival. A little girl with a shock of red hair. Sally told her
that this was a good omen. "A sun child." Katherine was elated. Quin was
so happy to see Katherine smiling. "My, my." said Nel "What a beautiful
baby." Karl was smiling "Praise the Lord and all His ways." As they
gathered around the bed. By the next day Katherine was up and washing the
baby and singing to her.

Nel thought she should rest some more. "I am fine Nel I need to do this.
I will take it easy I promise." "So have you chosen a name yet?" "Yes we
have Katherine Nelly James. Quin insisted. But I am going to call her
Katy." "Nelly?" Nel was trying to cover her smile. "Yes, Nelly after my
dearest friend." The two women embraced. Nel was constantly after
Katherine to hold the baby and in the weeks that followed their friendship
grew.

Jacob didn't know if it was proper or not to visit Justice at Mrs.Jacks.

He had grown fond of her and knew she was a recluse since her brother's death. She was a prostitute and he knew it. There was a time in his life when he would have looked down his nose at her. But since he had left his home over a year ago things had changed in him. Jacob had held a mistrust of women since his late wife's betrayal. But he felt differently about Justice. Perhaps he thought it was because Justice was open about her life style and had no expectations of him nor was she judgemental.

He decided to take her some wild flowers, he had picked from behind the hotel. He hadn't seen her since Charles funeral almost two months ago. He was ashamed he had waited so long. When he arrived one of the girls answered the door. She was bare breasted and he didn't know where to look. "Why mister you never saw titties before." She laughed. "Too darn hot for a corset today.

You look'n for Nadine? She's with a fella but I am available." "I am looking for Miss Justice." he stammered. "Hell I am better look'n then old one eye." Jacob was quiet never saying a word.

She pointed to a room and went off in a huff. He was very nervous as he approached Justice's room.

He knocked softly. "Come on in. You can lay your money on the dresser." Justice said with her back to him. "I am truly sorry Miss Hamilton that I wasn't here sooner." She turned around and looked into Jacob's face. "Did you do as I asked?" "Yes I did." "Is it nice where he's at?" "He is under a lone pine tree and it is very peaceful there. I could take you there sometime if you want?" "I would like that." she said as she started to cry. Jacob felt compassion for her pain. He felt this urgency to comfort her. Reaching out he touched her face. She turned her face away from him. "No" he said softly. She suddenly embraced him burying her face into his shoulder. He lifted her face to his and kissed her softly. She responded. The two of them instinctively went to the bed. Jacob was a tender lover kissing her and touching her gently. Justice looked into his face. He was a mature man with deep set, green eyes, he had such warm hands, she thought and he made her feel for the first time in months. She fell into a much needed sleep. Jacob lay there, staring at her. She was still very beautiful her face was healing and her lips were no longer swollen. He was surprised at himself.

107

The last woman he had made love to was his late wife Rebecca. He wondered how he had fallen so far from grace. He quietly dressed himself. Leaving a note with money and her flowers. It read this money is for you to buy yourself a pretty bonnet. I am speechless. Respectfully Yours, Jacob Riley.

37
"I Know Who They Are"

Beatrice worried about Zacharia. As he became more melancholy. He wanted to live with her. He had grown tired of the pretense. He longed to call her mum. He threatened to run away if she didn't come up with a place for them to be together and soon. It was a hot dry day and they were sitting out in a meadow. Beatrice had put together a picnic lunch. She had spread a blanket on the ground. She had made his favorite butter cake with chicken legs and salt potatoes. He ate as if it were his last meal. She smiled as she watched him wolf it down.

It was then she noticed bruises up and down his arm. "Zacharia what is this?" she asked lifting his arm towards her. He pulled back quickly. "Nothing." He muttered. "This isn't nothing who did this to you!" "What does it matter to you?" He cried out. "But it does matter to me. Do you think I like living like this? You know I have a better chance of getting work if people think I am single." "But you aren't working the taverns anymore .You don't even sing? Why is that?" "I want to know who did this to your arm." "Mr. Cranston. He doesn't think I work hard enough in the kitchen. He calls you a whore. The last time he did that I hit him as hard as I could in his stomach, he just laughed and lifted me off the floor and threw me against the wall. I didn't care. When I am at his house, his wife doesn't treat me any better." "Oh Zacharia, I am so, so sorry why didn't you say something sooner?" "I thought we were going to California." "As of today you are through at the hotel." "But where are we going to go?" "You let me take care of that."

Zacharia hugged his mother tightly. Beatrice's mind was racing she didn't know where to turn. But she wasn't about to let anyone hurt her son like that again.

It was a moonless night and the air lay thick and heavy. Making it hard to breathe. Harp, was standing under the town sign Crooked Hat that he had made almost two years before. The town had grown and more people kept migrating there and staying. He thought a lot about money. He wanted to be as rich as August. He resented the way he was treated. He thought he deserved more. Being the overseer at the Logging Camp alone was a tedious job. It was growing late the young Indian had promised to bring women so where were they? He was about ready to head back to the hotel when he heard some muffled sounds coming from the wooded area. He squinted into the dark just as two young Indian men appeared.

They had three women gagged and bound with them. "What the?" grunted Harp. "Girls, whiskey!" The one native said as he thrust his hips to and fro. Two of the women were young and one was older and quite heavy.

"This is the best yah could do?" Complained Harp. "You give Whiskey! No, woman." Said the taller of the two. "Hold your britches." Harp reached down and pulled out a box full of whiskey. The natives quickly grabbed the box and pushed the women toward Harp. They were all tied together like horses. They then scarmbled off into the darkness.

Leaving Harp alone withthe women. He pulled out his gun to let them know he meant business. He walked them up to the hotel. "Get on in there." He swore. Kicking one of the women in the back. There were four men sitting at the bar. Harp motioned for them to join him. His hand held out for their money. He had a room set aside for them. Two of the men chose the younger women while the bigger woman was left to join in. It didn't much matter as the men repeatedly raped the women. By dawn of the next day Harp Miller walked the battered women out past the town limits and left them to fend for themselves.

Kachiri looked up when she saw the three women walking into the camp. They were supporting each other. The youngest one fell to the ground. She

109

ran over to them. She could see they had been beaten. "Who did this?" she demanded. They stood mute, no tears, and no emotions. Kachiri called out to her father. River Tree quickly joined her. He was shocked to see the condition they were in. Soon others had gathered around. Healing Fox asked for help getting the young women to his lodge. "I want to know what has happened here." River Tree spoke angrily. "Where have they been?" "Remember Navia's mother came to you yesterday asking for help. I know she was certain Navia had snuck off to see her lover. I told her I would talk with her. "There is something bad here." Kachiri warned her father. "I want you to talk with them Kachiri you have a way with words. See what they say and let me know. I will hold a council tonight."

River Tree found Shila working with a young horse. He asked him to join the council he told him what had happened. Shila said he thought that whiskey was involved. He went to see the young women. This made him very angry and he wanted to find the truth. He brought Night Wing to the council that night.

The people of the village were attending. River Tree asked Healing Fox to start by praying. The young women were not in attendance as they were still recuperating from their ordeal.

Kachiri was there and she asked if she might speak. Kocho had joined her as well. "It is with much sadness I say these words. My sisters have suffered at the hand of the white man. They told me what has happened. Shila is right they were traded for whiskey. It is with shame they spoke to me. The shame is not with them, but the young men of our village, who took them there. I am trying to get them to tell me who they are but they will not." Shila spoke up "I have warned you all about this whiskey you can see the darkness that it brings. You must speak up and come forward tell the truth. For if you do not you will suffer a far greater outcome." It grew silent no one was saying anything. When Night Wing stood up. "I know who they are." He spoke softly and hung his head.

38

"A Hat For Molly"

No one knew where the heavy rains had come from. This was unusual
for the high mountain plateaus. The main street of town was a sea of mud
and wagons could not get through. August was in a odious mood about it.
It didn't keep the local drunks from making their way to the bar.
Since Beatrice and Justice were no longer entertaining the men. The little
Opera House sat empty. Some of the miners complained about it. So
August ran an ad in the San Francisco Gazette asking for women, who
could sing. He decided he wanted to build a new hotel. One that housed a
restaurant, a barber shop and rooms for rent. He had already ordered a
gravity furnace from back East to heat the rooms and he was going to put
in water closets in the bigger suites. He wanted a better clientele and was
fashioning it on one he had seen in Boston years before. August had
ordered all of these things through the San Francisco Gazette he had
delivered twice a month through the post. It would be over a month before
he would get the supplies as it all had to be shipped by wagon overland.

Harp wanted to know what he planned on doing with the one they had.
August told him that he could take it over. It was too small he said for his
plans. He still dreamed about a railroad coming through Crooked Hat.
Harp, was more then happy with the news. He had plans of starting up his
own bar and renting rooms by the hour.

Beatrice and Zacharia were fighting their way through the mud laden
streets to the Café. They were drenched by the time they reached Maizey's.
She introduced Zacharia as her brother and that he needed to work. Maizey
said a young boy like him needed to be in school not wait'n on a bunch of
rough neck miners. The desperate look on Beatrice's face gave Maizey the
impression that this woman needed her help. "So yah say the boy worked at
the hotel kitchen?" "Yes mam." "So yah kin peel potatoes and carry heavy
bags, boil water and sweep floors?"
"Yes mam." She introduced him to Ki. "He look like strong boy. Ki can
use help pretty much." "You two can get along then I can use yore help."

"Thank you." Said Beatrice. The little spotted dog had taken up permanent residence with Maizey. He liked Zacharia licking his hands and wagging his stub of a tail. "Looks like Pepper has taken a lik'n to yah. That's good." "When can he start?" "He start now."Said Ki smiling. "Good I will come for you after work." Beatrice had secured a room at the home of a Mrs. Jensen. A widow who's late husband had been an assayer at the mines. Zacharia was content to again be staying with his mother.

Cederholms General Store was where everyone in town went. If you needed anything. The locals hung out and drank coffee seated by a wood stove at the back of the store. It was a two- story building with the store below and their living quarters upstairs. They had hardware, horse tack, and guns on one end. With food stuffs like cheese, pickles and cracker barrels and penny candies towrd the front. Pots and pans and dishes of odd sorts lined the shelves.

They also had a small apothecary. Mrs. Cederholm's loom was at the front of the store and her blankets and shawls displayed with sewing notions in the main windows. Beatrice's bonnets were on display there as well. Mr. Cederholm was a shrewd business man and had struck a deal with August giving him a percentage of his sales. He despised August throughly but knew that his business was flourishing in this boom town.

Beatrice was reaching for a bolt of calico on a high shelf but she couldn't quite get to it when she saw a man's hand pulling it down for her. She turned and faced Dr. Haveston. Thank you she said as she placed the bolt onto the counter. "How is Zacharia doing?" "Quite well actually." Beatrice said as she started to cut the fabric into large pieces to be folded and wrapped for a customer. "And you?" Dr. Haveston asked looking into her eyes. Beatrice avoided his gaze and said she was much better and the medicine he had given her had worked. "Is there anything I can do for you?" She asked him.

"Yes there is. I would like you to make a hat for Molly." "I am making summer bonnets with paper flowers and ribbons of your choice." She brought out an array of ribbon of various colors. "I guess this isn't going to be all that easy." He smiled. "Perhaps you could choose for me." She held

112

out a satin ribbon of pale pink adding a paper rose of deep red. "I like it. When can it be ready?" "By tomorrow afternoon." "Perfect." "Molly's birthday is sometime this month. She has been really melancholy as of late. It has a lot to do with her health. He said quietly. "I am truly sorry. I have wondered is she your wife?" "No, she is a friend, her late husband was my colleague and mentor at Medical School. He died of a heart attack.

He often asked that I watch over her if he should die." "So how long have you been together?" "Five years." "So you have no family yourself then?" As soon as Beatrice said that he became very quiet and said he must leave as he had an appointment to make. I shall see you tomorrow then. With that he walked out. Beatrice was puzzled at his behavior. He seemed to not fit in his surroundings. Something in his nature revealed his affluence. He incited her curiosity.

39
"Cooper"

River Tree knew that he had to deal with the situation. To be fair to the women who had been raped and their families. He questioned Night Wing about his knowledge of this. Night Wing felt responsible for not coming forward when he knew about the young men and the whiskey. He thought he could talk to them about its dangers. Never thinking they would follow through on taking women to the hotel. The evening was warm and still when Shila, River Tree and Night Wing went to the lodges of the two men responsible. They asked to speak with them. They questioned each man separately to get to the truth. Each man lied and blamed the other. River Tree then went to the lodges of the three women to talk with them about the incident. One of the youngest women was raped so violently that she hemorrhaged to death from her injuries. Shila went back to the lodges of the men and tore them apart until he found the whiskey. He was very angry. He took the bottles and smashed them against the rocks. River Tree tried to calm him. He called for a council meeting for the next day. Several of the elders attended. The two young men were there and the two battered women and their families.

During the meeting the men confessed to over powering the women and taking them to Crooked Hat. River Tree asked the women what justice would be for them. They told the elders that the men should be banished from the tribe until they were cured from the drink. The council agreed.

The men were frightened of this decision but Shila told them that was the law and they knew it. They were to leave by the next day. River Tree escorted them out of the village and they were on their own.

It was hot and sultry as the sun dipped behind the mountain. Night Wing decided to go to Crooked Hat. He knew that he would never return so he left a leather pouch full of his personal items in front of Shila's tepee including his favorite bow and his horse. He walked all the way to the town. It was growing late and Harp Miller was drunk as he staggered out of the back of the hotel. He leaned against the side of the building and urinated. He heard what he thought was an animal as he spun around to stand face to face with Night Wing. "Why you crazy bastard you'd like to scare me to death." He said buttoning up his pants. "What are you do'n here look'n for whiskey? What did yah bring me some of your stink'n beads?" Night Wing threw the young girl's shawl in Harp's face. "What the?" Spat Harp throwing it to the ground. "Young girl dead. Night Wing spoke in his broken English. "What the hell yah talk'n about you crazy Indian." "Whiskey bad, you bad." Night Wing took out his knife driving it into Harp's stomach deeply. He fell to his knees looking into the Indian's face. A look of disbelief came over him as he lay in a pool of blood with his eyes staring into the night sky. "Little Grass her name. You not forget." He watched Harp Miller breathe his last.

Night Wing with-drew his knife and let out a war cry. Reaching for the shawl, he ran off into the darkness of the mountain. While a pack of dogs howled and barked at the taking of a life.

It was early morning on her way to the café that Maizey came upon Harp's dead body. At first she stepped back in horror at the memory of her late husband. She muttered under her breath. "La vache" yah had this com'n you and that devil August Mayfield." She didn't touch him but went to the hotel to find August so she could tell him about his friend. August followed her out to the street. "I knew he was going to end like this whiskey and women don't mix." He rolled Harp over his eyes were still open. "Who do yah think done it?" asked Maizey. "Most likely one of those young bucks he's been trading whiskey too. Harp don't have no kin that I know of. Best get the undertaker out here to clean him up for burial. He never showed any signs of grief over the loss of Harp. But then thought Maizey this man ain't got a heart not like a real person.

"So yah ain't said much about Nate's murder of late." "I'll get to it now shut your face." "Who's gonna be the mayor?" "You are look'n at him." August said as he walked off. Maizey went on toward the café wondering what was going to become of the town with people getting murdered in the streets.

Beatrice was coming out of the store heading to the café to get Zacharia when she saw him for the first time. He was stepping down off the stage coach and helping an elderly woman down the coach steps. He was tall and had a youthful face. He had cold blue eyes and long auburn hair that fell in waves. He walked with a limp using a cane. She couldn't help but stare. He was the kind of man that people took notice of. He saw her looking at him and she quickly turned a way. "Excuse me Miss?" "Yes?" "I am looking for the Sheriff's office."

"It's over behind the Livery Stable." Beatrice pointed. "Thank you, Cooper Dawson." He said tipping his hat. He looked in the direction she had pointed. Beatrice decided to help him. "Let me show you it will be easier. Not meaning to appear nosy but what is your business?" She asked. "I am a Federal Marshall." "I see, where are you from?" "San Francisco. President Pierce telegraphed us about some hangings taking place here. No Judge or jury involved?" Seems one of the widows wrote to the President complaining about it. So here I am." They were soon in front of the stables. "By the way I did not catch your name?" "Beatrice Faye." "Pretty name." He told her as he ducked under the low beams of the veranda. She smiled at him and walked away. The whole time thinking, well now the law has finally reached Crooked Hat.

115

40

"Justice Takes A Lover"

Justice was affected by Jacob's kindness to her. She was used to standing her ground with brutish men. He was gentle and emotional. It was something she was not sure of. Was he just being sympathetic or did he mean all the things he whispered to her? The night they had laid together. She saved one of the flowers he had given her and pressed it inside of a book. Something she hadn't done since she was a child. It was growing more difficult for her to lay with other men. He made her feel good about herself.

It had not been carnal with Jacob but an act of love. He stopped by to see her a few days after the incident. The women teased him about favoring "old one eye" and that they could show him a good time. As they could see what they were doing. He chose to ignore their taunts. He was very nervous to face Justice thinking possibly she didn't want his favors. He had brought her flowers again. His hands were shaking as he knocked on her door. She opened it standing in her under garments. A young man standing by her bed was pulling up his pants. He grabbed his hat. "Sorry pardner." He said as he pushed past him out of the door. Justice had wished this had not happened. "You need to tell me when you are going to be here." She snapped. "I am sorry I can come back some other time." Jacob said awkwardly. In that moment it all became so unpleasant.

She knew she had hurt his feelings. "Look I am sorry. I haven't been sleeping well. I still have headaches." She said putting on her dressing robe pulling out a pouch of tobacco to roll a cigarette.

He felt desire for her again it was overwhelming. He asked if she would like to go with him. He had rented a buggy and would take her to see Charles's grave site if she were so inclined. She felt badly about Jacob seeing her like this. So she agreed. She quickly washed herself as Jacob sat watching her. She was so lovely he kept thinking to himself. His eyes drank her in. If only he could touch her again, smell her skin and hair. She washed her body in the water basin her skin was the color of ivory. Her long black hair hung down her back. She looked beautiful in the soft light of the room. She finished dressing rolling her hair up in combs. She placed his flowers in her water basin and grabbed her bonnet. As Jacob helped her up into the buggy she asked him if they could take the back road out of town. She wanted to avoid August Mayfield if she could help it. She hated him with a passion.

It was a beautiful day. Justice had become so reclusive since her brother's death. She took in the sun full on her face and took off her bonnet letting her long black hair flow in the breeze. They had arrived to the meadow and the lone pine. "He doesn't have a marker."She said softly as her tears fell. Jacob quickly went about gathering pieces of branches. He fashioned a cross from them and using his handkerchief he tied them together. He then used his hands to dig a hole to place the cross. He found a rock and pounded it into place. There he stood covered in dust and Justice started to smile through her tears. She took her glove and wiped the dirt from his nose and cheeks. He let her as he enjoyed her touch, smiling the whole while.

As he stood there. He realized he could not remember the last time he felt this alive. Justice looking at her brother's grave started singing an old hymn from by gone days. Jacob knew it well and joined in as they stood by the pine. Later they sat in the tall grasses together and Jacob told her of his boyhood in Ireland.

Jacob was the middle child he had two older brothers and two younger sisters. His family lived in the village of Dalkey just outside of Dublin. Jacob loved books and his mother could read. So every night by candle light she would read her children to sleep. She would even make up stories when the three books they owned grew tiresome. He was up by dawn helping his father at the brick yards. His job was to push the cart loaded with bricks to the work site. His hands were calloused and he had back problems for the rest of his life from the constant bending and lifting. Jacob wanted more from life. He begged his father to let him go to school. It was agreed.

117

His father wanted Jacob to be a teacher. It meant long years of work and saving money for Jacob to go to College in Dublin. Jacob worked all the time going to school and paying his way. His father was so proud of him when he graduated. He was the only one in the Riley family who had ever done so. The Great Potato Famine was upon most of Ireland and the Riley's needed to seek refuge. Mr. Riley was taking his family to Canada. Where he had found work. Jacob wanted to come to America. It was one of the hardest things he would do in his life saying goodbye to his parents and his siblings. Knowing full well, he would never see them again.

It started to grow hotter and the wind blew the dust across the meadow. Justice looked into Jacob's face. She wanted him to hold her she longed to feel his hands on her again. He knew and lifted her face to his and kissed her with abandoned. He gently pressed her to the ground and made love to her while the hot sun shown down on them from above.

41

"Saying Good-bye"

Ansleigh found herself hoping the young Indian named Shila would come back to see her again. She was lonely for company. Peter kept her days busy, but she longed for the company of a man. They had lived on the mountain for over two years. Thomas had promised to add a loft area to their cabin and to put in windows at the front. Which he never got around to doing. He was gone longer each time he went out trapping. When she questioned him about it. He would only become irritated with her. She found herself wanting to go to Crooked Hat even if it meant being caught by Clegg. One day she decided to make the trip. She saddled up the mare. Peter was a blonde toddler with his mother's blue eyes. He was old enough to straddle the horse with her. She dressed like a man as not to draw attention to herself.

It was early fall and the leaves were turning on the trees. The air had a coolness in it. She could smell the change of seasons. When they reached the town Ansleigh was surprised at what all she saw. It was much bigger than what Thomas had told her. People were out and walking down wooden sidewalks and she could smell food wafting from the cafe.

There was a big sign on the Opera House that read Miss Lena LeBaron straight from Paris, France and her review. Ticckets inside. A new hotel was under construction and it was huge. The sign read The Mayfield House. The old hotel had become a saloon. With rooms to rent. There was a tobacco shop a tailor and a bakery all in one building. But the one place that caught her eye was Cederholm's General Store. She dismounted the mare tying her to the hitching post. Carrying Peter on her hip. She pulled Thomas's leather hat way down over her eyes.

She entered looking about there was only one other person in the store. Beatrice spotted her and walked up to her. "Can I help you?" Ansleigh spoke in a whisper "I am looking." "Take your time I am here if you need anything." Beatrice said politely. She decided to buy some penny candy for Peter and some thread she needed for mending. It was then she spotted the bonnets. It had been so long since she had anything pretty to wear. Her clothes had become quite thread bare and she had taken to wearing men's trousers at the cabin. "Someone special need a hat?" Asked Beatrice. "Yes my sister." Beatrice saw through the ruse but played along. Thinking the young woman must be hiding out from someone. She showed her two or three bonnets. Ansleigh loved the lavender hat with the pink roses. "How much?" "Well wouldn't you know? This is the last one and it is from last year's stock. So how about half the price?" Peter was pulling at the ribbon and chewing the flowers. He was giggling and being funny as he pulled the bonnet over his eyes and played peek-a-boo with his mother. "Pretty" he said. "I think he likes it."Smiled Beatrice. Ansleigh pulled out her pouch of coins and paid her for the hat and the notions.

Beatrice found a hat box for her when Mr. Riley entered from the back of the store. Ansleigh almost froze in her tracks. Her father was still here and a store clerk?

"Mr. Riley." Said Beatrice. "Do you know him?" "No." said Ansleigh hastily. "The look on your face?" "He just reminds me of someone I use to know." She said thanking Beatrice and hurrying out the door. She panicked looking for her mare. When she felt a hand reach for her shoulder. "You forgot this." Beatrice told her just as Peter pulled his mother's hat off exposing her long golden locks. Ansleigh hastily grabbed the hat box running in the direction of her horse.

On the way home Ansleigh was crying. She missed her father and her sisters and her old life. She didn't realize how much till now. She was glad that Thomas wasn't there when she returned. She did not want to explain herself. Exhausted she fell into bed holding Peter in her arms with the hat box sitting on the small kitchen table. The next day would change her life forever. It was a mild day and the sun was out. She put her new bonnet on for fun. Peter liked it and kept telling her "Mama Pretty." over and over. Ansleigh picked him up kissing him on his face nuzzling him. "I love you Peter." she sang.

She started chopping more wood for the woodpile something she did every day. Getting ready for the cold months ahead. Little Peter had found a stick and was beating the ground and the fallen leaves with it. Neither one of them saw the Coral Snake when it slithered out from beneath the wood pile. Peter fell on the ground and was rolling in the leaves giggling. Ansleigh looked over at him smiling. "You silly child". She said.

Peter looked at the snake as it lunged toward his little face. It bit him between the eyes. He screamed in pain. Ansleigh dropped her axe and ran to him picking him up. She saw the puncture wounds and knew it was bad. "Dear God why?"She thought. She was frantic. Her mind was racing what to do? She looked at the sky "God, please don't take my son, please!" It was then as if in a dream Shila appeared taking Peter from her. He quickly cut small slits with the tip of his knife into the puncture wounds. He began sucking out the venom and spitting it out on the ground.. He placed herbs on the wound. Carrying Peter inside the cabin. He laid him on the bed covering him with blankets to keep him warm. Ansleigh followed him as if a specter. It didn't seem real to her. Shila tried to show her with his hands what it was he was doing. She could tell by his expression that something was wrong. Shila prayed and chanted and smudged Peter calling out to the Grandfathers. It was growing late and Shila never left the boy's side. Ansleigh sat by the bed and cried. Holding his little hand. She fell asleep.

When she woke Shila was still there. She touched Peter's face he was cold and she knew he was gone. She gently lifted him to her chest and kissed his little face. Her pain was so great she cried out like a wounded animal. Sounds of great pain emanated from deep with in her. Shila was silent and hung his head in sorrow. He stayed with Ansleigh all through the next day. Watching over her and tending to her chores. He took care of the animals and kept the fire in the hearth going.

He fixed her a meal she refused to eat. She laid in the bed holding onto Peter. Thinking that somehow he was just asleep and would soon awaken. Shila never interfered. Just kept a silent vigil over her. On the second day. Shila gently lifted the boy from her arms. She woke looking into Shila's face. She knew it was time to say good bye. She got out of the bed and followed Shila outside. Shila lovingly washed Peter in a near by stream. Ansleigh wrapped him in his little blue blanket with the flowers embroidered on the corners. Shila had built a small scaffold for Peter and carried him to the top praying and chanting over his body. Ansleigh knew that this way Peter was with nature and would travel home through the trees and on into the sky. A hawk flew down and lighting on a branch looked down at the child. Shila placed his hands around Ansleigh's face. Speaking in his native tongue he told her that the Great Spirit had taken Peter home. Even though she did not understand this language her soul did.

42

"Becoming A Ghost"

August didn't sleep well. He kept looking over his shoulder. It had spooked him that Harp Miller had been murdered. He thought maybe he would be next. He never felt close to him. Yet Harp had always been there when he needed him. He hired an armed guard to sit outside of his room and to keep an eye on this new property. He was having a house built but had to delay its construction to finish the hotel. He had taken up residence in the new hotel. Many of the miners made fun of it. Calling it "Mayfield's

121

Whimsy." Saying it was far too high falut'n for the likes of them. It had become a curiosity to most of the town's people. They had never seen anything quite like it. It didn't stop August from his dream. He knew that he could attract a better class of people; if he had the right businesses to bring them in. With the Federal Marshall staying on at the town jail. He knew he had to step lightly.

August was never a religious man but people were talking and complaining about needing a house of prayer. His plan was to hire a Pastor and build a church. It would give him a little more respectability he thought. Even though it went against his grain. Clegg, was back in town. August knew him to be a cunning man and fearless. With Harp gone he needed someone he could trust to keep him adrift of things. He met with Clegg and made a more than reasonable proposal of money. Clegg, was ready to settle in after being on the range for the past several months.

Thorton came back to Crooked Hat a week or two before Clegg. As soon as he had heard about the acting troupe he met with Lena LeBaron. The singer from Paris. She was actually a buxom brunette by the name of Jeanne Barret from Chicago, Illinois. Posing as a French Entertainer. She was talented not only as a performer but as a con artist. She liked Thorton and had him sign on as part of her troupe. August was never the wiser.

Katy was the apple of her father's eye. She was a sweet child. Her hair was a vivid red and fell in ringlets framing a freckled face. Her eyes a deep blue. She was spoiled by her parents and Nel who loved her as if she were her own. It did cause friction between her and Katherine at times. When she was disciplining Katy. Nel would often give her treats and tell her to never mind the ways of her mother. Katherine was aggravated beyond words when she did this. She was growing restless with the ranch. She longed for her own house and she missed her sisters. She complained to Quin about it. He felt obligated to the Garrisons. Karl was arthritic and it was getting harder for him to keep up with his work. He treated Quin as if he were his son. Quin had grown use to Karl's preaching and bible stories. He barely listened to him anymore. He was practically running the ranch as Karl relinquished most of his duties to Quin.

Katherine longed for company other then the Garrison's. She would go to Vineyard once a month to pick up supplies at the Dry Good Store. Vineyard was changing. Sheriff Patch had retired. Mr. Peevy still ran the hotel. Mrs. Fairdale's brothel had burned to the ground killing some of the girls. There were times when the tumble weeds rolling down the main street was the only life visible. It only made Katherine more desperate to leave. She wanted to travel and look for their own piece of land. She was becoming more insistent as the months past. Quin told her that he had to take a trip to Nevada territory. He was to meet with a man to purchase a Hereford bull imported from England. Karl said it would strengthen his herd's bloodlines. He told Katherine to plan on going with him. It would be a two day trip. They could leave Katy with Nel. She wasn't willing to do that so they agreed that they would take her with them. On the morning they left Nel was beside herself. She kept asking Katherine if they were coming back. She reassured her that of course they would return. Her obvious desperation bothered Katherine. Nel cried as she stood on the veranda and waved them off.

Had it been three years? Ansleigh stood in the doorway watching the last deer as it lept through the brush. She still grieved Peter. The scaffold had become weather worn and the blue blanket faded and tattered as it flapped in the breeze. She hadn't touched anything since the day that Shila placed the little body high on its perch. She knew when Shila was near as he would leave her healing plants and she had this sense of his protection. Thomas never did return from his last trip. It had been almost a year and no word of him. She continued on each day alone.

Taking care of the goats and chickens they sustained her. Her appearance was distressing as she had quit grooming herself. Her days all blended together and the seasons the only reminder of time. She was surviving and that was all that mattered. She longed to be with Peter and was slowly becoming ghost like.

43
"Look Into Your Heart"

Huittsu was carrying Many Horses child. It was the time of thunder and the earth was springing forth with life. It was Kachiri's and Kocho's wedding day. The village was preparing for the feast. Kachiri would be moving with him to his home in the desert region. Hapisteen did not want to see her daughter go yet she knew it was time. River Tree and Shila had received Kocho into their clan. He was a strong and disciplined man. He brought three horses for River Tree and provided fresh elk for the meal as a gift for Kachiri. In return Hapisteen had made a beautiful beaded sash for him to wear during the ceremony. Healing Fox led the ceremony and everyone was celebrating their union. Kocho was liked by many.

Shila was going to miss his sister but he planned on seeing her when he could in her new home. He thought often of the young white woman. He knew she was still grieving the loss of her son. That her spirit wasn't fully present. Her husband had not returned and Shila could not understand what had happened. He thought that it was possible he was dead and how would she know of it? He kept an eye on her when he was able to be sure she was safe.

The feasting and dancing went well into the night. Many Horses played the flute and the young girls danced and twirled as their shawls spread out like wings. The young men joining and stomping the ground with their feet. Shila sat on the ground staring into the campfire deep in thought. When he felt a hand on his shoulder. Looking up he saw Huittsu. She smiled.

"They are good together. They are well matched." "I wish them both harmony and peace in their hearts." Shila said still staring into the fire. It bothered Shila that Huittsu still lamented over him. He tried to avoid her and not appear to callous with her. He did love her but there was no passion or longing such as she felt for him. He was hoping that when her child was born it might change things.

He thought of Night Wing. Many Horses had told him that Mr. Miller had been killed. That the townspeople were saying it was an Indian though there was no real proof of that being the case. He said that there was law in

124

Crooked Hat a man by the name of Cooper Dawson was staying in the hotel. Sent there by the Great White Chief in Washington. People were saying that this Marshal was no one to go up against as he was undaunted by anyone.

River Tree found Shila and sat next to him. "It is good to have a new son in our family." River Tree was fond of Kocho and knew his daughter would be safe with him. He had wanted her to marry someone from their clan. But she had waited telling him it was not the right time.

"You and Kachiri are like your mother strong and willful." He laughed. "It is good I am a happy man this night. When will you take a woman?" "Father you ask too much."

"Many Horses is to be a father soon. I want this for you to." "It will happen in time." Shila was growing irritated with his father's prodding. "I must ask you what we are going to do about the white men that I have seen looking at the land where we winter. They have brought in their tools and are digging into the rocks there. I fear it is for gold.

If we lose this part of the mountain then they will not stop there in their greed they will want more." "I know Shila, Healing Fox has told me that it is going to happen against our wills. My fear is if we go up against them many lives will be lost. Remember when you were small. The Arapaho came and took our horses and burned our lodges. Killing several of our women and children. We called it the night of great sorrow. I had to kill a man who was trying to steal your mother. Grey Elk forbid any of us to seek revenge. He said there had been enough blood shed." "So we sit and do nothing?" "I did not say that Shila. You are young in the ways of life. I must think of many things before I make a decision over this. Grey Elk would tell me our first teacher is our own heart. "To look into my heart for the answers not my head." River Tree looked at his son. "Let's enjoy this beautiful night and talk of such things at another time."

44

"Gossip Buzzing Through Her Mind."

Beatrice looked up when she saw Molly enter the store. She was
surprised because Molly rarely went out side of her house. Batilda
Cederholm knew of her and was not happy about her being in their store.
She didn't want her daughters exposed to such a person. "Vat do you want
yah?" Molly's eyes widened she wasn't use to women talking to her. She was
treated as a pariah in the town. "I'll be need'n some Catnip if yah have any."
"I don't think vee do." Beatrice knew this wasn't true. "You need to go
someplace else yah. You can see I am busy." Then she started talking loudly
in her native tongue of Swedish. She was angry and Molly was agitated and
looked to Beatrice for consoling. Mrs. Cederholm went to find her husband.
Beatrice quickly reached in the porcelain canister and pulled out the Catnip
Molly had asked for. Wrapping it in brown paper. "Here take it, I will pay
for it." "I canna take it." "Please just go before she gets back." Molly
thanked Beatrice and left. There was something piteous about Molly and
Beatrice felt a kinship towards her. She hadn't seen the doctor since he
purchased the hat. She wondered how he was faring. She did like him
despite his drinking. Beatrice enjoyed working at the store it gave her some
respectability. But she yearned to sing again. She saw Thorton on stage with
Miss LeBaron at the Opera House. They were doing a one act
Play. It had become a favorite of the audience. Thorton wanted Beatrice to
join them. She decided if she were ever going to settle down in a house with
Zacharia. She would need to be seen as a proper woman.

Actresses were considered nothing more than prostitutes by most people.
Besides she did not want any dealings with August Mayfield. Beatrice
wanted something more from life and she wasn't sure what that was.
Cooper Dawson was making a name for himself in Crooked Hat. He was
now situated in the new hotel. He had Sheriff Daniels walking the streets
arresting drunks and vagrants. The miners and trouble makers were not
happy about this new lawman. August knew if he were going to put this
town on the map. It would have to be tamed to attract the right people.
Inwardly he did not like Cooper because he wasn't a man who could be

bought. He was planning on expanding his mining industry as he knew that the present site would soon run out of ore. He had bought a parcel of land near the Armagosa River. It showed promise of bearing gold he had hired two Geologists to explore it. They said it was rich in placer deposits. They built a wing dam in the stream bed to keep the water flowing to one side while they excavated. That is when they found the residue of gold in the bed rock. The only problem being it was in Shoshone territory. That did not deter August. If he had to kill a few Indians to get what he wanted so be it.

Beatrice was carrying home a basket full of fabric she needed to make her bonnets. She would then go and bring Zacharia from work. She stepped off the planked sidewalk twisting her ankle. The sharp pain made her catch her breath. She started to hobble down the street when Cooper Dawson came to her aid. "Miss Faye it looks like you could use a hand here."

He lifted the basket from her. "Are you heading home?" "Yes Marshall Dawson I am." She grimaced as she spoke. "Well then if you don't mind." He placed the basket under his arm and had her lean on him as they made their way to Mrs. Jensen's place. He made her sit on the veranda and take off her high laced boot. Her right ankle was swollen black and blue. "What am I going to do? I can't afford to miss work. I need to go and fetch Zacharia." "Zacharia?" "My brother he works at Maizey's café out by the mine." "I know where it is. I can fetch him here." "I don't mean to put you through any fuss." He ignored her and helped her into the parlor. "I'll see you later." "Who was that?" Asked Mrs. Jensen peeking from the hallway door. "Marshall Dawson." If you don't mind my saying he is a fine figure of a man." Beatrice didn't answer but sat down on the sofa still holding her boot in one hand.

When Marshall Dawson reached Maizey's he knew Zacharia right away. A small boy with unruly black hair and his mother's eyes was throwing stones against the side of an outhouse. "I have a feeling you are Zacharia? How did you know that?" He asked looking the Marshall up and down. "A bird told me." He said jokingly. "Your sister Miss Faye sent me to bring you home." "Where is she? Is she alright!" suddenly Zacharia was worried. "She twisted her ankle pretty bad and I am here to help. I am Marshall Dawson."

"Are you a real Marshall?" "Is there any other kind?" "I mean there ain't no law in this town. People get shot and hung all the time. He said picking up a stone and throwing it across the street. "Really?" "Anybody that goes up against Mr. Mayfield does." "That's why I am here to see to it that the law is dealt with fair and square."

As they were walking past the General Store. The Marshall said "I hear tell they have all kinds of candy in that place." But then you wouldn't be interested would you?" "I have to save my money. Me and my sister are planning on moving out of this place." "Well what do you say to me treating you and you keep saving that money." Zacharia started liking this fellow as he followed him into the store.

While Marshall Dawson was there he told Mrs. Cederholm that Miss Faye would need a couple days of rest as she had twisted her ankle pretty badly. Batilda looked at him quizzically, wondering what tie he had with Beatrice. The gossip was already buzzing through her mind.

45

"Clegg's Rage"

Clegg was obsessing over Thorton. Ever since their last job together Thorton had become distant and moody. That was the reason he left early and came back to Crooked Hat. Even though Clegg was the one apprehending the horse thief. He shared the bounty with Thorton. Clegg had a jealous side to his nature and felt like Thorton owed him his allegiance. He was now working for August Mayfield. He did not trust the man but then he was being paid very well. He liked staying at the Mayfield House it reminded him of his days in San Fransisco. His penchant for finer things would never change. He ordered a new set of clothes from the local tailor. He started a ritual of having the town barber giving him a shave twice a week. He ate his meals in his room as he thought it cleaner. He decided it was time to see what Thorton was doing since his return. He had been avoiding Clegg and he didn't like it. So he went to the Opera House during a performance. He sat way in the back of the theater watching Thorton's every move.

He delighted in the way he took and held one's attention. He was so elegant for a young man witty and intelligent. All of the things Clegg yearned for himself. After the show was over he sat in the back watching Thorton from afar. He noticed him laughing with a young actor. Placing his arms around the actor's shoulders. They slipped behind the curtains. Clegg got up from his seat walking to the front he jumped up on the stage. He pushed the curtain aside.

It was dark and he was trying to make out the figures milling around backstage. His heart was pounding and he had a bitter taste in his mouth. He had a feeling about this he couldn't shake. He walked down the back hallway to a small dressing room. He could hear laughing which was unmistakably Thorton's. He pushed open the door to catch the two embracing one another. Clegg could feel the heat of his jealousy rising in a blinding rage he punched the young actor in his face and grabbed Thorton by his long hair. He shoved him down the stage steps and half carried him out of the building. Thorton was terrified of Clegg's rage and did not know what to say.

They made it back to the hotel. Clegg made threats on Thorton's life. He took him roughly and injured him in the process. Then he drank himself to sleep while Thorton laid next to him wide awake and in pain. He felt trapped and had to be free of this man whatever it took.

Both Ingrid and Gilda Cederholm were at the marrying age. They both had seen Marshall Dawson at their father's store. Each one secretly coveting his attentions. Batilda wished they could go back East where she would tell Sven their daughters would have a better choice of suitors. They had heard about the upcoming community dance and wanted to attend.
August had planned a dance for the miners and their families. It was to be held at the Opera House. There was a large room in the back where they held town meetings and it was big enough to house the dance. This was in late October before the snows would start. He wanted to get people there as he was planning on telling them about his new mine.

129

It would be operational in the spring in the Armagosa River Valley. He did not want any mention of it being Indian Territory. He needed workers as the present mine was nearly depleted of its ore. He had to move quickly to insure that he had the manpower he needed. What better way he thought then to offer bonuses and a dance to put everyone in a good frame of mind.

He hired Lena LeBaron to sing and a small group of musicians from her show to entertain. He also had a surprise for everyone on that evening. The news quickly spread around town about the dance. People were curious and pleased as this was the first gathering of its sort in Crooked Hat.

46
"The Town Dance"

The night of the dance had arrived. Several of the miners and their families attended. The room was full of laughing and talking. There was a long table set up with punch, cakes, cookies and other baked goods. The three musicians, a piano, fiddle and a banjo were playing old reels and waltzes for those who wanted to dance. It was mostly women and children but a few men were dragged out there too. Lena LeBaron sang at intervals. Thorton sat in the back of the room. He was sullen and quiet all evening. Seated on a small platform were August, Clegg, Sheriff Daniels and Marshall Dawson. Beatrice had come bringing Zacharia. Jacob Riley and the Cederholms along with Dr. Haveston, Maizey and Ki were in the crowd. About an hour into the festivities August called everyone to his attention.

There was a short stocky man with pinc-nez glasses and a long white beard standing next to him. He introduced him as Reverend Bigelow from Missouri. He was to be the new town minister with a church and small rectory being built on the back road out of town. Several people applauded as the Reverend introduced himself. After that August let everyone know his plans for the new mine in the Armagosa River Valley. There was an agreement voucher on the platform that men could sign that were staying on. August told everyone the truth about the situation at the old mine. To his surprise most of the original crew had signed up for the new mine. Each man received a bonus.

No one ever mentioned it being in Indian Territory. August was making sure of that. Beatrice was wearing a pale green dress with a large lace collar that she had made herself. Her hair was done up in a bun with ringlets aside her cheeks. Zacharia told her she was the prettiest woman there. Zacharia had his hair cut and a clean pair of flannel trousers and a white shirt and a black cravat at his neck. Maizey said she didn't know who that handsome boy was. Maizey wore the one good dress she had for special occasions. A Calico print in dark blue. She said she would most likely be buried in it too, as it was her only "Sunday go to meet'n dress." That she owned. After the speech everyone continued on with the dance. Beatrice found Thorton and sat next to him on the bench.

"What is going on? You look terrible are you not well?" "I really don't want to talk about it." "I haven't heard from you since your return." "I know but seriously I do not want to talk about it." He got up leaving her alone and went outside to drink from a bottle he had in his pocket. Beatrice sat there staring up at August she really did hate the man. The few times she saw him since their altercation he looked straight through her like glass. Which was fine with her. Dr. Haveston approached her and sat down next to her. "I haven't danced in years but if you would be willing I am asking you for this dance?" "But of course." They both danced the waltz Zacharia looked on in amazement. He had never seen his mother do the waltz before.

Dr. Haveston kept smiling at her. Beatrice looked into his face and blushed. She knew that she liked him and it was hard not to be coy. She no sooner sat down when Cooper Dawson asked her to dance. He told her he knew the old reels but had to stay away from the waltzes. Since his injured leg wouldn't allow certain moves. "Yore sister is the belle of the ball Zach." chortled Maizey. "Belle-femme." "Yeah men have always liked my mum." "Yore?" Maizey asked. "My sister. My mum she died a while back. The men liked her a lot." Zacharia was rapidly trying to recover his mistake and making it sound even worse. "If yore ma was as pretty as your sister I kin

131

see why." Beatrice started back to Zacharia when they started playing "Lorena" a sad song that she use to sing in the shows. In that moment an over whelming feeling of sadness came over her. She felt a man's hand reach for hers. It was Dr. Haveston "Please one more dance?" He gently led her around the dance floor looking into her eyes. He was a very good dancer and she let herself be led as the music filled her senses. She hummed along to the song. She missed singing.

Ingrid and Gilda kept flirting with the Marshall. He was feeling uneasy and kept finding every excuse to avoid them. He still ended up dancing with them both while Mr. Cederholm looked on beaming. The Marshall, soon tired as his injured leg was prone to arthritis. Giving him an excuse to sit the dance out. Jacob was thinking about Justice the whole evening. Wishing she could be there. But he knew she was ashamed of the way she looked and prostitutes were not welcome. He often wished he knew who had maimed her. Because he would have killed them.

It wasn't in Jacob's nature to be violent. August sat on his chair that overlooked the dance. He was self satisfied as he watched. He told himself that whatever it took he was going to have the railway come to Crooked Hat. He could fore- see in the probable future his town becoming another Baltimore or St. Louis. A gateway through the Sierra Nevada's to California. Clegg excused himself to find Thorton. He walked outside to find him laying on the ground. He was wreathing in agony. "What is it?" Clegg asked. "Leave me alone!" Thorton pleaded. It was then Clegg noticed Thorton's pants were soaked in blood. Clegg carried him in his arms to the hotel. He was afraid of losing him. Laying him on his bed, he promised to return. He than went back to the dance to find Dr. Haveston.

47
"Transgressions"

August had sent the Geologists out to check on the Armagosa site and to report back to him. He had hired two old miners as watchmen. They were set up in an old shack. It was a frigid morning in the valley as they made their way by horseback to the river. When they arrived they saw several lances stuck in the ground every few feet. Painted in reds and blues with feathers and bird skulls attached to them. It was a territorial warning for them to stay off this land. The two men went about their work and pulled the lances out of the ground. They knew that Mr. Mayfield wasn't going to be happy with this news. Two Arapaho scouts were watching the two white men as they marked out the site. They sat silently on their horses keeping their eyes on them. Clayton asked the old men when the Indians had started doing this. They told him they would come mostly at dusk and place their lances in the ground then disappear. They never bother us they were told. Burton was more aggressive by nature. "We need to tell Mr. Mayfield to contact the army and show these heathens who owns this here piece of land it ain't them for damn sure." Clayton saw no reason to start stirring up trouble. "Let sleeping dogs lie." He told Burton.

Pepper was growling and barking as he protected Maizey. "Pepper what is your problem?"She asked as she reached down to pick him up. "Tais-toi.' She was heading to the General Store when she came upon August Mayfield. Pepper did not like this man. "You best keep that beast out from underfoot or I will have to shoot the little bastard."

He told her with his hand resting on the grip of his gun. "He's be'n my protector is all. I know it's been a while August was wonder'n if yah heard anyth'n about my Nate? Did anybody see anyth'n? "Look Maizey it's time you let that one go. I'm way to busy to be worry'n about such nonsense." "You seem to forget Mr. Mayfield if'n it weren't for Nate and me. You'd never have come upon this mine." "Maybe so but I am the one that's making something out of this cow pasture. Besides I am going to need you cooking out at the new mining site come spring? So you better be plan'n on it you and that Chiny man of yours." Pepper bared his teeth as August walked past. Maizey didn't want to move she liked it where she was at. She didn't tell him that she had been offered a job cooking for the bakery. The owners were building a coffee shop with small dinners available. They wanted a community café and bakery combined. Maizey liked the idea and

133

Ki would still be with her there. She wasn't sure how to handle this with August.

Beatrice missed a couple days of work with her sprain and was back to the store using a cane. Gilda was learning how to make hats from Beatrice. She liked Beatrice and would have her sing for her when there was no one in the store. Gilda sang along with her she had a good voice and Beatrice told her so. She was a young woman full of dreams. Her parents were overbearing when it came to her and Ingrid. Ingrid was very shy and she was jealous of Beatrice.

Gilda wanted to go to the Opera House and see the shows. But her parents would never allow it. They told her only fallen women were involved in the theater. Beatrice never talked about her theater days as she did not want to lose her position with the Cederholms. But it was not meant to be. One day Ingrid came upon Beatrice and Gilda singing. Beatrice was showing her some hand gestures to use with her songs. "You can not do this yah! If poppa sees you Gilda. You are being shameful I vill have to tell mama." Gilda grew angry with her sister. "Vat harm is this? Singing is goot for the soul. Ingrid smirked "I can see vere Beatrice has brought the devil to you."

"You are jealous and that is a sin. You can not bring harm to my friend yah. I vill not let you." "Look I am so sorry." Beatrice said softly. "I do not see any thing wrong in what I did. It will not happen again I promise." "It is too late." Ingrid said with an impudent tone to her voice. Mr. Riley walked in at that moment. "Is there something wrong here?" He asked looking at the three women.

"It is nothing." Gilda said defending Beatrice. "You must know Mr. Riley this voman is bad. My friend Sarah told me how she vas vit Mr. Mayfield and sang at the Opera House before vee came here vit mama." "What has that got to do with her ability to work? You don't see her at the Opera House do you? Gossip is not a good thing." He warned. That only fueled Ingrid's jealousy more. "You say dese things because she is pretty. I am

134

going to tell mama. I must protect Gilda." "No Ingrid you cannot do this!" Gilda scolded as she followed after her.

Beatrice looked at Mr. Riley. He looked back with concern in his eyes. She sat down feeling very frustrated, knowing full well this had cost her, her employment.

Reverend Bigelow's little church had opened its doors. A large group of the town's people were attending. August was there for its opening ceremony but never intended on stepping his foot in there again. His ghosts lived there and were as a constant reminder of his transgressions.

48
"In The Spirit World"

Ansleigh was pulling hard on the young sapling. She was trying to pull its roots out to place a stake for her chicken fence. She had recently lost part of her flock to a fox. She had to keep the chickens cooped up. She was thinking of making a trip to town to buy more wire. The sapling wasn't budging she pulled again and it snapped back hitting her full in the face. She was on an incline and she fell striking her head on a rotted log. She lay there for a while. She stood up and was very dizzy she kept trying to focus her eyes. One of her chickens got out and started to run for the bluff. She saw the hawk circling overhead. She picked up stones from the ground and tried throwing them at the predator. Her head was in a lot of pain. She went after the chicken and tripped falling down a deep ravine. She fell several feet.

The only thing that saved her was a large branch that jutted out from the ridge. She lay there looking up at the sky. She wanted in that moment to die and she closed her eyes. Shila found her there the next day. He was able to pull her up and and back to safety. She wasn't responding. He tried different things to awaken her but it was useless. He knew he needed Healing Fox to help him. So he laid her across his horse and rode back to his encampment. People came running up to Shila looking at the white woman he had in his arms. Huittsu was really surprised at what she saw. She

135

wondered where this woman come from had and how it was that Shila was carrying her into their village.

Healing Fox sensed his coming and came out from his tepee. As soon as he saw Ansleigh he motioned for Shila to bring her into his lodge. Shila laid her gently down on a blanket. "I felt your presence." Healing Fox told him. "A hawk flew over and I saw you in a vision." "She's been asleep for sometime and I cannot awaken her." "That is because she is in the spirit world. I fear she does not want to return." Healing Fox said touching her face. "This happens when people are sad." "She lost her son and has not been the same. I have kept watch over her." Shila squatted down across from Healing Fox. They both sat quietly.

"This is the woman in your vision is it not?" "Yes. It is. She has a husband and he has been gone for several moons now. It has made her crazy being alone." "It is not natural for one to live alone." Said Healing Fox. "She needs to be with her kind." "Can you help her?" "It really is up to her she has to want to live. I will keep her here and pray about this. You are welcome to come and sit with her. I will teach you an old medicine way that brings the spirit back to the body. But first you must fast and prepare yourself." "I want to do this." Shila replied. "I will return in the morning."

Ansleigh was floating above her body she thought she must be dreaming. She kept going toward a bright light and she saw little Peter. He was happy and smiling at her. Her heart was full of joy and she wanted to stay here with him in this beautiful light. Then she saw her mother standing next to Peter. Her mother emanated much love and spoke softly and the whole space resounded with her words. "Ansleigh it is not your time. You must go back." "No." cried Ansleigh "no!" But something kept pulling at her like a force she couldn't overcome.

"No" she cried then she opened her eyes to see Shila bent over her. "No, I want to go back please." she pleaded. Shila looked at her with compassion and sat watching as she cried. He took her hand and held it gently. She fell back to sleep. Ansleigh had decided to live.

49

"Penny Candy"

Thorton was very ill. Clegg had Dr. Haveston at the Mayfield House to
attend to him. "This young man has a tear in his rectum and a very bad
infection. I would suggest you take him to Pigeon Grove they have a small
Infirmary. They can better care for him there." Dr. Haveston knew exactly
what had happened but kept tight lipped about it. He knew Clegg was not
the type of man you argued with. Thorton was weak and running a fever. "I
wish to stay here if I could. Please I do not want to travel." Clegg told him
he should follow the doctor's advice that he would be paying for his
treatments. "It's my decision and I want to stay here." Thorton said angrily.
"I can try to treat you but I need medicines that I do not possess." "What is
it you need?" asked Clegg. "I will provide you with whatever is necessary."
Dr. Haveston wrote out a prescription for the medicines he would need.
"The Infirmary will have these." "I can leave today." Clegg told him as he
looked down at Thorton. "Yes, the sooner the better." "Consider it done."
Clegg reached down touching Thorton's shoulder. "I am sorry." He then
walked out the door.

The doctor started putting things back into his satchel. Looking at
Thorton. "I know this is none of my business." "That is right it is none of
your business." Thorton said. "Perhaps but if I were you. I would end this
relationship while you still can. I will check on you tomorrow." Dr.
Haveston went down stairs into the hotel bar. He ordered two whiskey
shots. He ended up staying the rest of the afternoon. Drinking himself into
oblivion.

As Clegg rode his horse out of town he found himself deep in thought.
He regretted what he had done. It was too late for apologies to Thorton and
he knew it. What had driven him to such an act of violence? Billy kept
coming back into his memory. He had lost Billy's affections to another man.
He did not want to face that again. But in the process he had lost the very
thing he longed for.

It was late afternoon as Katherine and Quin rode into Crooked Hat. They had the bull loaded into the wagon. Which made it slow going on their trip back. They had been told they could find a place to sleep and find provisions there. Katherine liked it right away as soon as she saw all the shops. For a few moments she was reminded of Philadelphia which seemed so far away to her. She did send posts to her sister Martha from time to time. To let her know how she was doing. Martha wrote back to her addressed to Garrison's ranch. Telling her that she had a little boy and another baby on the way. She was content in her marriage. She would always ask about their father. Katherine was surprised to learn that he had set out to find her. She missed Martha and Ansleigh.

They ended up staying at the hotel-saloon as the Mayfield House was more than they could afford. Quin secured the bull at the livery stable. Katherine was hesitant to take Katy in the hotel as it was a rough place. But she was looking forward to sleeping on a real bed and they were able to bathe as well as their room had a tub. They all slept on the bed together but got little rest as the drunks and rowdiness kept them awake.

The next morning they walked to the bakery and had coffee and fresh sliced bread. Katy loved it. Quin told Katherine that they would spend some time there and head back to the ranch the following day. She told him she needed this and thanked him. The first thing she wanted to do was go to the General Store. She saw the bonnets in the window and had to try one on. She was surprised at the size of the place when she entered. She walked over and picked up a bonnet. Gilda saw her and offered her assistance. Katy was trying them on too and giggling. Katherine smiled and hadn't remembered when she felt this good.

Katy spied the penny candy and tried reaching for the jar with her chubby little hands. She stretched on her tip toes almost pulling the jar onto herself. When a man's hand grabbed the jar. He then held it out to her. "There you are sweet heart, help yourself." Mr. Riley said softly as Katy took a piece of candy. "Oh you can take more than that." Katy was shy but couldn't resist as she reached for more. "No Katy!" She heard her mother say. "You need to ask first." She walked over and picked her up. She then looked up and stared directly into the face of her father.

50
"Maizey's Café"

Justice was feeling nauseous she couldn't help notice that she had not been going through her monthly cycles. She knew she was with child and she knew it was Jacob's. She seldom let the men she was with go that far. You had to know how to protect yourself. She was surprised she had gotten careless. She decided to go see Dr. Haveston and be sure she was all right. This was her first pregnancy. Nadine had become her closest friend at the bordello. The other prostitutes were abusive towards her. Saying she would scare away their customers. Which was not true because she was still lovely despite her wounds. She told Nadine that she was expectant. Nadine said that wasn't good because Miss Francie the madam usually fired the girls when they got in trouble.

"You could always get rid of the kid." Nadine told her. Somehow Justice couldn't quite bring herself to do that. A part of her wanted this baby. She was very fond of Jacob. How was she going to tell him about this? She had to make plans and the baby was forcing her to make decisions about her life. She decided to pay a visit to the doctor. He confirmed her fear. He told her she was most likely two months a long. Her venereal disease was gone and that her health was returning. In spite of all that she had been through. He asked her what her plans were. She told him she didn't really know. Maybe she would go back to New Orleans as her and Charles had left friends there. The doctor told her that if she needed anything at all to contact him.

He would try and help her if he could. After Justice left that day she felt more secure knowing Dr. Haveston was a friend. As she walked back to Mrs. Jack's place. She felt a sudden glow of contentment come over her. For a moment she felt tremendous love for this baby and Jacob.

Maizey was having a hard time dealing with being alone. She still grieved the loss of Nate. She worked hard and was exhausted by the end of the day. Ki was a rock for her. He never complained, he was responsible and reliable. She would never find another like him and she knew it. She remembered back to the day they met. Nate was loading his wagon with supplies for their café. He dropped a bag and before he knew it a man was at his side helping him finish the loading. He was tall and thin with raven black hair that he wore in a long braid down his back. He had high cheek bones and a pleasing face. Nate had thanked him and asked his name and where he was from? "Ki Lim." He told him in his broken English from China. He came with his wife and son. They had fled Northern China to escape the Nian Rebellion and the flooding of the Yellow River. It wasn't until after Nate's death that Ki finally told Maizey the truth about his past. His wife and son both were killed in an explosion in California. Ki worked with explosives for a mining company who had hired him. The day of the accident his young son had run into an area that men were setting up explosives. His wife ran to grab him but not before it went off killing them both. Ki said he wandered for a couple of years. Finding work wherever he could. But he felt empty inside.
A man he was working with had told him about Crooked Hat and how Mr. Mayfield was looking for all kinds of help to build his town.

That day when he met Nate and Maizey he had just arrived. Nate hired him right on the spot. Maizey felt a kinship with Ki as they both had lost people that they loved.

Zacharia was a favorite to Maizey she would talk gruffly with him but secretly she adored him. He was a hard worker and listened when you spoke. But he was stubborn. He hated emptying the grease barrel with all the left over fat from cooking. He would try and leave and pretend he forgot to empty it. Hoping Ki would do it instead. Maizey knew his scheme and would scold him every time. He would begrudgingly do the task. The men liked him and called him "Short Stack" after the fact that is what he would eat every morning with the men before he started working. Sometimes Maizey would catch Zacharia staring at her in an odd way. As if

140

in deep thought. She would usually throw a towel at him or ruffle his hair. "Get to work. I ain't deal'n with no loafers no siree."

Zacharia was surprised to see his mother one afternoon her face was swollen from crying. She had come to pick him up as usual. He knew something was wrong.

Maizey was standing there next to him and had to ask Beatrice what was troubling her? "Yah ain't sickly are yah? "No, Maizey it's not that. I lost my job." "What?"Exclaimed Zacharia. "That can't be." "I wish I could tell you differently. But the Cederholms have let me go." "Why?" "It's complicated." "Je suis navre' *(I'm sorry)* That Mrs. Cederholm is a persnickety old frump and her husband is a snob if'n there ever was one. They think they own this town with that store of ther'un." Maizey was trying to console her.

"You have to admit they supply the town with much needed dry goods." Said Beatrice. "So what are you going to do?" Asked Zacharia. "I am not sure but please don't say anything to anyone, Maizey. I can't afford to lose my lodging with Mrs. Jensen. "You aint got ta worry yore pretty little head off about me. Well look who's here." Maizey said as she wiped her hands onto her apron. It was Gilda and she was upset. "Miss Faye I am so sorry. My sister can be so spiteful. I feel so guilty it's my fault zat you got in to trouble yah. If I hadn't asked you to show me dose routines." "No, it isn't your fault I knew better when I did it."

"Please let me help you. Mr. Riley is talking with poppa right now to bring you back." "That is kind but he doesn't want to lose his position over me." Maizey quickly asked if it would change anything with Zacharia's job. "You will see him in the morning Maizey. I got myself into this and I will get myself out." She took Zacharia by his hand and headed down the main street with Gilda keeping pace at her side.

51

"Vision Quest Revealed"

Ansleigh had been in Healing Fox's lodge for several days. She was awake and eating well.

141

Shila was there every day to check on her. When she had first arrived she was confused and kept falling into sleep. Healing Fox taught Shila how to work with her giving her sacred herbs and praying over her. He had to call her spirit back as she was near death. She knew that she had been spared and felt a bond with Shila. She had never been in a tepee before Healing Fox had a spacious lodge. All kinds of dried plants hung from its ceiling. Animal skulls and bird wings hung from the walls. In the center of the conical dwelling was a large fire pit. Colorful blankets and hides carpeted the ground. Facing east was an altar with a huge Buffalo skull placed on a bed of pine and cedar boughs. She could smell the aroma of the pine and cedar it gave her a feeling of well being. It was early morning and she was alone. She crawled over to the opening and peered outside. The sun was in her eyes and she was trying to make out where she was at. She stood up feeling a little light headed and still weak from her ordeal. She looked around her and saw a circle of tepees and they were situated near a small creek. She walked over to the creek and bent down to get a drink and to wash her face. She looked into the stream and was shocked at what she saw in her reflection. Her face was thin and her hair was long and matted. It was if a stranger was staring back at her. She quickly refreshed herself. She wanted to find Shila to tell him that she wanted to go home.

As she stood and turned around she startled as she looked down into the eyes of a young native girl. She stood there staring at Ansleigh as if she were some strange creature. Ansleigh was still dressed in an old shirt and trousers that had belonged to Thomas and she was bare foot. Soon other children had gathered around her. Ansleigh felt trapped she was not use to being with people. Huittsu appeared and chased the children away scolding them. She looked at Ansleigh and offered her hand. Ansleigh could see this young woman was carrying a child. As her stomach was already quite large. She accepted and followed her to her lodge. When she went inside. Many Horses was working on carving a flute. "You sit." Said Huittsu as she spread a clean blanket on the ground. She then offered her a pottery cup with a sweet drink in it. Ansleigh took it and sipped slowly its flavor was pleasant. "I am Huittsu, husband Many Horses." "I am Ansleigh, husband Thomas." She replied. "Where did you learn English?" "We go Crooked

142

Hat to big store." Many Horses listened but did not speak. Huittsu showed her the hair ties and beadwork she had made to sell. "These are beautiful." Huittsu gave Ansleigh a set of beaded hair ties. "Oh I can't take these they are much too lovely." "You take." scolded Huittsu. "I give." Ansleigh felt self conscious about her hair. For the first time in months. She suddenly realized how long she had been in grieving for her dead child.

Huittsu told Many Horses to leave. He gathered his things looking down at Ansleigh and left. Huittsu looked at Ansleigh "Hair!" She told her as she mimicked combing it. "I am afraid my hair is beyond help." "I help." Huittsu told her as she gathered a gourd and some herbs and placed them in a basket. She made Ansleigh follow her. They went to a place by the stream a long walk from the village.

It was early summer and the flies were out and butterflies were flitting among the Arrowleaf that grew in the meadow. There was a small waterfall there. It was a warm day. Huittsu had Ansleigh kneel down over the stream as she tediously worked unsnarling her hair. Washing it several times in the stream and adding the herbs to it. Soon Ansleigh's long blonde hair was glowing in the light of the sun. She felt wonderful. Shila came walking up to the women. Huittsu welcomed him. Shila was very still as if entranced. As Ansleigh stood up to greet him. Her hair was moving softly in the breeze with the waterfall behind her. He found himself in an altered state. Here was the young woman from his vision quest with hair the color of the sun. "Shila!" Spoke Huittsu. Bringing him back from his thoughts. There was a long silence between them. Ansleigh whenever in his presence felt a strange connection too.

52

"I Have To Work"

Beatrice did not want to tell Mrs. Jensen about losing her job but she felt she owed her honesty. Mrs. Jensen was a quiet woman but very likeable and kind hearted. She had a daughter who lived back East and she missed her.

143

Having Beatrice and Zacharia there gave her a sense of family. She told her not to fret that she had a home there as long as it took for her to find work. Mrs. Jensen would have a meal each evening prepared for Beatrice and Zacharia. Every Sunday they had a special dinner together Beatrice would help cook too. Which Zacharia loved? Beatrice went to the mining office to see if they needed help. They were hiring sorters. Who would sift through the gravel and minerals after it had been excavated to look for remains of gold; that may have been missed by the miners? She would work from sunrise to sundown each day. For little wages. Spending hours standing and stooping. The one good thing about it was she got to have breakfast with Zacharia every morning at Maizey's. She would come home each night and fall exhausted into bed. Gilda would often visit her on the Sabbath. She told her how Mr. Riley tried to talk her parents into taking her back. Beatrice told her it didn't matter because her heart had gone out of it.

Gilda was singing at the new church. She was happy and wanted Beatrice to come and hear her sing. She told her she would. Beatrice was bound and determined to get enough money to buy a home for her and Zacharia it had became her obsession.

She was having problems with her ankle again the pain was severe. She had to leave work early one day and was limping so badly she didn't think she could make it home. She sat down along the side of the road and took off her boot. Her ankle and foot were badly swollen. She started to feel discouraged about her situation. "Miss Faye is that you?" She heard a man's voice from behind her. She looked up into Dr. Haveston's face. "For a moment I wasn't sure. Not use to seeing you in men's clothing. Why aren't you at the General Store?" "Because they think I am a fallen woman." She said sarcastically. "I am afraid they are a little too puritanical for my liking." He told her looking down at her swollen foot, he knelt. "Let me take a look at that." Beatrice winced in pain. "It's a bad sprain is all?" "My dear this is more than a sprain you have a broken ankle that has healed the wrong way." "What can I do?" "To be honest the ankle has to be re-broken then set and put in a cast to heal properly." "No, I can't. I mean I have to work."

"I do not think you have a choice in the matter. If you let this go, you will be a cripple for the rest of your life. Eventually you won't be able to

144

walk at all." "Then I need surgery?" "Yes." "I cannot afford it. Not on the wages I am making." "Do you like to write?" "Why do you ask?" "Could you write prescriptions out for me, make out bills, take inventory and do my bookkeeping? I need an assistant. Personally I detest that part of my job." "Are you serious? What about Molly?"

"She is getting worse. She spends most of her time with the young man you met at my house. I really do need help. If it makes you feel any better you can work your debt off as part of your job.

I will give you an advance so you can quit the dreadful job I fear you have taken. You can start working after you recuperate. So what do you say?" Beatrice was quite taken with his offer "I think it is in my best interest to say yes."

"Oh and one more thing I do request that you wear a frock. The clothes you are in are not very becoming." He smiled. He helped her up gathered her into his arms and carried her to his carriage. He took her to Mrs. Jensen's house. Carrying her into the house and sitting her down. "I shall call on you tomorrow." He said and left. Mrs. Jensen stood in the hall watching. "Who was that?" She asked. "Dr. Haveston." "I have to admit the fellows do seem to favor you Miss Faye."

August was now the richest man in the Nevada Territory. He possessed the deeds to two gold mines, a Logging Camp and had his own Fur Trading Company. He sat drinking a cup of coffee, prepared by his man- servant Cheng Fa. He liked sitting next to the window looking out at the street below. He was situated near a mahogany mantel ornately carved with the heads of four lions two on each corner. It dominated the sitting room. Over the mantel hung a painting of a large sailing vessel at sea. He had it shipped all the way from New York. He was especially fond of it. The windows were large with heavy damask drapes looking out at the main street. An oriental rug graced the floor. There was a large oak desk and Rosewood Regency chairs lined the wall. A cherry wood dining table with matching chairs. A glass chandelier hung from the ceiling.

His bedroom was quite large with a four- poster bed. A walnut wardrobe held his clothes.

A large painting of a reclining female nude adorned the wall. A Parquet floor had been installed by a master craftsman from Boston. There was a water closet and a bathing tub in a small room adjacent to his bedroom. His suite was the talk of the town. Very few were privileged enough to see it. This was a side to August that no one knew. He had grandiose ideas for himself. He had recently entertained the idea of marriage. He wanted children to bequeath his legacy to. He had decided to put a post in the San Francisco Gazette. A publication he would get twice a month. He was explicit in detail with what he was looking for a young educated female, good looking and willing to have children.

53
"Beginnings and Endings"

They stood there for what seemed like an eternity looking into each other's eyes. Katherine was so happy to see her father she began to cry." Father, I am so sorry." Jacob came around the counter and hugged his daughter tightly. "Me Katherine it is so good to see you safe." They were speechless at first. Katy looked into her grandfather's face and smiled. "Can you be with me?" He asked. "There is so much I want to tell you." "Yes, let us find a place to talk." "I will return." He told Gilda. She watched Jacob as he left. She didn't realize he had a family. He never talked about it. They decided on the town bakery and eatery. Katy was happy as she loved the sugar bread. "She looks so much like you and I can see your mother in her too." "Quin wanted her named Katherine after me. I call her Katy most of the time. I prefer it that way." "However did you find your way here?" She asked. "To be honest I don't know. I no longer work with the men I hired to track you. I realize what a mistake that was. I went through me savings. I don't know when I will go back. Martha writes and is home sick for me she says. She has two children I have yet to meet." "I know we have stayed in touch." Katherine told him as she wiped the sugar from Katy's face. "So do you live near by?"

"Quin and I live out at the Garrison Ranch on the Utah border. Two days ride from here." "Do you like it there?" "Not really I am hoping we can find our own property soon.

California I keep hearing is the place to be, near the ocean." "You don't think you would ever go back East then?" "I like it out here. The mountains are beautiful. I really want to go to California." "And Quin?" "He likes it at the Garrison Ranch. We argue about it. A lot has happened to me since you saw me last. I didn't realize how well we lived in Pennsylvania until I left. I have changed. Life does that." "I know Katherine I have been a fool and I am sorry even fathers can be wrong. At first I was angry about your leaving the way you did. But I have learned to let it go." It was extremely awkward for Jacob to say what he really felt. But he knew it was the right thing to do. "You are me first born and I love you." She looked into his eyes. "I Know." "I think about Ansleigh. I was too possessive of her I know that now." "I worry about her too." Said Katherine. Just then Quin walked in. Little Katy jumped off her mother's lap "Pappa!" She cried. He picked her up into his arms. He stared unbelieving into Jacob's face. "Mr. James." Said Jacob offering his hand. Quin, hesitantly shook his hand. "Please join us." Jacob pleaded. They stayed most of the afternoon talking about all that had happened to them on their journey to Crooked Hat.

Thorton was on the mend Clegg had returned with the medication that Dr. Haveston told him he needed. Within a week Thorton was sitting up and able to walk about the hotel. He was told not to lift anything heavy for a while. He rarely spoke to Clegg. His anger was lethal toward him. He felt betrayed and would not tolerate the abuse any longer even if it meant his death.

He told him that he was strong enough to return to his room at the boarding house. The day he left Clegg pleaded with him to stay. He told him that it would never happen again. "It doesn't matter I am through with all of this." Clegg grabbed Thorton by the arm. "I will not allow you to leave I will see you dead first." 'Then I suggest you do it now and get it over with. Because being with you is like death to me." He let go of him. Thorton walked past him and out the door. Clegg, could hardly breathe. He spent the rest of that week alone in his room, in a drunken stupor. He had never been able to handle emotional pain.

54
"Mayfield's Law"

It was late and most people were a sleep except for a couple of drunken miners being thrown out of the old hotel. The two natives worked quickly setting small fires on the roof of the hotel. They wanted to be sure it was going to burn to the ground. They knew that the man called Miller was long since dead. But they wanted to seek revenge on the whites. Who brought the whiskey and brought them to shame and dishonor among their people. Even though they were ostracized from their village. They knew that news of their deed would get back to River Tree and that is all they really wanted to accomplish. They had been drinking heavily and their bodies were painted for battle. They let out a few war cries and rode through the main street. Screaming as loudly as they could. The sky was a blaze with the fire. It had been a hot dry summer. So the hotel went up like a tinder box. The two old miners stood their mouths agape as the natives raced up and down the street. Soon people were coming out calling out fire! The natives then disappeared into the dark. August was beside himself with rage.

"It were'n those injuns done it." One of the old miners told August. "Damn those savages. They won't get away with this." He told Clegg to mount up and see if he could track "those son of a bitches. I'll hang every last one of them!" "I will first thing in the morning." "Now damn you now or I'll shoot you where you stand!" August threatened.

Clegg asked the old miners where they last saw the natives. They pointed and Clegg soon was saddled up and in pursuit. The town had no fire control an over-sight on August's part. Harp use to warn him this would happen someday. They used barrels of rain water to keep the livery stables nearest the hotel wet. Several men using buckets of water worked till dawn fighting the fire. Two people were burned to death in the upstairs of the building. By daybreak all that was left were the charred remains of the old hotel.

Katherine, Quin and Katy had fled to safety. Jacob made it out and was over joyed to see they were all safe. Katy kept crying she was hysterical. Quin held her and kissed her. She wouldn't stop. Jacob asked to hold her. He started humming an Irish lullaby to her. She stopped crying. Katherine looked at her father. "I remember you singing that to us at night." It was good to have her father with Katy she welcomed it.

August told everyone that had been staying at the hotel that they would have to find lodgings with the miner's families. Until he could get this settled. There was no way he would invite them to stay at the Mayfield House. Jacob told Katherine that he would settle them in with Maizey until they had to leave.

Marshall Dawson wanted to know who had started the fire. He talked with the two old miners. They told him all they knew and that Clegg was sent out after them.

Clegg was a good tracker and he caught up with the two natives. They were encamped in a small canyon. He could tell they had been living there as there was an array of animal pelts, bows and meat on a drying rack. They were sleeping off their drunk. He quickly tied the hands and feet of each man without wakening them. Then he shouted at them to get up kicking them in their sides. They were surprised that one man had captured them without a fight. He pulled his gun and forced them onto their horses. He had the horses all tied together. "If you try any thing I will kill you it's all the same to me." He started out bringing them back to Crooked Hat.

By the time Clegg reached town it was early afternoon. Men were already clearing the charred pieces of wood. August wanted it all cleared out of there. As soon as Clegg started down the main street. Everyone stopped working. August was smiling broadly.

"You did it. There will be a bonus for you my friend." Men started gathering around the two natives. August walked over and pulled the younger of the two men off his horse. He began kicking him violently in the ribs and stomach. "You killed two of my tenants you mangy damn injun." The young man started crawling on his stomach to escape August blows. The other native urged his horse and pulled away from Clegg. He started

149

cantering his horse away from the angry mob. August pulled his gun and shot him in the back. "Get my ropes damn it. Now!!!" His hired gun went off to the stables to get the hanging ropes. By the time news had got to the Sheriff. The Marshall was fastening his gun holster on. "Aint no use in do'n anything." Sheriff Daniels told him. "Once Mayfield get's that blood lust go'n there ain't no stopp'n him."

"We'll see about that." By the time Marshall Dawson had gotten to the men it was too late. The two young natives were both hung on the same tree. August had a look of satisfaction on his face as if he had done something worthy.

"Look Mayfield I warned you. You cannot hang a man without a trial and a jury to prove their guilt. Then a Judge hands down a sentence." "Maybe you are an Indian lover but I am not. They killed two of my people and burned down my property. It ain't happen'n. Now if you want to play lawman go right ahead. But I have the right to protect what's mine." August told him spitting on the ground next to Cooper's boot. "I will have to make a report on this." "Like anyone is going to care about two heathens?" "That is where you and I differ Mr. Mayfield. I see them as two human beings and so does the law." "I don't know what they taught you at your fancy law school. But it aint got a dang thing to do with the way it really is out here. Each man for him self."

"That is more then obvious when it comes to you." Said Cooper angrily as he walked back toward the town.

55
"Mail Order Bride"

Dr. Haveston had performed the surgery on Beatrice's ankle. She was recuperating at Mrs. Jensen's place. Mrs. Jensen was a nurturing person. She took to nurse- maiding Beatrice with a relish. To her it was like having her daughter back. She had grown very fond of Beatrice and Zacharia. The doctor told Beatrice to take this time to heal and not worry. Gilda would stop by to check on her. She told her all about the hotel fire and August hanging the young Indian men. Beatrice was appalled at the news. Inwardly she abhorred August even more with the passing of time.

Marshall Dawson wrote to a Judge in Washington that he knew. He felt compelled to do some thing about the senseless killing of the two natives. August had the land cleared of the old hotel and set about building a Firehouse on that very spot. The townspeople were for once in agreement on his venture. August hired a Fireman from San Fransisco to come to Crooked Hat and teach a volunteer group of men how to deal with fires. The Fireman was bringing a Steam Pumper with him. It had to be hauled overland. Tin Pan opened a small bar next to Maizey's cafe. With a big sign in bad lettering that read Tin Pan Siloon it was no more then a shanty he built himself. But it afforded the miners a cheap place to buy a drink.

Katherine and Quin were more than ready to leave after the hotel fire. She begged her father to come with them back to Utah. Jacob wanted to be with Katherine and his little Katy. But he felt he shouldn't leave Justice. He never mentioned her to his daughter. Thinking she would never understand. He told her that it was better that she go ahead with her family.   He promised to write to her. When he had saved enough money. He would come visit her where- ever she settled before he headed back East. Katherine cried and told him how sorry she was for everything. He told her not to be. He could see that Quin was a good man. That he had been the one who was sorry for misjudging him. The day they left Jacob felt an emptiness he couldn't shake. He felt a deep desire to see Justice. He went to Mrs. Jacks to visit her taking her a box of confections form the bakery. Nadine answered the door. "So where you been?" She smiled. "If you are looking for Justice, she's not here." "Is she out then?" "Nope she doesn't live here no more."

"Could you tell me where she is staying then?" "I am sorry but she didn't tell us where she was go'n. Look if you need someone to take care of yah I am available." "No thank you I am not interested." "Suit yourself." Nadine said walking away. Jacob felt a sense of abandonment. He thought to himself where could she have gone and why?

August had received all kinds of letters from the ad he had placed in the paper for a mail order bride. Some contained explicit offers of sexual favors.

151

Others were more formal. He finally came upon a letter that was discrete in nature.

The young woman was originally from Delaware and had moved west with her brother to be a school teacher. But she said she had wished to marry and had no desire to end a spinster. Her name was Mary Karen. August liked the way she wrote and decided from her description to have her meet with him. He sent her monies to travel.

By two weeks time Mary was on a coach headed to Crooked Hat. On the day she arrived August sent Clegg to bring her to the hotel lobby. It was the very same day that the new Steam Pumper arrived and Mr. Lordes the Fireman from San Fransisco. Mary was quite nervous about meeting August. Clegg warned her to be prepared to speak her mind with Mr. Mayfield as he could be harsh with people. She met August in the hotel dining room. She was quite captivated with the hotel. In fact it was the most beautiful building she had ever been in. Mary was a petite plain looking woman with dark brown hair and grey eyes. She had a pleasing voice and was very intelligent. August was hoping for her to be more attractive. But her wit and personality made up for her lack of beauty he thought. They spent the afternoon talking and he took her to the mine and the logging camp to show her what he had created. He was very frank about his wanting children. They agreed to meet the next day and discuss the arrangements of their contract if they were to marry.

When August returned from being with Mary he met with Mr. Lordes. By then several of the town's people had gathered around the Steam Pumper it was causing quite a commotion. Mr. Lordes showed him and the crowd that had gathered how it worked. Discussing how many men he would need to operate it. August decided to hold a town meeting at the Opera House where he was to choose the men he wanted as firemen. He thought to himself that Harp would have approved.

The next morning he met with Mary Karen. He had given it his consideration.

Although he found her un-attractive. She was young and at the child bearing age. He felt she would most likely produce enough children for him. They met in the hotel dining room and over tea he told her that his decision was to marry her. Mary wasn't sure about him as she felt an unexplainable foreboding. However she was more than seduced by his wealth and power. They had come to an agreement that they would marry that weekend at the little church at Mary's request. She was to sign a contract. Stating that all of his properties and wealth would go to his children after his death. Mary was to have the deed to the Mayfield House and nothing more. She agreed. They had a private wedding with only Clegg and Mr. and Mrs. Cederholm in attendance as witnesses.

They had dinner in the hotel. August was roaring drunk and kept bragging about the railway coming to Crooked Hat. He was determined to make it happen. Clegg, looked over at Mary whom August literally ignored that night. She looked so small and fragile to him. She kept forcing a smile at August and their company. But he knew she was miserable. Clegg, finally said it was time for everyone to leave so the honeymoon could begin. Mary followed August to the bedroom this was her first time in his suite. She wasn't prepared for the elegance of it. This was also her first time with a man and she was nervous and a bit frightened. August didn't give her a chance to undress. He threw her on the bed and took her quickly. He then fell onto the floor a sleep. Leaving Mary to take care of herself. She was shaken and confused. She was in physical pain. This could not be what the poets wrote about in the books she read. She crawled into the bed still dressed and fell into a fitful sleep.

56
"Leaving The Camp"

It wasn't long before word had reached River Tree. About the two young men of their village being hung by Mr. Mayfield. Many Horses learned all about it from the Cederholms. They told him and Huittsu not to return until tempers had settled down. Many of the miners were upset over the loss of their friends in the hotel fire. River Tree was angry over this incident. But he also felt the young men had brought this upon themselves. A young warrior by the name of Broken Lance, a cousin to Night Wing told him that he wanted to take some young men with him to seek revenge, for what the white men had done. They argued at the council meeting over the hanging incident in Crooked Hat. Most of the elders did not want to start a war over this. River Tree felt what Mr. Mayfield had done was wrong. He told the council the two young men brought about their own death. Broken Lance wanted to know if they were supposed to sit by, watching while the white men took over their winter encampment grounds. River Tree suggested they talk with these men and work out a peaceful agreement with them. Broken Lance told him it was unwise if he thought that would work with Mr. Mayfield. He was known to be a cold hearted and ruthless man. Broken Lance said that he and his friends would be ready to defend their homeland if necessary. River Tree was trying to avoid blood shed if he could.

Ansleigh was feeling strong again. She had become friends with Huittsu and Many Horses. They taught her how to work with beads. How to make a flat corn bread and pemmican. Shila secretly admired Ansleigh for her strength of character and he noticed her kindness towards others. He taught her how to use a bow and arrow to hunt. Ansleigh had been with the Shoshone for a month and she felt it was time to go back to her home. Shila had been taking care of her animals while she was gone. She was very grateful to him. She had learned a few Shoshone words, simple things but it helped with communicating. Hapisteen made a special meal for Ansleigh before she left. Several of the people that Ansleigh had made friends with attended. Ansleigh gifted Healing Fox with pemmican she had made. For Huittsu she had made a small beaded fan with quail feathers. Many Horses a beaded pouch for medicine. Everyone was pleased. There was drumming and dancing and they taught Ansleigh the Grass dance. Huittsu couldn't help noticing Shila's attentions to Ansleigh and her heart grew jealous. In the morning Ansleigh was packed and ready to return. Shila came to take her back to her cabin. Huittsu hugged her goodbye and said she hoped they would meet again. Ansleigh was fighting back her tears. River Tree and Hapisteen were there to see her off as well. Hapisteen told her. "Yei Nanisundehai hebie" (*There is much to thank Him for*) Ansleigh returned the blessing. It was an hour's ride to her home from the encampment.

Shila barely spoke on the way back. When she reached there everything looked the same, just as she had left it. She was surprised to see she still had chickens in their coop. She noticed the fencing was reinforced. The goats looked healthy and she knew whom she had to thank for all of this. Shila told her in the few words she understood to be safe. If she needed him to come to the village. He told her that in the winter they would be moving their encampment to the big river.

Before he left, he gave her a beautiful leather shoulder wrap designed with beads and porcupine quills. He told her it was from his mother. Ansleigh's face lit up with a smile. "Shila I have something for you." She reached into her pouch and pulled out a necklace made of leather and strung in the center was an exact likeness of a grizzly bear. It was standing up on its hind legs. It was carved out of a piece of Rosewood that Healing Fox had given her. It took her the whole time she was there to finish carving it. Shila took it into his hands stroking the smooth finish of the wood. He felt a strong connection to this talisman. Ansleigh looked into his face waiting to see if he liked it. He had her put it around his neck. He looked deeply into her eyes. No words needed to be spoken his look said it all. He quickly mounted his horse and left. Ansleigh wrapped the shawl around her shoulders and walked into the cabin. There leaning against her table was a beautiful bow with a quiver full of fine arrows. She knew it was from Shila. She then broke down and cried. The loneliness came flooding back and she felt trapped.

57

"Letting Things Go"

Beatrice's first day at work for Dr. Haveston was very confusing. She
soon learned he did not keep very good records. When people stopped in to
see him. Half the time she could not find any record of them having been
there; even though they reassured her they had been. So she started a
system for him that was much more organized. It took her over a week to
finally get all his paperwork in order. Most of the time people could not pay
him so they would barter. He accepted their offerings of work, food and
whiskey. She soon learned that despite his alcoholism he was dedicated to
his profession. Being gone for days at a time tending to his patients. Giving
them care and medicines with no charge. Molly could be very hostile toward
him. He would give her money to run the household. She then spent most
of it on Opium. Beatrice found the house to be depressing and walked
home for lunch each day. Dr. Haveston mentioned it to her. "I know the
house is not pleasant is it?" "I prefer to take a walk to strengthen my
ankle." "I know I am ashamed it wasn't like this at first. Molly really was a
good housekeeper. She just quit caring. If I paid you extra would you be
offended if I asked you to put the house in order?" Beatrice didn't say
anything. "I am sorry. I didn't mean to offend you." "No, it's not that. I feel
as if this is Molly's domain."
"It's not her house I am letting her stay here. As you can tell I have let
things go. Since you are here I feel more like trying again." "Trying?" "To
make this more of a doctor's office.

I use to have a thriving practice when I lived in New York." "What
happened, why did you leave?" "I can't tell you that I wish that I could.
Please accept my offer and I will be sure you are more then compensated
for your time."

Beatrice started working on the house early each morning. Usually Molly
was asleep and did not get up till mid-day. She washed the windows and put
up new curtains she had made. She cleaned out the cupboards and washed
all the plates and cups. She even scrubbed the floor boards on her hands
and knees. Dr. Haveston was impressed with how the house looked and

felt. It was a far cry from Beatrice's first visit there. The patients were remarking on how nice it was to the doctor. He richly rewarded Beatrice for all her hard work. Upon returning from lunch one afternoon Beatrice came upon Dr. Haveston and Molly having a heated argument. "So I suppose you will be sleep'n with her if you haven't already. You think I am not good enough for the likes of you? Reggie was a smart man he taught you a thing or two he did!" "Molly, you know how I feel about him, why do you do this to me? I am my own man." "You can na hold a candle to me Reggie."

Molly screamed into his face. "You think yore so high hat n'all. I am think'n yah haven't told your little tart about yore past then?" Beatrice had walked in during the course of their argument. She felt embarrassed and quickly went into the doctor's office. He was soon to follow.
"I am truly sorry you had to hear that. Molly talks out of her head when she is on the drug."

"You are always making excuses for her rudeness why?" "I owe her that." "How long has she been an addict?" "Right after her husband died." "The doctor?" "Yes, Dr. Reginald Browning. He was a head of the hospital where I worked. We became colleagues. He met Molly in Dublin on a trip there to visit his brother.
He brought her to America and I stood up for him at their wedding. She never got over losing him. She was quite lovely in those days. She would help me at my practice. At first it was drinking. When we moved here, she found out about the opium dens. She has been going to them ever since. Her friend Durwin got her started. That is why I don't like him." "So what happened to you? How did you lose your license to practice medicine?" "I really don't want to talk about that." He said angrily. "Please let's work if you don't mind." He refused to talk any further.

Mary couldn't help thinking how foolish she had been to marry August. He was cold toward her. There was no intimacy between them. He would drink heavily before he slept with her. Taking her roughly and sometimes hitting her if she didn't respond the way he liked. Then leaving her alone in the darkness with no comfort or affection of any kind. She was with child within the first month of their marriage. He was elated when she told him. Her loneliness was obvious to everyone. She followed August

157

around like a servant. He would make fun of her in front of others. During her pregnancy he took to prostitutes again. He found her repulsive during this time and told her so.

Thorton was back working in the theater with Miss LeBaron. He had become close friends with the young actor Aaron.

He kept away from Beatrice and Zacharia and become somewhat reclusive. Something had changed in him after the incident with Clegg. He was thinking about escorting Miss LeBaron on a European tour she had planned. August was hiring a new singer from California to entertain. Miss LeBaron was not the type of person to play second fiddle to anyone. She told August of her plans. There was to be one last show before they left.

There was a large crowd that night. Spirits were high. August was in the audience with his wife.

Clegg was seated in the back row. He had to see Thorton one more time before he left. Beatrice was there as a guest of Marshall Dawson. The show was well received and ended on a good note. Miss LeBaron thanked her patrons at the curtain call and wished them all her best. Clegg waited outside of the stage door. Waiting for Thorton.

When he appeared Clegg's heart was racing he could barely contain himself. He stepped back in the shadows when he saw Beatrice and Marshall Dawson talking with Thorton and Aaron. When they left Thorton squeezed Aaron's hand and told him he would see him later.

Clegg stepped forward "We need to talk he said in a quiet tone. "I have nothing to talk to you about." Thorton said pushing him aside. "It can't end like this." "You are the one that ended this and to be honest it was the best thing for me." "I'll not see you again?" "I doubt I will return to this hell hole." Clegg felt desperate. "I have changed you will see. Is it money you want? I will give you anything. I will never lay a hand to you again I promise." His eyes were tearing.

"You are pathetic you know that. I once looked up to you. Not anymore. If you don't mind. I have someone waiting for me."
Clegg stood there watching him walk away as his rage burned within him.

58

"Night Of The Wolves"

It was a cruel winter. River Tree had moved his village to the Armagosa River Valley. Healing Fox had warned him that many would die in the mountains. The valley had a mild climate in the winter and there were several wetlands to sustain wildlife. Huittsu had a baby girl the first week after their move to the river. She named her Moon Rising after the full moon that was out on the night she was born. Many Horses, was proud of his daughter. Shila was happy for them and he had made a beaded leather pouch filled with healing stones and a small carved bird talisman. This would protect Moon Rising as she matured. Huittsu was grateful for this honor.

The parents of the young man who had been hung were still seeking revenge for his death. They went to Healing Fox, asking him to do something as River Tree had turned a deaf ear to them. Healing Fox told them he would not go against their leader. He too felt their son had brought disgrace to their people by his actions. There was a growing unrest among the people. The geologists were back working on the site and had a small encampment set up. Each day the young men from the Shoshone and the Arapaho could be seen watching the white men at work.
Sometimes short skirmishes would break out between the opposing tribes as they were natural enemies of each other. This made the geologists uneasy as they knew that this could lead to a serious problem once they started building the mine in earnest.

Ansleigh was struggling with the weather. She had lost more of her chickens to freezing temperatures and she lost two of her goats. She had made a lean too for the goats and her mare during the fall season. She ended up bringing the chickens inside to save them from the brutal cold. She was rationing her food. She still had pemmican and salted fish. She melted the snow for drinking water. Each day she would bring in her fire wood and dry it by the hearth. At night the wind would howl around the corners of the cabin. One morning she could not get out as the snow had drifted against her door. Thomas had built a fruit cellar so she went down through the small area under the cabin. She managed to pry open an area that was used to circulate air in the summer months. She crawled outside. It took her awhile to dig through the snow to her front door. Later that night as she lay trying to sleep. She heard the mare whinny and the goats were bleating. She knew something was wrong. Then the dreaded cry of the wolf could be heard just outside the cabin. She couldn't let them kill her mare.

She made a small torch using the fire from her hearth. Dressed warmly and grabbed her rifle. She slowly opened the cabin door. There was a full moon. So she could make out shadows in the moon's light. Then she saw the wolf pack. The alpha male was lunging at the mare.
The mare was kicking and squealing in fear. Ansleigh saw the goats they were both dead and the wolves were feasting on them. She waved her torch in front of her trying to ward off the wolf from her mare. He then turned on Ansleigh soon two other wolves had joined him and they were circling around her. She kept waving her torch at them. She backed up against a tree so they could not attack her from behind.

Just then a clump of snow fell from the tree and put out her torch. She quickly aimed her rifle and shot at the alpha male killing him instantly. The pack started fighting over the goat's carcasses. Ansleigh saw her chance to save the mare. She untied her and grabbed her mane trying to mount her. When she felt a sharp pain in her leg. One of the wolves had bit into her and was trying to pull her from the horse. Ansleigh was no match for the strength of the wolf. The mare was rearing and Ansleigh lost her grip. She knew this was a fight to the death. The mare broke away leaving Ansleigh on the ground. The wolf was trying to get at Ansleigh's throat. She managed to get her knife from its sheath and just as the wolf tried sinking its teeth into her. She pushed the knife deep into its gut. The wolf rolled off from her and ran off into the woods. The pack started circling her for the kill. She stood up holding her knife ready to face death.

When one by one the wolves started dropping as the arrows found their mark. Then he appeared it was Shila. She was so glad to see him. He could see her leg was bleeding profusely. He walked over to her and lifted her into his arms. He took her into the cabin. He ripped off her pant leg and went about cleaning the wound. He wrapped her leg with healing herbs and made a bandage from one of her shirts. He then made a strange tasting drink it was very bitter. Shila told her she must drink it. The drink made Ansleigh sleepy. Soon she was nodding off. When she awakened Shila was sitting on the floor near her bed. He told her that he was taking her with him to his people. Ansleigh resisted saying that she could not leave that she must find her mare. Shila was determined she was going with him. He put the three chickens in a satchel.

He carried her outside and there was her mare already saddled. He put her on her horse and placed the reins in his hand so Ansleigh could not leave him. It had started snowing again and a blizzard was coming in from down the mountain. Shila knew he had to get them to the river as soon as possible. They rode as far as they could in the storm. Shila found a stand of pines and he stopped. Digging a trench using his knife and his hands. He made a hole big enough for him and Ansleigh to hunker down in. He put his arms around her for body warmth. She was burning with a fever from the wolf's bite. Shila knew he was wrestling with time. As soon as the storm ceased he placed Ansleigh on his horse in front of him. Leading her mare from behind. As he knew that she was too weak to ride alone. It was slow going through the deep drifts. They made the Armagosa River by nightfall.

When he came into their camp Healing Fox was there to greet him. They were going to put Ansleigh into his lodge. Huittsu had heard the commotion and walked over to see who Shila was carrying in his arms. When she saw Ansleigh a feeling of intense jealousy came over her. What was this devotion Shila had for this young woman?

59
"Making Changes"

Crooked Hat was in the grips of one of the coldest winters ever. People were huddled inside their homes trying to stay warm. The streets were drifted high with snow. So wagons could not get through not even the coaches. Everyone was on foot. August was comfortable in his hotel. He would look out his window at the main street below and watch people as they struggled with the weather.

Mary was expecting her baby within the month. August would not touch her during this time. They ate their meals in silence and he spent a good deal of time at the bar. He liked playing poker and occasionally paying a visit to Mrs. Jacks. The mine was closed until the weather cleared. One of his foreman told him that there were problems at the Armagosa River site. The geologist sent word about trouble with the natives. So August decided it was time he went there himself to check things out. He took Clegg with him.

Jacob was miserable since Katherine had left. No one knew where Justice was. He missed her more than he ever realized. He was in love with her. His days were slow since most people were not venturing out in the cold. He spent his time doing bookkeeping and helping at the General Store. He had enough money put aside to leave Crooked Hat to head back East. He planned on visiting Katherine before he did that. He often thought of what it might have been like had he met Justice when he was younger. She treated him differently then Rebecca had. She made him feel whole.

There were times when he wondered how his life would be back in Philadelphia. He would be with Martha and her children and yet he felt something was missing.

Maizey carried Pepper through the deep drifts each morning on her way to the café. She had made up her mind about working at the bakery. She would make more money and work less hours. As all she had to do was cook, and not worry about running a business. The owners told her that she would have full say over the dining area. She was to be in charge of what was going to be served. Maizey had earned a reputation as being a good cook in the town.

She had thought about Ki and she wanted him to have the little café that she and Nate had started. Ki was surprised and grateful for the offer. He said it would be hard not to have her there running things. She laughed and told him that he was a hard worker, a good cook, and he would do just fine. Besides he had Zacharia to keep him in line.

162

She also knew that there would be problems with August over this but she would deal with it when the time came.

Beatrice was only going to the doctors a few days a week during this time due to the weather. Zacharia still worked with Maizey as the miners ate at the café as usual.

Thorton had left with Miss LeBaron right after Thanksgiving. He had stopped by at Mrs. Jensens one afternoon to see Beatrice and Zacharia. Beatrice couldn't help noticing how thin he was.

He was morose and kept fidgeting during their conversation. "I don't know why you have been avoiding Zach and I?" "Time just got away from me I guess."
Beatrice knew something was not right with him. "Thorton what happened to you? The truth!"
"Look I am here is that not enough?" "What about us? Our plans for California? Now you are off to Europe with Miss LeBaron?" "Yes, I have always wanted to go abroad and now is my chance. She is very generous." "What about your Mr. Clegg?" Thorton grew very quiet he looked down at the floor. Please do not mention that man's name to me ever again do you understand."

She knew then that something really traumatic must have happened between them. She had never seen Thorton this agitated before. "I promise I will write. We will be gone for most of the year. I will come back for you and Zach. You know that I love you both." He kissed Beatrice on her cheek and held Zacharia in a long embrace. Then he left without a word. Beatrice stood in the kitchen pouring herself a cup of tea deep in thought as Thorton's words still rang in her ears. Mrs. Jensen entered the room with Gilda Cederholm at her side. "It is so goot to see you Miss Faye I have missed our visits. Poppa is in a most foul mood vith this veather." "I can't say as I blame him. So what brings you out in this cold?" "Lets have some biscuits and honey ladies what do you say?" Mrs. Jensen chirped. "That vould be lovely yah. I vant to ask your opinion about a certain matter."

"So how can I be of help?" "Mama is having a party next veek for Christmas eve. She is clearing the back of the store for dancing. My parents have invited several of their patron's yah.

I feel so bad that you cannot be there." "Just leave it be." said Beatrice. "The ladies are bringing guests and I vant to invite Marshall Dawson is that goot? I know that he likes you. That is vhy I vant you to say it is alright vith you?" "I can see no harm in that." said Beatrice pouring more tea into Gilda's cup. "I lay no claim on him he is a good friend is all." "Tank you so much." Gilda squeezed Beatrice tightly. As they sat eating there was a knocking at the door. "Who could that be I wonder and in this bitterness?" Mrs. Jensen got up to see who her guest was. When she returned Marshall Dawson was with her. She looked at the two women and her face reddened. "I see I have interrupted a meeting of sorts?" "Please do sit down Marshall Dawson. Let me take your coat." Mrs. Jensen started to reach for it. "Would you care for some tea?" "No, but thank you I can't stay. I wanted to speak with Miss Faye if that is all right? May I have a word with you alone?" He asked awkwardly.

Beatrice was surprised at his being there. "Yes? Excuse me please. I will see you in the parlor." He followed her into the room. "I wanted to ask you if you would care to join me on Christmas Eve.

They're having a service and party out at the church. I would like to bring you and Zach." Beatrice didn't know what to say. She really liked the idea of going with him. But she did not want to hurt Gilda. She valued their friendship.

"I need to tell you the truth." "Yes?"He looked down into her eyes." It seems that Miss Cederholm is going to ask you to her parents for a party that night." "That is a nice thought but I prefer to keep your company." "Could we do both?" "How do you mean?" "I will go to the church with you. Then after you can see Miss Cederholm at the store." "Do I have a choice?" He smiled. "You would be doing me a favor in keeping a friendship and she doesn't have to know we had this conversation." He was quiet and Beatrice thought she may have gone too far. He feigned displeasure then in a joking manner told her "I think I can do that." He took her hand and kissed it. When they entered the kitchen both Gilda and

Mrs. Jensen looked at them in suspense. "Is everything all right?" Asked Mrs. Jensen. "But of course." Said Beatrice. "Marshall Dawson asked my opinion on a certain matter and I think he needs to talk with Miss Cederholm alone." Gilda started to blush and tripped as she got up from her chair. The Marshall quickly helped her from a spill. She looked up into his face. Her heart was racing and she felt faint. He felt her nervousness and offered her his arm. Gilda led him into the parlor but not before he looked over his shoulder at Beatrice. She just sat there sipping at her tea trying to hold back a smile.

60

"She Couldn't Have Gotten Far"

Katherine wasn't happy about returning to Utah and the Garrison ranch. She talked with Quin on the way back about her wanting to go to California. She even thought she might be able to talk her father into joining them there. She had grown to love the mountains and the beautiful weather. When they reached the Garrison's Nel heard them coming she raced across the front yard "I knew you'd come back."She cried. Lifting young Katy from her mother's lap. Karl came out of the house welcoming Quin home. He looked over the young bull standing in the wagon and gave his approval. That afternoon they all sat down to a feast that Nel had prepared. Karl told them how each day Nel would go to the window looking out and hoping for their return. She had been preparing several dishes ahead of time to serve when they came home. "You are home the Lord is good." Nel smiled. Katy was giggling and kissing Nel on her face. It made Katherine uneasy as she knew that the old problems would start up again. Which made her even more determined to move far from the ranch.

The next day Katherine fell back into the old routine again. She never told Nel about meeting her father on the trip. She didn't want to start a problem with it. They were coming onto the Holidays. Thanksgiving the women spent two days in the kitchen preparing the meal. Nel brought out her best linens and special plates she saved for just such an occasion.

The hired hands and a Dutch family that lived not to far from them joined them on that day for the meal. The food was getting cold as Karl had turned the grace into a sermon. Finally Nel started clearing her throat and others followed her lead to get him to shorten it. After a hardy meal the men sat about the fireplace and talked about politics and the coming of the transcontinental railroad to the west. Nel and Katherine were busy cleaning up the dishes and the table. Katherine mentioned how she had heard good things about California.

Nel resisted her by saying that she heard only outlaw's deserters, Spaniards and renegades inhabited the place. No fit place for a lady. Katherine's ire was up and she blurted out that when they could she and Quin were going there. Nel's face dropped and her pain was obvious upon hearing those words. "You just can't leave Karl like that after all he has done for you." "It works both ways." Katherine said bitterly as she lifted Katy up into her arms and retired to her room.

Several days passed while Nel and Katherine went about their chores not speaking to each other. Quin asked Katherine what the problem was. She told him the truth. He chastised her for it. Saying they had no solid plans about leaving for California especially with winter coming on. It did not stop Katherine from her plan. Even if it meant going it alone with Katy. Christmas had arrived and Quin brought in a beautiful Cedar tree which the women decorated with strings of dried berries and paper cut out snowflakes. Katy helped in the process. Nel and Katherine were under a friendly truce with Christmas upon them. It was a blustery winter day.

Quin and Karl spent most of the morning securing the livestock out of the high winds. Nel had made Katy a rag doll and Karl made her a top carved from wood. Quin gave her a wooden rocking horse he had made. Katherine made her a lovely white dress from fabric she had purchased at Cederholms. She had embroidered the neckline with tiny red roses. Nel was impressed. "My mother taught me how to embroider. My sisters do well with it too." She then gave Nel a delicate lace handkerchief she had tatted herself. Nel gave Katherine an old Bible that she said had belonged to her father. "I noticed you didn't have one and thought you could start read'n it

166

to learn the word. Any good mother should do that don't you agree?" Katherine wasn't going to argue the point. "Why don't we have dessert? I have grown hungry." Quin pulled Katherine to him and kissed her gently on the lips.

My dearest wife now for your gift. Katherine looked at Quin smiling. He handed her an envelope. She carefully opened it. Reading it she was overcome with joy. "Is this what I think it is?" "Yes." "However did you manage this?" "When I was in Crooked Hat I met a man traveling through who was working for the government. He told me that they are looking for men to help build a reservoir for a town that is going up near San Francisco. It is only a few miles from the ocean. They will give parcels of land to the workers for doing the work. I wrote and received this in the post last week. I was waiting for Christmas to surprise you." "Oh Quin." She kissed him and held him tightly. She then looked over at Karl and Nel. Karl was in agreement.

He told them he would miss them but it was time for Quin to find his way in the world. Nel was furious. "Karl you never told me of this!"! Her tears started. "Why didn't you say someth'n?"
"Because Nellie I knew you would get upset like this. It is the Lord's birthday don't spoil things." Katy seeing Nel cry went to comfort her. Nel picked her up kissing her face. "My little angel whatever will I do without you?" Katherine felt badly and didn't know what to say. Nel gave Katy to Quin and went off to her room for the rest of that day.

Things were sullen and quiet after that. The next morning Katherine got up early to help Nel in the kitchen she wanted to have a talk with her about their leaving. First she was going to check on Katy like she did every morning .She noticed Katy was not in her bed. She thought she must be with Nel or Quin. So she dressed and hurried to the kitchen. When she got there. Quin and Karl were both sitting at the table. Quin was ashen. "What is it?"Cried Katherine. "Where is Katy?"
"We don't know." "What do you mean you don't know?"

"Nel is missing and we think she may have taken Katy." Karl said almost in a whisper. "No! No! She cannot take my baby." Katherine became hysterical. Quin tried to calm her.

167

"Why aren't you out there looking?" "We have been up since dawn trying to track them. We plan on getting a posse of men to help. She couldn't have gotten far in this snow." "Dear God."Katherine cried. She ran out into the snow racing around the yard crying out for Katy. Her eyes were wild and she was soon covered in snow as it stuck to her lashes and covered her long dark hair.

She looked spectral like standing there. Quin had to wrestle her down and carry her over his shoulder to get her into the house and warmth.

61
"He Is The One"

August rode into the camp late with Clegg by his side. The weather was mild and it was a respite from the frigid cold of the mountain ranges. The young geologist and camp foreman, named Clayton heard them ride in and walked out to greet them. Reaching up to August mounted on his horse he shook his hand. "Mr. Mayfield it is good to see you." "So Clayton I hear you have run into some problems here?" "The Arapaho and the Shoshone have been dogging us." Said Burton as he climbed out from his tent. "They haven't done anything, mostly sit on their horses and watch." Said Clayton lighting his pipe. "They are planning something." Burton added. "Why's that?"Asked Clegg. "I know Indians and how they think. This is their land as far as they are concerned." "I don't want to fight 'um over it but I will be damned if they try and stop me. I will get the Army in here if need be." August said spitting tobacco on the ground. "I would meet with the Chiefs first." Clayton said. "Might be able to work out something with them." Burton scoffed. "Ain't no parley'n with them except at the end of a gun barrel?" "Let's see what yah got go'n here. I want to start drill'n by February." Said August. The men went out and walked around the perimeters of the tract of land. As they come back to their tent, a young Shoshone was there mounted on his horse. Clegg walked up to him and spoke in Shoshone asking him his business. They talked and then the young man rode off. Clegg told August that the young man was a scout. He told Clegg that their Leader River Tree wanted to talk with them.

"Looks like I will be here an extra day." Said August. "Clegg you and I will ride out in the morning." August had brought a couple bottles of whiskey and the men spent the night drinking and playing cards by the campfire.

August woke at dawn and climbed out of the tent. There waiting for him was the young native from the night before. August and Clegg saddled up and followed the young man to his encampment. Ansleigh was laying strips of deer meat to dry on racks when the men rode into the camp. August looked at her as he rode by. He was wondering what a white woman was doing in the camp. Clegg looked too. The camp dogs were barking and circling their horses. The young native told them to wait and he went to get River Tree. August had his hand on his gun as the dogs were snapping at his heels. River Tree appeared and said one word and the dogs scattered.

He invited the men into his lodge. The men sat in a circle crossed legged around the center fire pit. Shila was sitting next to his father. River Tree offered the two men berry juice to drink. They both accepted the drink. Then they all took turns smoking from a People's pipe as it was passed around. Clegg interpreted for August. River Tree asked him what his plans were concerning the land by the river. Shila remembered August from the time he traded whiskey to Night Wing. He knew that this was a man not to be trusted.

August told him of his plan to mine gold. He offered to share some of the wealth if they would agree to not interfere with his business. River Tree told him that gold was useless to them. They had been coming to this place for as far back as he could remember. He knew that the white men used explosives and he felt that harmed the Mother Earth. He also was worried about the destruction of trees and polluting of their water. August claimed it would be used in the mining area only. Shila spoke up and asked if he were speaking the truth? As he knew that he was responsible for the hanging of two of their tribesmen.

169

River Tree told Shila not to speak. August started getting angry. He told River Tree that there would be peace between them as long as they stayed put. That he had better tell the Arapaho the same or there would be war between them. Clegg was growing uneasy as he knew that August was crossing boundaries that he shouldn't.

Clegg thanked them and said it was time for them to leave. Before they left August had to know who the white woman was. We call her Dabai (sun). "Why is she here?" "She is here of her own will." River Tree spoke. He wanted August to leave as he felt the man had a bad spirit. He knew that Shila was angry. They quickly left and Clegg told August that they had better make tracks because he had offended their leader. "They want trouble I'll give it to them." snorted August as he mounted his horse. Shila told his father that this was only the beginning of a long road to sadness and great loss. That August was the one in his vision. River Tree told him he knew.

August stopped by Ansleigh on his way out of the camp. Leaning forward in his saddle he asked "You all right here miss?" Ansleigh feigned being mute. She knew intuitively these men were up to no good. "You struck dumb or someth'n?" "August we need to get out of here. I don't plan on having my scalp hanging on one of those lodge poles." Clegg urged his horse forward and August followed him out of the camp.

62

"Christmas Eve"

Christmas Eve was blustery and cold everyone was closed in. The Tin Pan Siloon was open at the mine. Old Tin Pan, opened it after the main hotel had burned to the ground. A few hardened drinkers were there. Maizey had invited Ki to her home for a meal. The church was standing room only and Reverend Bigelow was more than happy to see such a turn out. Some children sang Christmas carols and the retelling of the Nativity Story was shared. Beatrice and Zacharia were there with Marshall Dawson. Dr. Haveston came to the service late and Beatrice was surprised to see him there. She never thought of him as a man of faith. Beatrice was dressed in a pale blue suit with black piping and embroidery on the bodice. It was a dress she had wore in many of her shows. She looked most becoming in it.

After the service people gathered in the back where a table was set up with cakes, pies and punch. Zacharia had made at least three trips to the sweets table. Beatrice commented on it. "A boy after my own heart." Cooper mused. "I have a sweet tooth as well. I am so glad you decided to join me here." "I am enjoying it and of course Zacharia as you can see is making the most of it." Beatrice smiled as she watched her son. "So your brother is quite the man already. He is a hard worker." "Yes that he is. I suppose we should think about getting you to the Cederholms." "I almost forgot." the Marshall said teasing. "Look there is no reason for you and Zach to leave.

I will have the Reverend see you two home. I am only doing this because you asked me too. I want to see you again if that is all right with you? "I think I can do that." Beatrice told him as she helped the Marshall with his coat and hat. He tipped his hat at her standing for a moment looking into her eyes. He then talked to the Reverend and left. As Beatrice turned she almost bumped into Dr. Haveston. "Miss Faye, you look lovely. I didn't expect to see you here?" "Nor I you." She returned. "I didn't want to spend another Holiday alone." "And Molly?" "She is with Durwin. I noticed you were with Marshall Dawson this evening. Is he your beau?" "Not really just a friend." "He's a good catch for a woman. I hear he is a dapper dan with the ladies." "I wouldn't know." said Beatrice. "Would you like some punch?"Beatrice asked starting to walk away. "Yes in fact I would. He left early though?" "He had some business to attend to." "Shall we?" Dr. Haveston felt compelled to ask her these questions. He found her most attractive. They walked over to the punch bowl and Zacharia joined them.

Cooper was surprised at how many of the townspeople were at the General Store. It was bustling with activity. There was a long table laden with food. Mrs Cederholm was a good cook and she prided herself in that fact. Gilda upon seeing him immediately joined him taking his coat and hat. She was blushing and nervous about being seen with him and yet excited too. Ingrid was green with envy.

She stood back by herself most of the evening watching her sister and others. August was there with Mary and she was barely able to maneuver in her condition. He spent most of the evening talking with people about the new mine operating in the spring. Mary sat in a chair and was very alone. Gilda was having a hard time making conversation with the Marshall. She was extremely shy with him. He was polite and stayed with her talking occasionally with others. Batilda was pleased to see her daughter with him. Making plans in her mind about a possible courtship between the two. Jacob had volunteered to mind the food and drinks as people gathered around the table to eat. He was thinking about his family on that night. Missing his daughters. He looked forward to the weather changing. So he could make his trip home. He kept thinking about Justice and worrying about her. He didn't understand how she could have left without saying a word to him about it. He missed her most days. It wasn't about their lovemaking but feelings that went much deeper for him. She felt like a missing part of his soul.

As the evening wore on people started leaving and soon there were only the Cederholms and Jacob. He told Batilda to join her family and he would clean up and close the store before he left. She didn't argue as she was exhausted. Jacob was just putting away the last of the plates. When he heard what sounded like a light tapping on the store front windows. It was dark outside as he peered out into the snow covered street. Then he saw her a small figure of a woman huddled against the cold. He went to the door and unlocked it. "Come in." He told her. She entered. Jacob could not make out her features until she removed the hood from her face. It was her his heart pounded he was speechless. They stood staring at one another. "Justice my God where have you been?" He longed to hold her. I missed you more than words can express Jacob was barely able to control his emotions. She flung her arms around him and they kissed.

He was lost in the smell of her and her touch. "I have been so foolish Jacob." "Shuusshhh." He whispered putting his fingers on her lips. It was then he realized she was pregnant.

63
"Where Would I Go"

It was early morning and Ansleigh was hunting rabbit when Shila came upon her. She was completely dressed in an elk skin dress and leggings and moccasins. She had learned to trap from Thomas, and Shila had taught her about using the bow. She was a proficient hunter and trapper. She had been at the village for over a month. Staying with Hapisteen while Shila resided in Healing Fox's lodge. She liked living with the Shoshone they treated her like family. On certain days though she would find herself missing her sisters. Giving thought to the possibility of heading back East. She thought that Thomas must have been killed as he had not returned in almost a year. "Ansleigh." Shila spoke in his native tongue as she understood most words. He asked her to go with him that day as he had something he wanted her to see. She agreed to go. They traveled by horseback to the foothills of the mountain a day's ride.

It was very beautiful High Mountain ranges could be seen with snow caps and a high chaparral with a dense outcropping of trees. Shila took her down into a canyon where a river cut through. He spoke of flash floods in the spring coming through there. This is the time to gather a rare healing herb that grows out of the rocks. He told her dismounting his horse, they walked them as far as they could. Then it was on foot the rest of the way. He pointed to a small green plant, moss like in appearance that stood out from the snow. He knelt down asking her to do the same.

He offered tobacco from his pouch to the plant. His way of thanking the plant kingdom. He prayed and chanted teaching Ansleigh the same. She listened and followed his lead. After gathering the plants. Shila walked her to the top of a high bluff. When they reached the top Ansleigh was awe struck by the vista before her. She could see way off into the distance. The snow capped peaks. Shila told her that this was a hard winter for people living in the mountain regions. He felt better having her there. He told her that he had done a Vision Quest here. Ansleigh was curious about the Vison Quest and wanted to know if women ever did them? He knew of women who did especially those who were healers. She wanted to learn more about this as she felt called to do so. Shila said he would speak to Healing Fox about it. They both sat on a rocky knoll looking out at the mountains. It was quiet and Shila again felt a deep sense of peace as he looked over at Ansleigh. She was radiating a soft white light all about her being. He knew in his heart that she was good medicine.

Jacob locked up the store and took Justice with him to his room at Mrs.Clancy's Boarding House. They both huddled together against the wind. It was a bitterly cold night.

He knew how prudish Mrs. Clancy was and didn't want her to see Justice. He took Justice to the window by his room. "I will be with you wait here." He walked in as usual.

Mrs. Clancy hearing him peeked her head out of her room and wished him a Merry Christmas asking how things went at the party. "All was fine Merry Christmas; see you tomorrow."

He hurried inside locking his door. He needed to get Justice out of the cold. He lit a lantern and going to the window pulled open the sash and he helped Justice climb into his room.

She was covered in snow and her stomach bulged out from under her frock. They both had to cover their mouths as they were laughing so hard at the situation. He helped Justice out of her clothes. He gave her a night shirt of his to wear. He looked at her nakedness. Helping her dress he was very gentle with her. He touched her long black hair and her cheek softly. "When is your baby due?" "Please Jacob." She whispered lay with me. She took him into her arms as they nestled on the bed. "Our baby is due in about a month I believe." "Our baby?" "Yes Jacob. I am so sorry I panicked." "Why?" "Because you are a good man and I am ashamed of my past. I never thought I would say this but I am. I am a common whore. The way I chose to live my life most men would not understand. You deserve better. After Charles was killed something changed in me. You made me realize how empty my life really is." "You could have come to me you must know that. I thought you had met someone else and left. Where did you go?"

"Nadine has a cousin that lives in Pigeon Grove. She wrote to her. I stayed with her for a while. I kept thinking about you. I missed you so much Jacob.

I decided with Christmas here I would visit Nadine and ask to see if you were still here or that you may have left." Jacob could feel the dampness of her tears on his chest. "I wanted to see you one more time."
"Justice do you love me?" "Yes you know I do." "To me that is all that matters. You have changed me.

I am not the man, I once was. I saw things narrowly and with judgment. You make me see the truth of things. I love you more than my life. Where would I go without you?" Justice had a hard time believing that Jacob really loved her all she knew was that when she was with him, the world stopped. "The baby?" "The baby is our bond and I cannot believe I am a father again at my age." He lay there, smiling. "Merry Christmas, Jacob." "Merry Christmas." He said as he fell into a deep and peaceful sleep.

64
"Katherine's Journey"

Quin and Karl had left the ranch to search for Nel and Katy. They had taken three men with them to help with the tracking. The weather was bad and made travel almost impossible. But Quin was not going to quit until he found her. Katherine could not sleep, and each day she would go out and walk around the ranch calling out Katy's name as if she expected to see her appear at any moment. The Dutch couple that lived near by had sent their oldest daughter to stay with her. She would struggle each day to get Katherine back inside out of the weather. To try and get her to eat. It had been several days and no sign of the men. Katherine could bare it no longer so she slipped out of the house one morning, saddling a horse to ride to Crooked Hat. She had to go to her father. She thought he could help.

It was a two day journey, she would find pines to shelter her and the horse at night. Falling in and out of sleep as she stayed in the saddle. By the time she had reached Crooked Hat she was exhausted from not eating or sleeping. When she found the General Store she was so weak she fell from her horse. Laying in the snow she kept trying to get the strength to get up. Gilda saw her from the window and went outside to help. She could not lift her so she went to find her father. Sven came out and carried Katherine inside. "Ve must get Dr. Haveston you go Gilda. I vill keep an eye on her." By then Batilda and Ingrid were there looking to help. "What is it?" Jacob asked coming out of the back room.

"Gilda she finds this young voman on the street Sven said. "I think this is your daughter yah?" Looking down athe young woman Jacob soon realized it was Katherine.

Dr. Haveston was with Gilda. Beatrice had come too. He asked if there was some place he could lay her down. Gilda immediately offered her bed. "Ve don't know this person?" Batilda offered. "Mama sometimes you need to think before you speak." Dr. Haveston carried Katherine up the stairs to Gilda's bedroom. Jacob was worried when she wasn't responding. Dr. Haveston told him that she had a strong pulse and her breathing was normal. He thought it was exhaustion she was suffering from. "I don't understand? Where is Quin and Katy?" "I am sure they are all right yah."Said Gilda trying to comfort him. Beatrice put her arms around him as the three of them stood over the bed watching the doctor. He asked if she could stay there until she was awake and he could safely move her. Batilda was not happy about a stranger in her daughter's bed. But Sven and Gilda were having none of her nonsense. Beatrice said she would stay if it was all right and help. Batilda and Ingrid still held their prejudice against her. Gilda held strong and said that both of them would sit with Katherine.

"After all this is Jacob's daughter." chided Gilda. Jacob stayed on sleeping down stairs in the store laying on a counter top with a blanket over him. The women sat in chairs next to the bed holding vigil over Katherine.

They woke to Katherine crying "Katy? Where are you Katy?" Beatrice walked over to her. "It's going to be all right. You are safe here." Gilda had awakened to the commotion. "Can I get you something?" Katherine looked bewildered as she didn't know where she was at. She tried getting out of the bed. "I have to go. You don't understand I need my father." Gilda had all ready went down the stairs to get Jacob. By then the Cederholms were awake and in the bedroom.

Katherine was trying to find her clothes. "I need to go you don't understand." She became hysterical. She darted for the bedroom door as her father entered. He took her into his arms. "I am here Katherine I am here." At that point everyone left the room to give them privacy. Katherine cried into her father's shoulder as they sat on the bed together. Then it all came bursting out of her. The whole story about Nel and Katy and what had transpired. Jacob was very worried about the situation and felt helpless to do anything. He would be there for his daughter in any way he could. It was then he knew what he had to do.

65

"Only Time"

Maizey liked working for the Freidans at the bakery. She missed seeing Ki in the mornings and teasing Zacharia. They did however let her bring Pepper with her. He slept by the ovens and begged for table scraps after lunch. He was fast becoming a mascot to the customers. She loved being able to make special dishes for people to try. She made a chili with Buffalo meat that was a favorite of many. She hadn't heard from August which was just as well. She checked on Ki the first week. He was frantic with the cooking but Zacharia was a cool headed boy and was his saving grace. As the weather started to change the miners were taking supplies to the new mining site in the Armagosa Valley. It was August's plan to keep a few men working the original site until it was not producing ore.

Emery Elizabeth Mayfield was born in January during a thaw. It was a difficult birth and Dr. Haveston told August that he doubted that Mary could have anymore children; as she had torn the muscle surrounding her hip. August was more worried about the fact he didn't have a son to become an heir to his fortune. Mary was happy to have a child of her own to love. It made up for the coldness of her marriage. Emery was a beautiful baby and everyone said so. This helped bolster August ego and soften his feelings toward the child. Mary would soon learn that the pain in her hip would bother her for the rest of her life.

Beatrice was in the office when Katherine visited the doctor. Katherine thanked her for being there for her.

Beatrice said she wished she could do more considering the circumstances. She offered to share her room at Mrs. Jensens. If she needed a place to stay as she knew how difficult Mrs. Cederholm was.

Katherine agreed. They would meet later that day to work it out. Beatrice couldn't help notice the worried look on Katherine's face after her visit with the doctor. Katherine told her she would see her later and left. Dr. Haveston looked out the window after her. "Maybe I shouldn't ask but is she going to be all right?" Beatrice inquired as she looked out the window next to him. "She is suffering from melancholia. Then there is the fact that she is carrying a child."

Justice was staying with Nadine at Mrs. Jacks but only as a guest. She was done with her former life. She needed time to be near Jacob.

It had been awhile since Jacob had seen or talked with Clegg. But he sought him out. He knew that he worked for August. So he went to the Mayfield House to find him. Jacob found him in the bar. Oddly enough he didn't fear him as he once had. A renewed sense of himself was emerging. He asked Clegg if they could talk. "Well if it isn't the school master with the run away daughters." He said sarcastically. Lighting a cigar as he spoke. "I realize we did not end on the best terms but I need your help." "You are asking me for help?" Clegg, laughed. "I am serious I may not like you but I do admire your skills. I need help tracking a woman who has taken my granddaughter." "Your granddaughter you say? Do you have money?" "Yes I have a savings I will pay you if you find her otherwise I won't." "I got to admit it took guts to ask me for help again. But seeing I did not find your daughter I owe you. Don't look so surprised.

I do have a code I follow. Besides if I find them, we will discuss money then. What are you drinking?" Jacob and Clegg sat and drank as they discussed his plans to find her. Clegg, knew August wouldn't like his going but he wanted to do this. He needed time away from Crooked Hat. He had grown restless again.

Marshall Dawson found out about Katherine through Gilda. He decided to visit Katherine at Mrs. Jensen's place. It also gave him a chance to see Beatrice again. It was a Sunday afternoon and everyone was there. He found Katherine to be sullen and quiet. He asked her questions about Mrs. Garrison and what led up to the actual taking of her child. It only created more desperation in Katherine talking about it. Katherine told him that her father had secured the services of Mr. Clegg to track for them. The Marshall told her that he would do whatever he could to help her. He planned on holding a meeting at the Opera House and bringing this to the attention of the townspeople. He wanted her to be there. She agreed. He ended up staying the afternoon and having dinner with them. On Mrs. Jensen's insistence. Before he left that day he asked Beatrice if she would walk with him. Zacharia wanted to go too. But Beatrice told him better some other time. The afternoon was cold and frozen ruts lined the street as they stepped over them. They walked the full length of Main Street and out into the mining area. He wanted this chance to be alone with her. He hadn't said a word since they left the house. "You are quiet." she said. "Yes I have been thinking." "What about?" "You." "Good thoughts I hope?" "Yes only the best concerning you. I have been seeing you for sometime now. I want to know if I could court you.

"I realize you have no father to ask. I could ask Zach I suppose." He laughed. "A brother's blessings would be good."

"Zach really likes you." "And what about you?" "The feeling is mutual." "So are you saying you would accept my proposition?" "I think I would like that, yes." He took her by the hand and kissed it. "Good I shall see you on Sundays if that is all right?" "But of course." "Next Sunday it is then." he said as they continued to walk through the melting snow back into town. Beatrice hoped she had done the right thing. She knew that Gilda would be hurt. She worried about her past and not telling him the truth about Zacharia being her son. Only time would give her the answer she sought.

66
"True Spirit"

Healing Fox sat across from Ansleigh as she purified herself in the Sweat Lodge. She was going on her first Vision Quest in a few days and was preparing for it.. Shila had a place he thought she should go to for her safety. Healing Fox told him it was not his place to interfere with her spirit. Shila was growing more involved with her as time moved on. His father was starting to worry about Shila's relationship with the white woman and the fact she was still married. The people of their village were starting to talk about it and protest. Shila had never touched Ansleigh in an intimate way or forced himself on her. He held her in the utmost respect. She was the woman in his vision and he was letting spirit show him the way.

It was early spring and the trees were budding the village was getting ready to move back to the mountain range for summer. Ansleigh followed Healing Foxes directions on what she should do. She had fasted and Hapisteen gave her blessings and encouragement on the quest she was about to undertake. Hapisteen held Ansleigh in veneration. She felt there was something special about her essence.

Ansleigh left at dawn that day on foot to the mountain area that Shila had taken her to find the sacred plants. It was growing dark by the time she reached there. She was tired and hungry from not eating. She had to maintain her discipline. She drank little sips of water from her gourd and that was it. The first night she built a small camp fire and slept wrapped in her blanket.

She woke to the chirping of birds in the dawn. She knew this was the day she must stay awake. She walked the area looking for the right place to pray and cry for her vision. A large red tailed hawk flew down in front of her circling then perching on a limb high overhead. She spoke to him and then looking down at her feet was a perfectly shaped flat stone. She sat on it crossed legged and it felt good. She thanked the hawk for helping her and closed her eyes. Soon she was uncomfortable and wanting to move, her legs and back ached and she was hungry. She fought the urge to sleep and knew this was the part that Healing Fox told her was the real test of her

180

endurance. By nightfall she was starting to think of her life as it played out before her mind's eye. She thought of her sisters whom she missed. When she came to the memory of Peter she cried deeply. Her heart she thought would break. Then she asked about Thomas. It was as if a dark cloud descended and she was walking in a place with no boundaries. It was frightening, she felt so alone. She kept seeing the bison and blood everywhere on the ground. A dark figure appeared before her in the shape of a man. His skin was blue and his arms were more like wings. His head was that of an Eagle and his eyes held a light that started to stream out from his body and encircled Ansleigh. She instantly felt her spirit leave her body, she was floating in a gray area .When she felt a hand reaching for hers. She looked and it was little Peter he was smiling and so happy to see her. He gave her a feather, it was then she snapped back into her body. Opening her eyes in the palm of her hand was a hawk feather. Ansleigh looked around and noone was there.

She sat staring at the feather for a long time. It started to rain as she looked up into the sky and the rain washed her face. She sat in the rain not moving. When she heard it. A sound like thunder she had to stand up as the earth was starting to shake. She felt the urge to walk to the edge of the bluff. There she saw the flood of water coursing through the canyon. The rain starting washing from under her feet making her lose her footing. She felt herself starting to fall forward. Thinking this was her end. When she had a vision of Shila, he was standing across the ravine. A red tailed hawk was perched on his out stretched arm. Letting it go it flew over to Ansleigh. She was chanting and felt an unseen force lift her to safety. The storm was over as quickly as it had started and the sun came out. She looked and the hawk feather was still in her hand. She knew then her power came from the bird nation.

67

"They Was Head'n West"

Clegg left Crooked Hat packing provisions for a long stay. He did not know how long it would take him. His instincts told him that Nel would most likely want to be in a populated area. She was use to living with people and being taken care of. He started out for Utah camping along the way.When he reached the Garrison Ranch. Karl and Quin were there. At first Quin held him at gun point. Not knowing if he meant harm. When Clegg asked him if he were Quin James? It took him by surprise. "Your wife Katherine has sent me to help." Quin was relieved to hear her name. He was worried sick that she had left him. Clegg told him that she was well and staying at a boarding house in Crooked Hat to be near her father. Quin invited him to the house where he met Karl Garrison. The men sat and talked about the situation. Clegg asked several personal questions regarding Nel. It made Karl uncomfortable to answer them. He told him that he never knew of his wife to harm anyone. That she was a quiet and reserved person. Clegg explained the more he knew of her habits, it would make it easier to find her. He asked to spend the night and leave early in the morning. Quin wanted to go with him. Clegg told him that he worked better alone. The next morning after a cup of coffee with Karl he set out. He circled around the ranch to see if he could find any old tracks or anything that looked like a lone horse trailing off into the mountains. He did this for quite sometime when he noticed a small footprint in the mud. That of a child.

He dismounted squatting down to get a closer look. This was what he had been looking for. It gave him an idea of which direction Nel had taken. He headed north and watched for horse tracks which he picked up easily. About ten miles out he saw what looked like a doll laying in the tall grasses. It was one that Nel had made Katy for Christmas. He tucked it away in his saddle bag. He rode until sundown. Finding a secluded group of trees, he set up camp. He made a tin of coffee and ate some hard tack. When he heard the sound of cracking twigs. He pulled his gun and stood up. It was Quin leading his horse toward the campfire. "Good way to get killed. You want to warn a man when approaching or get your head blown off." "I know you don't want me to go with you. But I need to. I want to find my little girl." "You might as well join me for now. But first thing in the morning I want you out of here. I work alone." "I can help. I know how to handle a gun. I won't be a bother." "The only thing that you will do is slow me down and take my mind off my business. Tracking is hard. It takes all of my attention. If you want your daughter back than I suggest you let me do my job." The two men settled in talking about their past and the situation. They drank coffee which Clegg added a shot of whiskey to and bedded down for the night. When Quin woke in the morning. There was no sign of Clegg.

He couldn't understand how he left without his being aware of it. He didn't want to go back to the ranch. So he broke camp and tried tracking Clegg's horse. He soon became lost.

He spent the rest of that day trying to get out of the dense undergrowth of the trees.

He saw what looked like a piece of paper flapping on a low -lying branch. He reached for it. There was a note that read: *If you find this message then I know that you are trying to follow me, don't. If you start riding to your left of here .You will find an old logging trail. Stay on it .You will reach Pigeon Grove*
Clegg

It wasn't what Quin wanted to hear. He was undecided as to what he should do.

Clegg started thinking perhaps Nel was planning on taking a coach out of Nevada territory. It had him worried. He knew it was urgent that he stay on her trail as long as he could before losing light. There was an old Inn that still ran coaches about a day's ride. He kept watching her tracks. He made the Inn by early afternoon the next day. An old timer by the name of Frisco Dan ran the Inn. He was bent over with arthritis and almost stone deaf. Clegg needed to change horses and take a rest. Frisco eyed him warily. "Frisco Dan be mah name. You be a stranger to these parts?" What kin I do yah fur?" There was an older man and woman sitting at a small table. She was drinking coffee and the old man was snoring. He asked Frisco for a bottle of whiskey if he had it. "What?" "WHISKEY" Clegg said in a loud voice. As he joined the woman at the table. Frisco brought Clegg the bottle. "That thar'n will be five dollars mister." Clegg reached in his vest pocket and gave him a five dollar gold piece. He lit a cigar and drank straight out of the bottle. The old woman sat silently staring at him. "Well darl'n have you seen a woman and a little girl with red hair on your travels?" "Who wants to know?" She finally asked. He drew a silver dollar out of his pocket, spinning it on the table in front of her.

Her eyes never left it. She hit the sleeping man with her elbow. "Hank." He jolted awake. "What in tarnation." He looked over at Clegg. "This man is ask'n bout that lady and little girl we saw yesterday." Clegg told her about Katy and Nel. "That be them all right." Hank said spying Clegg's bottle. "Frisco." "Who? I caint hear yah". "FRISCO" Clegg said again. This time he got up and grabbed the cleanest glass he could find at the bar and poured Hank a drink. "Now tell me what you know of them." Urged Clegg.

"She told us it was her granddaughter and they was go'n back east for a visit to her son's place." Clegg was suspicious, as he knew that Nel had fabricated the story and was not going to let on about her true location. He wanted to know when the coach left. "A little bit after Hank and I got here." "She weren't on it though." "What you talk'n bout you old fool course they was." "Nope she had some fella wait'n for her. Cuz I saw his wagon down by the bridge when we got here." "What did he look like?" Clegg asked as he poured him another shot of whiskey. "He was a young'un with someth'n wrong with his face all red it were." "So what makes you think she went with him?"
"I had to take a leak so I goes out to water a tree and I sees her and the little one. Climb'n up on his wagon. They went off." "Which way?" "They was point'n west." "That's what I figured." Clegg said as he grabbed the bottle. "I need a fresh horse right quick." He shouted into Frisco's face.

Within the hour Clegg was back on the track again this time heading west. In no time he found the wagon tracks and was hoping to catch them. He couldn't help wondering who the young man was.

68

"The Past Comes Darkly"

Jacob hadn't seen Justice in several days. He spent time with his daughter and at work. He missed her and had to see her. So one evening he went to Mrs. Jacks. He took with him some lavender water and a box of bakery goods from Maizey. Nadine ushered him into her room. Justice had been crying her face was all swollen. He placed his gifts on the dresser and drew her into his arms. "What is it?" "I thought you were upset about the baby and didn't want to see me again." "Why would you say that?" "I am sorry. I got caught up with Katherine and the situation with me grand-daughter. Please forgive me." He kissed her and whispered I love you in her ear. Sitting down in a chair pulling Justice onto his lap. He took the combs from her hair letting it fall down her back. He nestled his face into her shoulder, caressing her breast. "I miss you." "What are we going to do Jacob? The baby is due anytime. I was thinking maybe I will go to New Orleans and stay with my cousin." "Why? I can't let you go. Life isn't the same for me without you in it. Is it me? I realize I am older and my profession doesn't pay all that much." "Jacob, do you think I care about that. I worry more about my past coming between us." "So answer me this. Do you still want to live that kind of life? Would you really be happy with just one man loving you?"

"Jacob, you are the first man I have ever loved." Jacob kissed the nape of her neck. "I want to marry you if you will have me?"

There was a silence between them. He looked into her eyes and tenderly kissed her face. "Yes" he heard her say almost in a whisper. "Is that a yes?" "Jacob you don't know how hard that was for me to say. But I will say it again yes."

Molly was screaming at the top of her lungs and throwing plates across the room. Beatrice had heard her from the office and came running in. Ducking to keep from being hit. "Molly, what is it?"
"He ain't go'n ta leave me. I won't let him. He promised to watch over me" She was drunk and high on Opium. "Who's going to leave you?" Asked Beatrice. "Aubrey he's all I got. You com'n here all dressed in them high

185

falut'n clothes. Pretty n' manners. Like you was somebody. I lived proper once. Me da was a mason. We lived in a house in Dublin with a fence and curtains ta the windows. Me mum died from Scarlet Fever. Me da left after that." She looked wild and stood swaying back and forth. "Now he's dead too." She was unconsolable. "Who's dead?" "Durwin, I found him dead lay'n on the floor all cold and white. The Chiny men carried him out to the back and left him. He needs ta be buried." She bent over in pain and vomited on the floor. "You need to sit, let me help you." Beatrice got her to sit at the table as she proceeded to clean up the mess.

Dr.Haveston had entered the house looking for Beatrice. He saw the situation and told Beatrice that he would clean it up. Before she said anything. He told her that he knew about Durwin as he had him in his wagon in the back. Molly hearing his voice stood up and walked over to him and wrapped her arms around him. "I know."

He said trying to comfort her. "I will be sure he has a proper burial. I need you to lie down and rest." He took her to her bedroom and helped her into the bed covering her. He walked back out and Beatrice helped him clear the room. "What happened?"

"He died from a heart attack it happens with Opium." "Will she be all right?" "I don't know. If I lived in the city I could put her in a sanitarium. As it stands she is in kidney failure and will soon be bedridden. I can only hope she goes quick." "She's that bad?" "Yes."
"I am sorry I wish it weren't so." Beatrice picked up the last of the broken plates off the floor. "She knew. She's always known that this addiction would eventually kill her. It is a slow suicide. When we first came out here. She stopped for a while. She took care of the house and seemed content. If you could have seen her when I first met her. She was so lovely." "Do you love her?" "Yes but not in the romantic sense. We don't have anything in common. We argue a lot. She really loved Reggie. When he died that is when her melancholia and addictions started. My wife at the time was." He stopped suddenly in mid-sentence. "Your wife?" Beatrice asked. "I am sorry I get confused." He went off into the office. Beatrice could hear him

looking for his bottle. Her frustration at his refusal to talk about his past was maddening.

69
"The Time Has Come"

Kachiri and Kocho were there to greet them. When her father River Tree brought his village back to the mountain area for the summer months. She had a baby with her. Her son. Hapisteen was so happy to see them and to hold her little grandson. His name was Rabbit. They all worked to set up the encampment and River Tree held a small feast to welcome his new grandson. Kachiri asked about her brother Shila as he was not there. Her mother told her that he was with Ansleigh. Taking her back to her cabin in the mountains. Kachiri wanted to know all about her. "She is a good medicine person. Your father worries because the people are talking about Shila's relationship to her. She is still married to a man by the name of Thomas." "Does he love her?" "I think he does. But it cannot be as she is taken and not of our people."

Ansleigh knew it was time to return to her home. But she was emotionally unprepared for the sense of abandonment she was feeling about Shila leaving. He felt it too. He helped her rebuild her chicken coop as she had spared two of her chickens from her stay at the village. Everything was as she had left it. Shila cleared the tall grasses and vines that had grown since her leaving.
He had left her with healing herbs. She was very proficient herself in knowing the healing plants and their uses. Healing Fox told her she had a gift and to use it. Shila had spent two days with her. Sleeping outside. He left in the dawn of the third day.

He did not say goodbye as he knew that it would only bring her pain. He worried for her welfare. When she walked outside that morning she knew he was gone and she wept.

Kachiri was glad to see her brother. She was staying the week while Kocho went hunting with River Tree for deer. She asked him about

187

Ansleigh. But he did not say much about her. He liked his little nephew and enjoyed holding him. It was good to see his sister again.

Huittsu was glad to see Ansleigh gone from the camp. It meant she could see Shila again. She had grown secretly jealous of Ansleigh and her relationship with Shila. She had spread rumors among the women saying that Ansleigh was a crazy person and not good for their clan. Many ignored her but some believed it to be true.

Ansleigh was very lonely that first week back. She worked around her cabin repairing what needed to be fixed. She planted a small garden covering it with wire fencing to keep the animals out. The hardest times for her were the nights. She missed Hapisteen and River Tree they had been very kind to her. She would dream of Shila and wake crying. She missed him so much.

She decided to go to Crooked Hat as she needed supplies. She had a few furs she had cured to trade. She packed the furs and hitched her mare to a dog cart and headed out hoping to be back by sundown.

When she reached town she could not believe how it had changed. It was like a small city. It brought back memories of Philadelphia. She needed to see if there was a place she could trade her furs. She decided to go to the General Store. Hesitating before she entered as the memory of Peter flooded her thoughts. He was with her on her last visit there. Ingrid was behind the counter wrapping smoked fish for a customer.

Ansleigh looked around and decided to ask about her furs. "Excuse me miss do you trade furs here? Or know of someone who does?" "Vee do take furs. But my poppa he is who you talk to. I vill get him." She left through the back door. Ansleigh stood looking at the ribbons and notions while memories of Peter flooded her memory. She sighed heavily. Sven approached Ansleigh asking to see her furs. She took him outside to her cart. "These are very goot furs. Who does these?" "I do." Ansleigh told him. "I need supplies can I barter with you?" "Yah, you can get vhat you need." He knew that the pelts were quality and would bring a good price. Ansleigh proceeded to purchase hardware and food items she needed. She also bought some fabric as she decided to make herself a dress.

She was wearing a shirt of Thomas's and a pair of trousers. She even bought some penny candy. Sven helped her carry her things out the front door and loaded her small cart. She wanted to ask him if Jacob Riley was still working there but decided against it. She thanked him and started down the street. When she heard a voice call out behind her "Ansleigh is that you?" Turning she saw her father coming towards her. Jacob then stopped dead still not believing his eyes. Neither of them were prepared for this. "Ansleigh." He sputtered. "I...I ...don't understand? Is it really you?" "Father? I can't believe it either." He wanted to hold her but he wasn't sure if it was the right thing to do.

Ansleigh jumped from the cart and threw her arms about him. "I have missed you." "Me too." Sven stood watching from the store front. "Sven I want you to meet my daughter Ansleigh." "So she does exist after all." he smiled. Shaking her hand. "Now you have both your girls God is goot yah! " Ansleigh questioned what Sven had said. "Katherine?" "Yes, Katherine is here." Ansleigh was excited upon hearing this news. "Where is she?" "Staying with a friend." Jacob said. "Can I see her?" "Go you go!"Said Sven. "Take your daughter to her sister. I vill be fine. Go."
Jacob helped Ansleigh into her cart. "Follow me it isn't far." When they got to Mrs. Jensen's, Ansleigh sat in the cart she wasn't sure what to say. Jacob told her it would be all right that Katherine would be so happy to see her. They knocked on the door and Mrs. Jensen answered. She was surprised to see Jacob and with a pretty young woman at his side. "Is Katherine here?" "Yes she is helping Zacharia with his reading." She ushered them into her parlor. When Katherine looked up at first she did not recognize Ansleigh. They both looked at each other. "Katherine, it is me."Ansleigh spoke suddenly becoming overwhelmed. She looked at Katherine who appeared aged from the last time she saw her. "Ansleigh I can't believe it is you." They rushed into each other's arms. They both broke down and sobbed. Jacob stood looking on while tears welled in his eyes.

70

"Ki's Farewell"

Ki was finally becoming accustomed to handling the meals for the
miners. There weren't as many eating there as before. They were traveling
to the new site to work. He really missed Maizey and found himself feeling
in low spirits about it. Even Zacharia couldn't cheer him up with his antics.
August had told him to plan on setting up a café in Armagosa Valley before
summer was out. He was closing this one. It didn't matter that Ki owned
the business as far as August was concerned. He had little to no rights
because he was Chinese. "You should go and see Maizey. Maybe she can
find you work at the bakery." said Zacharia. "She no need Ki there. I go
with Mr. Mayfield." "You should stay here Ki. Mr. Mayfield is a bad man."
"Why you say that?" "He is that's all. Old Nick will have his soul I can tell
you that. I am going to start work at the livery stable Marshall Dawson got
me a job there. I won't be go'n until you close down." This only made Ki
feel worse. After they finished for the day Ki decided to pay Maizey a visit.
It had been awhile since he saw her. It was early evening and the sun was
setting. The trees were in full bloom and the meadows were full of
Buttterfly Mint. Sometimes Ki would remember China and the little village
he grew up in. He thought of his son often. Knowing that his pain would
last a lifetime. When he reached Maizey's Pepper came bounding off the
porch. Wagging his nub of a tail and wanting Ki to pick him up. Ki reached
down and held him in his arms. Pepper licked him in the face and was
overjoyed in seeing him.

"Pepper where in tarnation did yah go?" Ki heard Maizey's voice. When
she stepped down off her porch. "Ki? What are yah do'n here?"
Miss Maizey good to see you." "Good to see you too." She gave him a
quick hug. "Is everything good with you Mon Cher? She wanted to know.
"Ki be fine." He smiled. "Come on in. I'll fix yah a cup of coffee." He
followed her inside. The house was small but tidy. Maizey had made it really
homey with curtains and a linen table cloth. Knick knacks of porcelain were
on the mantle. She even had a small piano in the corner. "You play?" He
inquired. "Heck no, but someday I am learn'n. It was hauled out of the

hotel the night of the fire. Mr. Mayfield gave it to me." Ki sat down at the table and she poured him a cup of coffee. "Now yah tell me true. What is ail'n yah? Yah didn't come all the way out here to see me." "I come to see you." He then went silent. "Ki, I've known yah awhile, this ain't like you. What happened?"

He told her about August and shutting down the café. Maizey fussed about August not honoring the deed to the café. "I should have shot the man when I had the chance." She grumbled. "I no go with Mr .Mayfield. I go to California. Find work there. Maybe on railway." "Yah mean break'n yore back. They kill men on those things. Fella don't make squat fur wages. Besides I don't want to see yah go."

They sat there in silence as they drank their coffee. Ki found it almost impossible to tell Maizey what was in his heart. But he knew the time had come to speak his truth. "Ki, know you pretty good. I know we not the same. I am Chinese, people make fun of me. I not say words right." Ki you make more sense ta me than most folks I know. Yah are an honest man." Ki looked down at the floor. Then slowly into Maizey's face. He had grown close to her and he knew her in ways she could not fathom.

"You live in Ki's heart. You good to me. I not forget." He was struggling to say the last few words before he left. "I not want to be Alone." Maizey was taken by surprise. She wasn't expecting Ki to say these things. Especially involving her.
She got up from the table to hide her tears. She walked out to her porch. It had grown dark.

Ki followed her out. "You not be happy with Ki? You believe words? They come from inside me." He put his hat on and stepped off the porch. As he walked away he heard Maizey. "Ki, don't yah leave do yah hear? Don't yah dare leave me?" Ne me quitte pas *(don't leave me)*. He turned toward her. She walked up to him throwing her arms about him. He hugged her back. They stood there in the dark in each other's arms.

71

"War Dance"

It was a hot and windy day at the Armagosa River Valley Gold Site.
Clayton was bent over washing and sifting fine stones through a sieve
looking for gold residue. When he saw the shadow of Dog In Moon. He
looked up. Dog In Moon was mounted on a horse, he threw a lance at
Clayton it landed near his leg. He did not miss his aim was intentional. He
spoke some angry words in Shoshone. Clayton knew he was being
challenged. He tried to sign that he was peaceful and did not want to fight.
There were two other young boys who had joined Dog In Moon that day.
When Burton walked up behind him. Carrying a rifle he aimed it at Dog In
Moon and then shot it off into the air. Dog In Moon's horse reared.
Knocking Clayton to the ground. Burton shot Dog In Moon wounding him
in the side. Dog In Moon then galloped off.

Burton shot one of the boys in the back as he tried to escape. A miner
had joined them killing the other boy. Two young natives lay dead on the
ground while their horses went scrambling. "Are you crazy? Now you've
went and done it!" "He was try'n to kill yah." "No! Shouted Clayton. "He
wasn't and he had the chance. We better warn the men back in camp,
because we will have company soon and they won't be friendly." He was
furious with Burton as he walked back toward their encampment. By the
time Dog Moon made it back to their village. He was near death. Huittsu
saw him hunched over on his horse. He fell off once the horse stopped.
Huittsu saw that he was mortally wounded and went to find Shila. By then
others had gathered.

Shila was summoned and immediately took Dog In Moon to his lodge.
He knew that he was not long for the world as he was bleeding to death.
He cleaned his wound and made him as comfortable as he could. He then
sent for his family. Dog In Moon told Shila about the two young boys that
had been killed and were still there at the gold site. They spent the night
praying over him. He died in the early morning hours. Dog In Moon was
well liked by many. His loss was deeply felt. The two young boys who had
went with him that day were not even men yet. The women keened for two

days. His final resting place was high on a scaffold in the deep woods where others were placed before him as well. River Tree called a meeting with the elders. There was a lot of anger that night especially among the young men. Some of the people were still angry over the hanging of their tribesman the year before. They wanted to know how much River Tree was going to allow before he took a stand. He did not want to see war and death befall them. As he knew that the whites were quickly out numbering the natives in the region. He remembered August telling him that he would leave them alone if they did not interfere with his work. River Tree cared nothing for gold. But he felt a growing resentment toward the whites and their greed for the land and their lust for gold.

He told the elders that he needed time to pray and make a decision about what to do. He ended the council meeting and went back to his lodge. Hapisteen was there to greet him. He told her he needed to be with her. As they laid together that night in each other's arms he told her of his fears. She listened and gave him comfort through her words. She told him to speak with Healing Fox.

The next day River Tree went to Healing Fox and they shared a pipe and prayed. They prayed for the souls of the two young boys. Healing Fox told River Tree that he could not hide from this responsibility. That the white men were aggressive and would not stop until they got what they wanted. He told him he must have a plan. He could choose not to fight and lose the respect of his people. Be easily taken by the whites. Or take a stand to protect what he could of their homeland. Either way there was no winning. He must follow his spirit. "For in the end that is all you truly have."

Shila went to find his father later that day. He rode up into the mountains knowing a spot his father favored. He found him there. He was sitting crossed legged on a ledge looking out over a mountain range. He had been crying. This bothered Shila because he rarely saw his father's tears. He turned his horse to leave when he heard his father say "Come join me." Shila dismounted and joined his father on the ledge. They sat in silence for sometime looking out at the beauty of the valley. "I have walked these mountains since I was a boy. My father and his father as well. I love it here.

My heart is too heavy to think I must fight for the right to be here. When it should be every man's right to live as he would see fit. Yet I know that the Grandfather's are asking me to have my voice heard for the benefit of the earth and the spirits of the young men." "So what does this mean?" Shila asked.

"That I will no longer stand by and let them kill my people. I am calling for a war dance and it sickens me."

72

"Past Regrets"

Ingrid Cederholm secretly enjoyed the fact that Marshall Dawson was seeing Miss Faye. She had always been jealous of her sister's beauty and her father's favoritism of her. When she would see Beatrice and Cooper together she would run and tell Gilda every little detail. Marshall Dawson, had been courting Beatrice for sometime. They would eat at the hotel on Sundays and take carriage rides out into the country. Most of the time Zacharia would tag a long. Beatrice liked Cooper but she wasn't in love with him. Gilda stopped seeing Beatrice. She felt betrayed by her. She still carried feelings for the Marshall. Her father tried to get her to see some of the young men of the church, but Gilda simply wasn't interested.

It was mid June when Thorton Blythe showed up at Mrs .Jensen's looking for Beatrice. Mrs. Jensen was surprised to see him. She told him that Beatrice was working for Dr. Haveston and he could find her there. When he walked into the doctor's office. Beatrice was surprised. She wondered why he was back. He told her that Miss LeBaron had fallen in love with him and she could not understand his lack of interest in women. The arguments got violent and she tried to kill him one night stabbing him in the chest. After a month of healing in a German hospital he decided to come back. He really missed Beatrice and Zach. He booked passage on a Clipper ship, heading to New York. From there he took the railway as far West as he could and then a coach to Nevada. He was all excited about the railway and would talk of nothing else. He begged Beatrice to join him in

194

California as he was thinking about finding work in the advertising trade. He met a man aboard the Clipper ship who was in the business. He told Thorton that with his good looks and his command of the English language he could go far. He would be selling medical supplies in San Francisco door to door. And in no time he figured he would be able to start his own franchise.

Beatrice was angry with Thorton and told him so. "You take off on a whim leaving Zach and I to fend for ourselves and now you come back hat in hand. Expecting that I will drop everything and go with you. I am seeing Cooper Dawson at present. Zacharia looks up to him. He is a steady man and he has aspirations of going into politics." Thorton was feeling jealous and annoyed at her remarks. "So do you love him?" "I am fond of him." "That is hardly being in love now is it?" Thorton said sarcastically. "I have a good position with the doctor here and he pays me very well." "So this is it for you? I thought you were the one that wanted more out of your life." "I do but not in the way, I once did. Things do change." Thorton was disappointed in Beatrice's attitude toward him. So they talked about meeting for dinner later that day. Thorton wanted to see Zach.

Beatrice was tending to Molly while she was there .She had become bedridden with her kidneys and was having problems breathing, she had emphysema. She coughed up blood and had to use a bed pan as she was too weak to walk.

Dr. Haveston wanted to move her to Pigeon Grove and the Infirmary. But Molly begged him to let her stay with him. At first she was rebellious with Beatrice taking care of her. She would swear and throw things at her. She refused to eat. She knew she was dying. Beatrice was firm with her but she felt compassion too.

Shortly after Thorton left that day. Molly cried out to Beatrice. She was coughing so hard she started to strangle on her blood. Beatrice was frantic all she could do was hold Molly's hand and speak comfort. "Please" Molly begged. "I need Opium." It was against what Beatrice thought was right but she could not bear to see a person suffer so. She locked the office putting up a sign as closed. She hurried toward Mrs. Jacks and the opium den that was housed near by. Once there she purchased the opium and hurried back to the doctor's house. Molly had her pipe and went about preparing the things as she had done so many times before with Beatrice's help. "I know you think badly of me. But it's between me and God now. Me sins have been many and I wish I had a priest to confess to. The things I am gonna tell you are for your ears only." Molly started to relax and drift a little from the pipe.

She wanted to say what she felt had to be said as she lay dying. "I know you don't understand about Aubrey and me." "Does it really matter?" Asked Beatrice. "Yes it does. He needs to stop drink'n or he'll end up like his brother dy'n at twenty from the drink." "I was but a lass of eighteen when I met Reggie and we married. He was so much older then me he was. When I came to New York I was scared. I didna know anybody. Reggie was the head of the hospital there and worked long hours. He introduced me to Aubrey who was young and good look'n. He was newly married with a young son. His wife Esther was a snob." Molly started coughing again as the blood spewed from her mouth. Beatrice cleaned her as best she could. Molly reached for her hand. "Please hear me out. Esther liked nice things expensive things. She was all about the social life. She liked me Reggie she did. I could tell.

Aubrey was kind to me and listened to me complain'n all the time. So one night we go to a charity ball. Reggie all dressed in fancy clothes he was and handsome.

"He got to drink'n and didna want to leave. He asked if Aubrey would bring me home. We all had too much drink that night. Aubrey brings me home and walks me to me apartment. I know it was wrong. But I invite him in for a bit of coffee. I was so lonely so I throws me self at him. Kissing him and want'n him someth'n awful. He kissed me back but then he stopped. "Esther" he says. But I was hav'n none of it. I started undress'n in front of him. We both ended up mak'n love."

She fell silent for sometime. Beatrice sat there trying to imagine how it all happened. "But then comes the worst of it." Molly said as her wheezing became more labored.

"We have a visitor that night. It was Esther she had followed us back from the dance. She looked at me in me chemise and called me a common whore she did. But then she laughed. Say'n that Aubrey and I deserved each other. She had contacted a lawyer for a divorce weeks before. Told us that she was pregnant with Reggie's child. Aubrey was furious he hit her hard in the face. "You can go to hell" she tells him and walks out the door.

Aubrey left me to go and find Reggie. He found the two of them together in a hotel room. And her with Aubrey's little son. He told me he pleaded to get Esther back he didn't want to lose his child. Reggie told him ta leave or he'd have him arrested. It were then that Aubrey went crazy choking Reggie. Esther tried to stop him. She reached for a kerosene lantern on a table and smashed it on Aubrey's head. Me Reggie liked his cigars and when the oil hit the ash. The flames went up. Reggie was on fire."

By then Molly was exhausted from the telling of the events and her tears fell. "God forgive me for what I done." She reached for Beatrice's hand squeezing it tightly. She took a deep breath and passed on. Beatrice could feel Molly's hand slip away. She sat there in the quiet of the room. Her heart going out to the young woman laying there. Beatrice didn't remember how long she sat there until she heard her name being spoken. She looked up it was Dr. Haveston. "She's gone." He said as he bent down and kissed Molly's face. Covering her with a blanket. He thanked Beatrice for being there with Molly at the end. "Did she say anything before she died?" "Yes she confessed to something that happened a long time ago."

"Did she talk about Esther?" "Yes she did." "Then you know the truth of things." "What really happened to Reggie? He didn't die from his heart like you told me." "No he died in the fire along with my wife and son. The only memory I have of it is choking Reggie and then Esther hitting me with the lamp. My skull was fractured and my eyes were full of kerosene. I saw Reggie staggering and the fire consuming the room. All I could think of was saving my boy. I blacked out when I came to I was in the hospital. A young man risked his life to save me that night.

I wish he had let me perish. The hospital not wanting the scandal made up the story about Reggie having a heart attack. The papers read that I escaped while trying to save my wife and child from an unfortunate accident. Three other people perished in the fire that night. There isn't a day goes by that I don't relive those moments. If only I hadn't taken Molly home that night. Stayed out of it. My son might still be alive. He stood there staring down at Molly while tears burned in his eyes. "There will be a place in hell for me." Beatrice didn't know what to say. "Don't look at me like that I do not deserve yours or anyone's pity.

I started drinking heavily after that night. Lost my practice and I didn't care. Molly's guilt was worse than mine. She haunted me with it. The two of us trying to forget something that never should have happened. We stayed together because I don't think anyone else would have us. Now you know about my ghosts."

"If you want to leave my employment I understand. I need to take care of my friend. You can go." Beatrice looked at him and said. "I plan to stay and help you. I think Molly would have wanted that."

73

"The Woman I Love"

Katherine and Ansleigh were inseparable that week. Mrs. Jensen was pleased to have a house full of people. She spent each day cooking for everyone. Beatrice had taken a sabbatical from the doctor's office. She had spent two days helping him set up Molly's funeral. Reverend Bigelow held a service for her at his church. Beatrice, Ansleigh, Katherine and Mrs. Jensen were the only one's there along with Dr.Haveston. He buried her high on a cliff overlooking a mountain valley. She was very fond of that spot. She once told him it reminded her of Ireland. Beatrice knew that he needed time to grieve. But she also worried about his welfare.

Ansleigh and Katherine were reconnecting and Jacob was grateful to have his daughter's back. He decided it was time to have them meet Justice. He planned a small dinner at "Maizey's Corner" as her new café was being called. The bakery was thriving and a lot of the draw was Maizey being there. When Ki went to Maizey's home that night he had packed his things and was going to leave Crooked Hat to find work. He wanted to say goodbye and let her know how he felt. Never imagining that she had feelings for him. He ended up spending the night with her. They both knew they did not want to be apart. They also knew that people would not understand their being friends and living together. It could cause serious consequences for them both. So they agreed to tell everyone that he was a hired hand living on at her place. Maizey had a small out building she fixed up into living quarters for Ki. He very seldom stayed there because every night under the cover of darkness he would join her to sleep.

He secretly became her new business partner and they both cooked and ran the little café.

Jacob told Justice about Ansleigh and how happy he was to have both his daughters with him. She was pleased for him but feared meeting them in her condition. They were not married and what would they think? "You are the woman I love and that is all that matters to me. They will have to make up their minds about this." "What if they don't accept me?" "Then they will have to live with that decision. Because I choose to be with you for the rest of me life, where-ever that takes me." Justice started worrying about her looks and fretting. Jacob was bound and determined to have her meet them. She started to get ready to go with him that day. Then at the last minute she balked. "I am so sorry you feel this way he told her but I will respect your decision." He left to meet with Ansleigh and Katherine as decided. They were happy to see him never knowing what he had originally planned. Katherine asked if he were all right because he seemed so quiet. They ordered their meals and as they were eating a young woman approached the table. "Jacob." She said modestly. "Miss Hamilton." Jacob was elated that she decided to meet him. He introduced his daughters and pulled up a chair for her.

There was an awkward silence. Ansleigh and Katherine were wondering who this pregnant woman was? She obviously had been in some kind of trauma by her appearance.

Katherine knew she couldn't be much older than herself. "So how do you know each other?" inquired Katherine? Ansleigh sat saying nothing. Jacob didn't mince words. He said with pride. "I want you to meet Justice

Hamilton, my fiancee." His daughters looked at him in shock. Justice started to rise up from her chair.

Jacob took her by the hand and pulled her back down. "Yes this is the woman I love and intend to marry. She is carrying my child. If there is any problem with my decision then say so now?" Ansleigh and Katherine looked at each other. So is there to be a wedding? Asked Katherine. "My father getting married I never thought I would see this day." "What changed in you?" Ansleigh wanted to know. "Yes what has happened here?" Katherine intervened. "How did you meet?" Jacob knew now was his chance to make amends to his daughters. The four of them talked into the evening about their lives and all that had befallen them. Maizey told them they could stay as long as they wanted. She and Ki were preparing food for the next day. During the course of the conversation Katherine burst into tears over her loss of Katy. Ansleigh and Justice were quick to console her. Jacob sat and listened to the women talk all the while holding Justice's hand. Before the evening ended there was talk of a proper wedding for their father as both women liked Justice.

74

'She Knew Who He Was"

Marshall Dawson helped Beatrice onto her horse. They were going up into the mountains that day. It was hot and windy as the dust devils twirled down the main street. They passed the livery stable when Thorton walked out with Zacharia. As soon as Zacharia saw the Marshall he ran up to him. Asking where they were headed. Someplace cool the Marshall told him. Looking at Thorton he said "So I see you are back from Europe. Did you get tired of those French boys?" He laughed. Beatrice was surprised to hear him speak like that. "No actually I am here to talk Beatrice into going to California with me." "I might have something to say about that. Wouldn't you think?" The Marshall said in a serious tone. "We'll talk later." He slapped Beatrice's horse on the rump with his reins. They cantered off down the street.

During their ride Beatrice grew quiet not saying much. "I wish you had told me about the doctor's woman dy'n. I could have been of help. Sometimes I think the two of you are a little too cozy for my liking. Why don't you say something?" He asked in a demanding voice. "I've never heard you talk like this before." "I speak my mind is all? You will have to get use to that. I want to be sure you are loyal. I will have it no other way." Beatrice started to feel her throat tighten. Here was a side to Cooper she hadn't seen before.

Ansleigh didn't want to leave her father but she knew she had to go back to her cabin. She explained that she had left livestock and a garden to fend for themselves.

She would stay for the wedding then she had to leave. Jacob did not want to see her go. He worried about her safety. She assured him she would be fine and would return within the week. She needed to see if Shila had been there. She missed him. The ceremony was set for a Sunday afternoon after regular services. Reverend Bigelow had asked Gilda to sing for the wedding. She was more than happy to do it for Mr. Riley. As she was very fond of him. That afternoon it rained. Unusual weather for that time of year. Justice was wearing a pale blue dress that Nadine had let her borrow. It barely fit over her stomach. Katherine braided her hair and added bits of flowers and blue ribbon. Justice had misgivings about the wedding. She wanted so much to be a good wife to Jacob. But she wasn't sure she knew how. Ansleigh told her that she was glad that her father had met someone who cared for him. She told Justice that she knew him to be loyal and had never known him to raise his hand to anyone. "It's putting up with his Irish temper that she would have to watch for." Mrs. Jensen and the Cederholms were there. Beatrice and the Marshall, Thorton and Zacharia and of course Nadine. Maizey and Ki had prepared a luncheon for afterward. Ingrid made a snide remark to Reverend Bigelow about Justice being pregnant and it being a sin. He looked at her and calmly said "Remember it was our Lord who said "Ye who be without sin cast the first stone." Ingrid grew indignant and went back to sit with her mother where she continued to sulk.

Jacob looked at Justice and he thought she never looked more beautiful than she did at that moment. He was thinking of the journey that had brought him to her. How he had changed. Much of his anger and feelings of retribution had fallen from him like a shedding of old skin and ideas. She had caused him to reawaken to whom he wanted to be.

After the ceremony everyone enjoyed the food. Gilda left early avoiding Beatrice. Ansleigh slipped away not saying goodbye to avoid confrontations about her leaving. The party was over by late afternoon. Justice and Jacob went to Mrs. Clancy's Boarding House to spend their first night together as husband and wife.

Ansleigh felt a deep sadness at leaving her father and sister that day but she knew she had to return and was hoping there was some sign of Shila having been there. When she arrived things looked different. Someone had secured the chicken coop. Fresh fire wood had been corded. There was a dark bay horse in her lean to. She reached in her cart and pulled out her knife. She then hid behind a tree and threw a large stone hitting the cabin door. Within a few minutes the door slowly opened a young man aiming his rifle walked out looking cautiously in every direction. He had long hair and a beard. Ansleigh knew immediately who he was, it was Thomas.

75

"Cloud"

Clegg rode into the small town of Cloud. It sat on the border of Utah and Nevada. It consisted of eight shanties and a tavern. He had been on the trail of Nel for over a week. Stopping only to sleep and up at dawn each day. It was easy tracking the wagon. They were always one day ahead of him. He had met a man camping on route. Who had seen Nel and a little boy. He said they were in the company of a young man called Dieter. Clegg was surprised at the mention of a boy? He wanted to know if they had said where they were headed. The camper said they had not. Clegg spent the night and the two men played cards and got drunk. He met an old hermit on his way to Cloud as he stopped to get water. The hermit told Clegg of the tavern where he might get help.

Clegg had decided to go to the tavern and ask around about Nel. The tavern reeked of whiskey and urine. Tobacco stains were on the floor where the men spat. There were three men stooped over the bar and they all looked up at Clegg when he entered. "So what kin I git yah spoke the bartender?" A crippled man with no teeth and hair that hung down his back in snarled knots. The whites of his eyes were yellowed and his skin ashen. His finger nails were long and filthy. "Nothing." Clegg wasn't about to drink from anything that came from this putrid place. "Ah bit of a dandy pratt yah are. Not use ta see'n the likes of yah in these parts." "I am looking for a woman and a little girl, came here in a wagon a day or so ago. Do you know of them?" "Meh bee, meh-bee not." Clegg pulled a silver dollar from his vest pocket.

The other three men suddenly took interest in him. "She be out at Dieter's place." one of the men spoke up. "Damn fool it were me he was talk'n to." Said the bartender. "I be the Mayor ah Cloud too. So I git the money." A quarrel ensued between the two men. Clegg pulled his gun. "I want to know where this Dieter lives and I will shoot the first man that argues." It grew quiet. "He be bout a mile from town head'n north. With ah big old dog tied to his stoop. So do I git the money?" Clegg flipped the coin high in the air while all the men scrambled to retrieve it.

Clegg wasn't sure what he might find. So he prepared his gun and had his knife at the ready. There stood the shack as the bartender had told him. With a very large dog chained to a post. He decided to see if he could enter from the back, avoiding the dog. Weeds were waist high around the house, broken whiskey bottles and trash were everywhere. He peeked in a small window at the back. He could make out a small child asleep on a cot. He figured the adults must be at the front of the house. The dog started barking loudly. It was then that Clegg opened the window sliding into the house. He walked quickly through the bedroom his gun drawn.

"Can you see anything?" Nel asked. "Someth'ns up. I ain't never seen Ted this upset before." The young man went to get his rifle when Clegg burst into the room. "I wouldn't if I were you." he warned. Dieter was a small man with a birthmark covering most of his face. "Sit down where I can see yah. Nel isn't it? You sit next to him. If either one of you move, you are both dead so don't try me." "Did Quin send yah?" Nel wanted to know. "Don't matter I am here for the child." By then Katy heard the talking and she ran to Nel crying. "There baby girl it's all right Aunt Nel won't let anything happen to you." Katy jumped to her lap. Katy was pale and looked ill.

She was wearing the clothes of a young boy and had her hair cut short. "So which one of you want to tell me what you were planning here?" They sat saying nothing. "I will only ask you again what you were planning." Clegg was getting angry. When they didn't answer, he shot the young man in his foot. Katy screamed." Dear God stop!" cried Nel. "What did yah do that for?" the young man winced in pain. Blood was oozing from his boot. "Dieter it's over." Nel sighed.

"Look mister we weren't going to hurt the child. I love her. Dieter is my brother and is innocent of any wrong do'n. It was all my idea. We was gonna lay low for a while then move onto Virginia. I want to go home. We was gonna raise Katy as our own." "What about Katy's mother don't you think she wants her daughter back?"

"She's young and can have more children. I never can. Look can't yah turn your head on this? I will give you every penny I have." "Nel don't talk nonsense how yah gonna make it to Virginia then?" Dieter asked. "In anyway that I can." Clegg looking at Nel told her "You should have thought this through. There is a Federal Marshall that is looking for you. So I would suggest you hand the girl over to me. I will pretend I didn't get to you. That is the best I can do. You are on your own after that." Nel started to cry. Katy kept touching her face and kissing it. "He's right sis let her go and we can head outta here for we get caught." "I can't let her go I got noth'n to go back to." "This is your last chance or I will turn you both over to the authorities." "I am leav'n for I bleed to death." said Dieter "I want yah ta come with me Nel." "Go!" warned Clegg "if I see your face back here I will kill your sister." "Nel." Dieter pleaded. "You go on I'm stay'n." "Stay'n for what!" "I need to say goodbye now go on." Dieter hobbled across the room and out the door.

Clegg knew that would be the last he would see of him. Some men value their lives more than others. "I need to get back and I am taking Katy with me." Nel wouldn't let go of Katy. Clegg fought with her trying to pull Katy from her arms.   Katy was screaming and the dog was barking loudly. Clegg punched Nel hard in the face. She went limp. He grabbed Katy and headed for the door. He shot the dog and jumped off the stoop.

Nel got up and forced herself across the room. Walking out on the stoop as Clegg rode off with Katy crying in his arms. Nel went back into the house.

76
"The End Of Peace"

Shila was sitting overlooking the gorge where Ansleigh had done her Vision Quest weeks before. He had an ache in his heart as he missed her. It had been several days since he had returned to her cabin. He knew that her husband was back. He watched him as he worked around the dwelling. He saw the look of sadness on Thomas's face when he saw Peter's burial scaffold. He could see no sense in leaving herbs as he usually had done before. He left quietly and came to this spot where he felt Ansleigh's presence. He was troubled over his father and the chance of war over the land. He knew that in his vision quest this was inescapable. He sat there praying and asking the Great Spirit for answers.

River Tree was restless and his heart was troubled over his decision. He met with Healing Fox the one man whom he trusted with his innermost thoughts. Healing Fox listened and then prayed over River Tree asking the spirits helpers to bring strength to him. He told River Tree to come with him they were going to take a journey, a day's ride. He told him to pay close attention to all the things he would experience and see on their trip. They left early in the morning. There was a haze over the meadows and birds were chirping and singing in flight. Butterflies and small bees were attending to the flowers and he saw a herd of deer bounding through the thickets. It was a beautiful day and peaceful. They stopped to refresh themselves at mid - day. Eating and drinking enjoying the bounty of the earth.

They reached their destination by late afternoon. It was the Armagosa Valley. Healing Fox took him to a high point overlooking the encampment of Mayfield's new mining area. River Tree saw a large area of old growth trees that had been cut down. Bare stumps were all that remained of what was once a beautiful forest. He looked up and saw a large crater that had been blasted into the side of the mountain from the use of dynamite. Tools and debris of garbage from food and waste lay about the encampment. There were carcasses of dead animals and buffalo that lay in a pile. Flies were everywhere. It was then that River Tree saw the charred remains of the two young boys that had been killed. They had burned their bodies leaving them for the dogs to eat. When they rode their horses to the river. Dead fish lay floating in the water a putrid stench was emanating from the area. River Tree did not understand. Healing Fox told him it was a substance (acid) that the white man was using to help dissolve impurities from the gold. It leached down into the water tables and into the river. As they rode a long there were dead deer and other small animals lying on the river's edge. Where the water had poisoned them.

It was devastating and the low energy that was coming from the earth was ruinous. River Tree had seen enough it was making him physically ill. The men left the site and headed back toward the mountains. Spending the night in a small cave before continuing on in the morning.

Over a campfire at night River Tree sat silently staring into the fire. After sometime he spoke. He thanked Healing Fox for the day's lesson. He knew that he must make a stand for the earth and the lives taken of his tribesman. It was with a heavy heart that the two men entered their camp the next day. River Tree called for a meeting of the council. That night he chose the warriors that would be going to attack Mayfield's Camp.

August had ridden out to the new site one afternoon. He had Cheng Fa and Tin Pan with him. They were to set up a chuck wagon and bar for the miners that summer. Some of the miners were complaining about Maizey not being there. He assured them that Cheng Fa was a good cook. Soon others had gathered around and were angry about recent events. Saying they wanted no part in murdering innocent Indian boys. The wives of two of the miners were already packing to leave. They said they knew there would be hell to pay for what had been done. August was surprised and wanted to know what they were saying? "Ask Burton." One of the men shouted. By then the two geologist Burton and Clayton were there to see what all the ruckus was about. Clayton spoke first. He told August how the natives had come out that day to try and scare them. He said they meant no real harm. Burton broke in swearing and saying that they were there to start trouble and someone could have been killed. A tall woman spoke up saying that the young boys were not armed. "I am not an Indian lover." She said but you murdered them boys plain and simple." The crowd started arguing amongst themselves and August fired his gun. "Enough!" He shouted. "Where are their bodies?" "They fed them to the dogs." The tall woman said. "My daughter is still having bad dreams over that." "Why in hell would you do that? Couldn't you have at least buried them?" "We was burn'n trash and decided it was a quick way to get rid of them." One of the miners told him. "Damn!" August said spitting tobacco to the ground. "There will be retribution I can tell you that." Said Clayton. "I didn't hire on for this. I would like my pay and then I am out of here." "Hold on now." August assured him. "I have personally spoken with their Chief. He told me there would be no trouble I think he is a man of his word." "If someone killed my sons I would come gun'n." Said Clayton.

"If some of you want to leave then do so. Anyone that stays on will get paid double and I will throw in a bonus at the end of the month." At that point a small group of miners, along with Clayton were ready to pack their things to leave. August spent the rest of that day trying to reclaim his workers. He told them that he would bring in gun men to guard the camp if that would make them feel safer. By the end of that day things had simmered down. August spent two days there to be sure he wasn't losing any more workers. He had a talk with Burton holding a gun to his head. He told him he did not want to hear any more complaints about his behavior. Or he would meet a swift and certain death. Burton knew better then to argue with August.

August put him in charge of cleaning up the mess the miners had made of the camp. On their third day of travel. Clayton and the group of miners who had left met their deaths at the hands of a small band of Arapahos.

77
"I Did It For You"

"Ansleigh?" Thomas inquired as she stepped forward into the light of the sunset. She was colored in rays of gold and her hair was long and shrouded her shoulders. She still wore the dress from her father's wedding. Thomas had forgotten how beautiful she really was. "I thought you were dead." she said flatly. There was an anger growing in her she felt betrayed by him. "It is a long story and I am sorry you had to suffer through the time alone. When did our son die? Why didn't he have a Christian burial?" "You weren't here so what does it matter? This way he is in nature not rotting in the ground. Her heart still ached for Peter. "In case you are interested he died of a snake bite." "We need to talk." Thomas said as they entered the cabin. Ansleigh could see he had been busy working. The cabin was clean and in order. He had made fresh coffee and offered her a cup. He stood before her and drew her into his arms he resisted and pulled away. "What is it? Are you really that angry with me?" "Yes I am." "I could ask where you've been dressed the way you are." "If you must know, I was at my father's wedding today." "Your father? Who's he married to? I thought he would have left by now." "Actually to someone who loves him." "I can see I have a lot of catching up to do." He sat at the table with his coffee. Ansleigh looked at him long and hard. She felt nothing for him. He was well dressed and wore expensive boots. "You might as well listen and hear my story. Then when I am done. You can decide for yourself."

"As you recall the last time you saw me I was planning on going higher into the Sierra's looking for Linx. Their furs are worth a lot of money on the market. I camped out for a week in one section trapped some coyote and fox. Then I got snowed in. I was stranded for days with little food. After the storm lifted I decided to head back here. That is when I came upon a young man camping for the night. Told me he was a leather maker. He invited me to join him. He had quail on the spit and a bottle of whiskey. I had some beautiful coyote and white fox furs attached to my pack mule. He really admired them. After a heavy night of drinking I fell into a deep sleep. When I came to the camp was empty. The young man was gone along with my horse, furs and the mule with all of my supplies. I set out on foot. Finding what food I could and sleeping in anyplace I could find out of the weather. I made my way to a river and decided to cross it rather then walking around it. At first I thought it was shallow and I could wade across. But there was an undercurrent. It sucked me under. I struggled to keep my head above water when a large limb that was caught in the current struck me in the head. The next thing I knew a young Chinese girl was tending to me. I found myself in a rather large tent. It belonged to a Mr. Braxton. The girl was his servant and lover. He told me that they had pulled me out of the water and brought me there.

He works for the Central Pacific Railways and was hired to go to California. He was a surveyor. He was traveling with two Chinese men." Thomas grew quiet and fidgeted with his cup. Looking down at the table he was ashamed. "I am so sorry Ansleigh. I know I should have left to come home to you and Peter. But I knew this was a chance to work with the railways." He had lied to Mr. Braxton telling him he was single and wanted very much to find work with the trains.

"Mr. Braxton's Uncle was involved with the Transcontinental Railways. He assured me he would find me employment. I followed them to California. I got a job as a brakeman on a steam locomotive running out of San Francisco. I loved it. I have enough money saved. We can build a real house and you can live in the city again. I did it for you and Peter. Ansleigh sat there looking at Thomas wondering who he was. It was all about him. Like everything he did.

78

"You Know Where To Find Me"

Beatrice spent a few days away from Dr. Haveston. She knew he would be drinking heavily and she felt helpless to do anything about it. As she stood in the kitchen with Mrs. Jensen they were talking about the wedding and how happy Mr. Riley looked that day. "It is a shame that Dr. Haveston can't find himself a nice young woman to take care of him. It's got to be hard for him all alone. I think it's harder for the men folk they depend on us for so many things." She said as she put a way the last of the supper dishes. "He took care of Molly. He is use to going it alone." "Maybe so but it don't make it right." At that moment Beatrice remembered Molly saying she worried about Dr. Haveston dying young like his brother. She couldn't shake her words. She decided to go and see him the next day.

It was late morning when Beatrice went to his office. She couldn't find him there. When she heard what sounded like muffled cries coming from Molly's room. When she walked in there was Aubrey sitting on Molly's bed. She had never seen him look so disheveled he reeked of whiskey. His eyes were red and his hair hung tangled about his face. He looked at Beatrice and asked why she was there. She told him she had come to see if he needed her help in anyway. "You are free Miss Faye to do as you please. I am through." "What do you mean through?" "With being a doctor with everything." "So you are going to sit here and drink yourself to death?' "It is my business if I wish to do so."

He reached for a bottle of whiskey from under the bed and drank it straight from the bottle. Beatrice stood there watching when suddenly she became very angry. She reached for the bottle smashing it against the wall. "Why did you do that?" He asked falling on his knees picking up the shards of glass, cutting his fingers. The blood mixing with the whiskey on the floor. Beatrice bent down trying to stop him prying the glass from his hands. Aubrey looked at her and wept. "My son, dear God my son. Why did he have to die?" It's because of me." Beatrice couldn't bear his tears.

On her knees she pulled him into her arms. Sitting on the floor she laid his head on her lap. Stroking his face and talking soothingly to him. He drifted off to sleep. She sat there and fell asleep as well. When she finally opened her eyes, it was growing dark. She gently moved Aubrey's head from her lap. Getting up she set about getting water to wash his wounds. She bandaged his hands as he slept. She made coffee and a small meal. He woke with a start "Molly is that you?"

Beatrice walked into the bedroom. "Do you think you could eat something?" "I am afraid I don't have much of an appetite." "I know but you must eat." She helped him stand and brought him to the kitchen. She made him sit he slowly sipped at the coffee. Then managed to eat a few bites of his meal. "I don't know why you are being so kind. I think you would be better off to not be around me right now." "I think I can make up my own mind about whom I choose to spend time with. You helped me when I was down on my luck. If it were not for you, I might never have walked again."

He looked at her not saying anything. "You are a good doctor and heaven knows this town needs you." "I don't care." He said burying his face in his hands. Beatrice reached across the table taking his hand in hers. "You aren't going to like what I am about to say. You have to let this thing go. Before it kills you. I see the truth of what happened even if you are blind to it." "Yes, that I killed my son." "Stop!" She said in a sharp tone. "It is true you should not have slept with Molly that night. That is not what killed your son. Your wife is the one who is to blame. She dragged her child to a hotel in the dead of the night drunk as she was. She is the one who smashed the lantern and caused the fire. Not you! Now you can see this for what it really is or you can live in your distorted view of what really happened. Personally I think you have punished yourself long enough." "I don't know." He said. "Well I do. When you are ready to see this for what it is. You know where to find me." With that Beatrice walked out the door.

79

"Nothing Prepares You"

It was late, past midnight when Clegg rode into Crooked Hat. He knew that Katy needed care. She wouldn't eat and was lethargic. He had camped out the first two nights. Then rode straight through without sleep to get her safely to her mother. He was exhausted by the time he reached Mrs. Jensens. He rapped loudly on her door. Beatrice was the first to answer. As soon as she saw Katy she lifted her into her arms. By then Katherine was awake and Mrs. Jensen and Zacharia had joined the group. "Katy oh thank God you are alive Katherine cried reaching for her daughter holding her tight. Everyone was pleased that Katy was safe. Beatrice asked Clegg if she could get him anything. He asked for a cup of coffee. Mrs. Jensen scurried around fixing food for Clegg and coffee. Katherine wanted to know what had happened and where he had found her. Clegg sat with them until before dawn. Recounting all that had transpired since he had left.

He didn't tell them that he had let Nel and her brother go. He said they had escaped. He had a strong feeling that Nel may have taken her life and he told Katherine she wouldn't have to worry about her again.

Returning to the hotel Clegg slept a whole day through. When Jacob learned of his granddaughters return. He personally sought Clegg out to thank him and pay him the money he had promised. They met in the hotel bar. Jacob placed the money on the table in front of Clegg. "It means a lot to have me grand-daughter back safe." Clegg didn't touch the money. "We're even now, you and I." He said taking a drink and looking into Jacob's eyes. Jacob knew better than to say anything more. "Good enough. At least let me buy you a drink."

They sat together for awhile longer. As Clegg talked about getting tired of working for August and wanting to head back to the old states. He said there was talk of a civil uprising over slavery. "It seems a Congressman by the name of Lincoln is causing quite a stir about it. They will be needing scouts." "You want to be involved in that mess?" "Why not." He said as he lit his cigar.

It took Katy a while to adjust. She had been traumatized by everything that happened to her. At first she wouldn't speak. Just sat staring. Her hair was close cropped to her scalp she was listless and pale. She cried a lot at night unable to sleep. Katherine was very worried about her. Beatrice suggested that Katherine should contact her husband and let him know what had happened. Katherine was already three months pregnant and starting to show. Katherine talked to her father and asked for his help. He was worried about Justice being close to having their baby. They were staying at Mrs. Clancy's until the baby arrived. But he agreed to go. She drew him a map telling him it was about a two day journey. Zacharia asked if he could go. At first Beatrice objected. But Jacob reassured her, he would be safe with him. It was agreed Jacob enjoyed the boy's company. They left on a hot and windy morning. Zacharia was excited to be going to Utah. The first day they made little progress as the heat was oppressive and the horses were stressed. They found shelter in a stand of pines. Setting up camp. They talked about many things. Zacharia told Jacob that he wanted to work on the railways. He heard the men talking about it at the livery stable. "What about your sister?" "Oh she'd be with me of course." "You have big plans for a lad. How old are you? Twelve soon to be thirteen." Zacharia boasted. "If I were a young man again, I'd think about that me-self."

They talked about Zacharias job with Maizey and the changes that had taken place. It was then they started talking about August Mayfield. Zacharia seemed agitated about the man. Jacob couldn't help noticing his discomfort in discussing anything involving August Mayfield.

On the third day they had reached the Garrison ranch. One of the ranch hands saw them ride in and ran to fetch Mr. Garrison. Jacob introduced himself and Zacharia to Karl. Stating his business and saying he had come to find Quin. Karl invited them in to his home. Jacob told Karl all that had transpired and that Clegg had indeed found Katy and that she was alive and all right." And Nel?" He asked. Jacob didn't know an easy way to answer the question. He told him what Clegg had said about her possibly taking her life. "She went with Dieter I knew it. She always wanted children. It's a shame because she would have been a good mother." Karl was having hard time trying to contain his emotions. Jacob asked about Quin. "Don't know

213

where he's off to. He left the same day as that fella Clegg did. Haven't seen hide nor hair of him since."

"That is why I am here to bring him to Katherine and Katy." "The Lord has his reasons for all of this. I wish I could help you. There's food to be had help yourselves. Stay as long as you like. I'm feel'n poorly. I need to lie down." Karl said as he walked off to his room. Jacob did as Karl had suggested. He then took Zacharia out to see the ranch and told him they would head back in the morning.

Quin did not do as Clegg had recommended instead he decided to find Katy whatever it took. Even if it meant the rest of his life. He doubled back and soon found tracks in the mud. He followed them. He spent the week heading in the direction of the tracks. Camping only long enough to rest. He wasn't sure most of the time but he kept at it.

It took him to a small dwelling deep into the woods. A hermit lived there and wasn't too happy to see Quin at his doorstep. Quin inquired after any people that may have come through there recently. The old hermit said in fact there had been a tall dark stranger on a buckskin horse that had asked him for water. Quin asked after his appearance. When he mentioned the dark mustache he knew it had been Clegg. The hermit told him that there was an old Inn not to far from there that he sent Clegg to. Quin was excited for the first time he felt maybe he was finally onto something. He wanted to get there before nightfall. When he arrived in Cloud the old bartender was closing down the bar and locking up.

Quin introduced himself and asked if he could answer some questions for him. The old man squinted up at him and asked him what it was worth to him?

"You young whipper snappers think an old man is supposed to remember things." Quin told him it was very important. He offered him money. "Come on in then." he told him. He set up a bottle and the two men talked. In the course of their conversation he learned that indeed Clegg had been there the day before. The old man told him about the woman and the little red haired boy. Quin wanted to know where he could find them. "Outta Cloud about a mile or so as the crow flies head'n north. Watch out for the big dog." He thanked him and was on his way. By the time he reached the house he saw the dead dog still tied to the post. He dismounted and pulled out his gun. He cautiously stepped up on the stoop. Calling out no one answered. With his gun drawn he entered the door wasn't locked. His heart was pounding and his mouth was dry. He looked about quickly there was a half empty whiskey bottle and a plate with leftovers on the table. He called out again. He started to feel spooked.

When he worked his way into the back bed room nothing had prepared him for what he was about to see. There hanging from the door with a belt about her neck and her face all swollen was Nel Garrison.

80
"He Thought Better Of It"

Emery was the apple of August eye. He bought her everything. She had a complete collection of dolls and children's books he had ordered from San Francisco. She wasn't quite a year old and he was planning her life. He had quit sleeping with Mary and she didn't mind as she was in pain most days taking laudanum to find relief. They kept up appearances but people knew their marriage was a sham. He decided to finish the house that he had started just before Harp was killed. It wasn't just any house. Using lumber from his logging camp and hiring a young architect from San Francisco to design it for him. With two master carpenters to do the labor. It was two miles from the main street and nestled in a panoramic view of the Sierras. It was three stories high with a wrap around veranda in the front. A cupola on the roof to look out at the mountains. He had five guest rooms a master bedroom and fireplace. Mary had her own room off to the side of the master bedroom. Emery's nursery was large and had a huge window that looked out at the woods behind the estate. The floors were all hardwoods and an elegant Persian rug adorned the main sitting room and his favorite painting of the ship at sea hung over the mantle. In the dining room there were two large canvases one of August dressed in his favorite tailored suit including a prop, a walking cane he never used. He had hired an artist to portray him without his scar and blind eye. He also had one done of Mary

215

with Emery sitting on her lap. The room was opulent with a hanging chandelier imported from France. A large dining table that sat twenty people. The kitchen was substantial with every convenience of the time.

He had his own chef a young Scandinavian and two housekeepers by the name of Mrs. Mulhoney and her oldest daughter Irene. They stayed in the servant's quarters at the back of the house. August favorite room was his study. He had a large oak desk and even though he did not read he had a library of books. He kept a collection of guns in a glass cabinet and had the heads of a Bison, elk and black bear he had killed mounted on the wall. The estate also had its own gardens and orchards, livestock and riding horses. He still kept his suite at the Mayfield House for private parties and prostitutes. All of this came with a price. August did not trust anyone and had made enemies along the way. Since Clegg wasn't all that dependable. He hired a gunman by the name of Butch Cady. He was of Navajo and Irish descent a skilled killer as his personal body guard. There were men who he paid to patrol his estate. The people of Crooked Hat despised him but in truth knew that he kept the economy thriving, August was, if nothing else a clever businessman.

Gilda could not stop thinking about the Marshall after all he had been so attentive to her at Christmas time.

She would see him from time to time at the church. He always acknowledged her presence. Ingrid wasn't too happy about his attentions with Miss Faye either. So she had come up with a plan. She sent the Marshall a note at the Hotel. Stating she was Gilda and wanted very much to have a private audience with him.

Could they please meet at the Opera House and she named the day and time. Signing it lovingly Gilda. She then told Gilda that the Marshall had asked for her at the store when she wasn't there. He left a note. Gilda read it. It was simple and to the point with day and time of their meeting at the Opera House. Gilda could not imagine why?

It got the better of her curiosity. So as Ingrid's plan unfolded her older sister did go to the Opera House. There were rarely any programs after Miss LeBaron left. The young singer August had hired left much to be desired.

216

She was a soprano and sang poorly. There were few people in the audience that night. Gilda nervously paced in the foyer watching for him.

It grew late she sat in the theater barely focusing on the show. She decided she had made a mistake and got up to leave when he entered. In the dark she saw his silhouette against the stage lanterns. As he scanned the room for sight of her. She quickly decided to leave exiting out the back door of the building. Cooper saw her and followed her out. "Miss Cederholm where are you going? Didn't you see me?"

"I didn't think you were coming." "You told me to meet you in your note if I am not mistaken?" "Note? I didn't leave a note." Gilda said. "You were the one." "I don't know what is going on here but I did not." They both looked at each other. "A prank I guess and a cruel one." Gilda said as she started to walk a way. "Wait don't go." The Marshall said as he took her hand. Gilda was flushed by his touch. "I shouldn't even be here. You are with Miss Faye." "Do you see her here?" "No, but I shouldn't be doing this." "Obviously you are interested? What do you say I treat you to a meal at the Mayfield House?" "Oh if my parents were to find out." "Nonsense I will vouch for you." Gilda was so enamored of him she felt giddy and said "Yes I will join you."

He took her to the dining area and bought her a meal with wine included. She had never drank before but he told her it was harmless and to try it. She sipped it making a face. He laughed. "Stay with it, it gets better." They talked and he told her of his plans to buy land and develop it. He never once mentioned Beatrice.

She was intrigued. She kept drinking and soon her head was buzzing and she felt a little faint. She told him she felt odd and should leave. He escorted her out of the dining area. She tripped over an urn in the hallway almost falling. He picked her up in his arms and carried her to his room. He did not want to send her home in a drunken state. So he laid her on his bed. She started to giggle about the situation.

He stood looking down at her. She was quite lovely lying there. An innocence about her. He knew that she was taken with him. She started to drift off to sleep. He started thinking about Beatrice whom he was strongly attracted to but she was becoming indifferent and he did not understand

217

why. He went back downstairs and drank at the bar. He was trying to figure out how to get Gilda home with out being noticed. After sometime he returned to his room. He decided to wake Gilda. He sat on the edge of the bed. Looking down at her when he felt her hand reach up stroking his face. "I need you to come with me." He said pushing her hand down. "I am taking you home." She sat up kissing him on his lips. For a moment he wanted to respond. But thought better of it. He ended up taking her back to the store. Kissing her on the cheek before he walked away. Ingrid stood watching them from her bedroom window high above.

81

"She Did Not Understand"

Shila knew that he should stay away from Ansleigh. He needed to see if she was safe. He rode to her cabin and under the cover of nature he hid while watching. He saw her working in her garden outside of the cabin. No matter what the outcome between them. He cared very deeply for her and he knew it. He made a bird like sound Ansleigh looked up she knew it was him. She shaded her eyes as she looked into the woods. She signed that she was good and made the gesture letting him know she missed him. She then quickly walked back into her cabin. For Shila it was enough and he left.

"So you look upset what's the matter?" Thomas asked as he sat working on a trap. "It's nothing." "You have acted strange ever since I got back. I found this." He tossed her the beaded cape Hapisteen had made her. "Do you mind explaining this to me?" "It was a gift." "A gift from who? I don't think they do this kind of work in town. And I am still wondering why Peter is where he is at without a decent Christian burial." Ansleigh could feel her temper rising. "You weren't here so why do you care?" 'Because he was my son." Her tears welled. "I fought to save his life that day. His little face was all swollen beyond recognition. He was in pain and there was nothing I could do." She wrapped her arms about herself trying to hold back the deep sobs that emanated from her being.

Thomas was distraught by her crying. "Look Ansleigh I am sorry I did what I thought was right at the time." Then he blurted out. "Were you living with an Indian here?" "Don't you go there? Damn you Thomas! Don't you dare? If you must know, I am friends with the Shoshone. They tried to help me with Peter. They saved my life. There was no one else." She could not bring herself to tell him about Shila. "I hope you are telling me the truth because if you have lain with an Indian. I will never touch you again I swear!"

Ansleigh could take no more she ran from the cabin and out into the woods. The branches and the briars tearing at her clothes. She ran until her lungs were burning. She had grown to angry to cry. She finally fell onto the ground exhausted. She lay there looking up at the sky. A red tail hawk flew down and lit in a tree near her. He stared down at her and called out as he flew off. She sat up and looked and there beside her was a feather. She picked it up and thanked the hawk and the spirits. She chanted a song that Hapisteen had taught her. She sat there in the peacefulness of the woods. Losing track of time. She did not want to go back and face Thomas but she knew she must.

As she headed back, she noticed smoke coming from the cabin. She started running toward it. She called out to Thomas there was no answer. Then she saw what was on fire. It was Peter's scaffold. She also saw that Peter's body was missing. She ran into the cabin. No one was there. Thomas had taken his belongings and his bay horse was gone with all of his trapping equipment. She sat in the doorway of the cabin and cried.

The next morning Ansleigh packed a few personal belongings and took her bow and quiver. She was dressed in her elk skins. She set the chickens free. Then got on her horse and rode toward the summer camp of the Shoshone.

Hapisteen saw Ansleigh riding into the camp the dogs were circling her and barking. She walked up to her chasing the dogs away. She was surprised to see her. Ansleigh dismounted her horse and walked to the waterfall. Hapisteen following. When she reached there she stopped.

Hapisteen could see that something was wrong by Ansleigh's behavior. The water made her feel more centered. She told Hapisteen in her native language as best she could about Thomas and how he took her baby away. That her heart was breaking and she did not know where to go or where she belonged. Hapisteen brought her back to her lodge. She made her some medicinal tea and told her to drink it. She said that it wasn't safe to be in the camp. That their people were ready to go to war against the whites at the Gold mine. Was there no one to be with her? Ansleigh felt like running but to where? She did not want to live in Crooked Hat even though she loved Katherine and her father. I want to be with your people I am happy here she told Hapisteen.

She told Ansleigh she cared for her. But it was not her place to interfere with her husband's decisions. "For your own safety you must leave." They could hear voices outside of the tepee Hapisteen lifted the flap and went outside. A young girl said she saw the white woman on her horse. Two of the young men said that she could not be in their camp if she stayed she would die. Hapisteen assured them that Ansleigh had only come to visit her out of respect and was leaving. By then Huittsu had joined them she asked what was happening. Ansleigh heard her voice and stepped out of the tepee. "What Hapisteen said is true. I am here out of respect for all of you. I do not wish to cause trouble. I will be leaving."

Hapisteen reached out and touched Ansleigh's hand and squeezed it. It was then that Huittsu spoke up. "You are not wanted here. You bring bad things to us. You are white and belong with your people." "I thought you were my friend?" Ansleigh started shaking from the hatred she felt coming from the group. Huittsu picked up a large stone from the ground and threw it at Ansleigh hitting her in the head.

She could feel the warm blood trickling down her face. Soon the other young woman threw a stone at Ansleigh as well. The young men joining in. Hapisteen was furious calling out to them to stop. Ansleigh started to run. She was frantic trying to find her mare, someone had taken it. Shila heard the commotion and stepped out of Healing Fox's lodge. When he reached his mother, he saw what was happening. He spoke in a sacred tongue those of the ancestors.

He walked up to Huittsu and took the stones from her hand. He was angry. The others knew better and threw their stones to the ground and

220

fled. Hapisteen nodded at her son in agreement. By then Ansleigh was running back into the mountains her mind frantically trying to understand what had just happened. She heard a horse running up behind her and bent down covering her head waiting for more blows. Instead a strong hand reached down to her. She looked up it was Shila and he pulled her up onto his horse.

82
"Jake"

Jacob and Zacharia were ready to leave the ranch that next morning. As they started out of the main gate, they saw a lone horseman heading into the ranch. It was Quin. Jacob was relieved to see him. For Katherine's sake. He had a large bundle strapped across the back of his saddle. They were soon to learn it was the body of Nel Garrison. Quin was exhausted as he rode straight through to get back. Jacob decided he would stay and help with Nel's burial. He would not allow Zacharia to see her. Karl was silent when he looked at her. He thanked Quin for bringing her home. Quin couldn't help noticing how this event had taken the life out of Karl. He was quiet all during the burial and service they performed. He seemed preoccupied as if somehow he wasn't really there. Their Dutch neighbors came for the wake and prepared a meal for the men. Jacob told Quin that Katy was safe and with her mother. A great weight had been lifted from Quin with those words.
After the funeral Jacob and Zacharia were ready to head back. Quin was going with them he was anxious to see his wife and daughter. Jacob admired him for what he had done.

"I don't know what to do and Dr. Haveston out of town." Mrs. Clancy was frantic as Justice had gone into labor. It was the middle of the night and what could she do? Justice was scared but she did what nature was intending. She had a wash cloth clenched between her teeth to help with the pain. She was drenched in sweat.

She begged Mrs. Clancy to go and fetch Miss Francie at Mrs. Jacks. "She is a mid-wife and can help me please." She screamed out in pain. "I can't go to that place for heaven sakes." She protested. Her husband had enough of her pretentiousness. He grabbed his hat and left. Within the hour. Miss Francie was at Justice's side.

Mrs.Clancy had to swallow her pride and her husband told her so. Justice had a long labor and she so wanted Jacob there. The baby finally made its arrival the next day at noon. It was a boy with thick black hair and big hands. Justice was so pleased. Wait till your father sees you. She no sooner said those words when Jacob came into the room. Miss Francie was tired but happy on a safe delivery. Mrs. Clancy was asleep in a chair next to the bed. "Well you did make it after all." Miss Francie told him. "I am going to leave the rest to you." "What do I owe you?" Jacob wanted to know. "Pssshh-nothing. Enjoy your little son." She said as she left. He sat on the bed and immediately kissed Justice. "I was so worried." He whispered. "I love you."
"He looks like you I think." Justice smiled as she looked into Jacob's face. He smiled. "And his hair he definitely got from you." Jacob said as he touched her face. "Can I hold him?" She lifted the infant up to his father. Jacob looked into his little face.
"A son can you imagine. What will be his name?" "You can name him." "No I want you to." "Jacob Charles Riley." Justice said softly. "I like it. Little Jake it is then. Me boy. Wait till your sisters see you."

Mrs. Clancy woke with a start. Seeing Jacob there made her uneasy. She took a peek at the baby smiling and excused herself. "I never thought she'd leave." He joked.

He put Little Jake into his mother's arms then he took off his boots and coat and climbed into bed next to Justice putting his arm across her and the baby. "I love you so much." He told her and fell fast asleep. Justice turned her face toward him and kissed him tenderly on his cheek.

Zacharia was so excited when he got back to Mrs. Jensen's he was full of stories about his adventure. Beatrice was happy to have him safely home. Quin found himself at a loss for words when he saw Katherine. Katy ran to her father begging to be in his arms. He held her tightly to his chest and tears were welling up in his eyes. He looked at Katherine. She stood there not saying anything. Beatrice and Mrs. Jensen left the room taking Zach with them. Quin was hurting but he didn't know what to say to her. Katherine broke the silence. "I was so angry Quin I am sorry. I thought you didn't care about me like you use to. That you didn't really care about being a father to Katy. How can you say that! Katherine what does a man have to do to prove his love for you?

I have been working to save money for the property, the deed is in your name. What more can I do?" Katy was getting upset with her parents arguing. She stared to cry. "No, no darl'n." Quin whispered kissing her face. Katherine becoming over wrought walked over to Quin wrapping her arms around him. "Please forgive me Quin. I don't know what gets into me. I do love you." "I know." he said as he kissed the top of her head.

The three of them stood there embraced in each other's arms.

83
"War"

It was the break of dawn when River Tree and the young warriors surrounded the Gold Mining Camp on the Armagosa River. He had planned on using the element of surprise to give his men the edge they needed. They had a few guns among them but mostly lances and bows were their weapons. He had torches ready to burn the tents and shanties. He sat astride his horse and looked down at the camp site. The same spot where weeks before he had sat with Healing Fox. He remembered the bodies of the two young boys and in that moment, he gave the signal to attack. They set the buildings and tents on fire. A little girl ran screaming from a tent with her night dress a blaze. Soon men and women were scurrying to take cover. Guns were fired and the fight for survival began. Burton was screaming and using profanity as he shot a young warrior from his horse.

There was hand to hand combat and arrows were finding their marks. Soon the entire camp was engulfed in flames. The battle lasted less than an hour and many dead bodies of men women and children lay on the ground. The miners lost many of their family members. River Tree called a retreat and before he left he buried a lance in the center of the camp. As a warning for the whites to leave the area. They picked up the bodies of those they could, as miners were still shooting at them. When River Tree returned to his village, he was dispirited. He had started out with thirty men and returned with eighteen. Hapisteen met him and brought him back to their lodge. She undressed him and bathed him. Smudging him and praying. He then left to find Healing Fox to do a sweat lodge.

River Tree needed to cleanse himself of the killing and the guilt he felt over the loss of innocent women and children. He never saw war as a way to make changes but he knew he was expected to avenge the lives of his people.

Burton rode into Crooked Hat that very same day to find August Mayfield. It was late by the time he found him. August knew something was up as soon as he saw Burton. He was still covered in the blood and dirt of battle. He told him all that had happened and that it was River Tree that was responsible. August was furious. He told Burton he would go with him, once he rounded up his hired guns.

By the time August reached the Gold mine the stench of death was everywhere. People were laid out for burial. Tin Pan was recruiting a burial detail. August rode up to the bodies not dismounting. The workers soon gathered around him. A young man spoke up. "You told us we would have protection. Where is it? My father lies dead and my brother. Can you bring them back?" "I am truly sorry for your loss. I will be sure you are more than compensated for this." "Money what good does that do them now?"

August's anger was growing. He told Pin Pan to make a list of the deceased and they were to have markers for their graves. He wanted a spot cleared to place a small cemetery. He called the remaining miners together. He told them if anyone wanted to stay he would leave his gunmen to keep watch. Anyone that wanted to leave they could. He would have Reverend Bigelow come out and consecrate the graveyard. He was planning on keeping the mine in full operation. If he had to hire an army to do it. He

224

would be damned if they were going to push him around. They will live to regret this day he warned.

84
"I Am Sorry"

Clegg stopped in at Maizey's to have lunch. He chose a small table in the corner. He preferred being by himself to eat. He didn't notice when he sat down that Thorton was sitting near by. He told Maizey he wanted some of her buffalo chili. His favorite dish. "Yah kin thank Ki for that he changed up ma recipe, it's much better than the old one." "Do you mind if I sit?" Clegg looked up it was Thorton. He stared at him coldly. "I heard you were back in town. So Europe was it as you had expected?" "Yes I just need to stay away from women." "What do you want with me?" "I need money." Clegg shook his head in disbelief "You are asking me for money? Why?" "I want to go to California. I have a business opportunity but I need cash to start. What kind of business? Thorton told him about the Medical supplier looking for a salesman to sell his product door to door. How it could lead to owning his own franchise. "You are sitting there telling me that you will be doing all the footwork so this here fella you met on a ship can take in sixty percent of the profits? That's bullshit. I thought you were smarter then that." "I am good at talking with people. It's something I would like to try. Besides you owe me that."

Clegg reached over and wrapped his hand around Thorton's neck. "I don't owe you a damn thing." Then he leaned back in his chair. Staring at Thorton he sighed. "How much do you need?" Thorton told him. "You will have to come back to my room I will see what I can do." Thorton hesitated at first not trusting Clegg. "Do you want it or not?" Clegg asked as he started toward the door. They left and headed to the hotel. Thorton knew he was tempting fate with Clegg.

But he was desperate to be out of Crooked Hat. Clegg had a small safe that he kept his valuables in underneath his bed. He pulled it out and took a stack of bills to pay Thorton. He thanked Clegg and said that he would be sending him payments until his debt was paid. "Don't bother." "What do you mean?" "I want to call it even. I am sorry for all the pain I caused you." "You don't have to do this." Thorton told him. "I survived." "I never have gotten over you and that is hard for me to admit. My temper is my road to perdition." He reached over and pulled Thorton to him. He kissed him passionately. "Now get to hell out of here." he yelled. Thorton left the room and hurried down the stairs. His heart was pounding and when he reached the outside. He ducked behind the building and vomited.

Thorton took the coach the next morning but before he left he stopped at the Livery Stable to see Zacharia. Saying good-bye was very hard for him to do because he loved his son. He couldn't keep up the pretense any longer.

He thought that this was probably the last time he would ever see him. He had an envelope with a letter addressed to Zach and one for Beatrice. Zacharia was happy to see him. They talked briefly about Zach's job. He told him about wanting to work on the railways and earning money to help his mother.

"Maybe we all can live together again like before." "I wish that it could be that way again Zach. But I have a job waiting for me." "You mean you are leaving again?" Zach looked down at the ground biting his lip. "I want to give you something be sure your mother gets this do you understand?" He handed Zacharia the envelope. He took it and looked into Thorton's eyes. Zacharia knew that something was different this time.

Thorton's eyes were tearing up. "Hey Zach I got to go. You treat your mother well do you hear me." He tousled Zacahria's hair with his hand. Then he walked away. Zacharia followed him out and down the street. He watched as Thorton boarded the coach. As it pulled away Zacharia felt with certainty he would never see Thorton again.

When he got home later that day he laid down on the sofa and stared at the floor. Beatrice noticed his behavior and asked him what was wrong? She felt his forehead and it felt warm. Mrs. Jensen said she had the cure for that a piece of her berry pie. He didn't want it he told her. "Zach you tell me what is going on?" He pulled out the envelope from his pocket. Beatrice looked at it. She knew Thorton's handwriting. "He wants you to read it."

She gave Zach his letter and asked him to read it to her. As he opened it a handful of money fell to the floor. There was a hundred dollars that Beatrice counted.

Zach
By the time you read this I will be on my way to California. I want
you to know that I love you . I always will. I have made choices that
were not always the best . But I have also learned from the
consequences. The main reason I have decided to move on is to save
you from the humiliation of what and who I am. I cannot live a
normal life, not the kind you want . The kind you deserve.
Someday when you are full grown you may look at this and
understand why I did it.
I want you to use this money for whatever you need. Whatever you
want to achieve in this life that is what you should do. Please be good
to your mother she loves you .
I will remember you for the rest of my life.
Your father,
Thorton Blythe

Zacharia looked up at his mother. "Why?" he asked. "Why didn't you tell me? You lied." "Zach please let me explain." "There is nothing you can say, you are a liar." He jumped up off the sofa. Running out of the house. Beatrice calling out to him. Mrs. Jensen tried to comfort her. "He'll be all right he needs to clear his head is all." Beatrice had dreaded this day and was angry with Thorton for doing it this way.

Clegg had packed up all his belongings. Leaving behind what he didn't need. He thought a lot about Thorton since he left. His life didn't have much meaning without him in it. He wasn't going to miss Crooked Hat or August Mayfield. He saddled his horse and rode due east. He was heading toward another war. He had grown used to the drama as men of his sort do.

85

"You Know I Will"

Shila took Ansleigh high into the mountains. He wanted to get away from the anger and hatred he saw in his people's eyes. They found a secluded spot in a deep ravine. Where he set up camp using what few provisions he had. He sat for a very long time not saying anything. Ansleigh slept on the ground, he had covered her with his shirt. As the air was cooler in this region. When she finally wakened she did not see him. She called out his name. He did not answer. She began to panic, had he left her? It was then that she saw him walking into the camp, carrying two rabbits he had killed. She told him she would dress them out. They worked together. Shila prepared the fire using mineral stones from his pouch. They ate and still Shila did not speak. Ansleigh finally broke his silence. In her limited use of Shoshone she asked him "Shila why did you bring me here?"

"I had to bring you to safety." He explained. "They were going to kill you." "But why? They were my friends." "There are no friends when it comes to revenge. That is why I am here. I need time to think to pray to the Grandfathers." He said he wished not to speak any further. Ansleigh did not understand Shila at times, he could be serious and moody. As the night grew near the air was cold. Shila told Ansleigh to wear his shirt. He had her lie near the fire. He then lay next to her for added body warmth. He was up at dawn and had gathered berries to eat. When Ansleigh saw him she smiled. "My mother used to make berry pie I can still remember." She savored the tart sweetness of the berries.

Shila would often look at her with discernment. "Where do I go from here?" She asked. "I cannot keep you from your family." I will return you to your father Shila told her. He reached out for the first time and touched her face.

"You know my heart." She leaned toward him wanting to kiss him. Their lips came so close to touching. But Shila pulled back. "Why?" Ansleigh wanted to know. There is much between our people. So much hatred and it is going to become worse. Shila struggled to let her know his feelings. "Thomas is gone and I am glad for it. And I love your mother and father." She took his hand in hers. "Is there no way?" Shila looked into her eyes "You are the one in my visions there is no other. I will take you to your father, so you will not be in harm's way." "What if I do not want to go?" Shila asked her to respect his wishes. They both cleared the camp and mounting the horse headed toward Crooked Hat never saying another word to each other. But as Ansleigh leaned her head into Shila's back she longed to always be with him.

They had reached the outskirts of town that day when they noticed a young boy walking down the road. The boy looked up at them. "It's you!" Zacharia said smiling. "You are the healer." "Remember me?" Shila acknowledged him. Ansleigh wanted to know what he was doing out there and not at work? "Don't matter none I am going to work for the railways." "What about your mother?" "I ain't talking to her." He said ignoring the question. "He is a great healer, he made me well again. I never forgot the bear. Why are you here?"

"He is bringing me home. If you wait Zacharia I will walk with you." "Can he come too?" "I am afraid not." Ansleigh sighed.

She slid off the horse. Looking up into Shila's face she touched his hand. He paused before he left holding her hand in his. Then he rode off leaving her and Zacharia.

Ansleigh asked Zacharia what was going on. He told her about his real father and how his mother withheld the truth from him. Ansleigh told him that she too had run from her father. Never thinking about all that could happen. She told him about losing her son and that the pain would never leave her. "Is that what you want to do to your mother?" "After all she was only trying to protect you. It isn't easy to be a woman alone you must realize that." Zacharia listened and decided she was right. He wanted to go to see his mother.

When they reached Mrs. Jensens. Beatrice was sitting on the porch steps. She cried in relief when she saw Zacharia. She hurried toward them. "Where did you find him?" "He found me." Ansleigh stood looking at him. Zacharia was feeling shame for what he had done. Beatrice gathered him into her arms kissing him. "Please don't ever do that again." "I am sorry mum." They all went inside. Jacob was there with Justice and their baby. Jacob was glad to see Zacharia safe. "I spent most of the day trying to find you and Maizey has a bee in her bonnet over this. You gave us all a bit of a scare." You need to make this right by your sister. "I know." Zachariah said hanging his head.

Jacob looked at Ansleigh with an odd expression on his face. She had forgotten that she was still in her Elk skin dress. Ansleigh looked over at baby Jacob smiling. "He is beautiful." Justice asked her if she wanted to hold him. Ansleigh reached out and placed the baby to her shoulder. "My little brother, he is so tiny. I forgot." 'It's all right." Jacob told her knowing she was remembering her son Peter.

"I know by the look on your faces, you wonder where I have been. I need to tell you some things about myself." She then proceeded to tell her father about Thomas returning only to leave her again. She spoke of Shila and how he had saved her life more than once. How she had lived with the Shoshone one winter. That she knew that there was a war about to start over Mr. Mayfield and his gold mine.

"I knew there was going to be trouble over this." Jacob said looking at Justice. "That man will meet his maker and account for all his sins." Justice said bitterly. Jacob had never heard her express any emotion involving August before.

He was told that the Sheriff was the one killing her brother. It had never dawned on him that August was the one responsible for Justice's wounds. She had told him it was a drunk that beat her. He stood there looking at her most certain that August Mayfield has something to do with this.

When Ansleigh asked about Katherine. Her father told her that they were going to California. They had left the day before to pick up a covered wagon in Pigeon Grove. They promised to stop back before they made their final journey to their property. Mrs. Jensen offered for Ansleigh to stay there until she decided what she wanted to do. Zacharia pleaded for her to say yes. Ansleigh accepted the offer. She was looking forward to being with her family again. They all ate supper together and talked about the situation with Mr. Mayfield and the Shoshone.

Before Jacob and Justice left that evening he asked to talk with Ansleigh alone. They went outside and sat on the porch together. Ansleigh watched as the lightning bugs flickered in the darkness. Jacob took her hand in his. "There are so many things I am sorry for." He told her. "I hope you can find it in your heart to forgive me.

I was so blind to things when you left. It took the journey here and learning to let go, that made me realize my weakness. Justice has opened me heart and I owe her everything for that. I am an old fool for starting a family again but I have never been happier." "I am happy for you father I am." "You mean that?" "Yes I do" "So tell me Ansleigh what about you and Thomas?" "There is nothing between us. He is dead to me.

"He took my baby he had no right." She said fighting her tears. Jacob pulled her into him. "Its all right me darl'n I am here." They sat together like that for a while. "Do you love him?" "Who?" "The young Indian man." "Shila, yes with all my heart." "Oh Ansleigh how can it ever be. A heart - ache you will have with this." "I know but I don't care. He is the one." Jacob sat silently knowing he could say nothing. "I could use your help." "Yes what is it?" I want to divorce Thomas. He will never return. And I feel I need to do this. Could you take me to Pigeon Grove to the Courthouse there?"

"Ansleigh you know I will."

86

"He Is My Son"

Beatrice heard from Mrs. Jensen that the Marshall was seen with Gilda at the Mayfield House. She thought she should know. "I do hope he isn't a masher." Mrs. Jensen told Beatrice. "It was probably a friendly chat nothing to worry about." Inwardly Beatrice was having reservations about Cooper. He had become increasingly possessive towards her. She didn't like it. Dr. Haveston had returned from Virginia. He was thinking of moving there and closing down his house.

231

It took him awhile to face Beatrice again. He felt ashamed of his actions and he wanted to thank her for her friendship. He went to Mrs. Jensen's to ask Beatrice if she would accompany him for lunch. He took her to Maizey's where they enjoyed a meal together. Beatrice couldn't help noticing how much healthier he looked then when last she saw him. He was dressed in a grey suit and a matching hat. He seemed more at ease and confident when he talked. He told her of his plans to move to Virginia. She asked him why? Aubrey told her about his father being there. "He is a stern man. We have always been at odds. You see he wanted me to have a practice there in Charlottesville. Instead I moved to New York and ended up marrying Esther. Which he was against from the start. Hind sight is I should have listened. He had paid for my education I owe him that."

"So why did you go back?" Beatrice wanted to know. "I felt I should see him again make amends for my sins. He still suffers from losing my younger brother Richard. He died from cirrhosis of the liver.

He wants to help me get my medical license reinstated." "That would be a good thing don't you think?" Beatrice added.

"To be honest I do love this profession. But my struggle is my alcoholism. I put myself in a sanitarium while I was there. My father visited me every day. He has inspired me to try. I am afraid the South will soon be involved in a civil war regarding slavery. President Buchanan will not take a stance on this issue. Our country is divided. All the more reason to be there for my father." "What about your practice here?" "It s not an easy decision to start over. But I must make an effort." He paused looking into Beatrice's face. "I wanted to personally thank you for all you have done for me. You are the reason for my return."

"I think you are the one that deserves to acknowledge yourself." "You treat me better than I deserve. I want to do something for you before I leave. I know how much you and Zacharia want your own place. I have signed over the deed to my house to you." He placed an envelope on the table. I need your signature to make it binding." Beatrice looked at him in disbelief. "I don't think I can accept this." "Yes you can. I want you to. The house is solid and will stand for years. If you wish you can sell it and use the money for whatever you deem right." "Why are you doing this?" "Please take it, it is yours." "Can I think about it?"

"Yes but I will be leaving within the week." Beatrice did not want to see him go. But she knew it was something he had to do.

It was late when Marshall Dawson climbed the stairs to his room. He felt as if some one were watching him. He looked down the hall before he unlocked his door. He then felt someone coming up behind him. He drew his gun and slowly turning around he saw Ingrid Cederholm standing there in the lamplight. "You want to get yourself killed?" he told her as she followed him into his room. "What are you doing here?"

"I need to talk with you." "You come to a man's room to talk?" "It is a matter of privacy." she said. Ingrid was nervous being alone with him. She wanted his attention and she had it. "So talk." "You must know that Miss Faye is seeing Dr. Haveston since he is back yah." "So?" "She use to talk about him to Gilda." "What are you getting at here?" "I think she vas sleeping vith him at his office." Cooper was becoming irritated by her gossip. "You know this for a fact?" "She had female troubles maybe she vas pregnant. The doctor he leaves town. Then he comes back to get her?" "So that is what you came to tell me?" "Yah I think a man should know these things. Ask her about Zacharia. He is not her brother." "How would you know that?"

"People talk in the town." By then the Marshall had, had enough of Ingrid. "You can leave now." He said coldly. "It is nice here, may be you can buy me a drink? I am not like Gilda. I can do things for you. I know how." "I think you need to leave and I will pretend I did not hear you. Or shall I have a talk with your father?" Ingrid was suddenly embarrassed. Her plan had not worked. She wanted this man. She knew that she wasn't pretty like her sister and Beatrice. But she could please him, she thought and maybe he would touch her as she longed for him to do. He stood there holding the door and his look of disdain ate at Ingrid's heart.

The Marshall decided that he must have a talk with Beatrice to quell his fears. He met with her the next morning. They went for a ride up to Beatrice's favorite spot a look out over a mountain ridge. She wanted to know what was so important that they meet in the morning. Cooper asked her if she was still interested in their courtship. He wanted to know if she cared for Dr. Haveston.

"Why are you asking me all of this? Has someone said something to you?' "Perhaps." He dismounted his horse. He helped her down as well. They both stood facing one another. "I want to know if you have ever slept with him." "No!" Beatrice said angrily. "He is my friend and employer nothing else." "You have never been pregnant by him?" "I don't need to answer these accusations." "I was told that Zacharia is your son is this true?" She was silent before she answered. She decided it was time for the truth. "Yes he is my son. From a relationship a long time ago." "Why didn't you tell me?" "I was waiting for the right time." "You lied to me!"
He grabbed her by the wrist and pulled her to him.

"All of this time I have been a gentleman with you. I thought of you in a respectful sense. You are nothing but a common slut." He kissed her hard on the mouth. She could tell he was getting excited. She drew her knee up hard and drove it into his groin. He let go of her bending over in pain. "You may think of me what you will. But no man will hurt me again." She went to her horse and rode off leaving him behind.

87

"It Is Through"

Shila went back to his people. Looking for his father. He was troubled by the energy he felt in the village. He saw young boys engaging in mock battles with war paint on their faces. He knew the men were preparing again for battle. He found River Tree with Many Horses they were working on making arrows. s father told him that he expected retaliation from the whites and they needed to be ready for them. Shila feared for his father and the death and sorrow that was sure to follow. River Tree said he did not expect a man of peace to be involved. But that he did need prayers of strength for their warriors to face the days ahead. Shila went to his mother Kachiri was there with her son Rabbit. He told his sister he needed to talk

234

with her. They walked to the water fall. The day was cool and early signs of autumn were beginning. He looked at Kachiri. He asked if she would take their mother back to the desert with her when she returned to Kocho. "I can sense the coming of death here it is strong. I want her safe." "You know I will do this. I must ask where you have been." "In the mountains." "I heard about the white woman. Why are you doing this?

There are young women here among our people, you only have to choose." "Kachiri why are you telling me what to do with my heart? Yes I could marry a woman of our clan. Would you have me unhappy and tied to a relationship dead at its center? I will be alone first. I have told her it can never be, is that not enough?" "Then you must also cut the cord." Kachiri warned him. "Not yet." Shila was angry with the situation.

They walked back to their mother's lodge. There they ate and talked of earlier times before the coming of the white men and their gold.

Rabbit was starting to walk and Shila enjoyed playing with him. As the evening wore on River Tree had joined his family. He said it made his heart happy that they were all together again. Shila told his father of the plan to take his mother with Kachiri to the desert home of Kocho. He was in agreement. At first Hapisteen resisted their request. River Tree insisted that she do this for him. She agreed if he would come to see her there. He conceded.

Shila wished his family a good rest as he went back to his tepee for sleep. His prayers were prolonged that night as he sought answers to all the things he knew were to come. He lay there unable to sleep thinking of Ansleigh and hoping she would be safe and how he would miss her. He often asked spirit what was the purpose of meeting her? Why place such longing in his heart? He saw her standing in the sun smiling at him. With her golden hair laying like a shroud about her shoulders. He started to drift off to sleep with this image in his mind.

He woke when he felt something rubbing against his back. He reached for his knife rolling over he placed the knife at the throat of the intruder. He could sense her in the darkness. Her lips sought his and she wrapped her leg over his thigh. She was naked. He could hear her heavy breathing.

He pushed her off from him. In the light of the fire pit he saw it was Huittsu. "What are you doing? What is this?" He was furious. "Many Horses has thrown me from his lodge. I have no place to go." "Where is your child?" "She is with his mother." He covered her nakedness with his blanket.

"I will be free soon and we can marry. If you will have me?" "Huittsu this is not what I want."

"It is because of her. The white woman. She has stolen your heart from me."

"No Huittsu I gave my heart to her freely." "It is I who loves you not her. I will give you many sons.

I will be a good wife and do whatever you ask of me." She went down on her knees and wrapped her arms about his legs. She touched him. He pushed her hands down. "You must not do this. I will speak with Many Horses about you." "It is too late. I told him of my love for you. He will not have me. I told him that you wanted me too." "Why? I do not understand why you have done this?"

"I love you so much." She cried. "Without you I will die." He lifted her to her feet. "You can stay with my mother tonight. We will talk tomorrow." He walked her to his mother's lodge. Hapisteen was not happy about the situation but for her son she took her in. She was to sleep next to Kachiri.

The next morning Shila went to talk with Many Horses. At first Many Horses would not let Shila into his lodge. Shila told him he needed to listen to the truth. "I will bring Healing Fox if you wish." Many Horses invited Shila in to his lodge. His mother sat there braiding Moon Rising's hair. She was a pretty child like her mother. Many Horses asked them to leave. She took the child and left. The men talked of their youth and their friendship. Shila told him that he did not understand Huittsu's motives. That he loved her like a sister and nothing more. That she had made up the story about them. Many Horses said he believed him as he was aware of her feelings for Shila. Even before they married. "You can be with someone but you cannot force their heart." "So what are you going to do?" Shila asked. "I cannot take her back.

Many people know of her shame. I will take care of Moon Rising. Huittsu will have to seek another if they will have her." Shila did not want to hear this. But he had to respect Many Horses' feelings.

Huitssu had brought this upon herself. He thanked Many Horses for listening and left. He wasn't sure what to tell Huittsu. For one moment as he walked back to his mother's lodge. He was thinking of marrying Huittsu to end the problem. Just before he was to enter the tepee a red tailed hawk swooped down and flew overhead. Screeching loudly. He stood outside the entrance looking up into the sky. He knew the answer.

He told Huitssu that day that she could stay with his family as long as she needed. That she would have to end the marriage with Many Horses and Healing Fox would perform the ceremony and cutting of the cord that bound them. Huittsu agreed and was hoping that Shila would forgive her. He told her it was over and to move on. During that week Healing Fox performed the letting go ceremony. Huitssu was happy to be free of him at last. She did grieve for her daughter. That night as Shila lay sleeping Huitssu again crawled into his lodge. She lay next to him and watched him breathing her heart was so full of love and desire for this man. This time she would be sure to do whatever it took to make him her own. She was getting ready to crawl back out before he knew of her presence. When he spoke "Huitssu why are you here?" She said nothing breathing shallowly as she edged her way out. "I will tell you this once. If you enter my lodge again un-invited I will not speak to you. I shall shun you is that understood?" She began to cry. He felt her pain but was angry at her refusal to listen to him. She spoke in a flat voice devoid of feeling. "Would you do something for me?"

"I know you do not wish to be my husband. Would you then give me a child? No one has to know. That way I will always have a part of you with me. I will then leave you alone."

"You ask me to do this? When in my heart I do not want it. You must leave I am through with all of this do you not understand? Now go!" he shouted. She crawled out and into the night running away from the village. Shila sat not sleeping until the dawn. It was Kachiri who found her. She had gone to the stream for water that morning. When she saw a body floating

237

face down. She waded out into the water and pulled it to shore. Turning it over she looked down into the face of Huittsu.

88

"Night Of The Mad Dog"

August was ready to retaliate for the skirmish at the Armagosa River. He had rounded up a group of vigilantes about fifty strong. He was paying them to fight and there was a bonus for any scalps they brought him. His plan was to attack River Tree's Camp at twilight. He was to be on higher ground watching from a distance. He did not want to be caught in the fray.

Shila was at a loss over Huittsu and the guilt he felt because of her death. He sat with Healing Fox and shared his feelings. He felt he should have taken her as his wife. Healing Fox told him that it would not have stopped her. "She wanted your soul and that is not the same as love." Shila would feel pain regarding Huittsu for the rest of his life.

The day of the Little River Massacre was quiet. People were eating their evening meals and preparing their fire pits as the day grew colder. River Tree had decided to rest and be with Hapisteen as she was to leave the next morning. Kocho had arrived to bring back his wife and son and take her with them.

Shila was helping guard the camp with the others as they rode the perimeter of the village.

This was the calm before the storm.

The camp dogs began to bark. The trees surrounding the encampment were set on fire. Horsemen entered shooting and burning lodges with their torches. People were fleeing, trying to seek cover as they were being shot at. Shila immediately headed to his father's lodge. Kachiri was lost in the bedlam she had went to comfort Huittsu's mother. Not knowing that men were just outside of their camp.

She wanted to get to her husband and son. The cries of the wounded and dying were everywhere. She covered her ears and ran blindly towards her father's lodge. A rider swung down to lift her to his horse. He stunk of

238

whiskey and his eyes were wild. She fought kicking and biting. Kocho was there and pulled her down as he jumped onto her captor. Killing him instantly with one powerful blow to his skull. She was frightened by the chaos and violence. Kocho kept telling her to be with him. To let go of the darkness she saw all about her. She followed him to her father's lodge.

River Tree was glad to see his daughter safe. He told Kocho to take his family and leave. Hapisteen was crying. She told him *Wastechilake* (I love you) He embraced her.

"Now go!" She looked back at him one more time before she left. Kocho had to fight his way through the melee to protect his family. Mounting their horses, they rode off into the river to avoid tracking and the fires. River Tree set about gathering some of the women, children and elders. Shila was there to help. They hid them among the willows and Shila found a gully where they had them lie down as he and his father quickly covered them with brush and fallen branches.

Returning they continued to assist those they could. In the midst of all the violence two small children were screaming for their mother. They were terrified. River Tree immediately ran to their rescue. Before Shila could save him. His father was stabbed in the back and then his throat was slit. He fell to the ground holding one of the children. Shila lept into the air grabbing his father's attacker by his throat and pulling him down. He lifted him over his head breaking the man's back. He then threw him into a burning lodge. The children were both killed by gunfire.

Shila wept as he carried his father's body to the river laying him in the tall reeds. Some of the women were raped and the men scalped. They had no place to go and were not prepared for this ambush. The night of the mad dog was upon them.

Shila was enraged as he felt the bear spirit within him. He continued to help those he could to safety. Then as quickly as it had begun the fighting was over. The vigilantes rounded up the remaining survivors. August then came down from his hide-out and made prisoners of the remaining few. Shila hid high in the crevice of two boulders watching. There were several of the vigilantes lying wounded and dead. August left them as he tied the

239

prisoners together and marched them out into the darkness. They set up a camp a mile from the battle scene. He left two men for burial detail the next day. It never happened because they were to frightened of being killed so they rode off never returning.

Shila did not sleep that night finding his father he sat holding him until dawn. In the morning the small group of survivors emerged from their hiding. They set about gathering the dead as the women keened. They found the mutilated body of Healing Fox he had been scalped and dragged by a rope through the camp until his body was a bloody carcass. Shila and Broken Lance created a burial ground higher up from the site. It took them two days to build the scaffolds and bury those who were burned beyond recognition.

Shila walked through this time feeling nothing. The camp smelled of burned flesh and flies were everywhere. The carnage was haunting. The black soot was in their lungs and on their bodies. It hung heavy in the early morning sun. Shila fell exhausted by the river. He lay there for hours. When he was awakened by a familiar voice.

He looked up and it was Many Horses he was holding the hand of his little daughter. "It is true then you are still with us." said Many Horses. He was badly burned over most of his face and hands. Shila stood embracing him. "It is good you are here." Shila looked into Many Horses eyes he realized at that moment that he was in great pain. "I will give you healing plants for your pain." "Can you give me a healing for my heart? We have lost much."

That night the people gathered to talk about where they should go and who would lead them.

They wanted Shila to be there leader and Holy man. Shila said he did not think he was ready for such a task. He was troubled and full of anger. He asked Broken Lance if he could take this responsibility. "I am not able at this time to do this. If you will be our leader. I will be there for you. Broken Lance did not want to take on such a responsibility. But he knew that Shila needed this time to heal his wounds.

Shila told the people that they should move under the cover of darkness to a place of safety. So the white man could not find them. "You shall be as a light in this darkness. Know your father is watching." Shila looked to see who had said this. Coming toward him out of the shadows was Night Wing.

89

"If His Spirit Wants"

The news was all over Crooked Hat about the killings out at The Armagosa River. Burton was bragging that "This taught those Indians where they belonged." "Manifest Destiny," was here to stay he told everyone. Some of the miners feared retribution from the Shoshone. Burton told them that Mr. Mayfield was taking care of that. He would bring in the miliary if necessary.

Ansleigh was residing at Mrs. Jensens. She was thinking about heading to California with her father and Justice. They were planning on moving with Katherine and Quin and starting a new life. That was until she heard about the massacre. She thought about Shila and his family. Her thoughts were they had been killed. She laid in bed at night muffling her sobs. August Mayfield marched the prisoners into town. There were men, women and children in the group. About twenty people. He wanted the town's people to come to the hangings. They were to take place at his hanging tree within the week. Mary told him this was not a good idea that people would hate him for this. He laughed at her. "They already hate me that is how I keep them in line. Fear is a great equalizer. When will you learn that the strongest are the rulers of this world? You best keep to yourself and let me take care of my business." She had learned not to argue as it meant a fist in her face.

Cooper Dawson was furious when he heard about the hangings. He went to August and told him that he could not allow something like this to take place. He offered to take them to a government reservation being set up near Utah. August lied and told him that he would think about it. But by the dawning of the next day he had already hung eight of the natives. When

241

Reverend Bigelow heard about it he gathered a group together to confront August. Maizey and Ki, Mrs. Jensen, Ansleigh, Jacob, and Mr. Cedarholm, Beatrice, Zacharia and Dr. Haveston were in the group of protesters. August had the prisoners bound and gagged. Tin Pan was the one that had built the scaffold for the hangings. August told them that he was the Mayor that the Indians had killed and maimed his workers. That this was justice being served. "Against women and children?" Beatrice shouted out at him. His hired guns were surrounding the site. "Shoot the first person that moves." August warned. He then proceeded to bring two women to the scaffold. Cooper wanted to stop him. Zacharia could take it no longer as he burst forward running he jumped on August punching him. Guns were cocked and aimed. Beatrice screamed out "No!!" Dr. Haveston immediately ran to help Zacharia. They shot him in the side and in his right leg. At that point Cooper stepped forward. "You shoot me and you will have the law here I guarantee it. How many people have to die before you come to your senses? This goes beyond revenge." August told his men to stand down. Beatrice had run to Aubrey's side. He was already incoherent. "Let me take the prisoners with me to Utah. What is there to gain by more killing?" "I want to be sure the Indians get my message."

"You've more then made your point. If you don't stop this, I will report your actions to the President. He already has your name under investigation." "This is an act of war."

"They are my prisoners." "No, this was a massacre. There is no legislation that defines this as a war." August did fear government involvement and agreed to let them go with the Marshall. They carried Dr. Haveston's body to his office. Beatrice knew that he was in a bad way. She held back her tears. Jacob lifted him to the examining table and opened his shirt. "Looks like the bullet went clean through. But he's going to need help. If he keeps losing blood like this." "Is he gonna die?" Zacahria wanted to know. "I hope not." Beatrice said holding Zacharia close to her. It was then that Ansleigh had an idea. "Keep him as comfortable as you can." She told Beatrice. "Zacharia come with me." Ansleigh gave Zacharia a pouch with herbs in it. "Be sure to apply this to his wound it will stop the bleeding. And if he can drink water as much as he can. I have to go. I will return."

242

Ansleigh was a day's ride from the summer camp she never slept. When she arrived she couldn't believe her eyes. The ground was black as far as she could see. The charred remains of trees and the over powering smell of burned flesh still hung in the air. It was quiet, no barking dogs. In the starkness of this place, nothing was stirring. She thought that it was too late and the survivors had moved on by now. She decided to ride through anyway in hopes of finding Shila alive. She knew that her life was in danger but she had to take the chance. It was then she saw an old woman rummaging through the debris looking for remnants of whatever she could find. She remembered Ansleigh from the winter she spent with them. She pointed her finger toward the mountain. Ansleigh urged her horse forward and went in that direction. She passed the burial ground and out of respect did not venture there. She couldn't help wondering if Shila or his family may have been buried in this place. She kept going.

She soon came upon a small encampment. Dismounting her horse, she cautiously walked toward the make shift shelters.

She recognized Many Horses but did not see Huittsu or River Tree. No sign of Healing Fox. She knew intuitively that they were gone. She squatted down and waited to see if Shila might appear.

"Why are you here?" She turned around falling to her knees. It was Shila standing above her. She told him as best she could about Dr. Haveston needing help. "You come here asking me to help the whites!" He said angrily. "My heart is broken and I am full of hatred. I want you to go from here. Return to your people." Ansleigh could only imagine what he must be feeling.

"Your pain is mine as well. You once told me that hate eats at a man's soul. Why then are you letting this destroy you? Can we not reach out past all of this? I am asking you to use your gifts. I know Healing Fox would want you to do this." "Tell him that, tell my father. They are both dead." Shila then smashed his fist into a tree. Ansleigh stood silent. She turned from him and started to walk a way.

She did what she thought was right, she could do no more. Shila walked up besides her taking her hand he walked her to safety. He mounted his horse and followed her as they rode on into the darkness. Ansleigh fell asleep on her horse. Shila stopped knowing he could not leave her alone. He carried her off her horse laying her down. He could not build a fire as it would draw attention. So he sat next to her as she slept. He knew it took courage for her to come to him. As much as he felt this bitterness, he could never feel it towards her. He soon dozed off. He had a dream where Healing Fox came to him. He told Shila that he must keep his vows of being a Medicine man.

He told him that he would be tested many times in his life. By the time Ansleigh was awake Shila was ready to leave. She looked at him with concern and then mounting her mare she headed in the direction of Crooked Hat. Shila watched her go. He heard branches and twigs breaking in the woods. He turned toward the sound. His horse reared up in fear. Shila slid to the ground. The large Grizzly appeared. He lumbered over to Shila sniffing his hand then rising on his hind legs he roared into Shila's face. Shila did not care if at that moment the bear were to take his life. The Grizzly slowly departed leaving Shila alone with his thoughts. He knew then he must help the doctor. He followed Ansleigh into Crooked Hat.

He asked her to take him to the doctor. When she arrived Beatrice and Zacharia were there with Dr. Haveston who was still unconscious. Zach was excited to see Shila and Beatrice remembered him from the healing. He told Ansleigh he would need to be left alone with the doctor for as long as it took and that he would need her help at times. "Will he live?" Beatrice wanted to know? Shila spoke. "If his spirit wants to stay." Ansleigh interpreted back to her. Shila asked Zacharia to help him by keeping intruders from interfering with his work. Zacharia said he would be more than honored to do so.

90

"Winter Of Replenishing"

Katherine was upset over what had happened to Dr. Haveston and told Quin that she wanted to leave as soon as possible. He was in agreement he feared for Katy and he knew that this was only the beginning of trouble between the whites and the natives. Katherine wanted her father and Justice to go with them. She wanted to leave within the week. They had their wagon loaded with supplies. Katherine was anxious to get to California before the weather changed. Jacob told them to wait until things settled down. He didn't think it was safe to travel just yet. Spring would be better he told her. Ansleigh won't leave until the doctor is out of danger. Katherine insisted that they leave. She would look for her father and sister when they could make it. She was adamant. Justice begged them to stay as well. They left early one morning without saying goodbye.

Shila stayed on for two days working with the doctor. Cleansing his wounds using healing herbs and prayers to bring him back. Dr. Haveston was sitting up on the third day and was able to drink and eat a little food. Beatrice was there the whole time with Zacharia. The doctor thanked Shila. He knew he would have died without his help. Shila wanted to leave to get back to his people. He knew with Night Wing's return things were going to change. Ansleigh rode out with Shila to the mountains. Before he left her. She asked if she would ever see him again. "You know I carry you in my heart. There is much between us that I cannot cross over. It is the same for you." With that he rode off.

Beatrice stayed on with Aubrey and helped nurse him back to health. He told her it would be spring before he would attempt to return to Virginia. Beatrice was glad he was staying. He feared that Mr. Mayfield had brought down the wrath of God with his actions. I think we need to be mindful these days. He asked her about Cooper Dawson, and she told him that it was over and as far as she was concerned it was for the best.

Jacob was upset over Katherine leaving without a farewell. He was very worried for them. Justice agreed that they should have waited until spring. Beatrice had finally signed the deed to the house. Aubrey was pleased. She told him that she wanted to invite Jacob and Justice to stay with her for the winter. With baby Jake they needed more room then what they had at Mrs. Clancy's. He was in agreement. Ansleigh stayed with Mrs. Jensen at her bidding.

245

Winter came early and people were more at ease as things had settled down from the upheaval of the fall.

Jacob and Justice were happy to have more space. Dr. Haveston as his strength returned took on a few patients as he was able. Beatrice helped him at the office. He decided to teach her how to dispense medicines, dress minor wounds and how to deliver babies. Beatrice felt as if she had found her calling.

Cooper Dawson started to see Gilda they would meet at the church on Sundays and sit together. Batilda was hoping that he was getting serious over her daughter. She wanted her daughters married and with families. One Sunday he asked Sven if he could court her and he agreed. Ingrid burned with jealousy. She was going to have her way whatever it took. Cooper had written to his superiors in Washington about the hangings. He finally received a letter from The Bureau of Indian Affairs.

They stated that it was unfortunate that lives were lost but what Mr. Mayfield had done was within his rights. As he was protecting his family and the citizens of his community. However if there were further complications to address the matter to them and they would administer to it , post haste. It wasn't what he had anticipated. He did not like August Mayfield and he knew there would come a day he would bring him down.

Shila went back to the encampment that day after leaving Ansleigh. He was troubled and missed his father and his spiritual teacher Healing Fox. He felt alone. When he arrived Broken Lance met with him. They talked about their future and how they would move forward after losing so many. That week Shila called a council of elders. There were only two elderly men left from their clan. There were older women and children. A few young men and young women that had survived the massacre. He chose among them who would sit on the council meetings. He put Many Horses in charge of making weapons. He asked Broken Lance to teach the young men how to fight and be prepared for any surprise attacks. He vowed that never again would they be ambushed. He would take on the responsibilities of his father as leader. As well as the medicine man for their group. Broken Lance was his alternate. When he was involved with healings and ceremonies. They stayed the winter on higher ground. Avoiding the possibility of

246

confrontations with the white men in the valley. During this time Night Wing asked Shila to consider making peace with the Arapaho. He had spent some time with them after he had left. He married a young daughter of a tribal elder and became friends with their clan leader. He had two young sons. Shila asked him why did you return here? Night Wing wanted to see Shila to thank him for saving his life.

He was sad to see what had happened. He told Shila that if they joined forces with the Arapaho .Then the white man would have a real threat to deal with.

He wanted Shila to attack the town of Crooked Hat. That would cripple the gold mine and chase the white men out of the area. Shila wasn't sure he wanted to risk anymore lives of his people. Also that his grandfather had been a long time enemy of the Arapaho. He wanted to live in peace and rebuild his clan.

Night Wing told him that he needed to think about this because the Arapaho were already planning on attacking the miners in the valley.

91
"Ingrid's Revenge"

It was close to Thanksgiving and Marshall Dawson and Gilda Cederholm were planning a Sunday wedding at the church. With Reverend Bigelow officiating. They had invited several of their friends and neighbors to attend. Beatrice bowed out as she was not involved with them anymore. Her life was busy with the doctor and the Riley's.

Sven and Batilda were happy about the union. The wedding was to be simple. They were hosting a party at the store after the ceremony. Sheriff Daniels was the best man and Ingrid the Maid of Honor. Just before the ceremony was to start Batilda kissed Gilda on her cheek. Telling her that everything would be all right. That men had to be tolerated and a good wife would listen and be obedient. She left the room to find a seat next to Sven. Gilda was wearing a light grey dress with a high collar covered in lace and pink cloth roses trimmed the bodice. Ingrid had styled her sisters hair and was attaching a small lace veil. "Vell you have vaited long enough yah." "I am happy and sad at the same time." Gilda said as she looked up at Ingrid. "Sad but vhy?" "Ingrid I know you like him too. I think you vill find the right one soon." She reached up squeezing Ingrid's hand. "So how do I look?"

"Pretty as you alvays do. This is not the time to say this but I must" "Say Vhat?" "Don't be mad at me but I must tell you." "So tell me!" "Back in the summer Marshall Dawson he invites me to his room yah." "Vhat are you saying?" Ingrid paused and she was feeling powerful as she held her sister in suspense. "He makes me drink. I have to do things for him." "Vhat things?" "Things that men like."

"He vas enjoying it too. Maybe I am pregnant? I don't know such things." Gilda looked at her sister in horror. Her whole world suddenly collapsed. She ripped off her veil grabbing her coat and bonnet she ran out of the church into the snow. She found an empty carriage and drove it out of the churchyard into town. She was upset and feeling desperate. Trying not to envision Ingrid and Cooper together. Where to go, what to do? Went racing through her mind. She decided to go and see Beatrice for some reason it made sense to her.

She stood out on the porch shaking. She pounded on the door. Beatrice answered. She couldn't believe her eyes. Gilda was hysterical. "Why aren't you at the church? What has happened?" Gilda could barely get the words out of her mouth when Justice entered the room with Jake on her hip. Gilda blurted out all the lies that Ingrid had told her. Beatrice calmed her down and Justice fixed her a cup of tea. "Is there a reason you came here?" "You know him, vhy did you leave him? I must know."
"The truth is he doesn't respect me. He changed once I got to know him. I knew that it would be a mistake to marry him."

"But I love him." cried Gilda. "I doubt he did what your sister said. I think she is jealous of you plain and simple. You are a pretty woman. If I were you, I would be looking for someone that you can trust." "Beatrice is right." Said Justice. "Can I stay vith you? I cannot face anyone not now."

"Yes you can. You can have my room. I will sleep on the sofa." Gilda went and curled into a fetal position on Beatrice's bed and fell asleep still in her wedding dress.

Cooper Dawson was furious at being stood up at the altar and embarrassed. The Cederholms were in shock. They asked Ingrid what had went wrong and where was her sister?

Ingrid again lying told them that Gilda confessed to not loving the Marshall. She tried to stop her but she ran off not knowing where. Before Cooper left the church that day one of the wedding guest told him his carriage had been stolen. They set out to find it. They found it in front of Dr. Haveston's place. Cooper told the young man to take it and leave. He would settle the matter. Knowing full well that Gilda was the one. He approached the house Dr. Haveston answered. Everyone was getting ready to sit down to eat. Cooper asked if Gilda was there and could he speak with her? The doctor told him that she was sleeping and that he should try again the next day. Cooper refused to leave. He demanded to talk with her. Gilda had heard his voice and walked into the parlor. "I vill talk vith you."

Dr. Haveston offered his office for their privacy. Cooper was furious as he lashed out at her for all the embarrassment she had caused him. She cried and told him every thing her sister had said about him. He said it was a pack of lies and that her sister was so ugly that even a drunkard wouldn't sleep with her. "If you take her word against mine then we are through." As he went to leave. Gilda grabbed his arm. "Please I am sorry. Can you forgive me?" She begged. He took her hand in his. They talked after that agreeing on a small wedding with no guests. They were married the following week in the General Store by Reverend Bigelow. With only Mr. and Mrs Cederholm in attendance. Gilda was through talking with her sister and after that they remained distant and non-relating.

92

"Things Are Not What They Seem"

Things seemed back to normal for a while. It was a week before Christmas and the snows were steady. There was a skeleton crew working at the Armagosa Gold mine and August was writing to the Railroad Companies trying to entice one of them to venture out west. He still had dreams of a railway station and bringing more people to Crooked Hat. He spent more and more time away from Mary and practically lived at the hotel. Mary was perfectly happy not to see him. She was enjoying the freedom and being with Emery.

Jacob had received a letter from Martha warning him to stay put as Philadelphia was presently engaged with the beginning of a Civil War. Threats were made that there would soon be an invasion of the North. Her husband had secured passage to Europe should the need arise. It was little respite from his fears. He had no idea how Katherine was doing and spring could not come soon enough for his journey to California. Justice surprised him with news of another baby on the way. Justice had never been happier in her life than she was with Jacob. She loved him so very much as she was fond of telling him. Jacob felt the same he loved his little family. He was still working at the General Store through out the winter. Ansleigh was restless and the days were long for her. She worked at the bakery making bread with the Friedans.

Dr. Haveston was troubled about his father and was thinking of leaving right after Christmas to be with him. He knew how the situation was there. Beatrice worried about him as his health was still fragile. With the Holidays approaching he wanted to take Beatrice out to dinner.

The hotel was the best eatery in the town. He asked her if it was all right as he wanted to do something special for her. She hated August but was willing to chance he wouldn't be there. It just so happened he wasn't. They had a full course dinner with wine. Beatrice was wearing a lovely burgundy dress with her hair swept up in curls. Aubrey told her he had never seen her look as enchanting as she did that evening. They talked about the Civil War and the present state of affairs with the Indians. He told Beatrice that he might come back. For what she asked him. Isn't it obvious he told her? She looked at him "Are you referring to me?" "Who else?" He smiled. Taking her hand in his. "I think you must know by now how I feel. Or am I assuming too much?" She sat there thinking about what he had said. "Unless you still have feelings for Marshall Dawson?" "No, no. If anyone knows about me, it is you." She told him. "You must understand that Zacharia is with me." "Yes?" "What you need to know is he is my son."

"That is not a surprise. I already knew." "How could you?" "He told me." "He told you? But why?" "It was when I was bedridden he came to sit with me and we talked. He told me about his father and how he wanted to leave and work on the railways. He is very grown up for his age." "He has had to be with me as a mother."

"You are a wonderful mother. Zach thinks you are." "To be honest I didn't realize how much having a home meant to me until now. I have traveled so much, no roots."

"It gets to be a way of life. I want more for my son." Aubrey leaned into her kissing her softly on the lips. She returned the kiss.

Christmas came and Maizey planned a get together at her house. Beatrice and Zacharia were there with Jacob and Justice.

They invited Mrs. Jensen, Ansleigh and Dr. Haveston. The meal was prepared by Ki he made Maizey sit and he did all the work. Everyone was in high spirits that day.

Singing Christmas carols as Justice played Maizey's piano.

Things were quiet at the Mayfield Mansion. August sat in his study getting drunk and shooting his gun into the fire place. Mary sat holding onto Emery at the oversized dining table laden with food they would never eat. Emery buried her face into her mother's shoulder she was terrified of what her father might do. He was often like this. Gilda and Cooper stayed in his room at the Hotel having food brought to them. He told Gilda he was thinking about leaving for Washington and taking a position there. With the Civil War starting he wanted to be politically involved. He told Gilda that she was welcome to come with him or stay with her family. That bothered her as she thought he was going to adore her. After their wedding night he became indifferent. She didn't understand.

251

He told her he was in no hurry for children and that she should do something to prevent it if at all possible. He would let her know when he was ready. Gilda knew that she had made a mistake. Some things are not what they seem.

 As people were celebrating. Night Wing and a band of Arapaho were on their way to the mine in the Armagosa Valley.

93

"Revenge Is Lost On The Sender"

Katherine was holding onto Katy and singing an old Christian hymn from her childhood. She tried not to look at Quin's body as it hung from a pole in the center of the camp. They had tortured him before he died. She kept thinking about her father and trying to keep her sanity for Katy's sake. But she was terrified. She wanted to go back to Philadelphia and her life there. If she had never left, perhaps Quin would still be alive. Katy had quit crying. She was listless. Katherine could feel her baby kick. Why hadn't she stayed as her father beseeched her to do? They were only a few days out when they were taken by a band of Arapaho. They captured them and rummaged through their wagon. Quin, kept begging them to take him and to let Katherine and Katy go. A young native kept touching Katherine. Quin couldn't bear to watch it and went up against him. They decided to kill him. Katy was screaming the whole time. Katherine became numb from the trauma. Her thoughts were about protecting Katy and her unborn child. It kept her alive. She was forced to work and to help the women of their tribe. All she could think of was escaping but how?

It was early morning when Night Wing and his band of followers reached the Armagosa Gold Mine they ambushed the workers killing them all. They ransacked the buildings and took what gold they could find. Night Wing said they could use it. He wanted to be in Crooked Hat while it was still light. They had brought guns with them as well as their bows and lances. He had selected some of the best fighters as he knew it was going to be a challenge attacking the town.

Shila had tried to talk Night Wing out of attacking the whites. He told him there would only be more loss of life. He knew that they would bring in the Army and they would be forced to give up their lands. The vision of his youth was playing out before him. He went deep into the woodlands and found a place to fast and pray. He needed answers. While he was there, a wolf came to his camp. She laid down across from the fire pit. He could see her amber eyes glowing in the fire light. He recognized her as the wolf he had pulled the splinter from. He saw in his minds eye Ansleigh and her people being attacked. Then he saw a large black raven as it swooped down and landed on a nearby rock. It looked at him and cawed. Night Wing was the reason for this. Revenge Healing Fox had told him would come back to you if you sought it. It was pointless and took away your personal power. Shila knew he had to move quickly. He went back to his camp and told Broken Lance about his vision and that he needed to go. He was leaving him in charge of the people. Two young men wanted to go with him. Spotted Owl and Deer Run. He told them this wasn't their fight. That he was going to try and stop a war not start one. They knew and wanted to be with him.

It was Sunday the day after Christmas. People were coming out of the church. The stores were closed except for the Livery stable and Cederholms. Tin Pan was weaving across Main Street with a Whiskey bottle in hand. He squinted his eyes as he saw smoke coming from the Livery stable. Then he saw the flames. Fire! He screamed racing down the street. Like a scourge they came from every direction. Shooting and smashing store front windows. They were on roof tops and hidden behind barrels and wagons.

They set Maizey's Corner on fire and broke into people homes stabbing and shooting. Scalping those they could. Night Wing was in the lead barking out commands of what he wanted. Soon people were running from their houses trying to find cover.

Cooper grabbed Gilda and carried her to safety he left her with a gun and told her to shoot and ask questions later. He went to find Sheriff

Daniels. He found him with an arrow through his neck slumped over his desk.

Jacob needed to protect Justice and Ansleigh. He hid Justice and Jake in the fruit cellar and made Beatrice go with her. Zacharia refused to go. He wanted to help the men. Jacob gave him his hand gun. Aubrey and Jacob barricaded the house and had their rifles loaded and aimed. Jacob told Aubrey he needed to go and get Ansleigh and bring her there. As he went out the back door. Ansleigh and Mrs. Jensen were already running toward him. He helped them inside. Ansleigh had her rifle loaded and was prepared to fight.

Ki and Maizey had both went to Ki's shed and watched the main house with their rifles ready. They broke into Cederholms looting and smashing taking food and whiskey. Batilda was terrified as her and Ingrid hid in the corner of the bedroom behind a screen. Sven was shot when he tried to defend his business. Several houses were now on fire and hand to hand combat broke out between the Natives and the white men.

Cooper rode out to the Mayfield Mansion to find August. When he arrived, he found Mary and Emery alone. Mary wasn't aware of what was happening in town. She told Cooper she didn't know where August was. One of the servants said they saw him leave that morning on horseback. Cooper made Mary and Emery hide in their cellar along with the servants. He made sure they were armed. He then headed back into town.

By the time Shila reached Crooked Hat several dead bodies lined the streets and half of the town was on fire. He wanted to find Ansleigh. He rode to the doctor's house. Dismounting he made his way around the outside. Peering in he could see Ansleigh with her father and the doctor. So he would not be shot. He made the bird call that he had taught her.

Ansleigh immediately whistled back. "It's him!" "What are you saying?" Jacob asked. "Shila he's here."

"I need to let him in. No it could be trap." Father he will not harm me. She went to the door and before they could stop her she slid outside. Shila was glad to see her safe.

He told her he must find Night Wing and try to stop him. He started to get on his horse when Ansleigh jumped up behind him. "You cannot do

254

this." He told her. "Then I will follow you." He knew she was serious. They worked their way slowly behind the buildings. Shila joined Spotted Owl and Deer Run. They remembered Ansleigh. Deer Run told Shila where Night Wing was. He was at the General Store and he was drunk on whiskey. Shila told Ansleigh to stay on his horse and wait, and to leave if danger threatened. He took Spotted Owl and Deer Run with him. They climbed up on the roof. Breaking out a window they climbed into the upstairs bedroom. Batilda clung to Ingrid closing her eyes waiting to die.   Shila signed to be quiet as they made their way down the stairs into the store area. Mr. Cederholm was sitting with his back against the counter his eyes still open. He had been shot through the chest. Shila crept silently, signaling to the young men to come in from the sides.

Night Wing was drinking heavily and three of his men were trying on Batilda's blankets and strutting around, they had been drinking too. Shila came up from behind putting his knife to Night Wing's throat as the young men captured the drunks.

"So Shila you are here." "Yes! You must stop before any more people have to die." "You are a fool like your grandfather Grey Elk. When there is a bear loose in the camp you kill it. It is too late. We must take what we can. Teach the white man that he is not our keeper.
"Kill me if that is your wish. I will not stop until they are gone from here." "That can never be."Shila said as he put his knife away." I want to help my people as I can. Not sacrifice their lives for my idea of what is right."
"Then you deserve to die as a coward!" Night Wing told him as he walked away and out the front door of the store. Shila followed him. Marshall Dawson was standing across the street with his gun aimed at both of them. He shot Night Wing in the chest and Shila dove to the ground then lept up to the porch roof. The Marshal was shooting at him.
Ansleigh rode to the side of the building. Shila jumped from the roof; then mounting his horse, they both rode off together.

94

"The Letter"

With Night Wing dead most of the natives retreated. They took his body and gathered the bodies of the wounded. The miners were out numbering them with their guns. By nightfall many of the houses were still burning. The next morning was a bitterly cold day. People were coming out from their hide outs. They had started a body count. Marshall Dawson saw to the burial detail. Dr Haveston set up a make shift hospital in the Opera House as it was still standing. Beatrice helped and Jacob. Mrs. Jensen was there wrapping wounds along with Gilda. Maizey and Ki fixed meals for the workers. Reverend Bigelow was housing people who had lost their homes at his rectory and the church. Batilda gave blankets, food and medicine to those who needed it. Everyone was coming together to salvage what they could. The question on most people's lips was where was Mr. Mayfield?

Shila took Ansleigh with him to his encampment. Spotted Owl and Deer Running were with them. When he returned, he called a council. He told Broken Lance and his people what had happened at Crooked Hat. Night Wing was gone and with him the ways of war. He was prepared he said to talk with the white men in Washington. He knew that the white men were warring among themselves over slavery. He did not want this fate for them. He told them that he would still be their leader and give spiritual council. He would not be devoured by hatred and sought peace. "Those who wish to fight I will not stop you. It is foolish to think we can win against something that is like a mighty fire devouring everything in its path. Soon we will be asked to leave our mountain home.

To a place that is not familiar. You must remember our ancestors. They live on in us. Who you are can never be destroyed, who you are is free. No man can take that from you ever."

Shila spoke of Ansleigh saying she was there to seek refuge and was going to write to the great white father in Washington asking him for help. A small battalion of soldiers rode into town later that week with August Mayfield in the lead.

Marshall Dawson and Tin Pan were there to greet them. The Marshall wanted to know where August had been during the fight. He told him that he had went to Pigeon Grove to find a messenger to reach a small outpost of soldiers in the Sierras. "How did you know we were going to be attacked?" Cooper asked. "I didn't." Was the reply. "You mean to tell me you left your wife and daughter to fend for themselves?"
"That Marshall Dawson is none of your concern? Now leave it! Before I say someth'n I will regret. I need help sett'n up quarters for the soldiers."

During the week that followed people were busy tearing down the burned buildings and boarding up broken windows and repairing their houses. The weather was not cooperating as snow storms were hampering their progress. Many of the miners were moving out with their families they'd had enough. They weren't waiting around for another Indian attack. August promised them double their pay. Only a handful of men took the offer. August decided it would go better in the spring. He was enraged over the Mayfield House being destroyed. But he told himself that when the railroad came through he would build an even bigger hotel.

Ansleigh was staying with Many Horses mother while in the camp. It bothered her that she could not be with Shila as people looked down on her. After all that had happened she could not blame them. So they could be alone with each other. Shila decided to meet Ansleigh in the mountains. Freshly fallen snow covered the ground. The sky was blue that day with the sun's light glancing off the snow. They rode up into a pine forest. Ansleigh told him that she must return to her father as he would be worried. She was grateful for the time she got to spend with him. She told him that she would write the letter and put all the things Shila had told her into the message. They sat on their horses looking into each other's eyes. He reached out taking her hand in his. They squeezed their hands together tightly.
The Arapaho's tried attacking the town a week later only to be defeated by the soldiers. This time everyone was ready for them. That would be the last time the natives attempted to fight them. As Shila had predicted. The Government would eventually force the Indians to reservations in the East.

257

95

"In The Aftermath"

The long winter was finally over. Spring was drawing near. The soldiers had left Crooked Hat, and rebuilding the town was in full force. Many miners and others were leaving .They had lost money and family members on that day of Night Wing's revenge. The people that stayed were doing so because they wanted to and not because of August Mayfield. Maizey and Ki turned the Opera House into a restaurant. Batilda Cederholm kept the General Store opened. She had both her daughters there to help. Marshall Dawson had left for Washington as he had planned. Gilda stayed behind. She really didn't care if she ever saw him again. She was impassive toward Ingrid and would remain so for the rest of her life. She ended up as a spinster never remarrying. ·

The Livery stables and coach line had to be rebuilt. Tin Pan opened a small saloon at Mrs. Jacks which was also the only hotel in town. Miss Francie had left taking her girls with her to Pigeon Grove. The church and rectory went unscathed and the town's cemetery was at its new location there. August Mayfield was bound and determined to bring back the town's distinction. His mine wasn't producing as it had been. He kept it open with a skeleton crew at best. His logging camp had closed and the fur trade was the one business that kept him going. The railroad was his only chance at redemption. He continued to write asking for help and he took a trip to San Francisco to find speculators to back his dream.

Dr. Haveston went to Virginia to be with his father. Beatrice and Zacharia stayed on at her house. Beatrice kept the office open administering medical aid to those she could. Hoping that Aubrey would one day return. Mrs. Jensen had moved in with them. She had lost her house in the fires. The Civil War had broke out and President Lincoln was trying to abolish slavery.

Clegg was killed at the battle of Antietam one of the bloodiest battles of The Civil War under the leadership of General George Mc Clellan. It was during this time President Lincoln had drafted The Emancipation Proclamation.

August still had Butch Cady working as his body guard and kept a few hired guns around his home. He never got over Harp's murder. It haunted him along with the many people who had met their deaths at his hand. He drank heavily and was verbally abusive to Mary and would beat her in his drunken rages. He was kind to Emery as she was the only light in his dark mind. Mary stayed on because she was not going to lose her rights to his wealth. It came at a high price.

Jacob decided to go to California to find Katherine and Quin. He had a bad feeling about their fate. He made Justice stay behind with Jake until his return. He did not want to endanger their lives. Justice stayed with Beatrice after he had left. He never did find Katherine. The land they owned was occupied by squatters.

They told him they had never seen or heard of Quin or Katherine. Jacob knew then that they must have been killed. He never would get over losing them. He returned to Justice and his son. He asked Justice if she wanted to go back East with him to live? During this time he was approached by some of the townspeople. They wanted him to teach their children.

They were willing to eventually build a school house they told him. Meanwhile they would set up a classroom in the assayer's old office. Justice wanted him to do this. Jacob was content to be teaching again and Justice had a baby girl. Followed a few years by another son. Jane and Thackery Riley. They would live in Crooked Hat for the rest of their days. Building a small house near the church. They took a trip one summer with their children to Pennsylvania to be with Martha before she died. Justice loved Jacob deeply. They were close until the end.

Thomas Andrews went on to become an engineer for the railroads ending up in New York State. He never remarried. Thorton Blythe died young from complications of syphilis in the slums of San Francisco. He had died penniless.

Maizey did finally learn who had killed Nate. It was shortly after Night Wing's attack. Ki and Maizey had set up a make shift kitchen in the Opera House to feed the wounded and the workers.

259

Tin Pan was drunk and mouthing off like he did when he drank. Zacharia was helping that day. He put a spoon full of scrambled eggs on Tin Pan's plate and started to pour coffee into his cup. Tin Pan staggered back and the hot coffee spilled onto his hand.

He swore and struck Zacharia in the face. His mouth was bleeding. Maizey saw what had happened and taking a broom she started to beat Tin Pan with it. "You son of a bitch don't yah touch my boy do yah hear!" Ki stepped up and intervened. "You and that Chiny man sleep'n ta-gether ain't natural."Cursed Tin Pan. "Yore late husband would be shamed I tell yah." "Don't you bring Nate into it." "He's dead defend'n the likes of you he spat." "What yah carry'n on about?" she asked. "Got his throat slit by August Mayfield." "How'd yah know that?" "I was there plain n'simple. "Nate he was carry'n on about you. Drunk he was and stupid. He pulled his gun on August made him git down on his knees. Told him to say he wus sorry fur all he had done to you. August wus skeered. Nate pulled the trigger his gun didn't go off. So August grabs old Nate by the knees and brings him down. Slit his throat quicker then a pig can squeal." It grew quiet everyone had heard Tin Pan. Maizey hit him hard in the face and ran out. 'Il est mort!" *(He is dead)* Ki went chasing after her. Maizey went home that afternoon got her rifle and rode out to the Mayfield Mansion with Ki in hot pursuit. He managed to catch her horse and pulled back on her reins. "Yah let me be. So help me God I am gonna kill that man." "Maizey it no good. It not bring back Mr. Townsend. He gone. My wife and son they gone. Hate make me crazy. I no lose you too."

The look on Ki's face made Maizey stop. She loved Ki and knew if she did this he would be involved as well. After that day Maizey no longer hid the fact that she loved Ki and they were openly together. There were a few people who complained about their relationship. But oddly enough most people accepted it.

96

"And In The End"

No one ever knew that Katherine and Katy were still alive. Katherine had a baby boy the winter of her capture. She named him Quin after his father. Catching Bull was a leader among the Crow. He had spent some time with the Arapaho after the attack on Crooked Hat. His sister was married to one of the elders. Upon seeing her, he thought Katherine was very beautiful. He went to the tribal council and told them he wanted her. He offered two ponies and a rifle he had to take her. It was agreed. With Katy and her baby son she was taken by Catching Bull to his home in what eventually became the state of Montana. Catching Bull was good to her. Katy never got over her childhood traumas and would spend her entire lifetime under her mother's care. Katherine eventually had four more children by Catching Bull. She never tried to contact her family. She had resigned herself to her fate. Her children were her life. She spent the rest of her days with Catching Bull. The Crows remained sovereign for many years.

Crooked Hat survived despite people leaving and attempts to destroy it. It was August Mayfield's dream. But it couldn't have happened without the people who stayed and built it. After the news spread about August killing Nate Townsend most people shunned him. He spent days alone in his study seldom sober. He was fanatical about the coming of a railroad. That would solve everything he had convinced himself.

Beatrice couldn't believe that Zacharia was eighteen and getting ready to head to Baltimore, Maryland to work on the railroad. He had written to the railroad office there and was offered a job. Beatrice and Maizey went to the Coach station to see him off. Maizey loved him like a son. Beatrice couldn't stop crying and Zacharia told her he couldn't leave if she didn't stop the fussing over him. He promised he would write and wanted her to come and visit him once he got established. He hugged her long and hard and Maizey too. The women were in tears as he got on the coach. Waving his hat out the door when the driver pulled out. With Zacharia gone Beatrice was considering moving herself to California as she originally planned. She told

Maizey there was nothing holding her anymore. Maizey said she would be sorely missed. You are not making it any easier Beatrice scolded her. Wrapping her arms about her. Beatrice was leaving her house to Jacob and Justice. They had made a room for Mrs. Jensen she was family.

On the very day she was packing her personal things and arranging the house for her move. Mrs. Jensen came to her and said there was someone in the office to see her.
Beatrice was irritated by the interruption. "Tell them I am gone." "He is most persistent." She told her. "Oh all right." Beatrice followed her into the office. A well dressed man stood with his back to her, looking out the window. "I am sorry sir but I am no longer taking patients." He turned toward her. "Would you make an exception for me?" It was Aubrey. Beatrice stood dead in her tracks. She didn't know whether to laugh or cry. He held out his arms and she embraced him. "I can't believe it's you! Why are you back?"

"I have come for you, if you will have me?" It had been five years since she last saw him. She was happy to see him looking so well.
He told her about the war and that it was finally over. He had volunteered as a medical surgeon for the wounded Confederate soldiers. His father had died the year before. He went and established his license and was practicing medicine in Virginia. He had been sober for over five years. Beatrice was suddenly overwhelmed. She wasn't sure how she felt. He told her he would stay until the end of the week. Mrs. Jensen insisted he stay with them.
He did and he visited families he had known and went to Molly's grave site. In the evenings he would dine with Beatrice. She still insisted on packing to leave for California. Mrs. Jensen told her to follow her heart. She loved her and would stand by any decision she made. Finally Dr. Haveston had to leave.

His coach was leaving the next morning. He once more implored Beatrice to go with him, and become his wife. He told her he loved her. She wouldn't answer. She went to bed early that night unable to sleep as thoughts raced through her head.

Aubrey went to say goodbye before he left and there was no sign of Beatrice. With a heavy heart he moved on. At the station he packed his luggage onto the coach. He kept looking hoping Beatrice would at least come and see him off. The driver hollered for everyone to take their seats. The coach lurched forward and he heard a woman's voice calling out his name. He peered out and saw Beatrice running behind the coach waving her arms to stop. Aubrey jumped from the moving coach landing on his knees. Beatrice caught up with him. Helping him up they looked into each other's eyes and he pulled her to him kissing her without reservation.

Within the week she left Crooked Hat behind her somewhat reluctantly as she left old friends. They were married in Virginia. Beatrice helped Aubrey with his practice and they lived in his father's house. She had three children with him. Two boys and a girl. Aubrey never touched another drink as long as he lived. Zacharia eventually moved to Virginia to be near his mother. He married a young English woman and ended up being the Station Master in Charlottesville.

One night after dinner August Mayfield walked out to the horse barn. He was checking on a mare that was ready to foal. He looked over into the stable where she was laying in labor. He was excited because the sire had been a thoroughbred. This breed of horse was becoming valuable as excellent race horses. This was a new venture for him. He stood there deep in thought when he felt someone come up behind him. He turned slowly and was about to say something when he looked into the face of a young Spaniard.

"Senor Mayfield?" "Yes?" "This is from my father. It has been along time coming to you." He then thrust a large knife deep into August stomach. "So you do not forget. His name was Valdez Aquilar." With that he walked away leaving the knife inside of August. As August lay dying the last thing he saw was the foal coming from his mother's womb.

Mary found him later in the barn. At first it surprised her but then she thought this was the only way August Mayfield's life could have ended. She had come to bring him a letter. In her hand was a letter addressed to August from the Trans-Continental Railroad stating they were indeed interested in making connections through Crooked Hat.

"Deep Into The Woodlands"

Ansleigh had returned to Crooked Hat after her stay at Shila's encampment. To be with her father. She told him how much she loved Shila and that she would stay on to be near him. Jacob wanted her to be happy but thought she should find a young man there to marry. He warned her it would never be possible for her to be with Shila. She wouldn't accept that as her heart knew better. During this time she never heard from Thomas so she went to Pigeon Grove they had a courthouse there. She applied for a divorce and was granted one on abandonment issues. Jacob went with her as a witness. She did write to President Lincoln asking for an assembly with him involving Shila. A month after she received a letter and was told to contact the Indian Affairs Office. She rode out to Shila's Camp. The two of them went to Washington later that spring. Shila met with a Mr. Long. Ansleigh was there to interpret for him. They were told that in lieu of recent events and the war ending. That the President was far too busy to worry about Indian affairs. To come back at a later time. They both were ushered out and asked to leave. Shila was angry and Ansleigh did not blame him. He was hoping for a treaty of some kind. An agreement where his people could stay on their ancestral lands. It was not meant to be and they returned.

Ansleigh was heart broken for Shila. He knew it was only a matter of time before they would be asked to leave their homeland. So he held a ceremony for his people praying and holding a give away feast.

Where they all gave something of value to all those who had lost much. It was at this time that Shila had to decide what to do about Ansleigh. He loved her and wasn't sure of leaving her behind. As he had anticipated the Army sent Indian scouts out. The scouts informed the various tribes they come upon that they would have to leave the mountains. If they went peaceably, they would be guaranteed a small acreage of land on what they were calling reservations. If not the Army would come and force them off. Those who refused to go were shot or chained together and forced to walk great distances to the reservations. That summer the Army sent troops to Shila's camp. They were forceful with the people and threatened them. Shila loved his people and told them not to fight back. To follow the way of (Tam Apo) The Great Spirit. To be proud of what they were, to carry this land and their ancestors in their hearts. One day in the future the white man will live to regret what he has done and the earth mother will be his teacher. This I know to be true. Do not let anyone take from you your heritage.

He gathered them together and they started their long trek to Utah where a government reservation was waiting. Many of the elderly died and a young woman who had delivered a still born baby was left behind to die. A Colonel mercifully shot her. They eventually arrived to the reservation after three weeks of walking. He could feel the broken spirit of his clan. The land they were allotted was barren and dry. No trees for shade no rivers only one spring to supply their water.

They built shelters out of rock and soil. In the first week three of their young tribe's men had hung themselves. A group of Morman missionaries came a month later taking the children from their parents. Telling Shila they were to be schooled and taught the ways of God.

Shila did not understand a God that would do this? He spent days in prayers and fasting asking the spirits for help. One night in a dream he saw Grey Elk. He was shown a beautiful woodland home and Ansleigh was standing next to him smiling. She opened her arms to him and he awoke. In that moment he knew he had to leave. He went to Broken Lance and told him about his vision. It is with a heavy heart I do this. I must leave here. "They will find you, you will be killed." Broken Lance warned him. "I do not care as my spirit cannot be bound. Until I will see you again." He embraced Broken Lance and disappeared into the desert.

Ansleigh was sitting on the porch with Mrs. Jensen they were cleaning elderberries to make pies. The heat was sweltering as they sat with their dress sleeves rolled up. Ansleigh heard him before she looked up. Shading her eyes with her hand she peered out. There sitting on his horse was Shila he stared at her quietly not speaking. She dropped her basket to the floor running out to greet him. He pulled her up onto the horse. Before they rode off. Ansleigh told Mrs. Jensen "Be sure to tell my father that I followed my heart." Then they were gone.

   He took Ansleigh deep into the mountain range of the snow caps. He had brought an extra horse, provisions and a blanket coat for her to wear. They didn't talk much that first night together. They both knew that they needed to be near one another and that was enough. They made a lean too out of Pine branches and slept snuggled together.

   In the morning Ansleigh eagerly reached for Shila .They lay in each other's arms. Looking into one another's eyes and kissing each others faces. He spoke to her in Shoshone (Neh ume chasuequanda Ndinokuda) "I love you." It was as if his spirit was finally free. He kissed her with much emotion. Their bodies entwined as they made love.

   Shila knew this was right on every level. He felt so deeply for this woman. Ansleigh felt so much a part of him as if he were her other half. They both had wanted this from the beginning. Now it was happening after years of longing and struggle.

   They spent several weeks in the high mountain ranges before moving onto California. On the day they left the high mountains they had a visitor early in the morning a large grizzly broke into their camp.

   Ansleigh was frightened. Shila was surprised to see his old friend. The bear sniffed the air and walked away. A good sign Shila knew. He had come to say goodbye. Shila and Ansleigh made their home in California.
Shila built a lodge deep into the woodlands. They lived there for many years. Ansleigh bore him two sons. From time to time Shila would venture to nearby villages to heal those who needed help. Ansleigh was often with him. Administering herbal remedies. The encampments were becoming scarce as the land was being swallowed up by greedy investors. Many old timers would tell stories of their past. They were fond of the legend of The Medicine Man of the Sierras and his golden haired wife. They called them Weda (bear) and Dabai (sun) the great bear and woman of the sun.